I have always loved you, I love you still, I always will.
We are One Mind, One Heart, One Soul
I know I will.

Dear Readers,

I'm often asked why I combined time travel with romance, of all things. I consider what I write to be stories of timeless love. Why is it that we all secretly believe, somewhere, the love of our life waits for us? I think it might be that beyond all our scurrying around for success, what we really want is to find our Twin Flame. Not that we can't be complete without it, but the complement of a Twin flame ignites magic in our lives, and combined, the power of such love can be astonishing, transcending even the dimension of time. This is the story of such a love.

When I set out to write about the Shakespearean era I was hesitant, having never ventured into this time period. My research sent me on a mind-blowing ride into the past as mysteries started to appear and threads of history began to unravel. Did I dare write about what I was discovering? The proposal for this book was accepted many months before *Shakespeare in Love* and *Elizabeth* were released in movie theaters, so the popularity of those productions encouraged me to keep writing.

I hope you enjoy this adventure as much as I enjoyed writing it. Come with me now, if you will . . . and watch as two souls, Twin Flames, recognize each other and create such a bright, wondrous light that nothing, not even time, can extinguish it.

Kindest regards,
Constance O'Day

Other Avon Books by
Constance O'Day-Flannery

ANYWHERE YOU ARE

Constance O'Day-Flannery

Once And Forever

AVON BOOKS NEW YORK

This is a work of fiction. Names, characters, places, and incidents either are the product of the author's imagination or are used fictitiously. Any resemblance to actual events, locales, organizations, or persons, living or dead, is entirely coincidental and beyond the intent of either the author or the publisher.

AVON BOOKS, INC.
1350 Avenue of the Americas
New York, New York 10019

Copyright © 1999 by Constance O'Day-Flannery
Excerpt from *Someday My Prince* copyright © 1999 by Christina Dodd
Excerpt from *Married in Haste* copyright © 1999 by Catherine Maxwell
Excerpt from *His Wicked Ways* copyright © 1999 by Sandra Kleinschmit
Excerpt from *The Perfect Gift* copyright © 1999 by Roberta Helmer
Excerpt from *Once and Forever* copyright © 1999 by Constance O'Day-Flannery
Excerpt from *The Proposition* copyright © 1999 by Judith Ivory
Inside cover author photo by Miko Miles/Fly Paper Graphic Designs
Published by arrangement with the author
Library of Congress Catalog Card Number: 99-94448
ISBN: 0-380-80170-1
www.avonbooks.com/romance

First Avon Books Printing: November 1999

AVON TRADEMARK REG. U.S. PAT. OFF. AND IN OTHER COUNTRIES, MARCA REGIS-TRADA, HECHO EN U.S.A.

Printed in the U.S.A.

WCD 10 9 8 7 6 5 4 3 2 1

For Cristopher...
my inspiration, my partner, my Twin Flame

Prologue

Journal Entry
15 May 1598

Long have my inner notes been lulled to whisper...until now, as I have been aroused by the reverberation that you, my ancient love, are approaching.

I have always loved you, I love you still, I always will.

And I know you are more than a dream, for I remember your tones, even in my waking, and your exquisite vibrations fill the very corners of my being.

We have orchestrated this, our music, for a thousand years or more. Our harmonizing chords striking deep within this One Soul shall serenade all things into infinity—a heavenly resonation—leaving such an impression upon the universe that the stars call out a billion ovations.

Listen now, My Beloved, our symphony seduces and implores, we return to us.

We are One Mind, One Heart, One Soul.

I reach to embrace you gently, but the sun's rise chases another dark velvet thief who has stolen my sleep, our song, and you from me, as I am left in these, my long waking hours, with only haunting echos of our refrain.

Yet I know I will find you, and our music will rise again, through eternity...

Once and Forever.

Chapter One

Maggie Whitaker always had a plan, a direction. Until now . . .

Okay, so she might just be having one of those mini nervous breakdowns, a mid-life crisis. Who could blame her? Her life had turned into a circus. Looking out the small window of the plane to the sunrise, she saw the dark sky giving way to shades of deep purple and rose, and she sighed in an effort to release the stress. She leaned her head against the backrest and closed her eyes. Everyone else was sleeping on this red-eye flight to London, yet her short nap had only produced a weird dream where she'd been walking in the woods and asking strangers, "Is it you? Is it you?"

Sheesh . . . even in her dreams she was unable to find peace. From some distant part of her brain she remembered a time, not so long ago, when her life had been normal. She recalled a feeling of safety in a great-paying job, a comfortable marriage. Her place within society seemed secure. How could it all have changed so quickly, she wondered, as the overhead lights in the cabin were turned on and people began to stir. Maggie smelled the aroma of coffee and stretched as best as she could, anxious to ease her sore muscles. Six hours in a cramped seat was no picnic, yet this adventure across the Atlantic had been her choice. Perhaps some might see it as irresponsible, though it felt like a lifeline had been thrown to her, and she would have been truly crazy not to grab hold.

Lifting her purse from the floor, she laid it on the empty seat next to hers. The least she could do was make herself presentable. She knew the routine. First breakfast, then they would land at Heathrow. Taking out her compact, she looked at her reflection and sighed again. The overnight flight hadn't helped her appearance, yet she knew the stress of the last year and a half had taken its toll, and there wasn't much she could do to hide it. She smoothed down her hair, trying not notice the fine threads of gray at her temples. In three days she was celebrating the big 4-0 and her life was a mess.

What are you doing, Maggie Whitaker? She looked at her reflection and snapped the compact shut, as if the action might stop the answer. Running away. That was what she was doing. There was a time when her job in television commercial sales had afforded her the luxury of buying designer clothes and eating at the finest restaurants in New York City. Now she was on unemployment; a gift from the state when her boss and mentor was fired and she along with him, when the new management team brought in their own staff. That would have been tough enough, had she not recently gone through a divorce and been paying alimony to her ex-husband . . . *the artist.*

She hadn't minded supporting him when they were married since her job provided them with a great lifestyle, and she was liberated enough to realize the man didn't have to be the breadwinner, but she'd never expected Eric to sue her for alimony. Especially since *he* wanted the divorce. Now the state of New Jersey was coming after her, along with the mortgage company, the utility companies, and every other institution she'd ever dealt with in the last eight years. It was enough to make her want to disappear, to slip away silently.

So that's what she was doing . . . disappearing for ten days.

Before closing her purse, she brought out the thick envelope postmarked Great Britain and again read the Victorian birthday card from her relative.

Dearest Maggie,

Happy Anniversary of the day you entered into this world. We have all been blessed by you and celebrate your life. How you have been on my mind this last month. I have heard through your mother that you are without employment and, of course, it seemed the perfect opportunity to send you this ticket. Please come to visit me, Maggie. One of my friends did a "reading" for me and it became apparent that you are needed here at this time. In fact, I believe it is imperative that you come here to England. Thus, I have enclosed a nonrefundable ticket for your birthday. It's time, Margaret Whitaker, for you to visit the place of your people. If nothing else, humor an old woman who misses her family.

I'll be waiting at the airport to meet you and show you my little bit of Paradise.

Love,
Aunt Edithe

Maggie remembered being stunned when she'd opened the envelope days ago and saw the British Airways ticket. It had been after another agonizing trip across the Hudson, where she'd been rejected again and told that advertising budgets were being axed. She'd cried her way through rush-hour traffic back into Jersey and realized she had no idea where to turn, what to do. All her contacts seemed useless. She was in trouble, and alone.

And then out of the blue Aunt Edithe, her late father's wacky sister, came to her rescue, inviting her to go joy-riding across the Atlantic. Maggie didn't know why her aunt seemed to favor her when they'd only met once, many years ago. Her aunt always remembered to send birthday and holiday cards, and she wrote letters that Maggie answered quickly. They had an unusual pen-pal relationship. Aunt Edithe, who gave up her life in New York almost thirty years ago to relocate to England and indulge in her eccentricities, wrote Maggie about her garden, her peculiar friends, her unconventional views, and always tried to get Maggie to visit.

Running her finger over her aunt's beautiful script, Maggie thought back to the way she had tortured herself over the decision to leave everything behind and just go for the adventure. All those years of being the good, responsible one, of trying to be nice enough, smart enough, understanding enough, talented enough, pretty enough, *good* enough, seemed like a colossal waste of time. It certainly didn't guarantee happiness, and she finally admitted she was tired of being the responsible one, always doing the right thing. After thirty-nine years of being the good girl, maybe it was time to be spontaneous. There was no safety in goodness, and that had blown her mind, making her question everything she had been taught. All of her belief systems appeared to be falling apart.

She really hated the victim mentality that seemed to permeate society, yet anyone who walked a week in her shoes would pack her bags for her and tell her just to do it. She had tried, truly tried, all her life to do what was considered the right thing. She had taken care of her husband, her widowed mother in California . . . everyone who ever came into her life and was in need. When her finances had taken a nosedive, so did her ability to bail everyone out . . . even herself.

She remembered the moment when she sat at her kitchen table and thought to heck with it all, or what everyone else thought she should do . . . for ten days she would be free, free to *be herself.* So she packed her bag, closed up her house, and took a cab to Newark Airport. She was about to celebrate an important birthday with her wacky sixty-one-year-old aunt in a foreign country and wish for some guidance. She could even put up with Aunt Edithe's strange philosophies and tarot readings for ten days of escape from the dismal circumstances of her own life. Bless her aunt's heart for coming to her rescue. Who knew what waited for her? Anything could happen, for it was certain she was now flying by the seat of her pants.

It was kind of a plan. She was turning forty, and she'd never done anything like this in her entire, regimented life. As irrational as it might seem, she was about to go joyriding into the unknown. Maybe it was time not to be a grown-up. Joyriding . . . at her age! She stifled a groan as the flight attendant rolled the beverage cart up the aisle.

It sure sounded like a mid-life crisis to her.

Heathrow was an experience of controlled confusion. She passed through customs with her cart and emerged into a huge space with ticket counters everywhere. It was so unlike American airports. Maggie felt lost in the sea of people and tried to make eye contact with several older women, who passed her with a look of disinterest. It was too reminiscent of her dream, where she'd been walking in the woods and feeling so lost as no one ac-knowledged her. Sighing, she wondered how long she should wait before she had her aunt paged.

An elderly woman was walking in her direction, and

Maggie smiled, even though this tall senior citizen didn't seem remotely familiar.

"Good day to you," the woman said, while lifting a cane and tapping her cart. "Now, please move this so I may proceed to my gate."

"Oh." Surprised by the matter-of-fact statement, Maggie quickly pushed her cart to the side, and murmured, "I'm sorry."

This feeling of being lost began to settle over her again, and she sensed the lack of sleep catching up with her, making her irritable. Really! She and Aunt Edithe should have come up with some arrangement, beyond *I'll meet you at the airport*. Maybe she should have her paged.

"Maggie . . . ?"

She turned quickly and was startled for just a moment as she gazed into the clearest blue eyes she had ever seen. A stately woman, with beautiful white hair that touched her shoulders in a loose pageboy and was dressed in a lovely deep gray suit, smiled at her with recognition.

"Aunt Edithe?"

Nodding, Edithe's smile increased as she opened her arms. "Welcome to England, child."

Maggie was wrapped in her aunt's embrace and, as she breathed deeply in relief, she smelled the delicate scent of Joy perfume. "Thank you so much for inviting me. It couldn't have happened at a better time."

Edithe pulled back and looked directly into Maggie's eyes. "I know," she whispered, with a gentle smile.

Maggie had the strangest sensation that her aunt, who did have some resemblance to her late father, really knew how desperate she had been feeling for the last few months. "You look . . . Well, you look absolutely wonderful. England must agree with you."

Edithe released her and smiled with affection. "It

does," she said simply. "Now, let's depart this madness and find the car."

Nodding, Maggie followed her aunt's lead through the maze of ticket counters to the exit and thought what a lovely surprise her aunt was. Suddenly, she no longer seemed so eccentric; rather Aunt Edithe seemed very interesting. For years, she'd written about her odd views on life, the earth, our placement in the universe, and Maggie half expected to see her aunt show up in flowing robes and crystal beads. Instead, her aunt looked like a very stylish, very charming older woman.

"I can't tell you how excited I am that you're finally here, dearest Maggie," her aunt said, as they waited to exit through the automatic doors. "We have so much catching up to do together."

Maggie noted that her aunt's voice held more than a tinge of a British accent, and she thought it, too, was a pleasant surprise. "Thank you for making it all possible," Maggie answered, as she pushed her cart through the opened doors and got her first taste of England. It was early morning, and lines of black sedans were waiting to pick up passengers. *How quaint,* she thought. The cabs looked just like those in the movies she loved when she was young. She watched as her aunt raised her arm, and Maggie thought she was signaling a cab. Suddenly a cherry red Jaguar stopped on the other side of the black sedans and Edithe motioned Maggie toward it.

She didn't know what to expect. Her aunt never spoke about her financial status, and she knew that Jags originated in England, but Aunt Edithe . . . in a cherry red one?

An older man came out of the driver's side, at the same time the trunk popped open. He was dressed in a very British style, all tweeds, with patches of leather on the elbows of his jacket.

"Malcolm, may I present my niece, Margaret. Isn't she lovely?"

The man smiled beneath a thick gray moustache and extended his hand. "The pleasure is all mine, Maggie. If I may be informal? Your aunt has told me so much about you, I feel as though we are already acquainted."

She shook his hand and couldn't help smiling back. He seemed so friendly, almost jolly. "It's very nice to meet you, Malcolm. And thank you for picking me up so early."

"Nonsense," he replied, taking her heavy suitcase and depositing it in the trunk. "Your aunt had us up hours before we should leave. Her anticipation was contagious."

Us? Was her aunt *living* with Malcolm? Maggie didn't know if it was lack of sleep, but she suddenly wanted to giggle and mentally congratulated Aunt Edithe. *She* certainly was a big surprise. Doddering, eccentric, odd . . . ? Hardly.

"It's a beautiful car," Maggie murmured to Malcolm, as he opened the door to the backseat.

The man grinned, and said, "Edithe created quite a stir when she purchased it."

Her aunt slid onto the front passenger seat. "I don't know why," Edithe said with a telling grin. "I supposed because I refused to be limited to the more sedate colors. I've still got some of the Yank in me. What did they expect? English racing green? I like this color. It makes me happy."

Maggie chuckled and sat back against the soft leather. This magnificent, red car belonged to Aunt Edithe? She was trying to align the mental picture she had carried for years. Her aunt was a cultured, refined older woman who was quite comfortable financially. Why, she could be the Queen Mum's lady-in-waiting!

As the car pulled away from the curb, Edithe turned

around and smiled with tenderness. "I would have known you anywhere. You have the Whitaker bearing, and those piercing blue eyes. Just relax, child. I know you're exhausted after that flight."

Child? Somehow the address was endearing, and Maggie knew her eyes were her best feature, but they certainly didn't have that sparkle Aunt Edithe's had. She smiled at her aunt, very pleased she had made the decision to come to England. "I *am* tired," she admitted, as they exited the huge airport. She looked out the window to the early-summer view and felt that surge of excitement grow. Something wonderful had already happened. Aunt Edithe wasn't weird at all.

"Are you happy, child?"

Maggie was startled and looked to the front seat and the back of her aunt's head. "I'm happy right now," she answered, smoothing down the material of her linen skirt. "If you're talking about my life in general, well, you know most of the details, and I guess you could say some improvements would be welcome."

Edithe laughed. "Very good. Stay happy, right now."

"That's my plan," Maggie replied with a grin.

Malcolm and Edithe exchanged glances and smiled at each other, as though some silent communication were taking place between them. Maybe it was just a look of affection, but Maggie had the distinct impression that her words had pleased them. She turned her attention to the passing scenery. In the next hour she learned that her aunt had a very full life in England as they talked about relatives and caught up on history.

Traveling on the left side of the road was odd, Maggie thought, as she gazed out the window. Kind of disorienting. Suddenly, she saw a sign that made her sit up and gasp.

"Stonehenge," she whispered, wishing that they could stop.

Malcolm heard her and chuckled. "I believe we have that trip planned. Much better on the weekend, when all this concert preparation is less. Don't think I've ever seen so much apparatus needed for something out-doors."

"It's an extraordinary event, Malcolm, no matter what the inconvenience. This disturbance," Edithe remarked as she gracefully pointed to a passing truck, "is well worth it."

Maggie watched as Malcolm nodded and changed lanes on the busy interstate.

"What concert?" she asked out of politeness.

Malcolm glanced at her through the rearview mirror and chuckled. "You are jesting, dear Maggie, aren't you? It's probably the greatest concert to take place since Woodstock. Stonehenge, Rock Reunion 2000. Every hotel room, B&B, even rooms in private homes have been sold out for six months or more. We didn't know you'd be coming at this time, and advance tickets have been sold out for almost a year."

Feeling foolish, as if she should know something and hadn't a clue, Maggie merely smiled back, and said, "I haven't kept up on music for some time, I'm afraid." She hadn't watched the news in weeks, nor did she have any interest in a newspaper, other than the Help Wanted ads. It was as if in some distant part of her brain she felt something familiar about it, like she had heard some-thing, but—

Her aunt suddenly turned around and looked back at her. "Oh, Maggie, I've been so looking forward to showing you around. There's a Renaissance Festival tak-ing place in an adjoining field from Stonehenge. It's too far away to see it, of course, but this place simply vi-brates with the energy. Tomorrow, we'll be meeting a few friends at the Festival. You do think you'll be up to it, don't you?"

Maggie's stomach muscles tingled in anticipation, and she grinned. Her aunt didn't leave her much room to back out, even if she wanted, which she didn't. "I would absolutely love to go tomorrow. Thank you for planning such a great beginning to my holiday."

Aunt Edithe smiled happily and turned back to the front of the car.

Maggie almost giggled as they passed the exit leading to the famous attraction. Now there was something she really wanted to see. Not that it held any deeper meaning for her than a neolithic sculpture upon the earth, but there was something mysterious about the place, though she'd only seen pictures.

Stonehenge.

Wow . . .

Even the name sounded magical.

Maybe there was something to this joyriding?

Chapter Two

*I*t was perfect.

She was delighted with her charming aunt. Aunt Edithe, it turned out, was nothing like she'd expected. Rather than being a bit of a loon, she operated a holistic health center, where she had a very busy hypnotherapy practice specializing in learning disabilities. Malcolm worked with her, and their practice provided them with the means to enjoy a comfortable life. Maggie had to admit the man seemed like a perfect companion for her aunt, and she realized she couldn't have asked for better guides on this holiday. A part of her worried that she was expecting too much and that her expectations might be unrealistic, yet she couldn't deny what she felt.

Something wonderful was already happening, she thought as she sighed with contentment.

Maggie, snuggled in her robe, was curled up in a huge armchair in front of the fire. A cup of tea sat on a lovely accent table by her side. Aunt Edithe, in a silky caftan, her legs pulled under her, was sipping Earl Grey and smiling into the crackling flames.

"I am so glad that we were able to transfer our relationship from paper to in-person," Aunt Edithe whispered.

"So am I. I feel very comfortable," Maggie answered, staring into the flames and feeling the affection in her aunt's words. "It's the oddest thing. Ever since we arrived here earlier in the day, I can feel myself relaxing, as though the muscles in my body are slowly unwinding. Kind of like a twisted rubber band."

"I'm glad you like my home."

Maggie looked around the comfortable, eclectic room, and smiled. "I do like it. It's lovely, and very peaceful." Rugs from Turkey lay under the overstuffed furniture. Carved bookends from Bali held together leather-bound books on shelves that surrounded the fireplace. An African mask hung on the wall, next to ornate sconces that held thick creamy candles. Dotting the tastefully papered walls and on every shelf and table corner, were varied antique frames bearing testimony to the time, love, and worldly travels Aunt Edithe and Malcolm shared. The entire room emanated comfort and peace, and was filled with the soothing scents of flowers from Aunt Edithe's abundant garden right outside the double French doors. Maggie knew she couldn't have found a better sanctuary to figure out her future than this lovely home in the country.

"Thank you for asking me to visit and making this possible. It was the perfect time."

Aunt Edithe grinned. "I did a little more than ask, I think. When I sent you that ticket, I was so afraid you might assume I was being manipulative."

Maggie laughed. "My ex was manipulative, not you."

"Ahh . . . love. The paths we take to follow it."

"I like Malcolm," Maggie said, thoroughly enjoying the opportunity to bond with another female. Her aunt seemed like a contemporary who was open and caring, and she realized it had been some time since she'd had this experience. It was nice. "You appear to have finally found the right path with him."

Edithe's smile became tender. "Yes. We have a good

life together. It's relatively quiet, and we have a wonderful group of friends here in Trowbridge. We've been together for eleven years this time.''

Maggie glanced at her relative. ''This time?''

Edithe sighed. ''Malcolm and I know we've been together before, in other lives, and live now in gratitude for each other. I think I wrote to you about my belief that everyone who comes into our lives is fulfilling a contract with us.''

''Hmm,'' was all Maggie could reply to that statement. ''I guess my ex's contract with me was to make me miserable.'' She always resorted to humor when faced with an uncomfortable situation, and a discussion of past lives or any other of her aunt's far-out theories was definitely uncomfortable for her. At least she hadn't brought out any tarot cards or started channeling. Yet.

Edithe chuckled at Maggie's answer. ''I'm sure there was something in the experience for you to learn. All our encounters serve our growth in some way. It will come to you, eventually, when the hurt lessens. So how's the love life now?''

It was Maggie's turn to laugh. ''Nonexistent. Love is not on my agenda.''

''What a shame,'' her aunt said in a thoughtful tone. ''Love *is* my agenda.''

''You have Malcolm. You didn't have a depressed artist who divorced you and then sued you for alimony.''

Edithe nodded. ''True. Malcolm is a blessing but, Maggie . . . how fair is it to judge all men by your experience with one?''

Shrugging, Maggie murmured, '' I know that. A part of me is glad the marriage is over. Living alone is easier than being with someone and feeling lonely. Besides, I have more important things to think about now. Like finding a job, paying bills, straightening out my life. If I'm introspective right now, it's because in my current circumstances it seems a little irresponsible to have just taken off on a holiday.''

Aunt Edithe chuckled. ''But what better time to take a holiday . . . when you truly need it? Seems to me that when we plan for such things, they rarely turn out as we had imagined. It's those spontaneous moments that have been special for me. I found out years ago that when I tried to force everything in my life, I complicated it miserably. But when I chose a direction and just allowed the universe to fill in the details, everything worked out so much better than I could have directed. I found it to be quite freeing, actually.''

Maggie listened to her aunt's words and tried to make sense of them. ''But isn't that what most people do? Take a direction and keep pushing until the goal is achieved?''

Her aunt laughed. ''I guess you could say I'm not like most people.''

Maggie joined her laughter. ''No, you aren't, Aunt Edithe. You are . . . unique.''

''I shall take that as a compliment. The very last thing I want to do is disappear into the masses, although I know how to do it when necessary.''

Maggie turned to her attractive aunt. ''When necessary?''

Edithe smiled softly. ''Doesn't do to stand out, you know. We human beings have such a need to fit in, to know that if someone else believes what we believe, then it must make it right, and we feel so much better about ourselves. If people think you're odd or different, then fear enters into the exchange, so my eccentricities are more private. I may reveal them to those I trust, such as you, dear child, in my many letters to you over the years. I'm sure you've been . . . curious, to say the least, over the ramblings of your silly relative.''

''I've never considered you silly,'' Maggie said,

though in her heart she had had many moments of such thoughts through the years. "Your letters may have been a tad . . . eccentric, as you put it, but they were always thought-provoking. You never really discussed your work, just your views. You know, I think I've secretly admired you. To leave everything and make a new life across the ocean. What courage that must have taken."

Edithe shrugged. "I suppose one could see it like that. Now it seems the most intelligent move I've ever made. It's when my life really began to make sense to me. Oh well." She sighed and looked back to the fire. "Everything happens as it should. For me, there are no accidents or matters of chance. I am just grateful I recognized the opportunity when it arose almost thirty years ago and followed through. I had a choice. To stay in the States, or leave to begin a new adventure. I chose the adventure."

Like me, Maggie thought, looking once more around the room and thinking of Stonehenge ten miles away. Just being here in her aunt's home in England . . . this was her adventure.

"It was the appropriate choice for me . . . to follow my heart," her aunt added, and sipped her tea. "That's how I make most of my decisions now, by following my heart. It's why I sent you the ticket. My heart told me you could use a break, and I could visit with you as you healed."

Maggie gulped her tea. "Healed?" Why did her aunt use that word?

Edithe's smile was filled with compassion. "Isn't that how you feel right now? Sitting here in this house, in front of the fire? Don't you feel yourself relaxing, maybe for the first time in years? There isn't anything for you to do here, except to relax, have fun, and heal, Maggie. And maybe have a reunion. Not just with me. With yourself. That's the kind of healing I'm talking about."

She felt a lump in her throat as she listened to her aunt's words. Was it from gulping the tea? That couldn't explain the ache in her chest as Edithe's words struck a chord within her. The very last thing she wanted to do was cry in front of her aunt. How odd that she felt so close, so quickly, to this woman. The years of letter writing had produced an intimacy that was rare for her. Usually, she was the strong one, the one who tried to fix everyone else's problems. Maybe that was an excuse not to face her own?

"I feel like I'm running away," Maggie murmured, as the stinging in her eyes increased.

"Good," her aunt answered in an emphatic voice. "No point in staying within something we perceive as not working. Did you know the Chinese symbol for chaos means opportunity? Your chaos may have provided you the opportunity to grow, to experience yourself now. Could you have changed anything by staying in New Jersey for this week?"

Maggie thought about it while blinking to ease her eyes. She really was fighting tears and took a deep breath to give her the strength. "Well, I could have tried to find another job, but it would have taken days to set up interviews. It's just that it seemed unreasonable to pick up and leave. Who knows, maybe I'm feeling a bit guilty."

"What I would consider unreasonable would be to stay in a situation where nothing was working," her aunt said, and looked at her. "You have an ascendant Aries moon. The ram. Your moon rules your emotions. Aren't you tired of trying to ram down the barriers, child, to make everything work the way you think it should? Don't you have a headache yet?"

Maggie laughed, picturing herself making running starts at brick walls that never tumbled, no matter how much force she applied. "I think my head is pounding from the effort. You're right. I need to heal. At least my head."

Edithe grinned widely. "Why, Maggie . . . that's where all healing takes place. In our minds, then it settles into our hearts. What is it that you want? Really want in life? Have you figured that out yet?"

"Hmm . . ." Maggie looked back to the fire and thought for a moment. "I want to be happy. And safe. It seems like I've spent my entire life searching for safety, some distant oasis of safety where I could finally freeze-frame it all and relax. Just stay there and be happy."

"*Bullshit!*"

Startled by the word and the force of her aunt's voice, Maggie turned sharply and stared at her relative who was staring right back at her. Edithe looked almost angry, and Maggie really wanted to cry, thinking she had somehow offended her aunt.

Edithe's words, when they came, sounded full of authority.

"There is no safety, Maggie. Safety is the lie we've accepted. If you freeze-frame something, it's done, finished. There's no more growth, adventure, life to it. Safety is the illusion. If you just follow these rules, avoid these foods, believe this dogma, accumulate enough money or possessions, you'll be safe. We'll buy into anything if we think it could lead to safety. Why, you don't know if when you go to sleep tonight you'll wake up in the morning. You could be hit by a bus crossing the street tomorrow, or fall in the bathtub and break your neck at any moment. All of this . . . *life* . . . could end in a moment." Her expression softened, as she added, "I'm sorry to have startled you, but in this case, it's the best way to get past the illusion. It's not as morbid as it seems, Maggie. It's taking the moment, and making it yours. I don't want to sound pessimistic, that you'll never get this moment back . . . but you won't, love. *Carpe diem.* Seize the day. And the day can be joyful, or miserable. It's your choice. There is nothing but this moment, dear child. This is it. Life. Right here. Right now. Anything else is the illusion of your past, which is over, or the imaginings of your future, which hasn't yet occurred. Though time itself is the illusion, for I think it's all taking place right now . . . it's where we place our attention, our focus, that determines what we experience.''

Her aunt's words seemed to echo inside her head, making her dizzy. "What do you mean? Nothing else is real, but right now?" It sounded . . . crazy.

"Isn't it?" her aunt asked. "You're worried that you must find a job. Why do you want the job?"

"For the money to pay my bills," Maggie answered, feeling her throat starting to get thick again as emotion crept into her voice.

"Just for the money?"

She thought about it. "Well, for the peace of mind it would bring. I'm so tired of the worry."

Edithe nodded. "I understand. So you want a job for the peace it might bring?"

"Yes." Where was her aunt going with this?

Smiling, Edithe asked, "And how did you feel moments ago, when we were staring into the fire? Didn't you say you felt peaceful in that moment?"

Maggie merely nodded, attempting to swallow the thick lump in her throat again.

"Maybe what you want isn't so much a job or even money. Maybe what you really want, Maggie, after all is said and done, is peace. And you can have that right here, right now. If you don't allow your mind to take you away from the present moment, where your life, child, is taking place. Don't worry about nine days from now when you return. Stay here in your mind, where your life is right now.'' Edithe smiled tenderly. ''And that's not irresponsible, Maggie. That is being responsible to yourself.''

Maggie felt like her aunt was confirming her worst fears, that being a good person and planning her life didn't guarantee anything. It felt like madness, like she had spent her whole life seeking something that wasn't real, a mirage that could never be reached. There was no safety. Even though she wanted to fight it, everything Edithe was saying made such sense, and her chest felt like it would explode if she didn't yell or scream or . . .

Suddenly, she couldn't hold back the tears, and they burst forth with such intensity that she covered her face in humiliation. It was embarrassing, and she wanted to apologize to her aunt, but the sobs were so thick she couldn't speak. All those years of worrying, about life, about her marriage, about the divorce, it all played out in her head. The months of rejection and sheer terror since she'd lost her job and then spiraled into financial ruin took their toll as Maggie continued to experience the convulsive sobs.

Being a good person didn't guarantee anything.

''I . . . I'm so sorry,'' she finally was able to mutter.

''Don't ever be sorry, sweet Maggie,'' her aunt whispered, still staring into the fire. ''Get it out. It's been a long time coming.''

She did. She sat in the chair and cried, cried for her screwed-up life.

It must have lasted two or three minutes. Maggie cried like a child, and Edithe sat in her chair, sipping her tea as she waited it out. Finally, when her despair had been exhausted, Maggie sniffled and wiped at her nose with the back of her hand. ''I am so sorry for falling apart like that,'' she managed to mumble. ''Must be the jet lag.''

Edithe set her teacup back onto the saucer, got up,

and handed Maggie a few tissues. She sat on the arm of Maggie's chair and smiled with such sweetness that Maggie felt like crying again.

Stroking Maggie's hair back off her forehead, Edithe gathered her into her arms and held her closely. "Shh . . . it's all right now," she whispered against her hair. "The reason I didn't hold you when you started crying is because I didn't want to anchor that energy around you, so you'd have to deal with it again in the future. You were releasing."

It felt so good to be held in a woman's arms, soft and comforting, and Maggie missed her mother. They didn't have many moments of closeness together, and she hadn't cried in front of her mother since she was child. "Maybe I'm having a breakdown," Maggie muttered, and laughed.

Edithe rocked her slightly. "Not in the conventional terms, but you are breaking down and releasing things you've held inside of you for too long. I'm honored you could do it with me."

"Guess you didn't figure on inviting me to visit and having me become hysterical on you."

Edithe chuckled. "Nonsense. You aren't hysterical. I think you aren't used to releasing. It can be a scary experience, but—"

"*Costly thy habit as thy purse can buy, but not express'd in fancy: rich, not gaudy: for the apparel oft proclaims the man.*"

Both women froze for a moment, then turned to see Malcolm at the doorway in a ridiculously theatrical stance. He was dressed in maroon tights, a short green jacket with gold piping and puffy sleeves, and a plumed hat atop his head.

Edithe burst out laughing and rose to her feet. "*Much Ado About Nothing*?"

"*Hamlet*, m'lady," Malcolm proclaimed, coming into the room. "Act one, scene three."

Maggie was stunned. She didn't know what to say. Wiping at her nose, she started to giggle at the sight of Malcolm, knobby knees and all, in tights.

He took his hat from his head and bowed to them with a deep sweep.

"You look wonderful, love," Edithe said, then walked up to him and ran her hand over his shoulder, feeling the rich material of his jacket. "Very . . . courtly this year."

"Yes," Malcolm murmured. "About time, too. The jester was wearing a bit thin."

Edithe giggled, and Maggie couldn't help smiling at her aunt's delight. Even though she had no idea what was going on, she could see the couple were enjoying themselves.

Maybe the wacky part was about to begin?

"Well, m'lady?" Malcolm asked, looking at Maggie. "What do you think of my attire?"

Chuckling, Maggie said, "I think you look fabulous. Is this for a costume party?"

Malcolm glanced at Edithe. "You didn't tell her?"

"Not yet," Edithe said, and looked down at Maggie. "I mentioned the Renaissance Festival tomorrow, but I didn't say we're all going in costume."

Maggie again wiped at her nose, used her finger to rub the running mascara away from under her lids, and sniffled. "How nice," she answered, hoping Malcolm wouldn't ask if she were upset, and then thought she'd feel silly walking next to him and her aunt dressed in period costumes. But what the heck . . . she didn't know anyone, and if it pleased Edithe and Malcolm to be in costume, then so be it.

"*All* of us, Maggie. That includes you."

She looked at her aunt, smiling Malcolm, and

laughed. "I don't think so. I'm not a costume person. You two have fun."

"Nonsense," Edithe said, and sat back in her chair. "It's the last day of the festival, and everyone will be dressed in the Renaissance period."

"Well, I don't have one." A wave of relief swept through Maggie at the easy out. Costumes. Role-playing. She didn't even like to play charades.

"Yes, you do," Malcolm said. "I picked it up this afternoon while you and Edithe were strolling through the garden and getting reacquainted. I laid it out on your bed before I tried on mine."

Maggie felt her easy out disappearing. "I really don't think I'd be comfortable."

Edithe nodded. "Well, we certainly want you to be comfortable, though I must say that most will be in costume. It's a tradition here, and such fun, Maggie, to get into the magic of that period. It takes place in the woods. There's a small village built, very authentic, and everyone speaks Shakespearean English. Actually, Elizabethan. There are actors, of course, who will stroll through the town and have an impromptu sword fight and such, yet with everyone dressed the part you never know who's an actor and who's a visitor. It can be a bit overplayed by the frustrated thespians, though some are very, very accomplished, but it's all in good spirit. Won't you at least look at your costume before you make up your mind?"

Maggie didn't want to look at any costume. Sleep was suddenly very appealing. "I thought we were going to Stonehenge."

"We'll make sure you get there before you leave," Malcolm said. "But it might be better to wait the five days until that concert is over. If I might make a suggestion, Maggie . . . Try on your costume. See how you feel. If you aren't comfortable, then don't wear it. The

Renaissance is a special time for us, and we do enjoy revisiting it. But that's us. You do what you feel is right for you.''

Smiling, Maggie picked up her cooled tea. ''Thanks, Malcolm. I don't know that much about the Renaissance, except through art.''

Edithe sighed with pleasure. ''Ahh . . . it's when civilization, at least European civilization, came out of the Dark Ages. When song, poetry, literature, sculpture, chivalry was reintroduced. And love. Romantic love was openly acknowledged. Civilization broke free of those bonds the Church had placed upon it, and thinking, creative thinking, was again allowed.''

She could only nod. Sounded like a good time in history, but she wasn't about to dress up in a silly costume and pretend she was going back into it. She had enough to do trying to live out her own history right now, let alone playacting four hundred years ago with a bunch of Renaissance fans.

''Just try it on, Maggie. See how you feel in the morning.''

Again she nodded to her aunt, for she wasn't up to discussing it further right now. She was already embarrassed by her show of emotion, and didn't intend to humiliate herself any more than she had.

''Shall we take a look?''

Edithe's expression was so hopeful that Maggie didn't have the heart to disappoint her. ''Sure,'' she said, rising from the comfortable chair after her aunt. As she passed Malcolm, she whispered, ''Hey . . . nice legs.''

He chuckled and answered, ''*Compliments are only lies in court's clothes.*''

Edithe laughed. ''Shakespeare again?''

''I don't know who said it,'' Malcolm answered, propping his hat upon his head and walking up to an ornate wall mirror. Pleased with his reflection, he smiled at himself. "I do have a noble bearing, if I say so myself. My legs are another matter entirely."

Edithe walked up behind him and touched his shoulder. She smiled at him in the mirror, and said, "I would know you anywhere. Whatever our souls are made of, yours and mine are the same."

Maggie watched as Malcolm turned and touched Edithe's cheek. "Emily Brontë knew, didn't she?"

"Yes, love, even though she was termed a spinster, somehow she knew." Edithe turned her face and kissed Malcolm's palm. "Now, let me show my niece her beautiful costume."

Maggie observed the interaction, and her heart constricted. Edithe really was blessed to have found her love, and she was happy for her aunt. So why did she have this sadness, that she might never experience that kind of love herself? Stopping herself from mentally going down *that* hopeless path, Maggie followed her aunt from the sitting room and up the stairs. She had enough to deal with right here, right now . . . like how to get out of wearing a costume.

She walked into the guest bedroom and stared at the dress laid out on her bed. Nothing could have prepared her for it. The gown of rich ruby velvet was simply breathtaking. "Oh, my . . ." Maggie murmured, going closer and touching the material of the wide skirt. "This is . . . so beautiful."

"It is," her aunt agreed. "I'm glad you like it."

"Who wouldn't like it?" Maggie insisted, looking at the gown and thinking she probably would look wonderful in it. Damn. Now how was she supposed to get out of wearing it tomorrow? The dress was lavishly trimmed with a gold embroidered and jewel-set border around the square neckline. An undergarment of elaborate gold-embroidery extended upward to a standing collar of thick, white, starched ruffles, the same smaller white ruffles appearing under the wide and deeply cut sleeves that must hang to the ground, cascading like trains on each side. The waistline slanted downward to form a broad yet deep rounded point and yards upon yards of ruby velvet, studded with hundreds of tiny seed pearls, billowed out to create the skirt.

"Oh, my," Maggie repeated. "It must cost a fortune. Those jewels look so real around the bodice."

Edithe laughed. "They aren't. And we're only renting it. It's fairly authentic in style though," her aunt said, as she picked up the dress by the shoulders and held it in front of Maggie. "Do you want to try it on now?"

Thinking about it for a moment, Maggie shook her head. "Not really. I feel kind of wiped from our healing session. No wonder you have a successful practice. You sure know how to get to the issue."

Edithe returned her smile. "I understand. Releasing can be exhausting. I'll just hang it here on the armoire, and you can decide later." Her aunt took the dress, placed it on a thick wooden hanger, and smoothed the material down. "It is lovely though, isn't it . . . oh! . . . I have something for you. I'll be right back."

Maggie sighed, already knowing she wouldn't be able to resist this dress. "Wow," she again whispered to the empty room. Never in her life had she worn anything quite so beautiful.

"Maggie, this is to complete your costume." Edithe returned and placed a twenty-inch strand of small pearls in her hands, then gently closed them around it. "They are very dear to me, child."

"They're incredibly beautiful, Aunt Edithe," Maggie whispered, fingering the tiny smooth beads. "Maybe I shouldn't wear them to an outside event. I would hate if something happened to them."

Edithe smiled. "Nonsense. I'm giving them to you. An early birthday present, child. They were given to me

many years ago by . . ." She smiled as though recalling
the event. ". . . by a dear friend, a wonderful teacher.
He said to keep them, to hold them, and I would know
when it was time to pass them along. It's time. Besides,
they're perfect for your costume. Wear them in happiness, Maggie."

She wanted to protest that it was too extravagant a
gift, but she saw the deep affection in her aunt's eyes
and smiled with awe and gratitude. "I will treasure
them," she whispered, feeling her throat thicken with
emotion again. "Thank you, and thank you for choosing
me. I'm honored."

Edithe fastened the pearls around Maggie's neck, and
the weight seemed to rest at her heart.

"Perfect, Maggie. Look in the mirror. You are radiant, child, simply radiant. I *knew* you were the one."

Maggie stared at her reflection and had to admit she
did look . . . younger, peaceful. She'd heard crying was
therapeutic, but a beauty treatment?

Edithe walked up to her and placed her hands on
Maggie's shoulders. "Rest well, dear Maggie. May your
dreams be sweet."

Turning, she kissed her aunt's cheek and hugged her.
"Thank you so much for our talk, and for handling my
hysterics with such grace. I have a lot to think about."

Edithe squeezed her in return. "Nonsense, child. We
were communicating. Plain and simple. It doesn't always have to be pretty. We just have to hear what each
other is actually saying. I'm glad I heard you."

Maggie pulled back and looked into her aunt's eyes.
"You really are a remarkable wise woman. No wonder
you work well with learning disabilities. I'm feeling a
little disabled myself tonight."

Edithe stroked her cheek and smiled. "We're humans.
We all become disabled once in a while. How else
would we learn what we're really capable of?"

Maggie laughed. "There's gotta be an easier way."

"There is, child. It's simple. Remember."

"Remember?" Maggie could feel her brows knitting in confusion. "Remember what?"

Edithe smiled. "Remember that this is just a stop on your journey, so throw away your map and just enjoy it. Don't take it too seriously. Remember that peace is a choice, and you have free will to choose it anytime you want. Do you remember joy, Maggie? What it was like to enjoy life with freedom?"

She thought about it. "Seems like a long time ago."

"One day you'll recapture that. When you do, you'll remember it all."

"I'm confused," Maggie said with a laugh.

Edithe joined her laughter. "Curiosity didn't kill the cat. Boredom did. Allow wonder to work its wonder. Seek peace, Maggie. Stay in the moment. That's all you need to remember now. Rest well."

Her aunt left and Maggie turned to look once more at the gorgeous dress. How could she not wear it now, especially after the gift of the pearls? Her aunt was the perfect hostess, and she knew in her heart she wouldn't disappoint Edithe. Sighing, she walked over to the bed and turned down the thick comforter. Even before she climbed onto the crisp cotton sheet, she knew she was defeated.

She had an adventure awaiting her tomorrow, exactly what she had wished. She just never thought she'd be dressed up like some rich Renaissance lady. Trying to relax, she turned off the light and ran her fingers over the pearls while staring at the shadow of the gown, hanging like a ghost in the moonlight.

She didn't even have to try it on to know it would look great, and she would wear it.

Giggling, Maggie shook her head and closed her eyes, giving herself over to the comfort of sleep. She envisioned Edithe and Malcolm and sighed . . . with a bit of yearning. Did she dare believe again . . . that somewhere, someplace, someone would really love her like she had always wanted? Was it real, or a myth women are fed? Edithe was real. The love she had with Malcolm was real. Maggie had actually *felt* it. Could it be that her disillusionment was fading, now that she had witnessed the kind of love she had been searching for her entire life? Was she actually opening up to the possibility again? It was scary, and a little exciting. Who knew what waited for her? Maybe she should just be more like Aunt Edithe and stop trying to direct everything. Just go for the adventure.

And she thought her life in the States was ridiculous? According to Aunt Edithe, there was no safety . . . and she was about to go on an adventure.

Talk about joyriding into the unknown.

Chapter Three

The woods were thick and lush with greenery, a canopy of emerald twinkling with bursts of sunlight. Maggie was in awe as she followed her aunt, whose elegant gown seemed to match the deep green of the leaves. Holding up the skirt of her own gown as she stepped along the dirt path, Maggie had to admit that she looked . . . well, great. Never in her life had she worn anything so exquisite. Her hair was pulled back into a pearl-studded snood that matched the tiny seed pearls on the dress. She became aware by the glances of those she passed that she must look pretty good, and she knew . . . even though the costume could be difficult to maneuver, she had never felt so feminine in her life. Almost everyone was dressed for the occasion. Some wore costumes as rich as her own. Others were dressed in shifts with laced girdles, boosting their bared cleavage, as if their breasts were being served up for inspection. There were knights and ladies, peasants and wenches, even children dressed in period costume. And they hadn't even entered the village yet.

"Good day, m'lady," a man in a black cloak, tights, and white ruffled shirt said, lifting his feathered cap and bowing deeply in front of her. "Thy beauty is announced by the sweet harmony of the birds."

The birds were chirping. Maybe it was a sound system, or something.

Even Malcolm's antics hadn't prepared her for such theatrical behavior. Slightly taken back by the handsome man, Maggie clutched the precious strand of pearls at her breast and chuckled. "Hello."

He stood upright and waved his hand toward the woods. "Welcome all, to our humble village faire. If thou would proceed along this beaten path and o'er yonder bridge, thou shalt succumb to many delights such as will tempt thy tongue . . . and thy purse."

Edithe laughed. "Why, thank you, kind sir."

They walked only a few steps more when they heard the man call. "Noble ladies!"

Both Maggie and Edithe turned back together.

"I dare warn thee . . . beware the dense woods, for such fine specimens, as yourselves, would certainly be tempting morsels for the villainous hedge-borne miscreants that oft lie in wait."

Maggie laughed and Edithe nodded sagely. "We shall heed your advice, sir, and we thank you for the kindness you've so graciously displayed."

The handsome man winked at Maggie, bowed to all, and turned to the next arrivals.

Still chuckling, Maggie murmured to her aunt, "They certainly do play the part well, don't they? Villainous hedge-borne miscreants?"

Malcolm laughed. "Ahh, but that's the best part, Maggie. The insults. Spongy, rat-faced foot licker, is a favorite of mine. Or mammering clapper-clawed maggot-pie is another that slips easily from the tongue. And then there's—"

"Malcolm," Edithe interrupted with a grin, as they approached the bridge. "Enough. Allow Maggie to discover those unique forms of address on her own. Besides, she looks like an angel. Can you imagine those words coming out of her mouth?''

Picking up the hem of her skirt, Maggie walked onto the wooden bridge and muttered, ''Mammering clapper-clawed maggot-pie. I'll have to remember that one the next time my ex calls and asks where his alimony is.''

Edithe overheard her and laughed. ''Oh, child . . . soon you will see the purpose behind it all. For now, just allow yourself to enjoy the day. Oh, look . . . already there's a sword fight.''

Maggie saw the village up ahead, and two men were swinging swords as they shouted at each other. Nearing the fight, she could hear more colorful insults that accompanied the clanging of metal against metal.

''Good day, m'ladies, m'lord.'' A maker of bows, arrows, and ornate walking sticks held up his wares, as though not in the least concerned that the duelists were rapidly making their way up to his tiny shop.

''Hi,'' Maggie answered, still not comfortable with the more formal way of speaking. She kept her eyes on the combatants, marveling at the choreographed fight. They really took this stuff seriously, she thought, but knew it was just role-playing. She turned to see Edithe and Malcolm placing bets as to the victor.

''M'lady?''

Feeling a tug on her skirt, Maggie looked down at the form of a child. The midmorning sun was shining so brightly, she had to squint to make out the long, loose blond curls framing a sweet young face. The little girl wore a pink rosebud head wreath and a simple white smock. She was barefooted and appeared to radiate.

The child giggled impishly and held up a perfect single red rose. ''For you, m'lady.''

Maggie leaned down and reached out her hand to take the stem. ''It's lovely. Thank you.'' Bringing the flower to her nose, she closed her eyes and inhaled the strong scent while wondering if she was supposed to pay the girl, if the child was a worker at the faire. "One moment," Maggie whispered with a smile, and turned toward Edithe.

"I didn't bring any money with me, and this angelic child just gave me a rose. Should I pay her?"

When Edithe and Maggie turned around, the child seemed to have vanished. Maggie looked through and around the crowd now encircling the sword fighters, yet couldn't see any trace of the girl. "I guess not," she murmured, as the gathering crowd made a loud "Hoorah!" of approval when one of the fighters knocked the other off-balance.

"It must be a gift," Edithe said, and returned to her position next to Malcolm, who was chiding the loser.

"*To arms! To arms! Ye brave! The avenging sword unsheathe, March on! March on! All hearts resolved on victory or death!*"

"Well spoken, sire," the victor loudly stated to Malcolm, as the crowd applauded the scene. Malcolm dramatically removed his hat and bowed lowly with a wide grin.

"All right, my scene-stealing noble . . . that's enough from this peanut gallery . . . let the *faire* actors continue their skits, my love." Edithe grinned and took Malcolm's arm, tugging him to move on.

"But that was Rouget de Lisle from the 'Marseillaise.' Only one of the greatest quotes for calling arms to—"

"Yes, my beloved," Edithe interrupted, "and you delivered it so well. Your dramatic training is quite evident, and always a source of joy to me; however, I confess, I do prefer it with fewer spectators present." Edithe placed both arms around his arm, laid her head against his shoulder, and hugged him tenderly.

"*Nothing great was ever achieved without enthusi-*

asm, madam. Emerson, 'Circles.' '' Malcolm smiled down at Edithe and placed his hand on hers.

"Maggie . . . this way," Edithe called back, as she and Malcolm continued on.

Suddenly, Maggie felt a wave of heat wash over her, and she drew away from the crowd. Gulping in fresh air, she walked toward a display of flowered wreaths with brightly colored ribbons hanging from them. No wonder she was hot, wearing heavy velvet and two layers of undergarments. How did women survive a Renaissance summer in all this getup?

Picking up a pretty head wreath of silky white freesia delicately laced with long dangling yellow ribbons, she stared at the artificial flowers and wondered if she could possibly find a tall icy Coke in a medieval village.

"Would m'lady like to try it on?"

Her attention was captured by a pretty woman, dressed in a pale blue gown with white-satin trim. She held up a silver hand mirror and, not wanting to be rude, Maggie couldn't see any way out of placing the wreath on her head. It did look nice against her dark hair, but she wasn't about to ask Edithe for money now. Why hadn't she thought to bring some herself?

"How lovely," the woman said, eager for a sale.

Maggie stared at her reflection. She already wore the snood, and the wreath was overdoing it, yet it might be a nice souvenir. Later, on the way out, she would ask Edithe to lend her the money until they returned to the house.

"It compliments you, m'lady . . . lovely and delicate."

This woman's really pushing for a sale, Maggie thought, and smiled back.

"It is very pretty, thank you." She took one last glance in the mirror, yet as she was about to remove the wreath, Maggie saw the reflection of scenery behind her blur and change, as if she were watching a special effect in a movie. The people, the shops, seemed to fade. There was only a lush green forest. She blinked several times and held her breath as another wave of dizziness washed over her. From the corner of her vision, she thought she saw the white smock of the little girl dancing by and quickly turned around.

Everyone was cheering the actors, yet she saw no sign of the child and she realized it was strange she didn't hear the cheers for a brief instant when she had looked into the mirror. Shaking her head, sure the heat and humidity were getting to her, Maggie removed the wreath and handed it back to the woman.

"It is lovely," she remarked again with a smile. "I'd like to buy it, if it's still here when I leave for the day."

"Shall I put it aside for you, m'lady?"

"Yes, thank you."

"Maggie! There you are," Malcolm said, leading Edithe by the hand. "Come along, dear girl. The maze has finally opened."

"The maze?" Confused, Maggie wiped the moisture on her brow as ladylike as possible and followed them through the village. She wanted to stop in some of the shops and check out the goods offered, yet it seemed that Edithe and Malcolm were on a quest.

Edithe slowed down and laced her arm through Maggie's. "This faire has been presented for almost a decade. A hedge maze was planted, and it's taken years to grow in, but now it's full. This is the first time it's been opened, and Malcolm and I want to see it before we meet our friends for lunch. It's just beyond the village."

The trio walked on amidst the throngs of people while Malcolm and Edithe described their excitement over the maze. Delicious scents wafting through the air triggered Maggie's tastebuds to watering. She thought her faintness must surely be from hunger, combined with the weight and heat of her costume. They passed through streams of smoke with the aroma of meats cooking on open-pit grills. Fresh bread baking in clay ovens and spices from Eastern lands filled the air. Calls to buy trinkets came from street vendors, while candlemakers dipped lengthy strings in heated wax. The tinkling sounds of wind chimes played against the rowdy laughter of armor-clad men lifting steins of what appeared to be ale. Peasant-dressed women spun dark threads by hand on long sticks. Jugglers, acrobats, jesters, and minstrels entertained along the pathway, while other peasants danced or watched in merriment. Nobly dressed men and women walked along, slowly eyeing the wares from gift booths and nodding to all they passed. Flags in assorted colors and shapes snapped in the light breeze as they made their way into a grassy clearing. The midday sun was intense, and the air was heavy with early-summer humidity from showers the night before. Strangely, Maggie thought she could hear the impish laughter of the little girl following behind her, but whenever she turned about, the child was not in sight.

This is too weird, she thought.

"The atmosphere is intoxicating, but the weight from this costume must be overheating me," Maggie said, pulling back from Edithe's grasp.

"Are you all right, Maggie?" Edithe held on with a concerned look.

"I'm okay. I just need to sit a moment," Maggie insisted, tugging on the high stiff collar. She couldn't still be dragging from the jet lag. She should have acclimated to traveling by now. Edithe and Malcolm assisted her to the end of a crude wooden bench where a family of tourists was also resting.

"I'm so sorry, child. Had I known the costume would be so burdensome, I wouldn't have asked you to wear it. Perhaps we should get you to a privy and you can at least remove the underblouse," Edithe said, standing and shading her eyes as she looked about for direction to the rest rooms.

"I'll get us something cool to drink," Malcolm stated, and darted off.

"I'm all right, really. I'll be fine after a cool drink." Maggie didn't want to tell Aunt Edithe about the dizziness she'd experienced, or the strange business with the mirror. She was tired, that's all. Traveling. Getting acclimated. That emotional discussion last night. No wonder her mind was playing tricks on her. She was not about to complain, since it was obvious Edithe and Malcolm were having a wonderful time, and Maggie didn't want to spoil their day.

"We can leave now, dear. We needn't stay if you're feeling—"

Maggie interrupted. "No, Aunt Edithe. Really, I'm fine. I want to see this maze you and Malcolm have been talking about so much."

"Only if you're sure you're up to it, child. I don't want you to push yourself if you're not feeling well."

Almost as quickly as he'd darted off, Malcolm returned. "Here ye are, m'ladies . . . this should do the trick. Freshly squeezed lemonade, ice-cold, to satiate any dry palate."

"Mmm, thank you, Malcolm," Maggie said into the paper cup as she began drinking. "Ah, this is much better." She finished her gulp with a lick of her lips.

"Perhaps we should move to the woods, where there's shade. You can rest a minute, Maggie. It's just over here." Malcolm pointed toward a path that began along a woods edge. "We could all use a rest, and there may be an empty bench."

"That's a good idea," Edithe answered quickly. "Maggie . . . ? Dear . . . ? Do you need help rising?"

Maggie sat, fixated in silence. She stared straight

ahead at the little angelic girl who was standing a few yards away staring back at her with another rose held up to her chin.

"There's that little girl again," Maggie said, standing up. "I think she's following me."

Malcolm and Edithe turned in the direction she was staring and saw only the hordes of people milling about.

"Where, Maggie? I don't see any child."

As a group of minstrels passed, blocking her vision, Maggie pointed and strained to see around them. "There . . . she's there—" Maggie stopped abruptly and looked startled. "Geez, she's gone. I swear, that kid gets around." Looking down to the ground around her, Maggie searched for the rose she'd been given earlier. "It's gone. I must have dropped it."

"Dropped what, child?" Edithe asked as she took Maggie's hand.

"The rose. The one that little girl gave me. I might have left it in the wreath shop."

"Well, I'm sure we can find you another. Let's get you out of the sun, dear."

From the corner of her eye, Maggie saw Edithe turn to Malcolm with a concerned look. Malcolm shrugged his shoulders, then gently took Maggie's other arm.

"I'm okay, Aunt Edithe. I think that little girl might have found it and wants to give it back to me. I've heard her following behind us all through the faire." Maggie's words trailed off as they entered the shaded woods.

"Here's a log you can rest upon, child," Edithe said as she led Maggie to it.

Nearly at once, they all sat down and sighed, Maggie in the middle.

"Ah, coolth." Malcolm grinned and closed his eyes.

"How do you feel now, Maggie?"

"Better." Maggie reassured her aunt with a pat on her hand.

They sat in silence for a few minutes, watching the passing crowd until Malcolm looked at his watch. "We've only half an hour before we meet our friends. Do you think you're up to going through the maze with us, beautiful Lady Margaret?"

She smiled at Malcolm's excessive language. "Sure." Maggie wanted to finish this mission and get out of her costume as quickly as possible. Thank goodness they all had a change of clothing waiting back in the car.

"All right then. It's just up ahead in a small clearing. Shall we move forth and be a—mazed?" Malcolm smiled wryly, then stood and held both arms out for his ladies.

Maggie giggled and thought he looked a little like the scarecrow from the movie *Wizard of Oz*.

"Let's." Edithe laughed. They continued down the path, arm in arm, very much like the characters in the famous movie.

"Come one, come all to Her Majesty, Queen Elizabeth I's, Great Maze of Pleasure." A very tall gentleman spoke in a theatrical tone and turned toward the trio. "Welcome, noble lord and ladies. Have ye come here today to be truly a-mazed?"

"We have, kind sir. 'Tis a pleasure we have patiently awaited for many a year now," Malcolm nodded in answer.

Maggie merely smiled, trying to be patient with the Elizabethan speech. Everyone but her seemed to be into it. She knew this wasn't what she needed, a maze . . . she was dizzy enough . . . but she would do it with Edithe and Malcolm. She couldn't wait to sit and have lunch with these friends her aunt was so eager to meet. She really was grateful for the experience, for she knew that not many women could say they were dressed in such a beautiful costume and given this opportunity. She just wished she felt better.

Malcolm paid the man, and they entered the maze. Many other participants could be heard around corners and over the hedge walls, laughing and calling out to one another. Maggie's heart really wasn't in it, but Edithe and Malcolm were almost giddy in their delight, and she hated to hold them back.

"Go on ahead," Maggie said to her aunt. "I'll just take my time and meander through. You two go and explore."

"We don't want to leave you," Edithe answered.

Seeing her aunt's eagerness, Maggie grinned. "Really, you lovebirds go ahead. I'll find my way around. Besides, if I get lost, I'm sure I could summon up a knight in shining armor to assist me."

Edithe smiled widely. "That's an interesting proposition, child. Be careful what you wish for . . . it just might come true!"

"Actually, that's the last thing I need," Maggie said with a laugh.

"She wants to walk alone, my love," Malcolm whispered into Edithe's ear.

"Ah, yes. For centuries mazes and labyrinths have been used for meditational walks. We'll find you on the outside, dear," Edithe assured her. "By the way, I've heard the trick to finding your way out, should you get turned around, is to keep your hand on the right wall consistently. It will lead you out." Edithe smiled, then turned away with Malcolm.

"Thanks, that's good to know . . . Now enjoy—" Maggie's words muffled off within the thick hedges and in a turn, Edithe and Malcolm were gone around a wall.

Maggie followed slowly in the same direction. She looked up to the sky and wished a breeze would find its way into the thick hedges, and couldn't believe she was in this maze, sweating her life away in a gorgeous costume, and starving. Thinking of all the calories she was burning, she wondered, who needs a gym workout? She probably should have gone ahead of them to get out quickly. Really . . . she couldn't imagine what all the "a-maze-ment" was about.

From behind her, Maggie faintly heard a childish giggle again. How unusual she thought, as it seemed to echo within the smothering maze. She turned, and from the corner of her eye caught a glimpse of the little rose child. There she was. That radiant, angelic child. She stood in the middle of a passageway, looking directly back at Maggie. The child smiled impishly and, without a word, appeared to beckon Maggie to follow her. Then she turned and disappeared down the path.

"Little girl," Maggie whispered, as though in invitation. "Hey, little girl . . . do you have my rose?" she asked in a louder voice, and quickly started off in her direction. Why had that child been following her all day? It was a mystery she wanted to solve. Maggie turned around the hedge wall, half-expecting to see the playful child, but she was gone. Could she have darted through the bottom of the hedges? Aunt Edithe and Malcolm were nowhere to be seen either. Maggie stopped to listen for anyone, but only an eerie silence hovered.

Suddenly, she felt terribly alone.

Spinning around, she vainly searched for anyone, but saw and heard nothing. "Hello? Hello?" Her calls went unanswered. She stopped abruptly in the path. She felt weak. Her heart was pounding, and her head felt light as it continued spinning. Grabbing at the starched collar of her blouse, she released the top few buttons and gasped in confusion. Now which way is to the right? Damn it. She'd turned herself completely around and everything looked the same. Okay, maybe she could use that shining knight right about now. She didn't care how or where he appeared, as long as he led her out, for the air was heavy and still, and Maggie found it hard to breathe. The heat was stifling, and she again clutched her high collar, fanning it back and forth from her neck. Her eyes closed as she felt the perspiration drip down her spine to gather at the small of her back, and her entire body tingled beneath the heavy costume material.

Great, I think I'm going to pass out, Maggie thought, opening her eyes and stumbling forward while hoping she was going in the right direction.

''M'lady.''

Her head snapped back at the childish whisper. Incredibly, the little girl stood right behind her. Twirling around, Maggie swore the giggling child was radiating with a weird light.

''Who are you?'' she whispered, attempting to slow down the hammering inside her chest.

''Follow your heart,'' the child said in a sweet voice, and plucked a rose petal from the flower she was holding. With a playful grin, she released the petal, then turned and ran down the path while dropping petals in her wake.

This kid's messing with my head, Maggie thought, leaning against the hedges while attempting to regain her bearing. She heard the child's giggle again and called out.

''Aunt Edithe! Malcolm! Help me . . . please.''

Silence.

Again she looked up to the sky and this time demanded some help, from somewhere. She couldn't do this alone anymore. All she wanted to do was rip the dress from her body and *breathe* again. Pushing herself away from the bushes, she began running over the scarlet petals.

Silence surrounded her as she rounded a corner and saw an empty pathway. Where *was* everyone? Why couldn't she hear anyone?

Rational thinking failed, and panic set in. Her heart

pounded harder, the pores on her body seemed to release a torrent of moisture, her stomach clenched in fear; her breath shortened, her limbs trembled, and the weight of the costume felt like it was pulling her down to the ground.

For the first time in her life she experienced claustrophobia.

She was trapped in fear.

"M'lady . . ." The child's voice sounded farther away, as if in a tunnel. "Follow your heart."

Confused, Maggie wondered if she really heard the kid or if it was merely her panicked mind playing tricks. Then something truly irrational happened, something that could not be explained. From all around her, every direction, she heard the child's voice.

"Follow your heart, follow your heart, follow your heart . . ."

Spinning around and around as each command echoed in her head, Maggie experienced a sudden lightness, as if she no longer had to struggle against gravity and push herself away from the earth. It was as though she were on an elevator at the World Trade Center and headed downward. The tightness in her muscles eased, and as she felt herself floating . . . she looked up to the sky, and the clouds appeared so close that if only she had the strength, she might be able to touch them. Whatever was happening was controlling her, and she was so weary of struggling, struggling with her life, her mind, all of it . . . flashes of her ex-husband and the alimony, her failed job interviews, the bills, the aloneness swirled together. It was bigger, more powerful than she, and she felt herself weakening, surrendering to it. The hedges appeared to fade away, and Maggie instinctively knew she had to get out or possibly fade with them. Gathering her last essence of strength, she started running toward the break . . . toward the light.

Grabbing up the hem of the wide skirt, she ran for her life. That was what it felt like, as every muscle in her body moved in perfect symmetry. She felt like a sprinter, effortlessly moving over the ground. Time seemed frozen. Nothing existed in that moment, save escape, yet she was aware that the faster she ran, the more rapidly the hedges began to fade away, like particles of light disintegrating into nothingness. It was freeing. It felt as though she were in a dream. She had no idea what was happening as she raced away from the dissolving maze toward the light ahead of her. Her mind instantly argued that none of this made sense. Stuff like this only happens in the movies. None of it was possible, yet she didn't care if she was losing her mind. She *had* to escape, and, through the light, she could see that the woods beyond were her only sanctuary. All she knew was that she must escape back to normalcy as she burst through the light and into the dense forest.

Miraculously, she was out.

Before she could even blink in relief, what could only be from the depths of a nightmare, a huge, hideous, yellow-toothed creature, with long black hair whipping back and forth through the air, appeared above her, screaming and frantically reaching out to tear her apart with long black arms. She screamed back in horror, and tried to move away from the monster. Catching her heel on the hem of her gown, Maggie felt herself going down. At once on the ground, she instinctively rolled over onto her stomach and covered her head. In any moment she expected death awaited her, as she would surely be crushed beneath the blows of this powerful creature.

"Thou fly-bitten, swag-bellied puttock!"

She was gasping for breath, inhaling the dust and dirt from under her mouth when she heard the angry yell that reverberated through the ground and rattled her already scrambled brain.

It *spoke*?

She dare not move, not even breathe. If this were a nightmare, and surely it couldn't be anything else, she wasn't about to add to the terror. This thing was directly on top of her as she could feel its hot, labored breathing on her neck. It was slavering around her head while snorting loudly, and she didn't move a muscle, not even inhaling, though her lungs felt like they would explode as sheer terror raced through her body. She would wake up any moment, her mind screamed. She *had to*!

"Damnation!"

Wait a minute, if this thing can talk . . . drawing upon more courage than she thought she had left, Maggie slowly lifted her head, fully aware she could be savagely struck down by the horrible beast. Looking up, pure amazement came over her. She was staring into the big brown eyes of a horse.

A horse!

She heard moans and looked beyond the animal to see a body. A man, rolled on the side of a dirt path, was clutching his knee as more colorful curses flowed back to her.

"Spleeny, lousy-cockered jolt head! Aww . . . heavens above deliver me from this vile, impertinent, ill-natured lout!"

Maggie sat up and began scooting and bouncing along her bottom away from the heated animal. Pushing herself to her feet, she brushed dirt, twigs, and leaves from her hands and backside while calling out, "Are you okay?"

He seemed to freeze with her words. Animatedly, still clutching his knee, he rolled over to stare at her in bewilderment.

She cautiously walked around the horse, giving it a

wide berth. "Sorry if I startled him," she called, still brushing debris from her costume. Her brain was fried, yet somehow she had to gather whatever shreds of sanity remained and slow down the pounding of her heart. She kept her gaze on the horse and cautiously made her way to the man. "How badly are you hurt?" she called out over her shoulder.

The man didn't answer, and she glanced in his direction. He was still staring at her, as though he'd lost his senses and, with one last warning glare at the horse, Maggie moved closer to the man.

Wow . . . that was her first thought.

Shoulder-length streaked blond hair framed a finely chiseled face. Eyes, large and of the lightest blue Maggie had ever seen, stared back at her, as though the man had seen a ghost. He was definitely an attractive, more than average, handsome man . . . okay, he was downright gorgeous, and she'd have to be dead not to acknowledge it. Since she was upright and breathing, she figured she was very much alive, and an instant attraction tingled through every muscle in her body, sending strong hormonal signals to each nerve ending.

"Are you all right?" she asked again, standing now a couple of feet away. Thrown by her reaction to the man, she nervously picked at more leaves sticking to the velvet of her skirt. "Can you get up?"

He appeared to recover and, through great effort, pushed himself upright while hobbling on his one good leg. Maggie wanted to reach out and help him, yet instinctively kept her hands at her sides. He wore dark brown breeches, a white shirt, ruffled and tied into a complex knot at his throat, and a deep green cape. A square-looking cap lay on the ground where he had fallen.

Gingerly testing his leg, he winced, took a deep breath, and bowed. "Good morrow, m'lady. I beg you forgive my slanderous outrages. Master Nicholas Layton, humbly at thy service.''

Maggie, still not recovered herself, blew out her breath in frustration. ''Nice to meet you, but *really* . . . considering the circumstances, I think you can forgo the formalities and drop the charade now, don't you?'' She was amazed that the man was continuing with the role-playing.

He glanced up at her with a quizzical expression before slowly standing upright again. ''Charade, m'lady?'' He winced in pain, hopping a few times to take the pressure off his knee, and added, ''I fear thou hast me at a disadvantage.''

He looked so comical, she wanted to laugh. Instinct told her that too would not be appreciated. ''What I mean is you're hurt. All the 'my lady' this and that isn't going to get you help. Just tell me where to go, and I'll find someone who can.''

Shaking his head, as though not believing his own eyes and ears, he spoke again. ''M'lady, it appears thou hast suffered thine own misfortune by the abominable actions of my steed. Why art thou astray in these woods? Perchance thou hast forgotten thy course?'' he continued, eyeing her slowly up and down.

She was aware that her gown was a mess, and there were smudges of dirt on her hands and probably her face. With as much dignity as she could muster, she adjusted the snood and brushed a stray lock of hair away from her eyes. ''Well, you see, I was in the maze and . . . and I guess I had an anxiety attack, or something. But I'm not hurt, you are. You can't walk back to the faire like that.''

She waved her hand out to the thick forest. ''Who runs this thing? Where's the manager's office? Is there a first-aid station? I'm sure they can get you help, a . . . a wheelchair, or something. Just tell me what to do.''

A glazed look came upon him. His mouth, though very nicely shaped, hung open, and his eyes, though only moments ago she had thought them gorgeous, now seemed vacant, only adding to the expression of senselessness on his face.

"Hey! Are you okay?" she asked, peering intently at him.

He appeared to snap out of it, and cleared his throat with unease. "Prithee, allow me to assist thee in mounting, m'lady. Despite that which you have witnessed, verily I tell you, 'tis not indicative of this beast . . . he is a most gentle animal."

Okay, he might be great-looking, but something was definitely wrong with the man. "Look, *Nick . . . I'm* not riding that horse! You've got to be kidding. In *this* getup?" She grabbed at the wide heavy material of her skirt and almost shook it at him. "You're the one who should be riding. I can help you up. You know, boost you up into the saddle and then you can ride back. I'll just walk back to the faire and find my aunt." She looked behind her to the woods and couldn't see the maze. Twirling around, she saw thick forests on both sides of the dirt road. "Where's the maze?"

"Maze?" He looked to the woods and then back at her as if *she* were the one making no sense.

Sighing, she placed one hand on her hip and stared at him. "The maze . . . remember? The Renaissance Festival? Did you hit your head when you fell?"

"Nay, only my knee has been injured. *My* mind functions most marvelously well. Perchance thou hast suffered some mental misfortune? Pray tell, a maze in the middle of a dense forest?" Bending down, he grabbed up his hat, dusted it off, and placed it on his head.

She would have laughed, except she could see this guy was really serious. "Look," she tried again. "I think you're a terrific worker, and I'll be sure to tell whoever runs this faire that even in the midst of an accident you didn't resort to modern speech, but we need to get you some medical attention, and I must find my relatives. I'm hot, hungry, and losing my patience. So ... let's just drop the *acting* for a moment, and I can either help you or you can give me some directions.''

"I am not an ac*tor*," he stated indignantly, obviously insulted by her words. "I am the third son of the Earl of Traherne. I have been introduced at court and formally educated by the masters of Italy and France. Presently, I have been summoned by the house of Amesbury to Greville Manor, and 'twas there I was on my way before you darted from the woods and commenced howling at my horse ... a shrieking woman who has yet to introduce herself, I might add, and now stands here to insult *me*." He took a deep breath and straightened his back, tugging down on the cuffs of his sleeves. "An actor, I repeat, I am not." He assumed an authoritative stance, going so far as to rest his injured leg to the ground, and fold his arms across his chest.

This time she had to bite the inside of her lip not to laugh out loud. He looked so funny, dressed in a costume and insisting he was *not* an actor. Everybody here was role-playing. And, of course, most were dressed like rich people, like him, the third son of the Earl of *Something* or other. At least when he was angered, he resorted to plainer speech.

She glanced at the horse and saw something that looked like a small guitar attached to his saddle. "Okay, you're not an actor. Then you play music? Is that your job? You're a musician?" Why this was so important to him, she had no idea, but she thought it could defuse the situation until they figured out what should be done with each other.

He lifted his square chin and looked down on her, as though he knew he wasn't making a great impression and was trying to correct that. "I enjoy music." Suddenly, he appeared to shake off whatever was bothering him, and commanded, "Who *are* you?"

Now she had to laugh. "Maggie. Margaret Whitaker."

"Lady Margaret?" His face took on an expression of shock. "Your Ladyship." He removed his cap, bowed lowly and continued with utmost courtesy, "I beg thy pardon. 'Tis an honor to stand before thee. Why art thou away in this wood? Thy presence was not expected until the week next. I am but a minstrel called upon by personal invitation of your esteemed aunt, the Countess Elthea. 'Twas she who implored I provide entertainment for your alliance to Lord Robert of Amesbury."

"Sheesh, what script are *you* reading from? This is really going to an extreme. Get it through your head, I'm not playing along with your game. Can't you just give it up?" Maggie demanded with irritation. "So . . . you're a minstrel. That's your gig here?"

"My gig? Pray tell . . . if anyone's speech is most confounding, surely Your Ladyship must take ownership of that observation."

Frustrated, Maggie waved her hands. "Okay, just forget it. Obviously, you aren't that injured and can make your own way back. Just point me toward the parking lot. I've got to get out of here."

"Parking lot? It is rightly known you are a visitor to your native England, having spent many years abroad, yet you are speaking with verbiage of which I have no knowledge."

He was at it again. She stared at him and clenched her jaw. "Drop it!" she nearly yelled. "Can't you knock off the role-playing for just a few moments? You Renaissance people are really weird, you know? What is it? You can't deal with life today, so you slip back in time and get lost in your fantasies? Well, you can keep it. I find this overplayed Renaissance speech extremely annoying. All I want is to get the hell out of this dress and return to sanity.''

He was adjusting his cape and staring at her. ''Remove thy dress? Lady Margaret, I have seen thee once at court, from afar I admit, but now you are possessed of a most distressful manner. Have you wandered afar, or come upon accident before thy arrival? You must return to the Greville Manor henceforth. Aye, I know there be highwaymen and poachers in this wood and—''

''Yeah, yeah,'' she interrupted. ''Villainous hedge-borne miscreants. I already heard about them when I arrived. How do I know you're not one of them? I was told to beware the woods. What *is* a miscreant, anyway? I'm telling you, it's impossible to communicate like this.''

''Your Ladyship, I would most honorably assist thee, if thou would but speak plainly.''

She stood her ground. It was becoming obvious the man must have whacked his skull. ''Was that supposed to insult my intelligence? Just because I refuse to be drawn into this role-playing?''

''By admission, thou art a most beautiful and confusing woman yet . . . manners be damned, Your Ladyship. You are making it impossible to treat thee with civility. I was extending my respect, while you are making it quite clear respect is not what you desire.''

She sighed. What was *wrong* with this guy?

If she heard one more *thee* or *thou*, she was going to scream. She didn't care if he looked like Sting in fantasy clothing. She didn't care how polite he was, or that he had just called her beautiful.

He was weird.

Really, really weird. . . .

Chapter Four

Maggie gathered what felt like her last shreds of patience and took a deep breath. "All right, Nick . . . let's calm down and concentrate on the present situation. What do you want to do? I can walk, but it's obvious you can't. Can you mount your horse?"

He hobbled to the horse, grabbed hold of the saddle, and made a valiant attempt. It was more than obvious he couldn't lift his injured left knee without great pain.

"Use the other leg," she urged, clenching her fists together to stop herself from helping.

"I cannot mount with my right leg. I would then be riding backward, Your Ladyship," he muttered with ir-ritation as the horse danced in nervousness.

"Then use the other side. Turn the horse around. Want me to do it?"

"No!" his word resounded through the woods and Maggie froze. He drew in a deep breath and added, "With all due respect, Your Ladyship, this horse is not trained to allow mounting from the right. He will only spin circles should I attempt what thou suggests."

"Well . . . I see only two options. You can throw yourself across its back and hang there like a sack, or ride backward. I'll lead the horse, if you tell me which way to go." There. That was as much as she could offer, considering she had caused the animal to throw him in the first place. "Make up your mind."

He looked back over his shoulder to her and all traces of patience and *civility*, as he called it, seemed to have vanished. She couldn't understand his attitude, since she was the one offering to help in spite of his reluctance to accept reality.

"I am *not* riding backward to Greville Manor. I would be the laughingstock of the entire court by week's end."

She crossed her arms over her chest and tilted her head to one side. "You know, you really have an ego problem, Nick, besides taking your job *way* too seriously. Look, maybe all you have to do is mount backward. Once you're on, I can hold the horse's head down and then you could . . . like, spin around in the saddle."

He turned at the waist, back to her. "M'lady, have you no sense at all? And have we been properly introduced that you should address me so informally? Has that memory completely vanished?"

She threw up her hands. "Okay, find your own way back. I was just trying to help, but if you're too full of yourself to accept my offer, then stand here. I'm getting out. I'll tell the first person I see to come back and find you."

They stared at each other for what seemed like minutes of tension.

"So . . . which way do I walk?"

He didn't answer her, just continued to gaze into her eyes with the strangest expression. It became uncomfortable, as though he were reaching inside of her and scanning her soul. Embarrassed at what he might find, Maggie shrugged, and said, "See ya, troubadour. I'm outta here."

She walked away, holding her shoulders and chin high. She was not about to stand around in the damn woods and argue with a man who was lost in his own fantasies. She didn't even care if he sang like Sting. He was nuts!

"Your Ladyship, you have struck out in the wrong direction . . ."

She stopped. Turning around, she began to pass him, and murmured, "Thank you."

"I shall attempt to mount, as you suggested."

Again she stopped walking and turned back to him. "I beg your pardon?"

"I repeat, I shall attempt to mount my steed, as you suggested. I am certain Your Ladyship heard me the first time. Your arrow has found its mark."

"My arrow?" Now what was he talking about?

He leaned his arm on the saddle, and began speaking as though to the horse. "The Lady Margaret requires complete humility, I see." He turned toward her. "If thou must hear it all, then so be it," he continued with a sigh, "my pride prevailed over my reason. Thou art correct. If I cannot ride, then you must lead me."

She smiled. "Thank you. I'm sure you'll do a splendid job of it, even backward . . . *Nick*."

He reluctantly grinned, as though he couldn't help himself, and Maggie saw the action completely transform his expression. She didn't desire anger from this man. Even though his manners were above reproach, something about him made her instinctively know that there was a strength, a forceful intensity about him that he kept under the surface, under control. She simply desired his attention in order to communicate, which wasn't going so well, she admitted.

She stood behind him, while he nearly hung on the saddle with both arms. Hearing his short gasps of pain as he stood on his injured leg, she wished she could do more than watch as he set his good leg to the stirrup. With one good bob, he began to lift himself, and once his bad leg was off the ground, he appeared to falter.

Maggie, not knowing what else to do, put her hands under his firm behind and gave him a shove.

"Hold his head down!" he yelled back at her as his cape fell to his right side and over her head.

"Oh . . . oh, yes . . . of course," she muttered, while throwing off the cape. Grabbing the reins, she pulled down. The horse lowered its head, and Nick groaned as he swung his bad leg over its neck and straddled the horse.

"Argggh . . . I swear by the fists of Thor!" His voice roared into the surrounding woods as he maneuvered his injured leg into position and settled onto the saddle.

Maggie winced in sympathy. Once she saw him sitting upright, she stood back and wiped her hands on her skirt while catching her breath. "There. Now, isn't that better? You're off your feet. In a few moments, your leg will ease up and we can start moving."

He wiped his forehead on his cape and looked around him in disgust. "I cannot believe this predicament. I must look the fool. I can only hope better fates are with me now and *no one* comes along."

"You're not a fool, Nick. A fool would stay out here with no hope of help. You overcame your pride and used your intelligence." There. That ought to make him feel better. But he did look pretty silly facing the rump of a horse.

He looked down at her and his eyes seemed to get lighter, almost a luminous, ethereal blue. "You may be confusing. You may even try a saint's patience, but you have shown your wisdom. And I thank you for reminding me that pride never serves, Lady Margaret."

She felt locked in his gaze, losing herself in the depths, and pulled back from the attraction by picking up the reins of the horse. "Well now, we'll just walk slowly, and soon we'll both reach our destinations. You just get as comfortable as possible. It can't be that far."

Nicholas Layton drew in his breath and stared down at the remarkable woman. She held her station as if she were the Queen herself, not budging an inch from her inner beliefs, and yet she was as contrary as a wildcat with a speech pattern that he was barely able to assimilate. The wealth of her bejeweled dress spoke of her rank and standing, yet she was also quite lovely in her feistiness, her spirited common sense. And she had called him to answer for his pride. Not many, save Francis, could have aimed so well to hit a target and not wound . . . too dearly. He mentally shook such thoughts out of his head. She belonged to another. As odd as this woman appeared, he was not to judge. He had heard the rumors from Francis last week that Lord Amesbury was marrying the Lady Margaret for the wealth she could provide Amesbury's dwindling coffers. Also, for several years the rumors at court were not kind, for gossips whispered that since Lady Margaret lost her husband, she was . . . peculiar.

Gathering his wits about him, he cleared his throat. "Even at a slow walk it shall take a bit of time," he said in answer to her statement.

"To get back to the faire? You're joking. Minutes, at the most."

"Faire? What is this faire you speak of, m'lady? Surely you can ascertain you are in the middle of a forest."

She turned to him and the expression upon her face was . . . not pleasant.

"I don't know how to get this through to you," she impatiently stated. "I am a customer at this Renaissance Festival. I'm here with my aunt and her companion, and when we entered the maze we were separated. Now I need to find them and—"

"You were with the Countess Elthea?" Pushing himself erect in the saddle and looking anxiously about the woods, he asked, "Where is she? Is she injured?"

"I was with my aunt. *My* aunt . . . not this fictional person you keep talking about. You still don't get it, do you? I'm not playing!"

He hadn't the slightest idea of how to answer this peculiar woman. Was she truly mentally unsound?

"Okay, let's just drop it and get out of here," she exclaimed with a dismissive wave of her hand, then wiped at her brow as she looked down the path. "Sheesh, it's hot. Hold on . . . don't turn around."

Of course he did, and was startled to see her releasing the closings on her garment. "Lady Margaret!" Shocked, he called out to her before she proceeded. Surely this woman was not in her right mind to be disrobing publicly!

"What? I'm just taking off this stifling blouse. How would you like it if you had to wear this getup?" She pulled at the delicate material around her chin. "If you turn back around, I can unbutton it and pull it through the sleeves. It's too damn hot to wear now."

Stunned, Nicholas watched her reach down under her bodice and then become most distressed as she pulled the material away from her body. She patted her chest, then clutched her throat. "My pearls! What have I done?"

"Your pearls, m'lady?" Still in a state himself, he could merely repeat her words as she worked at pulling the material of her underblouse through the sleeves of her gown. She looked . . . frantic, mad even, as she struggled.

"Dear God, what have I done? Where are they? I can't have lost them. I can't! Damn it. I can't do it like this." Trapped inside the material, she pushed her arms once more through the sleeves and stomped toward the woods. "Now turn away, and this time I mean it," she added as she reached behind her and began unlacing her gown.

He watched in astonishment as she walked behind a bush. Glancing over her shoulder to him, she shouted, "Turn around!" and he did. He stared down the path and simply could not believe what he was experiencing . . . thrown from his horse, a most unfortunate meeting with the Lady Margaret, seated backward upon his animal like a simpleton, and now witnessing the Lady Margaret undressing herself. What was Francis always saying to him? That all circumstances are meant to occur and are fraught with meaning? Well, he would like to get Francis's opinion of this afternoon's debacle. Imagine . . . Lady Margaret *disrobing*! He wished he could remember the gossip at court. Surely this type of behavior went beyond the realm of peculiar.

Just as those thoughts passed through his mind, Nicholas found himself turning his head ever so slightly toward the woods. He had to remind himself to breathe as he beheld a most astonishing sight. The scattered sunlight illuminated a wood nymph pulling down the top of her gown and removing her underblouse. He caught the tantalizing silhouette of her waist, her full breasts, the graceful line of her neck and bared arms as she pulled the blouse away and revealed herself to his spellbound gaze. She was . . . magnificent in her freedom, and the most outrageous being he had ever encountered. Male or female.

And he was mesmerized . . .

Lady Margaret quickly slipped her arms into her sleeves and pulled up the bodice of her gown to cover her nakedness. Not that much of a fool, he looked away just as quickly. Even though he was seated ass backward upon his faithful steed, he had enough wits not to be caught.

"Breathe, Nicholas. *Breathe*," he reminded himself,

acutely embarrassed to be in this situation and feeling his body immediately react to another man's woman.

"Oh, what have I done? Where *is* it?"

Her voice sounded near, and he straightened his shoulders in an attempt at composure. "What is it that distresses you so, m'lady?" He knew what distressed *him* and tried to wipe the amazing vision of this woman revealing herself from his mind.

"My pearls! I've lost them!"

He turned his head and looked down to her as all shreds of composure, any remote hope of composure, abandoned him. Without her underbodice, the Lady Margaret's breasts were deliciously exposed. No, not merely exposed, but framed by a square neckline bordered with jewels. What human being, awake, could *not* look?

"What am I going to do? I have to find them," she cried out, bending over to search the ground.

He didn't need to be asked. He averted his gaze without being told. Besides, if he continued to lose himself in her delights, he would also lose his ability to speak. Taking a deep breath, he wiped his forehead on the ruff of his shirtsleeve. She was right. It was exceedingly hot.

"Pray tell, Lady Margaret, when was it you last had them?"

She looked up at him. "I had them here at the faire. And in the maze. I must have lost them when your horse attacked me."

Immediately she proceeded to the spot where she had fallen. She bent over again and Nicholas cursed his body's response. This was a most delicate position in which to be placed. Shifting himself on the saddle, he looked behind him again and saw that she was now on her hands and knees, searching frantically through the dirt and leaves.

"Lady Margaret," he called out, hoping to make her

stop such foolishness. She didn't appear to hear him as she continued to pick at twigs and fallen leaves. "Lady Margaret, do not distress yourself," he again called, urging the horse with his feet to proceed forward.

It was most awkward, seated backward, yet Goliath sensed his direction and walked willingly. From some distant part of his brain, he saw himself, his position, his intention, and realized anyone observing would be rolling on the forest floor in peals of laughter. However, gentility, as he had been trained to believe, prevailed, and he proceeded closer to the woman.

Nicholas murmured to his horse and the animal stopped, not in the least concerned about what fools they looked, and lowered his head to the ground. "Lady Margaret, if you could but help me down, I can assist you. I am cursed by this injury and cannot dismount without aid." There. That was truth, spoken without pride.

She stopped crawling on the dirt path and turned her head to look up at him. His own heart seemed to catch at the expression of grief upon her lovely face.

"You don't understand," she cried, leaning back into a sitting position and punching at the billows of material that engulfed her. "These pearls are special. They're a gift. I *have* to find them!"

He thought she looked as though she were seated upon a ruby toadstool and marveled at her lack of decorum. Should anyone else come upon them, her seated thusly along a road, him seated backward upon a horse, they would think them surely mad. By the grace of Her Majesty the Queen, he wasn't so sure himself any longer.

"Help me dismount, and I shall assist thee," he again offered . . . anything to make her rise. Was she so distraught as not to realize her lowered position offered him the opportunity to behold her most excellent breasts?

"What?" She gazed up to him, as though his words

were finally piercing through her mists of madness. "Are you nuts? And go through that ordeal again to get you back up there? I'll find them. I have to. They must be here . . . somewhere. Damn it . . . what's happening? Why is *everything* so screwed up?"

He watched her cover her face with her hands, and she seemed to surrender as her shoulders sank in dejection. "Lady Margaret," he said in a low, gentle voice, "please do not distress yourself any further. I promise you shall have your pearls. Lord Robert will send someone to find them. If not, I shall scour these very woods myself. You shall have your proper jewels again."

Sniffling, she lowered her hands and stared at him with eyes that sparkled with unshed moisture. "You know, Nick, you might be weird, but you're really sweet. Thank you, but you just don't understand. They were given to my aunt by someone special, and he told her she would know when the time was right for her to pass them on. She waited years and years and deemed me worthy of them. *Me!* And now I've lost them."

"We shall find your maze then," he said, wanting to wipe away her grief. " 'Twas then you stated the pearls were still with you."

"Right. And where is this maze? I didn't run that far before your horse attacked me." She turned her head toward the woods. "Where is it?"

He had no answer for her. No maze that he had ever heard about existed in the forest. "My lady," he said gently, "my horse did not, and would not, attack you. 'Twas you who nearly ran him off the road. Goliath is a most gentle creature."

"Oh, right . . ." she muttered, pushing upward into a kneeling position, then grabbing her skirt and holding it up while struggling to stand. Sniffling, she said, "You'd have to have been in my shoes, Nickie. I thought the hounds of hell were coming after me."

Even the glimpse of her shapely legs faded when he realized what he'd just heard. She had called him Nickie. No one upon this earth called him that. It was an endearment his saintly departed mother used and one that melted his heart. "Forgive me *and* Goliath, Lady Margaret. Let us all depart this unfortunate place for more peaceful climes. Lord Robert shall indeed send someone to retrieve your jewels."

Walking toward him, the lady nodded and picked up her underbodice from the tuft of grass where she had dropped it. "You're right; maybe there's a lost and found office where I can file a claim," she murmured, blinking back tears as she held the reins and tossed the material embroidered with golden thread over Goliath's back. "Let's go."

"Ahh, Lady Margaret . . . ?" he called out as Goliath began to move. "Have you forgotten that I am turned in the wrong direction?" Surely he wasn't about to travel like this.

She was determinedly looking toward the woods. "I have to find that maze. They must be there. C'mon, let's hurry. I need to talk to someone in authority. Shit. I hope they're insured."

"Insured?" Again she was drifting into that strange speech pattern.

"It doesn't matter," she stated, walking faster. "They are valuable beyond money."

He had to hold on to the saddle to keep his balance as Goliath kept pace with the woman. "Lady Margaret. I *must* turn around."

"Oh, we'll get you turned around before we reach the faire. Just let's hurry right now. I don't want anyone to pick up those pearls and walk away with them. I would never forgive myself."

"And I shall never forgive you if someone should witness me in this confounding position." Really! He never would have mounted this way, had she not assured him she would assist him in righting himself.

She didn't hesitate in her direction. "Pride again, Nick?" she asked over her shoulder as she picked up her skirt and urged the horse to a faster pace. "These pearls are more important than your ego. Let's just reach someplace civilized, and I promise I'll help you then."

He simply could not believe her. She was the most unpredictable woman he had ever encountered, and he knew further entreaties would not be heard. She was determined now. Nicholas wondered if he could turn himself around, yet every time Goliath hit a rut in the road his knee reminded him that he was as good as lame.

They didn't speak until she reached a fork in the road. She began turning about to the left when he couldn't hold his tongue any longer. "We must proceed this way," he said, pointing in the other direction.

She stopped and stared down both paths. "I think you're wrong. The parking lot was this way . . . away from the village."

"That," he said emphatically, jabbing his finger in the air, "is away from the village. Your Ladyship's path will lead us back to the village, a much farther distance. We will find assistance *my* way."

She seemed to ponder his words. "Okay, so this is the way to a first-aid station? This is where the employees go?"

"I simply cannot comprehend m'lady's thoughts. Could you but speak plainly?"

She shook her head, as though *he* were the one unbalanced, and Nicholas drew up his shoulders and sat to his full height to prepare himself for her retort.

"Is . . . this . . . plain . . . enough? I . . . need . . . to . . . find . . . someone . . . in . . . charge."

He realized she was distraught, yet she was trying his patience beyond its limit. "Pray do not address me as though I am without the intelligence to know whence I came. The Lord Robert of Amesbury is in charge of this land, and he will be all the assistance you need, Lady Margaret.'' He didn't care how lovely she was, that the sight of her and her exquisite body made both his knees go weak, even his injured one, or that she had called him by his mother's childhood endearment.

She was odd.

Extremely . . . *odd.*

They proceeded in silence, and Nicholas was determined he would not break it. Surely, anyone observing would agree that he had extended himself beyond the realms of propriety. His chivalry was intact. Bruised a tad, sitting upon the rump of his horse, but intact nonetheless.

As they rounded a bend in the road, the horse suddenly stopped and Nicholas turned his head to see why they had paused. Lady Margaret stood, transfixed, staring ahead of her. Looking in that direction he saw Greville Manor, standing majestically beyond the woods.

"What is it?" she whispered. "Part of the faire? Wow, you guys get to stay there . . . ?"

He broke his vow of silence.

"Welcome to your new home, Lady Margaret."

She turned to stare at him, as though hit over the head with a battle-ax.

"*Huh?*"

"Your home, m'lady. Greville Manor." What was wrong with her?

"Okay, look, Nick . . . Maybe I'm not making myself clear here. I want to get back to *my home* . . . you know, back in the real world where there's air-conditioning and restaurants and phones where I can call for help. Remember the year 2000?"

Nick continued to stare at the woman, thinking Lord Robert of Amesbury was about to get the surprise of his life. Imagine being shackled for life to *her!* No matter how lovely she appeared, Lady Margaret could drive one mad merely by being in her presence!

The year 2000!

Chapter Five

"**N**ick . . . ?" She stared back at him. "You know what I mean, the modern world? C'mon . . . enough is enough." Really, the way this man continued to keep up the pretense of living in Elizabethan times was just ridiculous. Her new home? This castle? She wanted to laugh out loud, yet she felt her irritation momentarily turn to awe as she gazed at the huge picturesque building. It must be a museum, for it was kept in relatively good condition.

"I beg your pardon, m'lady?" He seemed to shake his head slightly while blinking, as though trying to bring some kind of sense into the situation.

Maybe there was hope, Maggie thought, as she waited for him to continue speaking.

"Lady Margaret, I have no knowledge of these *modern* things you speak of. I can only direct you to Greville Manor, your future home as the new wife of your cousin, Lord Robert. Let us proceed, shall we, after you fulfill your promise to assist righting me upon this saddle . . . surely, thou would not have me ride up looking like the court jester, would ye?"

She couldn't believe it. He was *still* insisting on this charade! "Okay, okay . . ." she said, exasperated, gathering more of the reins in her hands. "Let's get you turned around, if that makes you happy, and then I want to talk to someone else; someone who knows this is all a farce.'' There had to be someone at historic Greville Manor who wasn't steeped in this role-playing.

Looking up to him as she clutched the reins in her fist, Maggie directed, ''I'll pull his head down and you swing your leg around. Then you'll be seated correctly and only out of simple courtesy, for your taking me to some sort of civilization, I will keep this our secret. No one will ever know you rode your horse ass backward. Will that make you happy?''

He stared down at her and Maggie thought he might be tempted to throttle her if he didn't need her in that moment. Maybe she had pushed him too far, but really . . . the way he kept insisting that all this Renaissance stuff was real!

''Lady Margaret, that is not the first time you have addressed me as though I am witless. I pray thee caution; do not chastise me a third time.'' His statement dropped off in the afternoon air, just as a final command settles an unruly child. He focused his attention away from her and concentrated on shifting his seat while gingerly swinging his injured leg over the horse's lowered neck.

Maggie watched his determination break a light sweat onto his forehead as he stiffened with pain, closed his eyes briefly—as though accepting it—and continued with what she realized must be a very uncomfortable effort. When he had accomplished his goal, he sat quite still, opened his eyes slowly, and gazed outward, above her. She heard his controlled, heavy breathing amidst the hum of the warm afternoon.

''Are you all right?'' Maggie whispered, having to admire the way he handled his pain. Surprisingly, in the midst of the situation, she felt her confusing attraction return. That annoyed her even more than the man.

He stopped what looked like a meditation and, blinking a few times more, as though recalling she was still there, looked down to her.

"Yes. Thank you, Lady Margaret." He exhaled deeply. "You have been most helpful. We may proceed now." Inhaling fully, he placed his gaze back upon the hill toward Greville.

Maggie watched as a single bead of sweat trickled down his temple. As he wiped his sleeve against it, his demeanor seemed to soften.

"One might think m'lady would be eager to be rid of such a burdensome stranger."

Realizing she was still staring, Maggie completely released her hold on the reins as the horse raised its head and began to step on slowly. He must not be too badly injured to keep up this charade, she mused, then turned toward the beautiful castle. Shrugging, she started walking. "Whatever, Nick. I just need to find some help and get back to my aunt."

"I am sure your aunt, Countess Elthea, will be most pleased *and surprised* to see thee. Yes . . . I do believe this advent will cause quite a stir."

She wasn't going to answer him. So what if he was devastatingly attractive . . . nothing he said made sense. Directing herself on, she mentally repeated that all she need do was keep walking to the castle until she met someone who wasn't dressed four hundred years behind the times, someone who spoke modern English, even if they had an accent, somebody who wasn't caught up in this revival madness . . .

Anyone who held even a small concept of reality.

In the distance, she could make out men and women working in fields, some stopping their horse-drawn plows in mid-furrow to watch their approach. She found it amazing that this appeared to be a fully working Renaissance castle. They must have to pay the workers a small fortune to dress up and do work that a modern machine could accomplish in hours. When the British threw a faire, they went all the way, it appeared. She shook the thoughts out of her head and centered on more important ones. All she needed to do was find the manager of the place, get to a phone to call her aunt immediately, and then sanity would return.

Talk about an adventure! She hoped Aunt Edith and Malcolm weren't frantically searching for her.

The massive edifice once more commanded her attention. "This must have been quite a castle once," she muttered, breaking her vow of silence.

Impenetrable, large gray stones powdered with lime and thickly covered in ivy and moss loomed more than three stories above them. With both hands, Maggie shielded her eyes from the late-day sun to make out bright crested pennants dancing atop the barbican in the light breeze. Round corner turrets framed the entrance that beckoned with the sound of the hooves stepping across the narrow wooden bridge. This was probably the drawbridge a long time ago, she thought to herself as a cool breeze pulled her attention to the moat below. She saw their reflection interrupted by scattered lily pads on the dark surface, then focusing into the deep, she watched sizable fish dart about. How odd, she pondered, that everything seemed so fresh and clear in this moment, when she thought back to the stifling and hazy morning at the faire. She broke her gaze from the hypnotic water and took a moment to appreciate the artisans who created the ornately hammered black-iron straps adorning the massive arched oak doors that were beginning to squeak open. For an instant, her need to find someone rational was overrun with curiosity that insisted she venture inward to the interior splendor.

He'd given her a moment to admire Greville. "This is not a *castle*, m'lady. By comparison to thine own holdings, this is but a small manor house."

She refused to play into his continued rhetoric. "Well, whatever you Brits call it, they keep it in good shape compared to some of the others I saw when we drove through the countryside from the airport."

"Air . . . port?"

She wasn't about to start *that* conversation again. "Anyway," she continued, "I need to find someone who knows what's going on around here, and you need to get your leg looked at," she retorted, still hoping a little reality would bring him back to the present. "I'll do the talking once we're inside . . ." Her voice trailed off.

A tall, thin elderly man with a black felt cap, its brim folded up above his forehead, appeared. He was dressed in a long dark blue costume, brought tight around his waist by a wide leather belt with a large ring of dangling antique keys. As he pulled back the heavy door to reveal an expansive courtyard garden, Maggie almost gasped at the beauty.

"G'day, m'lord, m'lady," He spoke with utmost courtesy.

The fragrance of rose filled her senses. Every color dotted the yard at hand height. Someone obviously tended this garden with meticulous purpose, for it was incredibly lovely.

Bringing her attention back to the costumed man at the door, Maggie confidently smiled. "Yes, hello. I'm hoping you can help—"

"Thank you, good gentle man," Nicholas interjected quickly. "The Lady Margaret has arrived for His Lordship, Robert of Amesbury, and I, Nicholas Layton, have been summoned by the Countess Elthea. Please announce us at once."

Maggie swung around back to him with her mouth still agape; choking on what she wanted to tell the tall man, and with all the obscenities she could barrage Nick with in that moment.

"Immediately, m'lord," came a response.

The man trotted across the sunlit garden with the music of his keys jingling as he went toward what appeared to be the museum entrance. Maggie finally managed to blurt, "I can't believe you said that!"

Another servant instantly came to assist with the horse and, pretending to ignore her, Nicholas began his painful dismount.

Grabbing up her skirt, she hurried around the horse to confront him. "Why are you insistent upon playing this stupid game! I've got to get some *serious* help here . . ."

"I assure thee, Lady Margaret, momentarily it shall be yours . . . *agh*!" He winced as his feet hit the ground.

Desperate for someone—anyone—to understand her plight, she grabbed the shoulders of the young man attending the horse. "Look, where's your manager . . . your boss? Tell me, where's the nearest phone?" Bewildered, the fellow pulled back, as Nicholas nodded to him with a wink.

"Damn it . . . I saw that, Nick! Stop leading these people into your sick game!" Jerking back to the young man, she pointed to Nick, and insisted, "This man is delusional! He's fallen off his horse and hit his head. He needs first aid, and *I* need help getting out of this costume and back to my aunt in Trowbridge. Now please, tell me where the manager or phone is!"

Nearly terrified, the young man's eyes turned toward Nicholas for reassurance.

"Go on, lad . . . stable him up for the night, and don't go heavy on the oats," Nicholas directed.

The young man quickly walked off, turning to look back just once, and shook his head in disbelief.

"*Why* are you doing this to me? Is this your idea of

a joke?'' Maggie demanded spinning around, ''This isn't funny at all! Your entire charade is sick *and* borders on kidnapping!'' Stepping within inches of his face, Maggie forced him to lean against the outer curtain wall. ''Listen, buster, I've put up with enough of this ancient revival shtick, and now I'm pissed. I had better find a phone and someone from the *real world* quick if you don't want major trouble in your life. I have half a mind to press charges against you!''

Breathing heavily, she didn't give an inch as she stared straight into his clear blue eyes, certain her bravado would intimidate him.

He returned her stare with equal intensity, and she felt it run through her entire body.

''Lady Margaret, I assure you, I am not party to some grand plot against thee,'' he stated in a firm and slightly sarcastic whisper. ''I fear a far greater force is at work here, for I doubt you have been nipping at the brew, as I can attest through proximity of thy wisp, the bitter fragrance of hops is not detectable. As for explaining what ails thee, I cannot, for it is not of my doing. Perhaps after a rest and a—''

''I don't want a rest, and I haven't been drinking, you . . . you actor!'' She interrupted. She was pleased to see that his face held a hint of alarm at her insult and close proximity. She could almost feel her breath bouncing off him as she gritted her teeth, and sputtered, ''It ain't just you and me out in the woods anymore. I'm going to find some real help, and I don't want you interfering. Keep your mouth shut, until I find someone in authority here. I *am* going to get out of this madness, one way or another! Do you understand me?'' She was breathing heavily from her explosion.

''With all due respect, Your Ladyship, you speak in terms I am not familiar with . . . quite odd, in fact, and your demeanor is a curiosity which amazes me,'' he answered with absolute calm as he continued holding her glare. "And my mind doth ponder if even *you* comprehend the gibberish that incessantly spews forth." He tilted his chin up in mock defiance, and continued, "I happen to know exactly where I am, and who I am, and why I am here. Dare I marvel further . . . can you, Lady Margaret, say the same?"

"Odd? *I'm* a curiosity? You don't even know what year it is, Nick!" Maggie blurted.

"If the Gregorians are correct, it is the year of our Lord, fifteen hundred and ninety-eight," a woman's voice responded from behind her. "Welcome, dear cousin Margaret."

Maggie spun around to the voice. Nothing could have prepared her for the stately older woman. Long, platinum white hair was braided and coiled round her ears, and she stood erect, dressed in a long-sleeved gown of emerald green velvet adorned by ornate gold piping forming a V atop her hands, which she held out in welcome. Stunned, Maggie could only stare as the woman came closer and smiled warmly.

"Dear child, have you met with some tragedy upon your travels?" The woman's clear hazel eyes quickly darted beyond her guests. "Where is your entourage? Your servants and guards?"

There were no words, Maggie thought, to describe what she was feeling as she instinctively returned the offer of her hands to accept the welcome. It was too incredible. Whoever this woman was, she did a near-perfect imitation of her Aunt Edithe's voice, right down to the soothing tones and the endearment. She felt a wave of dizziness as she tried to comprehend what was happening, and, letting go of the woman's hands, Maggie took a deep steadying breath.

"Dear Nicholas . . . prithee, tell me what is transpiring here, for my beloved cousin appears to have happened upon most unfavorable circumstances. What grave misfortune has befallen the Lady Margaret?''

Maggie could only watch, dumbstruck and mute, as Nicholas hobbled forward and bowed before the woman.

''Greetings, Countess Elthea, I am most humbly at thy service and indeed, regret to inform thee, thy cousin has suffered a mishap of some kind, which she has been unable to explain to me. When I came upon the Lady Margaret, she was running from the woods . . .'' he paused, ''having endured a bit of a fright. 'Twas then we suffered a mutual misfortune whence my steed deposited me upon my path.''

Countess Elthea drew in her breath and began in a calm command, ''You are both injured then and must receive attention forthwith.'' She turned to the tall man who had opened the door, and added, ''Evan, please assist Master Layton and instruct Mary to prepare Lady Margaret's chamber at once, thank you. I shall arrange for the physician to be summoned.'' She looked back to Maggie, placed her arm around her waist, and smiled. ''We weren't expecting you until week next, but rest easy, child. . . . You are safe now.''

Before this travesty continued one moment further, Maggie spun from the woman's embrace and threw out her hands to halt everyone. She began in an exaggerated and slow tone. ''Ev-er-ry-bod-dy, hold it . . . okay . . . let's all calm down and attempt to communicate *reasonably*. This man''—she pointed to Nicholas—''this man insists on role-playing, as do all of you, I see. However, I am not part of this Renaissance revival. I only went to the faire to please others. I got lost in the maze and then he and his horse attacked me and then—''

''I beg thy pardon, my horse *did not* attack the Lady Margaret. She ran out of the woods shrieking,'' he continued with a stammer, ''. . . as, as though the hounds of hell were after her and—''

"*And then,*" Maggie regained the advantage after giving Nick a stern warning glare, "I helped him back up on his horse, because he hurt his knee when he fell, but then I realized my pearls were lost somewhere in the woods, maybe in the maze, and this guy"—she pointed again to Nicholas—"practically drags me here to this museum, *promising* I can find someone in authority who will help me get back to the Renaissance Festival to find my aunt so I can just go back to a quiet day picking roses in Trowbridge and end this entire trip into Bizarro World!"

The group stared at Maggie, all looking quite dazed.

She drew in an exaggerated deep breath, and added, "May I *please* speak to the manager of this place? I need a telephone, a car . . . just some way back to the *real world.*"

Breaking what seemed an eternal silence, the woman named Elthea abruptly turned her attention to Nick.

"What madness has befallen my cousin?" Elthea blinked suddenly.

Maggie didn't give Nick time to answer. "I am not *mad.* I am lost! And I am not your cousin. Look, you seem like a nice lady, but *my* aunt Edithe, who lives in Trowbridge, is probably very worried about me, so may I just speak to someone in authority please?"

"Authority?" the Countess Elthea repeated, turning to Maggie. "Dear cousin, pray tell, have you gone absolutely adrift of your senses?" Her brow furrowed slightly. "Your cousin, Robert, is the lord and thereby sole authority on these lands. He is ultimately responsible for everyone. Surely one knows that by right of his birth he represents Her Majesty the Queen in all matters."

"Ooh-kay, so where is this guy?" Maggie interrupted, preferring not even to ask questions about the rest of this woman's words.

Countess Elthea clasped her fingers together, trying to maintain her composure. "Why, Lord Robert is hunting at the moment. He's taken his falcons this morning and is expected back before our evening meal. He, as I, never expected your early arrival, cousin."

"I'm sure," Maggie muttered, blowing a stray lock of hair away from her eyes. "And there's no one else in charge around here? Nobody I can ask what the hell is going on, or why I can't seem to find anyone who *isn't part* of this Renaissance madness?"

Nick and the woman seemed shocked by her words, yet she couldn't have cared. It was *much* more mild than what she was really thinking. But now . . . enough *was* enough.

Turning around, she announced, "All right, there's got to be a phone around here somewhere . . . I'll do it myself." She swept past the onlookers and began walking through the rose garden, barely noticing the loveliness of the flowers, and stormed up to the huge door. She didn't even knock, figuring she had made it this far. The metal latch lifted easily, and Maggie pushed the door open and stepped inside. Her breath caught at the back of her throat when she saw the immense stone wall some twenty feet in front of her with a large, elaborate, and intricately woven tapestry hanging on it.

Spying oversize, dark wooden-paneled doors on either side, she quickly deduced that this was merely a foyer of some sort and wondered if she should take the left door, or the right, to find an office with a phone and perhaps someone with some sanity. She heard the sound of movement behind her and realized Nick and the others were following, so Maggie picked up her hem and hurried to the right door.

She entered a vast stone hall, a room so large that there were seven arches a good ten feet apart to support the roof. Three black-iron chandeliers, each at least six feet around, hung from the cathedral ceiling and dripped with molten wax from hundreds of candles. There were more tapestries hanging on the walls between the arches. She realized when she was in the foyer, she'd been looking at the back of a fireplace so enormous she could stand inside it, one that now burned with low embers. Against the farthest wall, a long table was set and had carved high-backed, dark wooden chairs all to one side, looking out on the great hall.

Before much more could register, Maggie heard the door on the other side of the fireplace quietly open, and the Countess Elthea came in alone. She smiled at Maggie, who then realized it didn't matter which door she had chosen, as they both led into this room.

Elthea slowly approached Maggie. She held her hands together at her chest, each palm resting against the other, as if she were terribly worried. "Margaret, there is no one save us here, and the few servants about the manor. Pray tell what happened in the wood," she implored. "Granted it has been many years since we have smiled into each other's eyes, yet your mother and I were as sisters to each other, and although I was not granted a daughter in this lifetime, I love thee as I would my own. You may trust me. I only have your best wishes in my heart."

Something about the woman made Maggie want to trust her. She gave off that same soothing energy as her own aunt Edithe. There was integrity in her eyes. But she had also gone along with Nick, which proved that she, too, was drawn into this madness, and Maggie couldn't trust anyone at this point.

"Really, thank you, that's a very sweet thing to say," Maggie said, as her eyes darted around the room searching for another exit. She saw doors behind the grand table at the far end of the room. The sound of her hard leather-soled flats clicked and echoed as she walked across the fine chiseled beige-stone floor. She added, "If you really wish to help me, then please find me a phone, a . . . call box, I think you Brits say. I need to make a call out to my aunt."

The woman followed her hesitantly, as though she were a wild animal and therefore unpredictable. "You wish to call out to your aunt, child? But . . . I am present."

"My aunt's name is Edithe, not Elthea," Maggie answered, proceeding toward the table. Everything was anciently styled, yet not exactly aged, as if someone had created the chairs behind the table within the last few years. They certainly didn't look four hundred years old. *This place is kept up very well*, she thought. *This Robert guy must be a good manager . . . but, hunting with falcons? That's a bit eccentric!*

Elthea's voice broke Maggie's mind from its rambling thoughts. "I know not of this woman in our lineage. You say there is a Lady Edithe, and she is your aunt?"

Finally, Maggie stopped walking and turned back to the woman who played the lady of the castle so well. "Yes, Edithe is my aunt, and I need to contact her. Will you help me?" she asked, just as the man named Evan entered the room carrying a large silver tray.

"Help you?" Elthea repeated, and then noticed her servant. "Aye, indeed, I shall help thee, dear cousin. Let us first rest a moment and partake of a small repast, then verily, you and I shall find the solution to all your concerns," she finished in a persuasive tone. "This I do promise."

"I don't have time to stop and eat," she stated flatly. "Listen, all I'm asking is to be shown a telephone. It's a local call, not long-distance. Or do you have a fax, a computer . . . any ability to contact someone on the outside of this Renaissance Festival?"

"Child," the woman whispered as though she had not

even heard Maggie's desperate request, "you must be half-starved. Please sit with me a short while and we shall unravel this mystery. How long were you lost in the wood?"

Again Maggie blew the stray lock of hair away from her face and figured maybe if she told this Countess Elthea the whole story, she would realize her predicament and help her get back to her aunt. "Geez, it must be hours by now." With resignation, she exhaled. "They're probably frantic about me being gone."

In spite of her incredible predicament, Maggie found that she began to like this woman's calming effect and figured if this Countess Elthea was employed here to play a part in a castle for wandering and lost tourists, she was playing it to the hilt. Maybe this museum really didn't have electricity or telephones to keep it authentic. In her opinion, and especially in her situation, that was taking it too far, but she knew there were areas of Europe that refused to modernize . . . and since she was in a foreign country and was obviously not making herself clear, Maggie decided to sit for a moment and gather her wits about her. Plus, the scones looked delicious and her stomach was growling. What could it hurt? "When in Rome, do as the Romans do," she whispered under her breath as the man placed the tray on the long table.

"Thank you, Evan. . . . Please leave us until I call for you again." The Countess Elthea nodded and smiled to him.

Maybe now, *one* of them could think clearly. There was, however, a nagging thought, one that kept demanding her attention. She realized she had been pushing it to the back of her mind while she attempted to communicate with these people. Plus, it was too damn scary to examine right now.

Still it refused to be denied and, suddenly, burst through all her defenses.

*What if she had somehow, by some crazy twist of fate
or something, been thrown back in time?*

What about the maze and that strange, ghostly little
girl who kept telling her to follow her heart? What the
hell was that all about? There had to be an explanation
somewhere. Did England harbor a town of loony people
who insisted on living four hundred years in the past?
How nuts was that?

It was *way too* bizarre even to contemplate, and she
again banished the insane thought while bringing her
concentration back to the woman seated next to her. She
almost wanted to laugh out loud . . . yeah right, time
travel!

"Perhaps, if you would dispel your disquiet, child,
here between family, your correct path will become evident. Once we have had a moment of respite, I am certain all will be crystalline. Please be seated, dear
Margaret, and we shall be peaceful and perchance discuss your coming celebration and new life here at Greville Manor with much joy."

"My life is not here," Maggie insisted, wanting to
avoid the almost pleading tone of the woman. She
looked out to the great hall. "I'm supposed to be on
vacation, my birthday is day after tomorrow, I'm visiting
my aunt . . . in a time and place much different than
here." She stiffened her back, and repeated, "So I can't
stay for more than a few minutes. I'm only a visitor here,
and I must get back to my aunt's home."

"Such overwhelming day for all of us, child," the
lady gently continued. "Simply quench thy thirst, then
make a decision."

"Okay," Maggie answered cautiously, pulling her attention back to the food. "But, remember, I can't stay.
If you don't have any way for me to call my aunt, then
I'll have to look somewhere else. I'm sure I could probably walk back in the direction of the faire before dark."

"What is this faire you speak of, child? There is the celebration for your marriage, but that is a fortnight hence." She poured what looked like a dark brown ale from a glass decanter into two silver goblets. Setting one at a place on the table, Elthea smiled up to her.

Maggie shot her gaze from the high-arched window she had been looking out for an approximate estimation of afternoon time, and back to the woman.

"The Renaissance Festival that's going on right now, outside Trowbridge, near Stonehenge . . . the one you're all involved with . . ." Maggie shook her head in frustration and silently decided this woman was so engrossed in character that she'd lost all sense of the present. "And a celebration of *my* marriage? . . . Not!" She crossed her arms in front of her, then swung them back in an umpire's safe gesture. She suspected all these actors had lost themselves in time and resigned herself to that conclusion. She then grabbed up the hem of her soiled gown and moved to the assigned seat. Right now, she could use a glass of ale to steady her nerves and food to calm her stomach.

Once that was accomplished, she would leave this place of insanity and find that faire or get back to her aunt in Trowbridge if she had to walk all night. She *was* going to solve this riddle, and she was never going to wear a costume again and pretend she was someone or something she wasn't.

Maggie waited until the woman served herself, then picked up her own goblet. It was stamped with a seal and one ruby was set into the eye of a gryphon. It looked pretty official, royal and authentic, but then what did she know about royalty? She knew her father's family came from England, but they were probably scullery maids, and not the privileged class.

"Cheers," Maggie said with a slightly mocking smile

and brought the goblet to her lips. "Here's to returning home . . ." she added more seriously.

"To the *home*coming." The Countess Elthea gazed at her and smiled in return.

The ale tasted very sweet, with a hint of ginger and orange, not exactly her choice, yet she didn't complain. She was thirsty and hungry and grateful for the hospitality this woman was showing her.

Elthea never looked away but sat next to her and smiled sympathetically. "Poor, dear Margaret," she murmured. "You have been through so much in your short life. It must all seem strange to return to England after so many years."

"Return? This is my first time here." Maggie couldn't wait to taste the scone, dripping with honey, and looked around for some cutlery. Finding none, she picked it up in her hands and took a bite. It seemed to melt on her tongue and her taste buds savored the unique flavors. This was definitely homemade.

"Yes, child . . . your first time at Greville Manor, and I can understand your confused state of mind. Assuredly, you need to rest." The woman bit into her scone and nodded.

Maggie looked into the woman's eyes and felt the muscles in her body relaxing, in spite of her situation. She took another gulp of wine to wash down the scone and to draw her attention away from Elthea's gaze. Although sympathetic, the woman was looking at her deeply, as if trying to read her thoughts.

"I will rest when I find my pearls, the faire, and my aunt."

"Pearls? Goodness . . . thy jewels were lost?"

"Yes," Maggie answered, feeling a comfortable weight descend upon her, like someone covering her body with a warm blanket. "They are precious to me, and I have to find them. I never should have worn them today." Why was she so tired all of a sudden? Had she been running on adrenaline and now it was all catching up to her?

"Be assured, dear Margaret, your possessions shall be recovered. When Lord Robert returns from his hunt, conceivably, he will set all matters right. I shall inform him of the miscreants who attacked your cortege. How many were traveling in all? Perhaps you could make a list of your belongings. Robert must know all that he is to recoup and, without fail, he will ferret out the perpetrators of this knavery and they shall be dealt with severely."

Maggie paused for just a moment to absorb this confusing woman's thoughts now in her head. "I'm sorry . . . Elthea, is it? Whatever story you're telling, it ain't mine."

She finished the delicious biscuit and wanted another, but thought that might be rude, since the woman only took a small bite out of hers and hadn't even touched her ale. Sipping the last of her own, Maggie sat back and sighed while wondering where to wipe her hands. They were sticky from the honey and the only thing resembling a cloth was the coarsely woven runner covering the middle of the table and another on the serving tray next to a bowl of water. Should she reach for it? She mentally shrugged. It was the least of her worries at the moment.

Holding her hands in her lap, sticky fingers up, Maggie said, "I wasn't attacked by bandits. I just got lost in the maze and then found myself on the side of a road, where Nick's horse nearly ran me over. Where is he, by the way?"

"Master Layton? He is being tended by the servants until the physician arrives. I shall see to him after I have escorted thee to thy chamber." Countess Elthea changed the subject abruptly. "Do tell more of this maze. Where might it be, child? Is this where you were attacked? To my knowledge, no estates, nor bailiwick for that matter, maintain a maze . . . and the wood is a most unlikely surrounding for such frivolities, is it not?''

Maggie sighed with frustration. ''Look, there was no *ambush by bandits* . . . I can only tell you that I was at a Renaissance Festival with my aunt and her companion, and we entered the maze together. They went on ahead of me and then I got lost and had an anxiety attack, or something, and then there was this child who kept calling to me, telling me to follow her, so I did and that's when the hedges started to fade and I ran toward the woods and Nick's horse attacked me,'' she rattled off, before she threw her hands up in the air, and continued. ''After that, I'm completely lost, since I can't seem to find a single person who speaks normal, contemporary English, or even knows of anything modern.'' She glanced rapidly around the room and abruptly turned back to the Countess Elthea. The motion caused a wave of dizziness. ''May I ask you a question?''

Countess Elthea had been listening carefully, merely blinking her eyes and showing little emotion. ''Ask me anything, child.''

''Do you work here? Is that why you're dressed like that and insist it's 1598? Are you an actor being paid to play this role?'' Okay, that was three questions, but she still wanted to hear this woman's responses.

Elthea swallowed deeply and seemed to be trying to formulate answers. ''Dear Margaret, I live here. I have lived here since I married the Earl of Amesbury, Robert's father, and have remained since his passing many years ago. Do I think the year is 1598? Aye. According to the calendars the monks started centuries ago, that is this, the year of our Lord. Am I playing a role?'' The woman leaned closer to her. ''Dear child, we are women and it was not so long ago in history that the church

deemed us worthy as human beings and granted us souls.
So yes . . ." The woman sat back. "To that question, I
would say all women have been playing the role assigned to us. Our good queen, Elizabeth, playing the
prominent role of woman, is giving a fine performance,
I dare say."

Maggie got a huge grin on her face. "Oh, I get it.
This has to be some gag. Okay, where's the camera?"
She laughingly jerked her head around the room, trying
to guess where it might be hidden. "This is just like my
aunt Edithe and Malcolm to play a joke on me." She
turned toward the empty room, and raised her voice.
"Hey, everybody! I get it! This is my birthday joke,
right?" She paused and looked back at the woman.
"Well, the jig's up, and you can all come out now!"

A prolonged silence followed after her echoed words.
Maggie didn't know if it was the ale or the woman's
confusing answer, but her head was now spinning, and
her body felt weighted, as if she were completely exhausted. Rallying her strength, she tilted her head and
asked the most ridiculous question of all.

"Is there a napkin I can use to wipe my hands?" She
held up her sticky fingers like a child, and felt slightly
tipsy in her speech. Wow, one little glass of ale wouldn't
do this.

Elthea said nothing in response to Maggie's outburst
and simply reached for the basin of water.

"This isn't *Candid Camera*, is it?" Maggie stated in
a tone of resignation.

The Countess Elthea still did not answer. Maggie
watched in dazed astonishment as the woman actually
began to take her hands and submerge them into the
lukewarm water. Elthea gently massaged her fingers,
then palms, and Maggie wanted to moan with the wonderful relaxing sensation. "Pull yourself together here,
Maggie," she said under her breath. Before she got any

deeper into this insane asylum, she had to start figuring a way to get out. Elthea lifted her left hand and patted it dry with a small silky handkerchief she pulled out from under the tray. She looked up from her service and smiled sweetly at Maggie when she released her right hand.

"Thank you," Maggie murmured, feeling quite pampered by the experience. Geez, she inhaled, realizing she couldn't relax now. This was too bizarre, and she had to get out of this place quickly. "But now, I must leave. I have to find the faire and my aunt. She will be very worried if I don't at least contact her or get back soon." She pushed the heavy chair away from the table and rose.

The room seemed to become fluid before her eyes, and she had to balance herself by placing both palms on the table. "Wow . . . maybe I shouldn't have drunk that ale. What was in it, anyway? It was awfully sweet, and I tasted ginger and orange."

"The drink? Simple mead, child, a weak honey drink. Come with me, dear Margaret, it is time to rest. A chamber has been prepared, and we are in full service to receive thee in a proper embrace."

Blinking, desperately trying to bring some focus into not just her vision but also her mind, Maggie spoke each word with deliberate intention. "I can't rest now, I have to . . . umm, to—" What did she have to do again? It took a few seconds to retrieve her thought. "Oh, yeah. I have to leave this place and find my aunt and get back to my own time. This isn't my time."

Why did she just say that?

"Look," she continued, as another wave of dizziness crashed upon her. "I don't know what's wrong with me . . . maybe if I just sit for a few more minutes."

"Settling for a rest in thy chamber is a most excellent idea, dear cousin," Elthea enticed. "I do fancy after all you have suffered this day, a repose is in order. You shan't be alone, child, I shall stay with you. Come this way,'' Elthea began leading as she stood and gently grasped Maggie's arms before she could sit down again.

Placing an arm around Maggie's waist, Elthea motioned for them to leave through the door Maggie had wanted to inspect when she first entered the great hall. But the oddest thing was how she found herself accepting the woman's guidance farther into this castle. Why was that? A little voice seemed to be telling her something was rotten in Denmark, and although she giggled internally at the irony of her own pun, she knew deep inside not all was as it should be. Yet, the thought of lying down for just a little while seemed so appealing.

The heavy oaken door hinges squealed and the sound carried across the great hall as Countess Elthea pulled it back. Beyond it, Maggie saw a winding staircase of stone, illuminated by thick candles flickering in large iron sconces. She allowed a groan to escape her lips.

''Come, child. We shall do this together. Step by step. It isn't far,'' Elthea encouraged.

Maggie concentrated on each step, leaning against the woman for support as her own energy seemed drained.

''What's wrong with me?'' she moaned as they rounded each step, merely to be faced with more stairs. ''Why do I feel so weak?''

Elthea sighed. ''I pledged to care for and be true to you, precious cousin. I beg, accept within my reason, I have your best interests at heart for I love thee dearly. Recall a time, long ago, when you were but a small child on sojourn just after your father died. You came to me in the night, frightened by dreadful mares. That eve, you were served a mildly potent drink which assisted thee to rest in quietude. Do you recall that night, child?''

With mental desperation, Maggie compiled the woman's words down to the only thing that made sense.

"I remember when my father died, but you . . . you were my aunt Edithe then," she stuttered. "It was the first and only time I met you."

At least she had the presence of mind to know that now she was really confused.

"Hush, dear Margaret, we share the same ancestry . . ." Elthea continued, "therefore, I confess, 'tis the mead that debilitates. I instructed Evan to blend a gentle potion which simply allows one to rest not only the body, but also the mind. Pray, do not conclude I am deceitful, child. When you arrived, most distraught, I realized I must take present matters into my own judgment, for it would never do to have thee in such an agitated state when your husband to be, Lord Robert, returns," she finished with a puff of exhaustion.

Maggie heard all her words, yet they registered as if everything were in slow motion, while this woman, and everything around her, was in real time. Three steps from the landing she halted and pulled back against the curved stone wall, while staring at the woman who held her in the unbalanced condition.

"Wait a minute . . . you drugged me?"

"Dearest Margaret, remember, if nothing else, I understand the loss of great love in this life, and how loneliness can play havoc with not only the heart, but the mind as well. When you arrived, ranting senselessly, after all you have been through, I felt there was no other alternative but to quell your state of delusion," the woman chided. "Regrettably, Nicholas has already observed your behavior, yet he is an honorable man and after I speak with him, I am certain no further word of your . . . your confusion will pass his lips."

"*You drugged me!*" Maggie's heart started racing as fear infiltrated her body and took hold. Her head was spinning. Her arms and legs felt like anvils were attached to them, making every step an enormous effort.

She knew if she didn't find a place to sit down soon, she was going to fade out.

"Please, Margaret, I am endeavoring to keep this unfortunate display away from the eyes of gossiping servants. It wouldn't do for Robert to think that you are not capable of making sound decisions. Your chamber is right there." She pointed to a large wooden door on the other side of the landing. "You must rest, child, and be able to receive Robert this evening."

Maggie found herself putting one foot in front of the other, desperate now to reach a bed. She tripped once and cursed at her gown. "Shit . . . how do you wear this stuff?" she mumbled, knowing she should be very angry and yet somehow feeling a companionship with the woman who had just drugged her! Damn . . . she *did* need a rest!

"Countess Elthea . . ."

Maggie heard the male voice and froze as she entered a long stone hallway. The man who had brought the tray, Evan, was closing a door and spied them. "So much for stopping gossip," Maggie managed to say, though her lips were enjoyably tingly.

"Oh, Evan is devoted to me," Elthea whispered, grunting as she again led Maggie toward the assigned room.

Evan hurried to them and flung open the door. In the recesses of Maggie's mind, she registered a huge bed covered in luxuriant furs, a fireplace at one end, and lit sconces on the walls. There was a table and a chair and an ornately carved wardrobe. *Nice place*, she thought . . . *to be drugged and held captive by some loony foreigners. This has to be a dream*, she thought, and was sure she would wake up in her aunt's bedroom.

She really wasn't the adventurous type.

"But if I'm not . . . you know, like dreaming, then what a crazy adventure," she said, right before being deposited upon a bed that she swore was filled with straw. "I should have stayed home and found a job and paid my bills and . . ."

Elthea was guiding her toward the pillow, and Maggie gave up her worry and just sank against the sweet softness. Rest, she thought, for just a few minutes, until she got her bearings back, and then she would give them all hell before she stormed out of the place.

She vaguely heard Elthea talking to the man who had closed the door and was standing by the bed.

"Oh, Evan, whatever shall I do? Robert is to arrive soon, and Lady Margaret is obviously not in her right mind. How can I keep her isolated until clarity returns? So much depends upon this union, yet I want Margaret to be fully aware of her decisions. She is like a daughter to me, and I wish only to protect her."

"M'lady, do not distress thyself. Should the Lady Margaret still be . . . indisposed when Robert returns, we shall simply say she is recovering from her exhausting trip. Anyone, especially a gentlewoman, would be taxed after such a crossing from the Continent. It would seem reasonable to wait a few days for their meeting."

"I do not know what else to do, Evan. The dear child has had so much grief in her short life, it is no wonder that she escapes in her mind. I fear Robert would not have patience with her if she continued to rave about such strange things. He knows she is still grieving for her late husband, though it has been many years since he passed. I only saw them together once, yet their union was blessed by such love it is no wonder her desolation has made her appear peculiar to some."

"I . . . I'm not this woman," Maggie mumbled, drifting off. She had heard their conversation and felt sorry for the woman they spoke of, but she was also determined they know she wasn't the peculiar one here. She merely needed to rest, and then she would be able to make herself understood and get back to sanity, safety. That's all . . .

Just as sleep was wrapping its dark arms around her, a thought passed though her mind.

She had asked for an adventure, to go joyriding into the unknown, and she'd gotten it.

A brief vision of her aunt Edithe flashed, and she heard her voice saying . . .

"Bullshit! There is no safety! You can't have an adventure until you lose your perception of safety."

If it weren't so bizarre, she'd laugh. Well, if her lips still worked, she would have laughed. Whatever was happening to her was one hell of an adventure. She felt like Alice in Wonderland, and she had definitely fallen down some kind of rabbit's hole. She only hoped when she awakened she'd be in her aunt's guest bedroom in Trowbridge, or back in New Jersey.

Anywhere . . . but here, on the other side of the looking glass.

Chapter Six

The soft strains of music entered her wild dreams, dreams where she saw herself racing through the woods with a handsome man. A part of her brain was sending signals that she must wake up, yet all Maggie wanted was to return to the man with such beautiful eyes, who professed to love her more than she'd ever thought was possible. Still the soft, quaint notes lulled her away, and soon she had lost him. Knowing she could never recapture such a wondrous dream, she began accepting, reluctantly, that it was time to awaken. Her senses became more alive, and Maggie smelled the faint aroma of food. Blinking, she stretched her arms and was about to yawn when her vision was captured by a continuing nightmare.

She couldn't believe it!

The guy from the faire was dressed in a new costume of burgundy and white, and he was sitting on a chair in the corner of the room with his leg propped up on a cushioned stool as he played a mandolin. And . . . and the woman who had seemed so nice and then *drugged* her, was sitting at her bedside sewing something as she slowly nodded in time to the music! They both looked so peaceful, so innocent, as though both were sane!

The woman glanced at Maggie and dropped her sewing to her lap. A smile Maggie would have sworn was real appeared.

"You have awakened, child. How do you feel?"

Maggie attempted to bring moisture into her dry mouth. It didn't help her mood to realize that as she was licking her lips the troubadour stopped playing his weird-looking guitar and was now staring at her.

Wide-awake, she pushed herself into a sitting position, and said, "I hope you both realize kidnapping is a major crime in any country. I demand that I be released!" It sounded so melodramatic, like something someone would say if they were in a movie, and that feeling of strangeness returned with force.

Why would they still be keeping up this elaborate charade?

"Lady Margaret, cousin, daughter of the sister of my soul, I would not hold you against your will, nor would anyone here." Elthea looked beyond her to Nicholas and smiled in acknowledgment before turning back to Maggie. "I ask your indulgence for aiding in your rest, child, yet I can see that you are still confused. Pray let us speak of this with a calm voice, so we may each be heard. I ask this with your best wishes in my heart." She delicately patted the center of her breast. "I will listen and speak through this."

Despite the chaos that was wildly running through her head, Maggie found herself nodding in mock agreement. What were her other options? She could make a mad dash for the door. The drugs had worn off. They might not catch her, but it was now dark, and she didn't see herself running through forest and stream in the middle of the night, searching for a Renaissance Festival and the year 2000. All she was certain of was the fact she wasn't about to be drugged again.

"O-kaaay," she rasped. She simply didn't know how to refuse such respectful logic and cleared her throat.

"All right. Where am I? What year do you think it is?" Wow. Maybe she was still a little woozy.

No one said anything. They were both staring at her as if she'd lost her senses. "Okay, so you didn't get it," she said, waving her hand. "Skip the last question and answer the others. Starting with, who *are* you people? And how dare you drug me to keep me here?"

Elthea immediately rose and started pacing the room, wringing her hands together and sending darting glances to the freshly attired *actor* in the corner.

Of course, she was still bound up in a soiled, bulky, uncomfortable costume. If she looked bad before, imagining what she must look like now made Maggie grind her back teeth.

"Well . . . ?"

The woman stopped pacing and grabbed the thickly carved dark wooden footboard. "Lady Margaret . . . I am your cousin, Countess Elthea. You are here to be joined in marriage to my son, Robert. Lord Amesbury. And this is Nicholas Layton, son of my fondest friend, Lady Anne. I sent for him, and you encountered him after running from the woods. Margaret, what happened in those woods? Now you must try to remember and tell us."

Maggie saw that Elthea really believed what she was saying and that Nick had believed it before the two women had even met. Something was very, very weird. As it was dark and she wasn't about to go running off in the woods in a foreign country, Maggie decided that she would answer their questions. *Just play along*, she thought. Since her reality was vastly different than theirs, and they couldn't even discuss hers, it was her only course. Play along . . . until she could escape.

"Okay, you want me to tell you my story?"

"Aye."

"About what happened in the woods?"

Elthea nodded, and even Nick leaned forward with interest. At any other time she might have laughed at him, but this was way too serious. Even the truth was too bizarre.

"And you won't interrupt?" She shot that question toward the singer, now trying to appear uninterested.

"Nicholas?" Elthea whispered to him, like a mother chiding a child to respond.

"I will not interrupt Her Ladyship's recounting of her unfortunate mishap in yonder wood. Does that satisfy Lady Margaret?"

"Your dry wit is not appreciated at this time, Nicholas," Elthea remarked.

He looked to Elthea and became contrite. "I beg your pardon. I will not interrupt."

"Thank you," the woman answered, then smiled encouragingly to Maggie. "Tell us, child. I am listening with my heart."

"May I have something to drink first? Something without drugs or potions. Just plain ole water will do fine."

Elthea hurried to a table and brought a large round tray to the bed. Placing it on the fur blanket Maggie had thrown off in her sleep, the woman then poured what looked like water into a heavy silver cup. She handed it to Maggie with the words, "I swear by all I hold sacred, this water is pure, taken from our well. I have added nothing."

She then removed a cloth and revealed a trencher of bread, soaked in gravy with a slab of meat on top. "Eat, child, and tell us your story."

Taking her chair and angling it better to see Maggie's face, Elthea whispered, "We shall listen without interference."

As incredible as it would sound to anyone if she dared

to express her thoughts, Maggie found herself liking this woman, a woman who admitted drugging her! It was crazy. Maybe she could secure not only Elthea's sympathies but her help in escaping as well? Hmm . . . she would think on that later. Right then, she had to pull herself together and entertain them. Well, she would tell her story, and it would be the truth.

Let's see how they handle that, she thought while bringing the cup to her lips.

The truth . . . It seemed a rare commodity.

Sipping the water, which tasted better than any water she could remember, Maggie deduced it wasn't drugged. She was so thirsty that she drank three cupfuls before again licking her lips and glancing at Nick.

A surge of feminine power went through her as she saw his stunned reaction to her subtle flirtation. Clearing her throat, she looked at Elthea.

"Well," she began, "it all started when my aunt sent me a birthday card with a ticket to England. Can you imagine? Me, either, especially since I'd just lost my job, but then I thought . . . what the hell, you know? I mean, what did I have to lose? A chance to get away from all that and visit with my aunt. You would have done it, right?"

She looked into their stunned faces and laughed. "Okay, no interruptions. Well-done, guys. Where was I? Oh, right . . . So I'm with my aunt and she says we're going to a Renaissance Festival, something she and Malcolm, that's her lover, have done for years and years. Now she not only has this costume for me, this very dress . . ." And Maggie waved her hand in front of herself, before ripping the snood the rest of the way from her hair. Shaking the length of it free, she glanced at Nick in the candlelight and was pleased to see him inhale deeply.

Brushing her hair back from her face, Maggie smiled at Elthea and continued.

"So you can see why I couldn't refuse to wear it, right? It is, or was, lovely before the woods incident. Anyway, the night before the faire my aunt also gave me a special strand of pearls that were precious to her. So we go to this faire and everyone is talking just like you guys, only even thicker sometimes . . . you know, all your *thees* and *thous* and exaggerated speech. Like, mammering clapper-clawed maggot-pie. There's one I remember!"

Elthea's chin dropped, but, to her credit, she did not interrupt. Nick, on the other hand, brought his fist up to his mouth and attempted to muffle a laugh.

"Anyway, so my aunt and Malcolm want to go through this maze. *Are ye prepared to be a-mazed?* That's what the man said at the entrance. Well, I've been a-mazed all right! I've gone beyond amazement into insanity, for nothing else could explain what happened after I entered. There was this little girl following me all day at the faire. She looked almost angelic and she gave me a rose . . ."

She spoke, without interruption, for the next twenty minutes. Sometimes, she would judge their reactions and then, seeing how shocked they were, would look out to the room as she related the sequence of events that brought her to this place.

". . . and then I was drugged and deposited on this bed and, well, here we are folks. That's my story, and I'm stickin' to it."

Her audience appeared stunned, speechless, and Maggie congratulated herself for giving a great performance. There was too much detail in her story for them to completely disregard it as the ravings of a crazed woman. Neither said anything for several moments. They just continued to stare at her and each other.

At least they didn't laugh.

Yet.

"Well . . . ?" she asked, reaching to pour herself more water. "Whatcha think?"

"Why, Margaret . . . your story is . . . incredible," Elthea murmured. "I don't quite know what else to say. What you have related is beyond my comprehension. Your verbiage at moments appears foreign, yet I do believe I have grasped that which you are relating."

Swallowing the cool water, Maggie smiled. "And that would be?"

Elthea stood and again began pacing, wringing her hands together, as though trying to word her thoughts carefully. "May I ask a few questions, child, before responding to yours?"

"Certainly. I have nothing to hide. Everything I have told you is the truth. My truth." She glanced at Nick and saw him staring into the fire across the room, as though he were lost in his own thoughts.

"This . . . this strange occurrence that took place in the maze, you said you were assisted by a child who was surrounded by light?"

"Well, I don't know whether you can really say I was assisted by her, or not. Guess that depends on the perspective. But, yes. She kept telling me to follow my heart and dropping the rose petals for me to follow. I'm telling you, it was all very odd."

"And then she led you to light, what you described as light, and the hedges, the maze began to disappear?"

"To fade," Maggie answered, looking at the roasted meat and wondering if there was any cutlery with this meal. What did they think? She was going to kill herself with a fork?

"You keep saying that we are playing roles, performing in some festival, yet I ask if, since you ran out of the maze and into the woods, you have met anyone who can substantiate your claims?''

Maggie gave up thoughts of food and turned her attention to the woman who was now facing her with a serious expression. ''Well, of course not. Everyone I've met has been part of this Renaissance Festival, or working with them.''

''You have seen nothing to confirm that you are not in the year fifteen ninety-eight?''

Maggie thought about it, and that scary feeling returned, those thoughts that she kept trying to ignore. ''I'm not an authority on that time period, but I have seen nothing modern if that's what you mean.''

''And by modern you mean something of your own time? The place where you claim you are from?''

''Yes.''

Elthea took a deep breath and glanced once to Nick before answering. ''Then I would say to you, child, to consider that you *are* in the year fifteen ninety-eight.''

It was Maggie's turn to stare.

''Elthea, with all due respect, that's simply crazy. People don't just . . . I don't know, time travel . . . Jump from one time to another. I don't belong here. I belong with my aunt, in the year 2000, where there are telephones, televisions, computers, cars, trains, planes . . . *forks!* Try and remember, indoor heating, stoves, bathrooms. You *must* know what I'm talking about!''

''The year 2000 . . . ?'' The words were spoken with awe by the woman, who looked as though she should be sitting down.

Maggie nodded just as Nick said, ''I told you her claims, my lady. Please do not distress yourself now when your voice of reason is most needed.'' He rose awkwardly and started to limp forward, using a long staff of twisted wood to assist him. ''May I serve you while Lady Margaret rests?''

Her clear hazel eyes became glazed, and the rosy flush left her cheeks as Elthea sank to her chair. Maggie quickly leaned forward and poured more water into the goblet. "Here," she offered. "Drink something."

Nick reached the bedside and took the cup from her hand, but not before his expression registered his concern for the older woman. "Calm thinking, m'lady," he urged Elthea.

The woman suddenly looked up to Nick, and her face appeared tortured. "Nicholas Layton, by all I hold true, this is not my cousin, the Lady Margaret."

"What?"

The sound of Nick's voice seemed to bounce off the walls. "Calm thinking, Nick," Maggie whispered, as the man shot her a look of high impatience.

"I thought over it this afternoon, and now I am convinced. I will grant you, she could pass as Margaret to someone who has not seen her in many years, but I knew my cousin and this woman's words and voice and mannerisms are too contrasting to be ignored. Lady Margaret is more . . . retiring, and would never be uttering what we have heard, nor are the eyes the same. It was what I first noticed, but dismissed, when you arrived. Under close scrutiny, the truth is revealed. This is not my cousin."

"Countess Elthea, what are you saying? Lord Robert is in the great hall now, drinking ale with his men and celebrating his forthcoming marriage! This has to be the Lady Margaret. I brought her here as such!"

" 'Tis a mistake I, too, would have continued to entertain, had we not just heard this woman's story. Nicholas, can you imagine Robert's reaction if I were to even attempt to explain this to him?" She held out her hand to take his. "Dear friend, the blood between you and him is already bitter. I now fear for your life, and the life of this woman." She looked at Maggie and smiled sadly. "I regret we have placed you in grave danger, child."

"Wait a minute," Maggie called out. "We'll just tell your son Robert that Nick, here, made a mistake, and then I'll be on my way, out of everyone's business . . . okay?"

"If it were only that simple, child." The countess sat forward in her chair, intently gazing at Maggie. "I must confess that upon *your* arrival, I dispatched a messenger to Lord Amesbury and his hunting party. He, and all present, were informed the Lady Margaret had indeed arrived earlier than expected. My actions, and your presence, have set myriad events into motion. For as well, presently there are other guests staying in the manor who are to attend the forthcoming betrothal feast . . . all of whom have been led to presume that the true Lady Margaret is with us this day. The news of your presence is no small matter."

Maggie began shaking her head. "But I'm not this Lady Margaret. You've gotta tell everybody, so I can get out of here and go back to my home!"

Elthea closed her eyes sadly and drew in a deep breath. "Please indulge me, dear Maggie, for just a while to explain further. This error is woven more deeply than you may comprehend."

The tone of dread in the woman's voice was enough to allow Maggie's permission for the story to continue. "Okay, I'll listen to your story . . ." and finished under her breath as she flattened the fur cover on the bed around her, "but I just don't understand what the big deal is here."

"Thank you, Margaret, for your attention," the Countess Elthea nodded. "Now, can you, for just a few moments, think of yourself as being alive at present, in this year 1598, and in this country?"

Her mind really didn't want to go there, but she conceded to the request. "If it helps, I'll try," Maggie said, and lightly closed her eyes.

"Great subterfuge has been taking place for more than forty calendar years, as powers from every land abroad have been attempting to influence our beloved Queen's throne . . . for absolute control, one religion and incredible monetary gains."

"Your Ladyship, is this a subject we should be discussing?"

"We have no choice now," the older woman answered Nick.

From beneath her lashes, Maggie saw Nicholas becoming antsy in his chair. She drew her attention more deeply to the Countess Elthea. Still, there was an almost vindictive thrill begging her to watch him squirm.

Elthea continued with a more serious inflection. "Our Queen has played an intricate, but winning, game of chess with powers in Rome and the English court, yet England remains vulnerable to many plots against Her Majesty's will and rule."

Through her squint, Maggie could see the countess turn away from her and stare into the fire.

"I am deeply saddened to admit, my son is parcel to at least one plot against the Queen's rule. Robert is, not so secretly, aligning himself with the Spaniards and the Church of Rome, while Nicholas and his camp are on the side supporting the monarchy, and Her Majesty's restored Church of England."

Maggie exhaled heavily. Religion and politics were subjects she had always avoided, yet the quiet tone of Elthea's voice began to mesmerize her.

"My son's marriage to my cousin would solidify our coffers; in addition, it will greatly improve Robert's political ambitions and power at court. He wishes to accede his father's title, Earl of Amesbury, for he cannot simply inherit this title through birth. Such a title is only vested by the Queen, and since the house of Norreys is in great favor with Her Majesty, Robert assumes this alliance with Lady Margaret will secure his title.''

''But I still don't see what this all has to do with me,'' Maggie interrupted with a whisper, her eyes now fully closed.

''Should it be discovered thou art an impostor, 'twould humiliate Robert no end, thereby endangering his interests at court, not to forget mentioning it would intensify his inherent dislike for my dear friend Nicholas. There is no telling what my son would do, but I warn you this . . . the wrath of Lord Robert of Amesbury is not one even his mother would risk.''

Maggie opened her eyes widely. ''You mean, Nick's head might be on the block?''

Okay, so maybe she accepted the minute possibility she was in an age of chivalry, and she figured that's how they dealt with people in those days.

''More than his own, I fear. Mine and very possibly yours.'' The countess sighed.

''I *don't* think so,'' Maggie interjected quickly, ''not *my* head, I'm just a visitor in this whole scenario you're playing out.''

''Thou must have faith in my words, Maggie. I jest not. Revealing your truth would make a mockery of his noble position. His plans would be ruined, and you would be held responsible. Verily, I tell you, this is quite serious,'' she ended, finally raising the vessel of water and drinking deeply.

Maggie didn't know what to say. She watched the woman's hands tremble slightly as Elthea brought the empty cup down and placed it on the tray.

''You guys are definitely wrapped up in this whole thing, aren't you?'' She looked back and forth between Nick and the countess, who appeared to be lost in their own worry, for neither answered her question.

Suddenly, Nick banged his fist on the bedpost, shaking Maggie and the tray on the mattress. Quickly steadying the decanter, she looked up as he began ranting.

"Heavens above, what have I done? How could something so simple become so difficult? All I had to do was answer thy request, m'lady, and return to my studies. Now I am embroiled in a madness of my own making! I should contact Francis. Surely his mind could resolve this dilemma."

Maggie could only watch in hypnotic wonder as the two argued between themselves.

"We're not involving Francis in this. At least not yet. Somehow we have to keep Robert away from this woman. We can't simply say she isn't recovered. He would still pay his respects, and after spending moments with her he would know something was afoot. We must delay . . . somehow."

Nicholas turned to the bed once more. "Who *are* you?"

She broke her silent trance. "Maggie Whitaker. I told you."

"Maggie . . . ?" Nick looked to Elthea and sighed while shaking his head. "Not even a Margaret. *Maggie.* Sounds like a serving wench."

"Hey, watch it, buster!" she retorted, anger starting to replace bewilderment. "My people may have been peasants, but they certainly didn't kidnap anyone, drug them, and then plan to thwart a coup! You're on thin ice now, Nickie, so I'd just shut up and let Elthea speak."

The older woman reached out to take Nick's hand in a pleading gesture. He groaned his displeasure and walked to the fireplace.

Looking back at Maggie, Elthea said quietly, somberly, "A disservice has been performed today, Mistress

Maggie, and for that I and my young gallant extend our sincerest regrets.''

Smiling, Maggie said, ''I accept your apology, Elthea. But please, just call me Maggie. Mistress Maggie sounds like a dominatrix, or something.''

''I'm sorry . . . ?'' Elthea appeared confused again.

''Nothing,'' Maggie said. ''I was just trying to lighten the mood here. I mean, if I could do anything to help, I would, but since this is—''

''You could assist us,'' Elthea interrupted, ''. . . for just a few days.''

''Assist you?'' Maggie was already regretting her last statement, meant only as a courtesy to this woman, who had finally accepted her story.

Elthea nodded as Nick pulled his gaze from the fire and turned back to them.

''Could you play a role, as you put it earlier?'' Elthea asked. ''Could you pretend to be Lady Margaret until I determine the whereabouts of my true cousin? The resemblance between you is uncanny, and you appear to be about the same age. It would be most helpful, and I'm sure I could explain the necessity for such extreme measures to my cousin when she arrives.''

''Countess Elthea! I must protest!''

''*Restrain your protest, sir!*'' Elthea's voice rose an octave, and her expression became unyielding. ''What is our alternative? I am speaking about not only your life and the life of this woman, but the lives of those you represent, who may be also endangered by this misfortune.''

She turned her attention back to Maggie. ''Will you assist us?''

She hated to be placed in this position since she was starting to really like Elthea and the way she took care of business, but . . . ''Elthea, my aunt must be very worried about me and no doubt has the police looking for me at this moment. I won't be able to help because I won't be here. I have to go home to *my* relative, where everything is normal and safe. I'm sorry I'll have to leave your relatives to you.''

''Oh, nonsense, mistress! You believe you are safe? Listen to me, you are not in the year 2000. You are right now, in this moment, living and breathing in the year 1598 and surrounded by servants who are instructed to report to Lord Amesbury any suspect behavior. It cannot be said anymore clearly. Either you are mad and able to envision a fantastic future, or . . . when you ran from the maze you ran into this time, into this year, and into the path of Nicholas. There is only one answer. Not both.''

Maggie could only stare at the woman for a few prolonged moments of tension. Finally, she said, ''How can you even believe that for a moment? Time travel is the fantasy. Living in the past is the fantasy. I just want to go home.''

''Child, do you believe in the unexplainable? You must, for what you have related to us is most certainly unexplainable, is it not?''

She would make a great lawyer, Maggie thought while shrugging. ''Okay, you've got me there. I can't explain what happened to me.''

''So you honestly, with your heart, believe?''

''Yes. I know what I experienced. I can't deny that.'' Where was Elthea going with this next?

The woman drew up her tunic slightly and sat on the bed, at Maggie's side. ''What I am about to reveal to you must remain in your heart also. It must never be spoken of again, for to do so would endanger not only your life, but the lives of many. Myself, included.''

''M'lady . . . !'' Nick's voice sounded alarmed.

''Hush, Nicholas. Critical times call for critical measures. None of us counted on this woman appearing or your assumption that she was my cousin. Now the die has been cast, and we shall have to see which way it falls, but we can use our heads and perhaps even gain an advantage while waiting.''

Elthea turned her attention back to Maggie. ''May I secure thy word, *Maggie Whitaker*, never again to speak of what I am about to reveal?''

Maggie found herself nodding. Something inside of her was opening up, wanting to help this woman. ''You have my word.''

Elthea nodded. ''I, too, believe in the unbelievable.''

Maggie couldn't help it. She chuckled. ''Well, I'm glad we agree on something, I guess.''

''I don't know how much more you will agree with, though. I also believe that certain people, for whatever reason, or by whatever means, can be reported to be in two places at one time. This I have heard, though I cannot say I have done so myself.''

''Two places?'' Maggie asked, seeing Nick shake his head as though regretting Elthea's words.

''Yes. There have been ... scripts, ancient scripts handed down from the wisest of souls and copies were brought to England after the Crusades explaining this miracle. Have you ever heard of the Knights Templar?''

Maggie shook her head. ''I don't think so. I'm not really up on the history of Britain.''

''This would be the history of the holy land, where such things were magical and respected. Here, in this country, the shadow of the Inquisition still hangs over the land and all are most hesitant even to speak of magic ... which of course there's no such thing. What one perceives as magic, is merely God revealing itself. Do you have a concept of God, child?''

''Well, yeah,'' Maggie said, very uncomfortable at finding herself neck deep in discussions of religion and politics. ''God is ...'' She chewed the inside of her cheek while wondering how to proceed. What did she really think?

"Exactly," Elthea said in an excited voice. "God just *is*."

"Okay." Sounded harmless enough to Maggie, and she was glad to be off the hook on that subject.

"How can we possibly try to paint a picture of God? God is the life force inside each human being and each blade of grass. All of creation. So if I use herbs to heal the sick, I might be using God, but there are those that would say such a practice was evil."

"You mean like a . . . like a witch? You're a witch, Elthea? That's why you drugged me . . . with a potion!"

The woman laughed and broke the tension. Maggie was glad, because she was beginning to get a little more than scared. This woman and her aunt sounded *too* much alike. In a show of support, Nicholas came to Elthea's side and placed his hand tenderly upon the woman's shoulder.

"Oh, child . . . how quick-witted you are!" She actually winked at Maggie before becoming serious again. "I am the Countess Elthea, widowed by the Earl of Amesbury, and mother to his son, Lord Robert.

"But I shall tell you of my beloved grandmother, a healer and saint upon this earth, who used herbs to assist many of the sick and dying who came to our family for aid during the dark ages of the plague. Marigolds cured inflamation of the mouth, wounds, and burns. Simple chamomile would relieve coughs and fevers, skin irritations, even liver complaints. These are natural healing elements and ingredients, which alleviated the many pains and suffering that had enveloped our world in her time."

"That much I think I understand, because I have a friend who is . . . well, sort of a hobby botanist." Maggie thought the comment would ensure the countess that she was listening to the history lesson.

"Well, all the physicians and the Church, with their barbaric rituals and rites, could not accomplish more than what my grandmother had. Word of her abilities spread far and wide." Elthea gestured with hands outward. "Many of the priests took word of her healings to Rome and Pope Paul III himself."

The countess paused for a moment. "And he had just established the Inquisition three years prior. I was merely a young girl of nine calendars. It was by those, the fearing and feeble-minded, yet all-powerful, my grandmother was accused of heresy. Verily, I tell you, the woman condemned herself when she dared to speak out against the ignorance and cruelty of the Church."

Maggie watched Elthea shake her head, seeming to surrender to the memories.

"So, this good woman was accused of being a witch, imprisoned for months in chained degradation, tortured unmercifully until she would have confessed to being the devil himself! After her cruel death at the hands of her inquisitors, her lands were seized by the Church, who only killed her to add to its coffers. Our title, tarnished by the accusation and public display of her murder at the stake, was allowed to remain in the family, but all our holdings vanished save for one small manor. This one that I was able to retain by marrying the Earl of Amesbury, a man of . . . of many talents who agreed with Bloody Mary's reign of terror for those who opposed the return of Catholicism. Upon Elizabeth's ascension to the throne, he promptly turned to the Church of England, though he secretly attended mass and forced all in his house to do so with him."

"Wait a minute. Hold on . . ." Maggie pleaded. "I'm confused. You're saying that your grandmother was accused of being a witch and was killed?"

"Yes."

"And then years later you married to keep this place?"

"Aye, yes."

"But your husband was playing both sides of the fence? Pretending to be Protestant, when he was really Catholic? He was like . . . a spy, a double agent?"

"Quick-witted and perceptive. Yes and now my son, through his own foolishness, is following in his father's footsteps by secretly joining ranks with the likes of Ambassador De Quadra in aiding the Spanish claim to the throne. A Catholic claim."

"And now you are plotting against your own son?" Maggie was shocked, for she couldn't see any maliciousness in the woman.

"I am merely the observer. I agree not with my son on many issues, yet I do love him. He is my blood, though it appears the blood of his father runs far deeper than my own. I am not plotting anything, nor was I, until your untimely arrival. Now I must plot a way to get you and Nicholas away from this madness."

"Do not distress yourself, m'lady," Nick whispered to Elthea.

"The only way I can see in this moment is to have you play the role of my cousin for a few days. And then, I promise you shall be free of us all. Would you assist me in this most dire of times, Maggie?"

She didn't know what to say. Her mind was reeling from the information she'd received and from all the crazy thoughts running through her mind. How could *any* of this hold even a shred of truth? It was beyond incredible. It was too bizarre!

"Countess Elthea, this woman could never hope to impersonate a lady. She is most distressing as she is, let alone a—"

"Hold it right there!" Maggie demanded, while shift-

ing her legs over the side of the bed and rising. She felt
dizzy for just a moment, until her body caught up with
her anger. Imagine the nerve of this guy. It didn't matter
that he was handsome. He was also a royal jerk! She
had faced down network heads, ego-crazed entertainers,
and even her depressed ex-husband. She wasn't about to
be called less than a lady by an acting troubadour!

Pushing her hair back off her forehead, Maggie tilted
her chin and stared down the man. "I will help you,
Elthea," she stated, while capturing Nick's resentful
glare.

The woman sighed with relief and touched Maggie's
arm in a show of thankfulness.

"Bless your heart, child. I will help you as much as
I can. Fill you in on family history and what you will
need to know to pass during your meeting with Robert.
Nicholas will tutor you in our social graces while you
recover tonight and tomorrow. I cannot postpone your
meeting longer than that."

Maggie blinked. *What the hell have I walked into?
How am I to make an escape after making this promise?
And this arrogant ass is going to be my teacher? In
social graces? It is absurd.*

She set her teeth as she stared him down. Why was
she sure this was going to be torture? One he would
enjoy?

Closing her eyes for a moment, she patted Elthea's
hand, and whispered, "I do this for you. Not him."

"I have not asked anything from you, mistress."

"Children," Elthea pleaded. "This is a time for unity,
not dissension. Both your lives depend on it."

Sighing, Maggie broke eye contact, and said to Elthea,
"I don't suppose you know what a bathroom is."

The older women looked up. "You wish to bathe? I
shall inform the servants."

"A bath would be nice, but I'm talking about . . .

well, a place to relieve myself." She refused to look at Nick.

Elthea jumped up and shooed Nick out of the room saying, "Verily, I should have thought of this. Here, dearest Maggie. The privy." She closed the door after Nicholas then walked over to another, revealing a small closet that looked like it might be a bathroom.

Maggie timidly peeked in and saw nothing but a carved wooden seat upon a stone shelf with a thin slit of a lead-framed window above it. It was just a primitive outhouse in the wall. A seat, a hole, some rags and a pot of water to wash it all down with. Maggie wondered when the joy part was gonna kick in, and how she was going to get back to sanity and indoor plumbing.

Yeah . . . she was getting really, *really,* tired of this joyriding.

"Thank you, Elthea," Maggie said weakly, and started to enter the small closet.

"Allow me to assist you," Elthea offered, and began unlacing the back of Maggie's gown.

When the heavy velvet gown puddled at her feet, Maggie looked into the woman's eyes, and said, "Elthea, you know one of us is right and the other is delusional. Both of us can't be right."

Elthea picked up the gown and folded its bulk over her arm. "Dear child, we have both spoken our truth this eve. You are not in the year 2000. I do not have sufficient knowledge to explain how this has come to be, yet only if I accept your truth . . . child, you have traveled back in time. Such a miracle does not happen by chance. It is certain, you are here for a great reason."

Maggie looked into Elthea's eyes and swore, for an eerie second, she saw the eyes of Aunt Edithe looking back at her. Blinking furiously to clear her vision, Maggie broke eye contact and shuddered.

"Excuse me," she muttered, gathering up her slip and stepping into the tiny space.

Sanity. Just thinking the word proved too much. Here she was, in some castle, about to pretend to be some Renaissance noblewoman, involved in thwarting some kind of a coup, and annoyingly attracted to a crazy man who insisted he lived four hundred years ago.

Yeah, sanity was just too much at the moment.

She sat with a moan of relief.

Actually, she couldn't have picked a better place to think about it. Sanity and how she could escape back to it. She would play along until she found a means of securing her freedom. Her world, her life, was out there somewhere. After what she had heard tonight, there was no doubt in her mind it would be up to her to find it.

At the moment, there was a more pressing need.

Chapter Seven

"**A**ye, Mistress Margaret . . . you curtsy more slowly to Lord Amesbury, in deference to his station. Once again, please. And this time hold your spine rigid." He actually had the nerve to pound the floor with the curved wooden staff someone had given him to use as a cane.

Oh, her spine was rigid, all right! "Hey look, *Nick,* there's no need for you to punctuate every directive by pounding your wizard stick on the floor. I'll curtsy, bow . . . whatever . . . when I'm ready."

"I *shall* curtsy when ready," Nick corrected her while examining the tip of his cane. "Mistress, thy speech is most deplorable."

Now she was grinding her back teeth together. "*You* may call me Lady Margaret," she said in an authoritative voice. "I need the practice."

His head jerked to the side and he looked to the ceiling, posturing as though he hadn't heard a word of her command.

She rolled her gaze. "Just say it. We both need practice so we don't screw up in front of Robert." Plus, she wanted to annoy him by taking a shot at his superior manner.

He turned to her with an I-know-what-you're-up-to

sly grin. "Thy speech is most deplorable . . . Lady Margaret?"

She couldn't help it. She smiled back. "That's better. Now, I *shall* curtsy." And she did, very slowly, with spine erect.

Wearing Elthea's dressing gown and heavy blue-velvet robe, Maggie felt foolish yet played along with all this ridiculous formality. She refused to consider that Elthea might be right . . . about time jumping.

This whole Shakespearean scenario had to be a Midsummer's Night*mare*. She giggled at her own pun.

She'd clearly been kidnapped by a bunch of Renaissance fanatics who insisted that it was 1598. *They really have a great setup*, she mused, looking around the darkened room. Everything, all of it, seemed authentic, from the heavily paneled walls to the thick curtains around the bed.

Of course, none of it could be *real*.

So why did that nagging thought continue to scare her? She hadn't seen anything modern since she'd run from that maze . . . and how does a maze just disappear? An entire faire? Her aunt Edithe. And Malcolm. Geez, *time travel*. She nearly said the word aloud, but she knew deep down inside, that if she really thought about it, her brain would have some kind of meltdown. So she'd continue to play along with them until morning, when she could see a way to escape back to where she'd come from. Reality.

"Well-done," Nick said, observing her long, slow curtsy.

She stood up. "Thanks. Now how do I address him? Lord Robert?"

"No. There is precedence, Mistress Margaret."

"Lady Margaret," she corrected.

"Do you know nothing of rank?" he asked in a presumptuous voice.

"Rank? Oh, you mean 'special' people elevated by birth and not by deed? There is a small group of people who hold on tightly to archaic titles, but most people think such a desperate attempt to believe one is superior to another is well . . . quite frankly, pathetic."

She walked to the table where, earlier, Nicholas had placed a small wooden vessel of ale. She was glad he'd brought it. She needed a drink. Then, with a defiant air, she filled a cup and continued the education of one Nicholas Layton about history in the future.

"Even your monarchy in my time is debated as meaningless. Your way of life is falling away, and everyone is more egalitarian. One's *blood* is no longer thought to be *better* than anyone else's. It is one's *deeds* that distinguishes one, not who one's *father* was."

There, she nodded and mentally congratulated herself for giving an articulate and intelligent answer. She was woman, "hear her roar"!

Nick sat down once more before the fire, and rested his leg on a short stool. He still held his cane and was examining the twisted, polished wood.

"Prithee, Maggie, thou art here, not in some fantastic future. This is the Golden Age of England, where precedence, preferment, and even attainder is law. Therefore," he stuttered, "if you are to be received and pass thy meeting with Lord Amesbury, you must learn it," he finished, exhaling deeply.

He had just called her Maggie.

He cleared his throat, and continued, "Now, precedence refers to your ranking, either above or below other people. An earl takes precedence over a baron, a baron over a knight and so forth."

"Hmmm . . ." she murmured. "So much to remember, instead of just saying hello."

And she said it without a tone of aggravation in her

voice. She smiled softly at him, yet her expression didn't deter his teaching.

"That is to say . . ." for an instant, he looked at her with an appearance of wonder on his face then went on, ". . . that an earl is the first to be introduced and also the first to lose his head should the occasion arise. Sir John Wallingham, whom you shall meet tomorrow, may be addressed as Sir John or Master Wallingham, but not Sir Wallingham. Margaret, do you comprehend this?"

Maggie blankly stared. "Why can't I just shake his hand, and say, 'Hello, Robert'?" she said, mimicking the action of shaking someone's hand.

"You will never pass your meeting with Lord Amesbury if you do not commit this to memory. Henceforth, I insist you cease your interruptions until you innately behave in accord with precedence. Formally you are known as Margaret Gray, Countess Norreys of Rycote. You may be formally addressed as Lady Norreys, but not Lady Gray or Lady Rycote. To address you as Lady Margaret, one must have a close relationship. Do you understand?"

"No." She began tapping her foot. *Behave?* Now he was really pushing some buttons. Yet, she restrained herself from a feminist barrage.

She watched as Nick blew out his breath with frustration. "Mistress, I am not such a dull teacher that you cannot grasp this simple form of address."

Maggie took her seat before the fire, a few feet away from him. "Listen, Nick . . . I don't mind playing this Lady Margaret person, but I'm not about to be filled with this ridiculous *precedence*. Do you know how insulting this is to the majority of people who are not titled? You are saying that by right of birth, you are entitled to special treatment. It just isn't so."

"Mistress," he said, obviously trying to maintain his patience, "I have received a classical education in the arts, in rational, logical philosophy, moral philosophy, and natural history. I even excelled in the seven liberal arts of grammar, rhetoric, logic, arithmetic, geometry, music, and astronomy. I have studied the faculties of law, theology, and medicine; surely I may instruct thee on precedence.''

Maggie held up her hand to stop him. ''Enough already! I'm impressed. I'm just saying that treating anyone as though they are better than I am, or worse off than I am, makes *me* uncomfortable. Somehow, *you* don't get this. In the real world, out there somewhere''— and she pointed to the darkened lead-framed window— ''equality of all is being practiced, or at least is the ideal. This . . . this precedence is antiquated superiority, and I have a right to object to it.''

''Object all you wish, mistress. However, you agreed to assist Countess Elthea in this most unfortunate of circumstances, and so you shall. You have only this night and the morrow to become Lady Margaret. Now, how would you address Robert when you meet him?''

''Wait a minute. I agreed to help Elthea, but you also have a stake in this, if I'm not mistaken. You and Robert aren't exactly friends, and you brought me here as his future wife, so, so your neck is on the line here, too.''

He gazed at her and nodded. ''I am as deep in this deception as anyone involved. And all for a moment of mistaken identity. Heaven knows how it shall all be resolved. Presently, I am concentrating my attention on your meeting with Robert. You must get through that before we worry about the future.'' He rose and tapped his cane once more on the floor.

''Now we shall practice your meeting once again, until it is so natural even you shall believe you are the Lady Margaret. Prithee, rise, sweet lady, and show me your curtsy.''

Sighing, Maggie stood up and closed the space between them. She kept his gaze as she slowly bowed before his chair, "Good day..." wait, the words boomeranged back into her skull. She quickly looked to the floor. His words, "sweet lady," momentarily interrupted her murmur, ". . . to thee, Nicholas Layton," she finished with a nearly crowning curtsy.

He was still staring when she finally looked up. Maggie was acutely aware that Elthea's robe was tight around her breasts, and her hair was cascading around her shoulders. It didn't matter that he was younger than she, or living in a fantasy. In that moment, when her gaze locked with his . . . she saw something that took her breath away.

She saw an acknowledgment of attraction.

He cleared his throat and held out his hand to her. Maggie placed her fingers inside his palm. Assisting her to rise, he muttered, "Well-done, Maggie. You are either a talented performer, or you have some of that dreaded blue blood racing inside your own veins," he mocked theatrically. "That was almost perfection," he finished with a wide grin.

"*Almost perfection*?" She couldn't help smiling, just a little, as they continued to hold each other's gazes *and* hands.

"You should lower your head when showing respect to a person of higher station, especially the male of the realm."

"Ooooh!" She withdrew her fingers and stormed away. "Give me a break, Nick. I am *so* sorry . . . no wait"—and she bowed once more—"forgive me, my lord, pray pardon my ignorance, I crave your forgiveness for my most atrocious blunder. The higher-stationed *male*! Ya know there wouldn't even *be* a male, had he not come through a female, so don't ask me to buy into male superiority now, 'cause this debate is one you're gonna lose, buddy."

She'd had to resurrect the feminist in her for his in-equality comment.

He laughed. *Laughed!* "Oh, mistress . . . you are in-credibly amusing. Our monarch at this time happens to be a queen, a woman . . . for years now, I have watched her play a labyrinthine political game with popes, the State nobility, and even her own Royals. I hold a deep respect for a woman's mind, however, these forms of address are strictly observed. It is well you should lower your head while addressing Robert, so as not to attract more attention to yourself, which is . . . I believe . . . *Lady* Margaret, the purpose of these late-night exer-cises."

Okay, so he had thrown her a little off-balance with that one.

"So . . . how come you can be in my room this late at night?" Maggie demanded, wanting to change the subject, as she felt herself being drawn back closer to him and she knew that was just plain crazy. It was like he was pulling her into his fantasy.

She was determined to regain the upper hand. "If we're really in 1598, then I'm sure, late at night, having a male guest in the private room of a woman betrothed to the lord of the manor ain't exactly kosher." As her words left her mouth a mixed string of frustration and dread entered her mind. She could *not* be falling for this guy, or his ridiculous *line!*

He merely smiled. "Kosher? I do not believe I am familiar with the term."

"It's a Hebrew term. It means approved." Maybe that would jar his memory. She had to convince herself that this boy was in a time warp of his own, and she wasn't about to go joyriding into that realm. He had to meet her in reality!

He nodded. "I will remember that. Thank you. I have a high regard for certain works that were written by Jewish authors. As for your question, if I understand it correctly, my presence here would be most inappropriate, should anyone, save the good Countess Elthea, have knowledge of it.''

Okay, she had him on this one. ''Well, think about it,'' she said condescendingly. ''What about the servants? Didn't Elthea say they were paid by Robert for information?''

Wait a minute. Her own words shot back to her. Was she actually *buying* that there might be some truth to this Monte Python-ish satire–fairy tale after all? Hardly. It was nuts, yet she couldn't deny that by all appearance, anyone else would say she was living in another time.

''The steward of the household, Evan, is most loyal to Countess Elthea. As for any of the others . . . Elthea is known to grace the palm with the sweet voice of an angel. I would think most in service here are rightly devoted to the lady of the household.''

All right, it was easier to secede and give him back the upper hand. Nodding, she walking to the table in front of the fire. Pouring herself another cup of ale, Maggie sighed.

''Well, Elthea certainly does have a way about her.'' Chuckling, she added, ''I guess you could say she has the voice of an angel.''

''I do agree with your observation, Mistress Maggie, though I was alluding to coinage. An angel is a common coin, worth ten shillings. As in any time . . . gold speaks, or speaks *not*, as in this case.''

''Interesting . . . bribes, or angels as you refer to them, come in the form of gold coins here.'' Maggie turned and retorted quickly, ''But I will agree there is something, well, different, perhaps angelic, about Elthea.'' Lowering her voice, she looked sideways to his profile and asked, ''Does she really believe she's a witch? Do you?''

As the effects of the ale crept up on her, Maggie watched him. He seemed to lose himself in the flames that flickered and danced while casting shadows against his incredible face. Maggie felt even more mesmerized as lights seemed to bounce around his blond hair, almost like a halo. She blinked several times to stop the silly notion and waited for his answer.

Fight the feeling, Maggie, she chided herself. *He's no angel.*

He continued to stare into the flames, wanting to center himself before he said another word. This woman was throwing his sense of balance into chaos. Ever since he'd met her she had been challenging everything he had learned and thought he knew.

Who was this incredible woman . . . this desirable creature standing next to him? He felt her gazing with eyes he'd known in all his dreams, now imploring him to answer questions that were better left unanswered.

Oh, how she vexed him.

Only hours ago he had thought her to be of noble birth and promised to his political opponent. Now to find that she was neither fell beyond his comprehension.

Now she was a mysterious goddess from the future.

On one hand, he was in grave danger for the possibility of Lord Amesbury's discovering he had caused this scandal. Yet, on the other hand, there was a greater danger in the realization he could not deny that this impertinent, incredible vixen was capturing something deep within him.

How improbable was that?

He needed some grounding and wished Elthea were there to assist them both. And now this woman asked a question that demanded integrity to answer. . . .

"Nick . . . ?"

"Aye, I heard your query. A witch? Nay, she is no necromancer. Do I believe Countess Elthea? Most assuredly, I would take to my heart everything she says. The lady is most respected in those areas beyond the physical as well as those taking place in this moment. She is a great teacher."

"A teacher? With students? I don't understand."

"Nor should you be expected to understand. Suffice it to say that Countess Elthea holds her own power in this household and beyond it. You needn't fear talk of servants for this eve. Nevertheless, I suggest when you feel the desire to express yourself, in an outburst of emotion, you might restrain the impulse . . . and whisper." He turned to her and smiled.

Surprisingly, she smiled back. Heavens above, who *was* this woman who claimed to be from the future? Who, in moments of timeless communication, seemed so familiar? As it was, he himself had trouble concentrating on her words and not the sweet depths of her eyes. He *knew* those eyes!

"I *shall* whisper, Nicholas, if *thou* might stop pounding the floor with *thy* cane."

He chuckled. In spite of himself, he liked her bold manner and poured himself another drought of ale. This was a woman who would stand toe-to-toe with a man as his equal. He was shocked to find that appealed to him very much. "Agreed. No more cane stomping. Shall we continue the lessons?"

She held his gaze for a moment too long, until both of them became aware that something was being said without words, they were both learning something, and it was something neither wanted to broach.

"Yes, sure . . . the lessons." She backed away from the fire and sat down in her chair. "I shall lower my head when I curtsy to Lord Amesbury."

" 'Tis done, then!"

He replenished their cups.

"But I will not consider him to be above me in station. Just so you know, Nicholas Layton . . . since I have finally agreed to this crazy role-playing, I will do it the best I can but that doesn't mean I have to *like it* or even agree with it. Got it?"

In his entire life, he had never met a more perplexing female or male, for that matter. Not even his teachers in France or Italy confounded him more.

"Got what, prithee?"

She giggled. It was a most enticing sound to his ears.

"Got it . . . you know, what I just said."

Now he couldn't help chuckling at her girlish reaction. She had the most amazing faculty of being a mature, seductive woman, yet maintained the sparkle of innocence. Yes, she would perform well, if given the proper training.

A part of him sobered at the thought of what they were involving her in . . . the subterfuge to preserve a monarchy and a queen's promise. He, himself, didn't quite comprehend how it had all come to sit upon his lap, yet he knew since he and Francis had pledged brethren, his entire life was a continual series of revelations. And now this woman.

"Got it," he replied in a thoughtful voice.

She smiled at him most warmly, and he emotionally confronted the newest divination in his life . . . she was not the Lady Margaret about to marry Robert, she was an eligible woman . . . but tarry his fleeting thoughts . . . was she? Perchance there was another who laid claim to her heart?

"May I ask about family, mistress? Thy mother and father . . . ? Siblings? Betrothal? Marriage? Have you no alliances or unions?" Perhaps his true intentions were cloaked well enough.

Her pause and knowing smile made him think perhaps not.

"If you are asking whether or not I am married, the answer is no. I am a free woman and intend to remain so."

"Ahh," he mumbled, and nodded, as though in agreement, though he wasn't at all sure what she meant.

"Free, at least for now," she added.

"You are free, this moment?" Astonishment flushed through him. "You are otherwise enslaved? I find that highly unlikely, m'lady," he answered, shaking his head in disbelief.

"Oh, I *was* enslaved all right . . . and I am not about to reenter the *institution* of marriage anytime real soon. I intend to remain free to choose any direction I please . . . until I find *my* prince charming." Her voice held a challenge. "If he even exists . . ."

It was much clearer now. "I see," he mused. "Mistress Maggie is her own woman."

She giggled, again invoking that contrasting innocence. "C'mon, Nick. Please don't call me Mistress Maggie anymore. Plain old Maggie will do just fine, especially while we're alone."

For an instant he was stunned when he felt her hand push playfully on his shoulder.

"I respect your freedom, Maggie, and have no desire to affront your reputation." He rose and began stretching his sore muscles.

"What reputation?" she asked with a laugh, and poured more ale for them both. "To you I am below your station and my reputation doesn't really matter. To me, you are playing a role, pretending to be something you're not, and so your reputation is ludicrous. It seems, Nicholas, we are at a stalemate of reputations. Why don't we both just relax, since our reputations with each other are shot anyway?'' She said the last words with the cup raised to her open lips.

She stood before him in the low fire's glow and began a slightly seductive sway; her gentle movement mesmerized him. Against an amber glow, her silhouetted form taunted him mercilessly. He knew she was merely lost in thought, yet still his body betrayed him.

He had never in his life experienced such honesty, such frankness, with a woman, especially a woman who was making him think thoughts of such passion that his heart was racing. But he knew Cupid had an ironic sense of humor.

Remain calm, Nicholas, he advised himself. While his heart yearned for his mate, the twin to his soul, and his gaze was openly cast . . . could it be, this goddess of a woman, slipped through time, only to meet his eyes and challenge everything he believed? His brain ached under the massive concept. Would the universe play such a trick?

He was falling deeper into her soul, and almost groaned as the recognition raced through his body. It couldn't be . . . ! All these seasons . . . and *she* finally appears? Maggie Whitaker, from the year 2000, about to be taken for Lady Margaret, was the one?

His twin soul? It was too preposterous!

Verily, he mentally admitted to himself, *I am bewitched.*

''I must take respite,'' he murmured, and sank heavily into the chair again.

''Your leg . . . or the ale?'' she asked in an impish voice.

'' 'Tis neither, Maggie.'' He sighed. ''I fear, a thing, much more infinite.''

He looked up to her and knew, within everything he held sacred, he was either losing his mind, or this woman had traveled through time to be with him. The ancient manuscripts, which he and Countess Elthea had read, spoke of such miracles. How could he explain this concept to her, when she was uninitiated in the mysteries? It would sound improbable . . . mad, yet he knew something she didn't.

He knew it was possible. How Cupid must be laughing.

She felt like a drunken Elaine from TV's *Seinfeld* on another date in the *Twilight Zone*. Here she was, an educated and single woman of the new millennium . . . okay, so her life in New Jersey was in a small rut . . . and this whole Renaissance thing was actually beginning to grow on her . . . *No*, she halted her thought process. *I'm not goin' there now.*

"Umm, what time is it, anyway?" She knew she'd better change the subject quickly.

He looked out to the window and began with great theatrical inflection. "With deep regret, I cannot tell thee that which you wish to know, m'lady . . . for the light has left the sky, and therefore, I cannot read the sundial." He turned back to her completely straight-faced.

Then burst out laughing.

"Maggie dear . . . we are a *modern* people, as you put it, and indeed, we have clocks which tell of the hour." His boyish grin beamed at the thrill of his prank.

"Funny, very funny." She tried to keep a straight face. Laughter spewed forth.

He sighed out of his laugh and settled his tone seriously. "I know not, if there is a clock in this chamber," he said, glancing around the room. "Perhaps I should request one of the servants to inform us of the hour."

"Oh no . . ." she broke in, warning, "No one is supposed to know you're in here with me, except Countess Elthea, remember?"

"Aye. Indeed, you have a rare clarity of thinking, madam, while you have been drinking."

Oh, that grin again. Damn. She knew she was getting in trouble now.

Maggie abruptly turned and walked to the window. "It's getting too hot in here. How do you open this thing?" She cursed under her breath as she dumbly struggled.

"Allow me, Maggie."

He limped to the window, and when the sensation of his shirt brushing lightly against her shoulder sent shivers down her arms, she had to hold back a moan. She backed away a step and watched him open the window with ease.

"There, m'lady. The breeze is thine." He gestured for her to sit on the sill, patting the wide gray stones.

Her bulky evening costume made her scoot up awkwardly into the small space. She was glad of the extra padding against the uncomfortable roughly chiseled stones. She inhaled deeply. The sensuous scent of an early-summer night filled her being. Exhaling slowly, she felt the cooling relief caress her heated skin. Crickets stopped singing long enough to allow an owl his solo in the symphony, then began their music again.

It was much more quiet here than at her home in Jersey. It was as though she could hear so much more . . . but more what? More quiet. Suddenly she realized the modern noises she was beginning to miss were actually assaulting. This was so peaceful.

She leaned her head against the widowsill wall and stared up at the sky.

"The moon is huge . . . and so many stars . . ." she marveled. "Mmm, it's really exquisite here."

Her sensuous dance with the night was abruptly interrupted with a bang.

"I beg thy pardon, Maggie. I meant not to disrupt thy

meditation," he said, bending over to pick up his cane from the floor.

"Oh, no problem," she assured him and quickly looked back out the window, hoping he hadn't seen she'd been startled. "Hey, do you know if people ever told time by the stars?" She thought that might be a possibility, since, in any age, you can't read a sundial at night. At least it was some conversation to break the embarrassingly silent situation.

His voice was a whisper of introspection. "Ah, 'time' you ask. Interesting concept, time."

She didn't know if it was the ale or the night, but she giggled. "Yeah, tell me about it!"

"You wish for me to expand on the subject?"

Inhaling deeply of the sweet night air, Maggie closed her eyes, and said, "Sure, why not. I've listened to some pretty unusual stuff already. Why should this be any different?"

He paused, and, even though her eyes were closed, she somehow knew he was bringing his thoughts together. She respected that. It was a pretty deep subject not many could discuss . . . including herself!

For some reason she really wanted to hear this man's concept of time.

"The Black Plague was instrumental in giving us a sense of time as we know it. Time had always been considered the domain of God before it. People thought of time in terms of day and night, the seasons, eternity. Clocks were not used to measure lives."

"Some people even sleep with watches, small clocks on their wrists," she murmured. "Where I come from, everything is regulated by clocks . . . what time you awaken, how long you cook your food, what time you arrive at work and leave, even our entertainments . . ."

" 'Twould be a slave shackle," Nick pronounced.

Maggie grinned. "I guess you could say that," she

said, keeping her eyes closed and enjoying the symphony of nature. "I'm sorry. I interrupted. The Black Plague introduced the invention of time. Because of death?"

"Aye. When the laborers were decimated, working hours were extended into the night. 'Twas then clocks and bells began to signal the hours. It was no longer God's time, but merchants' time that people lived. Anyone who has spent an hour walking through the woods knows time can expand and appear longer than to someone working an hour in the city. A dream may seem to span many hours but may actually last a few minutes. It is a concept that goes beyond traditional boundaries of time and space into the infinite nature of the divine. There timelessness is experienced."

"Okay . . ." Maggie listened, yet most of it was over her head. She could blame it on the ale, but it was the whole concept of time that confused her.

"Therefore, with knowledge of this *'Invention Of Time by Man,'* traveling through it could be quite probable. Would that not be dismantling our own illusion of time? Would not *you* agree, Margaret Whitaker?"

She opened her eyes and stared at him. This was getting much too serious. "Hey, if I'm really back in the year 1598, then I'm the *queen* of time travel, buddy!" she cajoled as she slipped off the windowsill and walked back toward him, playfully pointing her finger. "You oughta be bowing *deeply*, Master Layton."

He laughed. "Very well, *Lady Margaret*." His eyes were filled with merriment while he struggled into a standing position. He executed a perfectly drawn-out, elaborate, bow.

Sheesh, Baryshnikov had nothing on this guy when he laid it on. She reluctantly admired his grace of performance, especially with a bum knee. Still, he was a bit arrogant. Well, maybe not arrogant, but this superiority thing he was so hung up on could use a bit of balancing.

"Since I am queen, I am now superior to you?" she challenged as he rose.

He saw her challenge immediately and stared at her for a moment, as though testing where she wanted to go on this one. Maggie's answering grin was genuine. He nodded, letting her know he accepted, and then he grinned at her with the sexiest smile she had ever seen in her entire life and tomorrow she was going to be forty years old!

Oh, c'mon . . . her mind was rebelling as her body was shot through with intense sexual tension. It felt more powerful than when she had been young! And in an instant, she knew she had little to worry about turning the big 4-0 tomorrow. She had never felt more *alive*!

"If I am correct," Nick said as leaned his hand on the edge of his chair and examined his fingers, "if I have spoken my truth, and we are *together* in the year 1598, then you have traveled through time to be here. For me, there is no other answer. Therefore, you have experienced the power of something I cannot define. It is beyond my scope of language."

He slowly reached for his goblet and extended it in a salute. Once more their gaze was locked with such intensity that another surge of sexual tension raced inside of her, shocking her with its intensity. She was now keenly aware that she had extended a challenge to someone extraordinary. He might be an actor. He might be nuts. He might be an angel in heaven, and he might be a fellow inmate of life. Whoever he was, whatever his story, she knew he wouldn't hurt her.

There was no fear.

It was as though the space between them collapsed as their gaze deepened and Maggie felt herself opening to him with respect.

When he spoke, his voice sounded . . . real.

"I am in the presence of someone divinely . . . gifted. A queen, at the very least. Someone more, I think." His smile was humble, yet respectful of his own station in her presence. "I would bow deeply, Maggie Whitaker."

She was stunned. Rattled. Flattered. Hit for a loop, her mother would say.

So many thoughts ran through her head that she felt dizzy as she tried to maintain balance. This was about some challenge . . . right? Who had challenged whom on this one? It might have been the ale, yet Maggie had to admit that if she were stone-cold sober she would have felt the same thing.

Wow!

And she had thought she didn't go for that romance-hero kind of guy. She was too . . . what? Practical? She wanted to laugh at herself, yet knew she'd better keep it together as Nick sat down and invited her with a gesture to join him. He held out his hand to her, and as she placed hers inside his strong palm, she felt a jolt of energy pass through her, igniting her already inflamed senses.

She slowly sat in the opposite chair before the fire and tried to appear composed, even though her mind was telling her that the man of her dreams was sitting right across from her! It could not be possible. It couldn't! She didn't want to buy his story!

There wasn't anything called time travel. There wasn't . . . What was she? The queen of craziness? Because she'd have to be crazy to believe it! And yet . . . something *had* happened. She could no longer deny the existence of that little girl, the light, the disappearing hedges. It had happened, and she had been transported to the other side of the looking glass, where everything seemed so real. It was if she were the only single person since she'd left the woods who knew it was the year

2000. But she wasn't alone. This man was saying he accepted her story as her truth. He was merely stating his.

Now that sounded crazy.

Her brain seemed to crash with the concept and she had to force her lips to move. "And what if you are not correct?" She couldn't believe she was afraid of the answer.

He smiled tenderly. "Then you have learned precedence."

She sucked in her breath as his words struck another chord within her. A tender, sweet one that resonated so deeply that she felt her heart opening more.

"Do not mistake my bow as an act of submitting to another's power over me. It is not so, Maggie Whitaker. I am but acknowledging that I am in the presence of someone who also knows about power. And that may be a woman who travels through time or a queen who marries a country to save herself and her beliefs. Would you not agree it is the use of power that earns respect?"

"Of course." Her mouth was dry, but she didn't want to drink anymore ale.

"Also, I admit, when we met, I took offense at your assumption I was an actor. I believed I hid that well. Your choice remarks about ego were well received, m'lady."

As if reading her mind, he replenished her drink and handed it to her. She accepted the goblet and held it in her hands as she stared at him in the firelight. She simply could not believe she was falling in love. One day with this man and she knew . . . *knew* . . . that they were supposed to meet.

Their eyes locked. He was illuminated in the fire's glow, seductive in the magic light. What was that . . .

that wild racing through her body, as though she'd just connected to something important, something she thought she recognized in his face?

''Is it good to be queen?'' he softly whispered.

Chapter Eight

it was as though she were living a fairy tale.

When she had awakened it was to three costumed women bustling about her room, withdrawing the heavy curtains around her bed, lighting fires, serving her honey wine and delicious biscuits. She had been pampered, groomed, and left to ponder the incredible turn of her life. Sitting in a chair, gazing out to the rose garden below ... Maggie again wondered if she'd had a nervous breakdown and was actually sitting in an institution hallucinating. Yet, as her fingers touched the heavy, rich material of her gown, she realized that everything *felt* so real, looked so clear, even the breeze coming in through the window smelled more sharp, cleaner.

And what about last night with Nick! Now that was about as *real* as anything she had ever experienced. He was ... she fought for a word. Incredible. It had to have been the ale. Something. She could not be forty years old today and considering love with a singer who claimed to be living four hundred years in the past!

If she had gone crazy, she was certainly in a great place to be ''out-there.''

Inhaling deeply, Maggie looked out to the lovely rose garden and stood up. Even though she'd said she would help Elthea, she simply had to escape, for she found herself being drawn more and more into this fantasy. *His* fantasy. It was seductive. . . .

A mental picture of Nick wishing her a good night raced through her mind. She had thought, just for a moment, that he might kiss her. He had been staring at her mouth for the longest time, as though wondering what it might taste like. At least *she'd* been wondering, and that, alone, should be proof enough that she needed to find an escape. If she remained, Maggie feared she just might believe she had time traveled . . . and that would mean, of course, that she *was* insane and *should* be institutionalized! Her brain was starting to hurt from trying to analyze everything.

Dressed in her refreshed ruby gown, Maggie looked once around the chamber and walked toward the door. It was now or never.

What did Aunt Edithe say? There is no safety, nothing guaranteed, in an adventure?

Ironically, Elthea had scolded her with almost the same message.

Don't think about it now, she admonished herself as she pulled up the metal latch and opened the heavy door. Looking out to the empty stone hallway, Maggie moved forward and tiptoed to the stairway. She would just go down it, walk through the great hall, and out into the garden. Once there, she would meander toward the entrance to this place and run.

That was her only plan. It had to work.

She opened the door at the bottom of the stairs and entered in back of the great hall, behind the head table. Several people were working, sweeping and assembling tables, and some raised their heads and stared at her.

Startled by their presence, Maggie squared her shoulders and took a deep breath as she closed the door behind her and entered the massive room. She kept reminding herself to stay calm as she walked farther into the hall, and appreciated the high, stiff collar of her underblouse that forced her to keep her chin up.

Two women, sweeping, bowed and lowered their heads as she passed.

"M'lady," they whispered in unison.

Maggie smiled and nodded with a simple, "Good morning."

Several others followed the ritual, and she found herself smiling and nodding as she briskly walked past them. This was her first honest attempt at role-playing and she felt foolish. Maggie almost laughed at her nervousness. How can one be honest and be playing a role, other than herself? *Don't think*, her mind commanded, and she was reminded that her immediate objective was to get to a door, either door to the sides of the fireplace, and leave this crazy place that seemed so real.

Success!

Once out of the great hall, Maggie hurried to the main door and slowly opened it, wincing at the creaking of the old oak. Closing it behind her she inhaled the fresh air and immediately walked to the nearest rosebush, while attempting to remain as nonchalant as possible. She stopped and, while waiting for her heart to slow down the hammering inside her chest, sniffed the delicate fragrance coming from the pink rose.

She'd made it . . . at least so far no one had questioned her or tried to stop her. Encouraged, Maggie slowly walked to the next flowering bush and the next and the next, all in the direction of the gated door that would lead across a wooden bridge and to freedom.

She felt a twinge of remorse for leaving Elthea like this and more than a twinge about Nicholas, but none of it was really normal, and she needed to get back to normal people who took showers and had working indoor plumbing, telephones, and drove cars and spoke in a language that wasn't archaic. Oh yeah . . . and men who didn't look in her eyes and read her soul. Normal people. Her aunt Edithe would help solve this mystery, she thought as she inhaled the scent of another delicate rose. If there was a weird group of people that practiced living in the Renaissance, she was sure Malcolm and Edithe would know about it.

"The loveliness of my mother's flowers surely pales before thy own beauty, cousin."

Startled, Maggie, none too gracefully, stood upright and turned toward the sound of the deep male voice. A man dressed in dark green britches and a white shirt with intricate lace on the high collar and flowing sleeves was walking toward her with a smile upon his face. Behind him stood several men, who seemed pleased to be witnesses.

"Forgive me, Your Ladyship, for interrupting such a private moment, yet I could not help myself in finally making your acquaintance. I am most happy to see the blush of good health upon thy comely cheeks."

He stood before her and Maggie felt the pounding of her heart in her ears and in her fingertips. It was Lord Robert! She was sure of it, as his mouth held the same pleasing tilt as Elthea's. Now what was she supposed to do?

Immediately, she remembered last night with Nicholas. *Just change the names*, her mind commanded.

Slowly, Maggie lowered herself into a deep curtsy and bowed her head.

"I am honored, Lord Amesbury," she whispered, as a bird let out a loud cry above them.

"Prithee, rise, dear lady and allow me to gaze upon thy countenance, for I fear the small portraiture I have held these many months does thee no justice whatsoever."

Oh shit, now he'll know, Maggie thought, and took a

deep breath as she accepted his outstretched hand and slowly stood upright. Raising her chin, she gazed into his eyes and smiled, wondering if he would see she was an impostor and end the charade right then.

"Thou art far more lovely than I had expected. The years have been kind to thee, dear cousin." There was flirtation in his dark eyes and some kind of knowing in his full smile. He wasn't bad-looking ... at all. Tall, dark with a full head of hair that curled around his handsome face and quite sure of himself, too.

For some reason, Maggie didn't like being around him. It could be because Elthea and Nick had warned her about him, or it could also be that she wasn't all that fond of a man, even a good-looking man, assuming anything about her. For some weird reason, he reminded her of her ex-husband, physically, and in that barely contained arrogance of a man who knows how to get what he wants from a woman. She had to also remind herself that he, like all those around her, actually believed he was someone else and his someone else was betrothed to the Lady Margaret. What a web they all were weaving. It was hard to keep the roles in order. Now, how was she supposed to answer him?

"You are very kind, m'lord. Thank you."

Seemed polite enough.

"Your cousin, my lady mother, informs me you have suffered a misfortune while on your travels to Greville Manor. I pray you are recovered sufficiently, m'lady? Perchance, a recounting of your tale would enable that I might dispatch my guards posthaste to apprehend the scoundrels who accosted you, and your cortege. Such an affront upon a person of the nobility is punishable by—"

"Dear cousin Margaret," Countess Elthea called out, as she hustled through her garden. "Thou gave me quite a fright, I fear."

Caught for sure, Maggie could only smile with an odd
mixture of the disappointing failure to escape and immediate relief to be rescued. She was not doing well on
her own with Robert. "I was admiring your beautiful
roses," she murmured, as Elthea joined them and looked
cautiously from Maggie to her son.

"Good morrow, my dear lady mother. It appears our
lovely cousin Margaret shares thy passion for flowers."
He raised his mother's hand and lightly kissed her fingertips. " 'Twas here I happened upon her, a most inviting vision of loveliness she presented, that I was
compelled to seize such advantage and dispense with
formal introductions. You might have warned me my
future bride was so pleasing that the winged birds above
would sing her praises. I am most pleased." He glanced
to his cronies behind him and smirked.

Okay, now she really didn't like him. He not only
overplayed the part of lord of the manor, but he also
actually believed that his opinion of her looks was important. What arrogance! Immediately, she remembered
that he thought Lady Margaret was about to marry him,
and so he would flirt. She glanced at Elthea and recognized her pleading expression, as though begging her to
go along with the charade. There was something, almost
fear, in the woman's eyes, and Maggie found herself
bowing once more in answer to his compliment.

"Impetuousness can wither even the strongest of
hearts, my lord and son." Elthea gave him a mildly
chastising glance. "We shall make the formal introductions in the proper manner, Robert. Such an untimely
meeting before an audience is most unseemly, is it not?"
And she glanced to the men, who were still staring with
great interest. "Pray thee, allow me to escort this lovely
child from here and return her to her chamber, where
she may recoup fully from her arduous journey and pre-

pare for the coming festivities.'' She squeezed Maggie's hand.

Robert smiled to his friends, then bowed with great flourish. ''I beg your forgiveness, my lady mother and dear cousin Margaret. My heart overwhelmed my good senses.'' He took Maggie's hand and brushed his lips over her knuckles in an intimate gesture. ''Until this evening . . . when we may be formally introduced, then we shall feast and celebrate our betrothal with fine food and drink. Anon, m'lady . . .''

Maggie pulled her hand away quickly, grabbed her skirt, and curtsied with a quick bounce. ''Good day, m'lord,'' she whispered, while staring the man down. Nicholas might not approve, but she wasn't lowering her head to this pretentious man again.

''We beg thy leave, Robert.'' Elthea curtsied once more, pulling Maggie back with her.

''Come,'' Elthea said, ''I have sent for the mercer, the draper, and the stapler. You might be surprised at the quality one finds this far from court. As soon as your silks and linens have been selected, the tailor and seamstresses are prepared to replenish your wardrobe posthaste. Already the draper has arrived and is waiting in your chamber, dear cousin.'' Maggie knew that speech was more for an impression than truth. Elthea took Maggie's arm and looked back to her son watching their departure from the garden.

Neither woman said another word as they walked through the courtyard and back toward the main door. Just before they entered, Maggie distinctly heard Robert laughing with his men and one of them saying, ''Fie me, but thou hath lucked well again, m'lord. Not half as sorry-looking as thou had imagined!''

Maggie's back stiffened as she barely heard Robert's reply. ''I am pleased.''

''Child, do come along,'' Elthea encouraged, as Evan

opened the huge front door and exchanged an expression of relief with the countess.

Once inside the hall, Maggie pulled away from the woman. "I can't stay here! I have to leave and get back to my own people!"

"Hush," Elthea warned, and looked around the foyer for others who might overhear. " 'Tis neither the time nor the place for this discussion. Come with me to my chamber, that we might converse in private."

And so Maggie found herself back in the castle, back in the deception, and back into insanity.

"Prithee understand, the fabrics delivered are for the true Lady Margaret, and I regret our stapler cannot finish a new gown for you prior to this night's gala," Elthea whispered as she patted Maggie's hair, which had been twisted into a coronet. She checked the pins on the circle of diamonds that rested on top. "You are an angel, child," she breathed in appreciation of her creation.

Maggie sat frozen at the vanity table, unable to speak, just staring into the hazy mirror.

"Regardless, tonight you are so lovely, familiarity of thy raiment shall be overlooked. All shall be taken quite agog, I am certain, by your piercing blue eyes." Maggie could tell Elthea was trying to smile reassuringly. "Practice caution, child, for the eyes are the windows to the soul . . . and our deception must be convincing for tonight's performance. Once the feast has concluded, you may retire. Then an outing shall be arranged for you to search out thy . . ."—she paused—". . . thy maze and the illusions surrounding it."

Maggie spun around. "Illusions?" she asked with exclamation. "You simply don't understand that my people are out there," and she again pointed to the window. "There are people outside this place that don't act like

you, people who are normal! Just let me leave, and I'll
find them, Elthea. I can't go through with this charade.
Robert will find out I'm not this Lady Margaret. I know
almost nothing about the Renaissance, except what my
aunt told me, and that was about cultural freedom, not
about political maneuvering. I'm telling you, I can't do
this!'' Maggie turned back to the vanity, sighing with
defeat. She leaned on her elbows and rested her chin in
her hands forcing her face into a pout.

"You can, and more importantly, you *must*, child,"
Elthea said firmly and turned Maggie back to the mirror
as she finished dressing Maggie's hair. "For not only is
Master Nicholas's life endangered, but mine own wel-
fare is threatened by exposure. Can you not see these
cultural freedoms you speak of will be withdrawn if a
monarch takes the throne and is supported by the
Church? Rome would like nothing better than to keep
all but a chosen few in ignorance, for then power is
retained and those who sit in power in Rome are very
greedy indeed. This is not about you, dear child. 'Tis
history, in the making, and remember . . . history is written by the victors. Those who follow us shall only know
what the victors want them to know."

Again Maggie spun back around. "Listen, Elthea . . .
I can tell you. England stays Protestant. Rome never
again regains power here. There's your history. So you
and Nick and everyone else who are so worried right
now can relax because you're the victors."

Elthea rested her hands on Maggie's shoulders and
stared into her eyes. "Repeatedly, you have insisted you
are not of this age, but of a future world. I am inclined
to believe many things beyond my comprehension, and
such a thing has brought you to my home. And yet, these
remain dangerous times in our England. The Queen is
aging and has no legal heirs to ascend her throne. She
has spent her entire reign outwitting the Spaniards, the

French, the Papists, and her own nobility. By not marrying any earthly man and declaring herself married to England, she has safeguarded her reign, yet the throne is still vulnerable to the machinations of those whose only desire is power, not the good of the people. If you know the future, who sits on the throne after Elizabeth?''

Maggie stared blankly into the woman's eyes. "I don't know. I can't remember. And none of this really matters, because it's not real. History is over and—"

Elthea's fingers tightened on Maggie's shoulders. "You must cease this denial once and for all! I know not how you came to be here in this troublesome time, but you are *here*, not in the year 2000. Such talk is unbalanced, should anyone save myself hear it.'' She inhaled slowly. "On the morrow, I shall arrange for you to ride back to the woods and search for your fantastic maze, the faire, your relatives, yet I doubt their existence."

Maggie felt tears well up in her eyes, and her throat felt like it was closing. "I know they exist . . . somewhere. I had a life, and I want to get back to it. I must get back to it.''

Elthea closed her eyes briefly and sighed. "Dearest Maggie . . . how can I make thee comprehend 'tis best not to ask the 'why' in all things, but to accept them as possibilities. I know not how such fantastic things happen, yet I do know they have. I have studied ancient scripts, talked to mystical scholars, and have seen writings which mention beings who are verily unexplainable. Other beings traveling to us, bringing knowledge and wondrous messages. I am even told of a legend of paintings found within caves in France, telling of these visitors from the sky.'' Elthea paused, as if searching her mind. "Might they have been angels? Perhaps they were visitors from the future—"

"I can't buy this!" Maggie stood up and began pac-

ing the room. "You . . . you're talking about angels,
time travelers, UFOs and . . . and all kinds of stuff that
has never been proven. I am just a woman, who had an
anxiety attack and got lost in the woods. I didn't come
with any knowledge or great message. Nick brought me
here for help to get back home, and now I must insist
that you allow me to return when it's light out again."
She stopped and gazed at Elthea pleadingly. "Look, I'll
help you tonight. I'll go through with this feast thing,
and then I'm done. Tomorrow, I am leaving here if I
have to tell Robert myself that I'm an impostor. It that
understood?"

Sadly, Elthea nodded. "I have no desire to hold thee
against thy wishes."

"And you won't use anything to drug me . . . no more
sleeping potions?"

"I vow to honor thy decision, child. On the morrow,
thou shalt depart and hopefully find thy path home. But
that is anon. Prithee, be at ease this night, and walk a
while in Lady Margaret's shoes? Rather, you might find
this eve to be enjoyable, and an honor. This intense desire to leave quickly just may be vanquished."

Elthea continued with an inviting lilt. "You have
come to this place . . . to us . . . at this time, for a reason,
child. Perhaps it is to assist us in keeping Rome away
from the English throne . . . it may only be a personal
revelation for yourself. Whatever the reason, you are
here . . . in this moment. Seize it, Maggie."

Memories of sitting in front of the fire during her
small breakdown with Aunt Edithe flashed through Maggie's head. She closed her eyes in disbelief. The irony
was too much.

"This night is thine and all shall honor thee." Elthea
tenderly touched Maggie's chin. " 'Tis a burdensome
role you have assumed, yet I pray know in thy heart I
honor you, Maggie, and am in your debt."

"Okay . . . all right, Elthea," Maggie murmured. "I'll do it."

"Then let us depart this chamber, for I believe the festivities in thy honor have begun."

Maggie couldn't resist this woman's smile, nor her charm. Whatever delusions she was suffering from hadn't diminished her intelligence, her grace, and her kind heart. In any other time, Maggie knew she would want to be Elthea's friend, for she really did remind her of her own aunt. Smoothing down the ruby-velvet material of her gown, Maggie nodded.

"I guess I'm as ready as I'll ever be," she muttered.

"Well-done, child. Together, we shall enter the great hall and thy loveliness shall cause all to whisper the Norreys name with awe."

Maggie chuckled in disbelief. "Yeah, right . . . Poor Lady Margaret will be known as the silent one after this fiasco."

"I shall explain all to my blood cousin, the true Lady Margaret. You do bear a strong resemblance to her . . . enough that she will be astonished should she ever see you, as though she were looking in a mirror." She paused, then added, "But sometimes, silence is the best path after all. Who am I to know?" she asked, shrugging her shoulders.

Opening the door, Elthea whispered, "Thy reticence will be admired, especially by Robert, who does not seem to appreciate the intuitive side of the female. He shall be relieved that you hold no opinions of your own and thus he will be pleased to know his marriage will be a smooth one. Let it worry thee not, child. Smile. Bow. Murmur sweetly. Women have always known it does not always serve to show we have minds of our own. The punishment can be severe."

As they approached the stairs, Maggie stopped. "It

has always grated on my nerves that a woman with intelligence frightens men.''

The smaller woman took a dcep breath and looked around her to make sure they were alone as they continued down the long corridor. ''It's always about power, child. Never forget that. Power and control. Once, long ago, there was a strong religion dedicated to the Goddess. It is said 'twas through Her that life began. Yet, presently it is taught that oneself is to believe life came through a male, even if nature shows us that cannot be possible.''

They continued descending the musty stairwell poorly lit by candlelight.

''Oh, shi . . . oot,'' Maggie corrected her cursed stumble. She had thought it better to refrain from obscenities, since she was living vicariously as a noblewoman.

''Do be mindful of the treads, Maggie dear,'' Elthea urged in a caring tone.

''Sorry . . .'' Maggie whispered. ''You were saying, if it weren't for us gals, there'd be no guys . . . but that's not exactly what we're taught.''

''Aye, precisely, child. How better to ensure the female face of God remain obscured, than to deny the godliness of the female? Her Majesty, by marrying England, saved her own life and the throne from Rome's clutches. Yet, it is not yet secured without threat. Rome will never acknowledge that God is also female, for their whole structure would crumble and the cries of thousands upon thousands of women who perished during the Inquisition would deafen their ears and haunt them.''

As Elthea's words trailed off, Maggie found they'd come to a high-ceilinged room with ancient furnishings. On the length of the room there were massive, dark wooden tables against opposite walls loaded with bolts of beautiful fabric.

Maggie shuddered while gooseflesh popped up over her skin, as though a ghost had walked past her. "You're like an undercover agent, aren't you, Elthea? You're not working for the Protestants. Your interests are—"

The countess halted suddenly and brought a finger to Maggie's lips. "Hush. Do not speculate at this time. I smile. I bow. I murmur sweetly," she whispered, and parodied a demure curtsy, "for I am but a mere woman."

Maggie felt herself drawn into Elthea's energy, for there she saw someone to be admired. A woman with absolute integrity. She couldn't wait to speak with her in more depth, to find out what her story really was. "Tonight. You will tell me tonight?" Maggie implored.

"I shall answer all thy questions whence we return to our chambers. The greater irony is with us tonight, Margaret. Women may not act upon a theater stage, yet we are here, on a stage of Life. Shall we show this audience an extraordinary performance?"

"It'll be an Oscar nomination for me, I'm sure!" Maggie joked, raising her eyebrows.

A smirk came over Elthea's face. "I accept thy riposte as an 'Aye,' my dearest cousin, Maggie. And I speak this endearment even without proof of blood, for that which I have witnessed in thine eyes tonight confirms in me we are yet bound together in this struggle for balance. I am doing my part as I am shown . . . and likewise, thou art. Verily, I tell you, Margaret Whitaker is indeed, a lady. It is my honor to bow before thee." Slowly, with a graceful curtsy, she paid tribute to Maggie.

And in the moment as Elthea rose, Maggie recognized something inside of her that refused to be denied. Elthea was either the best actress in the world, or somehow, by some incredible circumstance . . . she found herself living with people who honestly believed they were in the year 1598. What had happened when she'd run from that maze? How could she have run into the Renaissance? This stuff just doesn't happen!

But this wasn't a movie. This was her life!

As they continued their journey through a network of small chambers, short hallways, and more damp stairwells, Maggie had to ask the question that was now resounding so loudly inside her she couldn't suppress it any longer.

"Elthea . . . you honestly believe that someone could . . . well, time travel, from one place to another? That they could time jump hundreds of years?" She could hear the desperation in her own voice.

Startled, Elthea grabbed Maggie's wrist, and whispered, "Calm thyself, child. Now is not the time, nor place, for thee to understand the deeper meaning behind this adventure. There is a feast prepared in thy honor, and that is our priority. Anon, we shall discuss all of this, and then thou shall make a more sound decision about leaving." She waved her hand out to the staircase. "Lady Margaret . . . thy presence is awaited."

Maggie found she was shaking and held on to Elthea's hand as they slowly descended the final stairway. It couldn't be possible. She hadn't time traveled into these people's lives, into this madness. She just couldn't buy into it.

The sound of conversation and laughter became louder as they approached the great-hall entrance. "Oh, Elthea, I don't know if I can do this. I'm not a good actor."

Elthea turned to her, before opening the door, and captured her frightened gaze. "Of course you are. Are you not a woman? Prithee, hear me clearly, you shall do all that is necessary *to survive*," she encouraged in a voice that was firm. "Maggie dear, how else are we still here, I ask, when our rights have but all been stripped away? I dare say our time will come again, but until such a time of balance, we will do what we must, for sanity and to ensure darkness does not reign freely once more. Now, prepare to greet thy peers, admirers, *and* opponents, Lady Margaret.''

The large paneled door was flung wide open before them by a servant.

The clamor slowly diminished until it stopped completely as they entered the great hall. Maggie became acutely aware all eyes were on her. The air was palatable with expectation. She could feel the blush creep up her neck to settle on her cheeks. Wow, what a huge guest list Elthea must have worked on, and how did she have time to plan all this? There were at least fifty people who'd stopped milling about, and this was only half the crowd Elthea said was coming to the wedding ceremony.

A clattering of cups and plates resounded as plainly dressed servants began moving hastily around the room pouring wine and checking tables. All these other people, well, they looked like normal people, just dressed up royally . . . as a matter of fact, the scene was almost exactly like what she'd seen at the Renaissance Festival.

Talk about déjà vu.

Chapter Nine

Wow. It was all she could think as Elthea escorted her into the huge hall. As she was led through what seemed to be a carnival of curtsies and bows, she couldn't help but notice the extravagant costumes. These must be designs of the Donna Karans and Bill Blasses of their day. Elaborately layered silk gowns of purple and crimson or cream, all gaudily decorated with jewels, pearls, and silk embroidery floated through the room. How the ladies managed not to bump into each other with their large, belled skirts was amazing to her. *My kingdom for a bowling ball*, she nearly chuckled out loud with nervousness.

Most of the men were in darker colors; shades of greens and blues, though some wore plain black, and one man, with an extremely effeminate manner, wore white entirely. He sounded like he must be the life of the party from the laughter around him.

What's with these huge starch-ruffled collars? Most guys she knew complained about a necktie. Ha! They should try and get around in one of these getups!

Don't start laughing now, Maggie Whitaker, she scolded herself. *No eye contact. Nod. Curtsy. Smile.*

She saw waist-length velvet capes draped over backs, like the one she'd seen on Nick when they met. But so many had their jackets or vests as garishly adorned as the women's gowns. *Geez, what these people would give for the invention of the sequin,* she mused. There was no wool or flax on these folks.

Obviously, this was uptown.

She really had to admit some of the costumes were incredibly beautiful, but the pompadour hairdos under high-crowned bonnets with jewels and plumes had to go. Some of the ladies wore high arched veils rather like wings over their shoulders. She'd seen them in paintings before, and always thought they were a bit silly. She was glad her hair was pinned up more simply and she wore Elthea's small diamond tiara.

Actually, she was beginning to think she might be a bit underdressed for the occasion, but she figured everyone knew the story about Lady Margaret losing all her belongings en route. Including her pearls. Damn. She wished she had them.

She saw Robert approaching, and the pounding of her heart became louder to her ears as the dispersing crowd made way for his advance.

Feet, don't fail me now, was her mental prayer.

Stay calm, she admonished herself, just as she also saw Nick walking behind Robert with a very attractive and young woman. It didn't help her nerves to realize she actually cared what Nicholas thought. Care? Hell, she was falling in love! A trickle of perspiration ran down her spine to remind her she was wearing the same dress he had met her in. Yeah, but at that time, it was covered with dirt because he'd nearly run her over with his horse.

It was clean now, and she had bathed and been given scented oils, yet Maggie felt like an object as everyone inspected her—the crazy widowed cousin who came to marry Robert, saving his fortune and supplementing his power. Poor Lady Margaret. What exactly was she getting out of the deal?

Maggie couldn't worry about that at the moment. Right now, the spotlight was on her.

Elthea curtsied and began the introduction of her distant cousin to her son.

"My lord, may I have the pleasure of formally presenting your duly betrothed, Lady Norreys of Rycote."

Maggie curtsied very low before him. "Thank you for receiving me, my lord Robert. I am most honored."

"Lady Margaret, may I present, my son, Lord Robert of Amesbury."

He bowed deeply. "Lady Norreys, we are graced by thy presence. Welcome to Greville Manor and thy new residence."

An asylum would be more like it. Control, she mentally warned herself. She had agreed to do this for Countess Elthea and Nick. She was bound to do it genuinely.

Robert extended his hand, and Maggie placed hers lightly upon his palm as the man dryly brushed his lips against her fingers. "And the honor is mine, sweet lady, that thou hast consented to sharing not just this feast, but as well, our lives. I trust the manor accommodations are to thy liking?" He led her to the table at the front of the room.

"Ahh . . . Yes, Your Lordship. Thank you, my chamber is . . . most comfortable." She turned her head slightly to be assured Elthea was close behind for support.

"It pleases me, thou art rightly pleased, Lady Margaret. Come, let us celebrate this night!" He called out for the musicians to begin playing.

She pulled that one off. *Maybe there isn't so much to this role-playing*, she thought.

A small group of men immediately struck up a festive tune, playing gourd-shaped violins and what appeared to be a small piano. It sounded like a harpsichord. She really wasn't into chamber music, but she didn't figure this band would know any Jackson Browne tunes.

Maggie prayed the shaking in her body would cease before it was transmitted to Robert. He was parading her in front of more men and women, who continued to bow and curtsy as they passed. She had to remind herself not to look into anyone's eyes, to smile demurely in acknowledgment, and to make sure she didn't trip on her skirts.

Robert continued to introduce her to an earl, several "Sirs," and many ladies. Nod. Curtsy. Smile sweetly.

Okay, she had it down now.

"And the acquaintance of our musician friend and poet, Master Nicholas Layton, has already been thine, I understand."

This time she did look in someone's eyes, and her breath caught at the back of her throat at what she was seeing. Nick's eyes seemed to probe her soul for just a moment, before he bowed, lowered his gaze, and murmured, "Lady Norreys, 'tis a pleasure to be in thy presence again."

Maggie found her smile was genuine. Just as she was about to offer her hand for his kiss, Robert's grip suddenly tightened. He conducted her through the room to the head table.

She was happy to see Nick again, though if she were honest, she'd just admit that Nicholas Layton was taking up way too much of her thinking lately. And how could he not, after that great night? *Stop it*, she again warned herself. *This is not the time to swoon over Nick when Robert was standing next to me. Sheesh! Swoon? I'm even starting to think like these people!*

Once seated, she exhaled her tension and thought she might just make it through this night after all, as a servant filled her goblet with wine. She couldn't help smiling at the young boy who shyly stole a peek at her face.

People began taking their places at the tables in the hall as the sound of conversation once more filled the room. She could just imagine the topic. Holding her chin higher, she glanced at Elthea. The woman was beaming.

"Thy early appearance took us quite by surprise, m'lady," Robert stated in a loud voice, as his gaze seemed to be riveted on her. It was obvious he wanted to be overheard.

"Lady Margaret, with regard to thy wardrobe . . ."

Oh no, where was he going with this?

"Perchance, you have seen the many fabrics delivered just this day? It was at my request our local mercer imported the finest silks for thy preference."

"Why yes, m'lord. Your mother was kind enough to show them to me earlier." She was glad Elthea had stopped her in that sewing room on the way down to the party.

"We employ an excellent French seamstress, and the mistress is well abreast of the latest fashions from Spain, Germany, and France. And a right industrious thing she is, I might add . . ." A couple of his cronies smirked along with him.

From the sound of it, he was probably having an affair with her. Even in four hundred years, not much had changed in that department. "Mmm," was all she could remark with the goblet of wine to her lips. Good thing.

"A fine new wardrobe and a much larger celebration is planned for thee. Thou art worthy of only the best, Lady Norreys of Rycote."

Okay, he wasn't going to get an argument out of her on that point. If the true Lady Margaret was going to suffer the rest of her life through all his egocentric comments, his shirttail-hanging cronies spying on her, and quite possibly his adultery with the manor staff . . . well, at least she could be spoiled in the comforts of luxury.

Still, she was glad it wasn't she, for no amount of luxury could make up for a bad marriage.

"I thank thee humbly for thy graciousness, m'lord," she said, confirming the deal for the other woman.

"As you may not be aware, Lady Margaret, I, too, have spent some time abroad . . . I do hope you might demonstrate the newest dances of France." He leaned slightly forward. "I make a marvelous student, and have been told by many that I have much grace and agility." His boast was met with surrounding approval.

She nearly rolled her eyes. What an ego. And now she had to spend the evening listening to it. It wouldn't bother her so much, except she had the distinct impression his words were meant for his cronies' approval more than hers. Much safer to keep her eyes cast down on her lap, because if she raised them, she just might find the courage to drop his arrogance a notch or two.

"As you wish, m'lord," she modestly responded.

What dances anyway? The only ones she knew would shock them. She might need a lot more than one glass of wine to make it through this night.

"Indeed . . ." Robert sounded pleased. Again.

It was obvious Act One had begun.

Nick watched her sitting next to Amesbury and found his back teeth gnashing in annoyance. By what right did he have to feel such discomfort in watching her play the role of Amesbury's betrothed? None, his mind answered, yet his heart was singing out to the woman, wondering if she, too, recognized the connection between them. Last night he had sworn he had seen it reflected in her wondrous eyes. Their discussion of time had been most informative . . . for them both. Countess Elthea had spoken to him earlier, confirming that such feats as transportation through place and time were plausible and there were records of instances in which it had occurred. The myths of gods had spoken of it, the Bible, the ancient mysteries he had been studying with Francis, his mentor, made mention of the immense power of the mind to manifest itself in two places, yet even that, as incredible as it might sound, could not deter him from pursuing this miraculous woman. Mistress Maggie Whitaker really was the one who haunted his dreams, who inspired his songs, who would complete his soul! He knew it.

What he had seen last night before the fire, as he instructed her in the etiquette of conversing with Lord Robert, had robbed him of reason. Either she was an accomplished actress, which he was less apt to believe, or she really had traveled from the future. But why . . . ? His mind continued to torture him. Surely not to play Margaret of Norreys for this night of deception. For what other reason would she have traveled back in time? He was most anxious to visit Francis to seek counsel on the matter.

"Nicholas, I am told thou art the one who intercepted Lady Margaret in the wood."

He blinked, bringing himself back into the present. "Aye. Her ladyship suffered a mishap in her travels, and I was fortunate to have come upon her in a time of distress."

Marjorie Radcliffe, a maid of honor and an earl's daughter, leaned closer to him, and coyly remarked, "How chivalrous of thee, dear Nicholas. Pray tell, is it true Lady Norreys is most peculiar? The rumors . . . ?"

He felt oddly protective toward the real Lady Margaret and especially Maggie, who sat next to Amesbury, with her eyes downcast as she played the meek future wife.

"I find Lady Margaret to be most enchanting," he answered truthfully.

"Beware, Layton," a male voice called from down the table. "Our host is most protective of his newest acquisition, I hear."

"I only pay the lady a high compliment," Nick answered casually, seeing the speaker was one of Amesbury's intimates. Montague. The man was reputed to be a sword for hire, a scoundrel of the worst kind. They were not seated all that far, as not to be heard by the head table. He would swallow his retort and protect his lady. He thought of Maggie as his. . . . Now he only had to convince her of that.

Suddenly tankards started pounding tables, one after the other, until the hall was resounding with the clatter. Nick looked to Maggie and saw Robert whispering the meaning. He also registered the horror upon her countenance when she realized that to stop the noise she must accept a chaste kiss.

Again, he ground his back teeth together in annoyance.

Maggie looked to Elthea, who smiled reassuringly then looked back to a guest farther away. Obviously, she couldn't ask for help with this. The whisper of "kiss" was beginning to creep up through the rumble. Seeing all the excited faces around the large hall, hearing the laughter of the men and women amid the banging of mugs upon the wooden tables . . . Maggie knew she was alone in this one.

She sighed. "One kiss upon my cheek, m'lord. Then ask for no more."

Robert looked affronted. "No more? But thou art my betrothed!" he said loudly and with forced laughter that his cronies supported.

"Not yet. I am here to discuss the terms of our marriage, am I not?" Enough with hiding her face and pretending to be some meek woman. She would soon scream if she had to sit through an entire evening next to this pretentious, arrogant windbag and listen to his hall of rowdy friends and his assertions of how *pleased* he was that everyone kissed his noble behind.

Suddenly, like radar homing in on her, she could feel Countess Elthea's petrified stare.

"The terms were arranged and agreed upon many months ago, Lady Margaret," Robert shot back suddenly in a serious voice.

"But . . . how could they be discussed, m'lord, when this is our first meeting?" There. She had them on that one. At least, that's what this whole introduction was for, wasn't it?

The banging increased as the man stared at her.

" 'Tis neither the place nor the time to amend our contract. I am satisfied our original agreement is unequivocal. I suggest thee also find comfort in the alliance terms forth written."

Shit. Now he's mad. Okay, maybe she was overstepping some proprietorial boundaries for the real Lady Margaret, but she figured maybe she might save the woman at least some defilement.

"Oh, do kiss me, Robert, so we all may eat in peace." She quickly recovered the original subject, and offered her cheek.

"Hoorah!" The room resounded with the cheer.

The kiss, when given, was . . . reluctant. Obviously, she had displeased Robert by not remaining meek. Well, at least now maybe Robert would get the idea he couldn't bully or take advantage of his bride-to-be. It was the least she could do, Maggie thought, for borrowing the woman's identity.

Maggie shook her head, yet watched as a servant filled her goblet anyway. Mentally shrugging, she decided to avoid Elthea's cautious looks and just be herself now.

Besides, nobody said Robert was gonna kiss her! She had more of a grasp of this formal language to get by now. She certainly had enough intelligence to hold her own, even with Robert. Talk about role-playing! But now . . . she was going to play it to the hilt. She might as well enjoy herself. It was a celebration after all . . . and in her honor.

Just as her confidence rose, Maggie looked out to the seated guests and spied a young woman leaning toward Nicholas with an expression of what could only be termed adoration. She found she was annoyed and had to remind herself to relax. What did it matter if a hundred young women looked at him like that? She was leaving this insanity tomorrow and would never see any of them again. Still, she had to acknowledge more than a twinge of curiosity about the woman and her relationship to Nick. They seemed pretty familiar with each other.

Realizing Robert was glancing at her, Maggie stopped her ridiculous musings and smiled. Okay, she'd probably ruined the man's night. *I guess it wouldn't hurt to be nice*, she thought.

Robert seemed pleased by her smile and picked up his goblet. "I drink this wine, savoring its sweetness, until my thirst may be quenched by something more delicious."

Whoa! Maggie mentally called out to him. He was taking this flirtation way over boundaries for a first meeting. Then she wondered if Margaret and Robert had written and become more intimate in letters. It might explain his outright seductive manner.

Great! And Elthea didn't inform her how close Elthea's son was to her cousin. Sheesh . . . it sounded like something from a daytime soap opera! Having sold airtime and received big bucks for those afternoon hours, Maggie mentally shrugged and figured every generation was probably dysfunctional. Why expect anything else?

"You haven't sipped to my toast, dear cousin."

Maggie blinked a few times, then picked up her goblet and drank deeply. It was way too confusing to figure out. Replacing the heavy silver goblet, obviously a family heirloom, Maggie then turned to Elthea, who was looking out to the gathering and smiling.

"Is that a real one?" she leaned over and whispered. "The smile."

Elthea seemed surprised and then a wider smile appeared. "Yes, child. That was real. I was just observing dear Nicholas, as he artfully dodges Lady Marjorie's advances. It would make a good match."

Maggie immediately looked toward Nick and saw him smiling at something the woman was saying. "How charming." Her voice sounded just a tad dull, even to her own ears, and she cringed, hoping she hadn't revealed more than she had wanted.

"Yes, it is charming," Elthea answered. "Marjorie would make a fine wife, yet I do believe my young friend Nicholas is searching for his dream."

Now *this* was interesting! "A dream? What do you mean?"

Elthea nodded to a man at a nearby table and turned back to Maggie.

"Have you not noticed yet, child, that Nicholas is a dreamer? That is his soul, wondrous and expansive and deep. I do enjoy being in his company. He reminds me there is hope."

Trying not to look at Nick, Maggie answered, "What does all that mean?"

"That Nicholas is a fine man, who has not closed his mind. He believes in something that cannot be corrupted, manipulated, or sold. Now you should return to your companion before he takes affront." Elthea smiled and turned to talk to the man seated next to her.

Maggie just stared at the back of Elthea's headdress, wondering what the heck had just happened. As she turned her attention back to Robert, Maggie couldn't help taking a peek at Nick. What was it that he believed in? she wondered, just as the man lifted his head and looked right back at her. It was as if the space between them collapsed, like nothing else existed in that timeless moment, except them and the almost tangible charge of electricity between them. Shocked, Maggie broke the gaze and brought her attention to the man at her side. Thankfully, he was watching a servant place a huge roasted leg upon his plate.

She barely had time to recover as her own serving was placed in front of her. Robert grinned at her, as though very happy with the meal. She could just guess.

He was pleased. *Again.*

"I am pleased," he announced, before digging into his food.

Maggie couldn't believe he'd said it, and she laughed without thought to the consequences. Immediately, she covered her mouth with her hand as those nearest her watched for Robert's reaction.

Slowly, as if considering whether or not to be offended, Robert said in a voice intended to be heard by all, "I am pleased by your pleasure at mine own, m'lady. This is a feast, for I am to be married!"

Cheers broke out and everyone raised their drinks in celebration. Even Maggie. It was a small price to pay for seeing that the emperor wore no clothes and laughing about it! At least she wouldn't lose her head. As soon as that thought raced through her mind she wondered why, and then remembered stories she'd heard that anyone who had dared to point out to those in authority that they, too, were human, often lost their lives for it.

Sheesh, she was starting to think like Elthea now!

Again, she lowered her gaze to her plate and vowed

to leave this place before she was swallowed in the fantasy.

Nick felt his whole body come alive with a recognition that raced through his limbs to settle on his heart. It was odd to experience this strange mixture of joy and dread, yet that is exactly what happened when Mistress Maggie Whitaker laughed at Lord Amesbury. Something within him cracked open, and he was even more sure that Maggie had traveled to this time for him. He had found her, after all. She didn't run into Robert out there in the wood. It was to him she announced herself, and he had to stifle his own laughter when he remembered her shrieks of terror when she'd emerged from the trees. But he held his station, for like all others present he feared that Robert's infamous temper would win out and was greatly relieved when the man handled Maggie's laughter with more grace than any expected. The cheers that followed were not so much for the man's words, as for not spoiling the festivities.

He, too, had raised his glass, but in his eyes and in his heart he was saluting an honest soul. He attempted to appear as though nothing extraordinary had happened, yet he knew within him that Maggie Whitaker had come to his time for a reason. Francis had drilled into him that there were no accidents. Everything had a reason to be. It was only one's perspective that could bring about clarity.

"She does seem an odd one," Lady Marjorie murmured, after the cheers had given way to conversation.

Nick shrugged his shoulders, as though the topic of conversation were of no importance. "I wish the lady happiness."

"You are *such* a romantic, Nicholas Layton," the lady cooed. "Have you a new song for us this night?"

"I have," he said, and stabbed another turnip.

"How delightful! I do so admire your talent, Master Layton, as does many a lady I would dare say."

Her maidenly giggle only seemed to annoy him. All he could think about was when Maggie was turning from Elthea and had caught his gaze. His heart was demanding his attention to listen as the words he had waited his entire life to hear resounded in his mind over and over and over again. . . .

She's the one.

Maggie felt like someone had punched her in the stomach. Her breath seemed trapped somewhere between her lungs and her throat. Her mind was reeling. Her hands shaking. What the hell was happening? She had felt his attention, like someone tickling her nerve endings. When she slowly looked up from her plate, Nick was staring at her. The woman at his side was talking to him, and yet he continued to hold her gaze across the space that separated them. It was as though he were speaking to her in her mind, demanding that she remember him.

This is insanity. Maggie again broke the contact and looked down to the turnips before her. She could not be feeling like this again . . . this urge to meld with another, to open her heart once more. Not now! And not with *him*!

Her mind ticked off the many reasons why she should banish such thoughts immediately. She hardly knew him. He was another *artist*, this time a singer! He was younger and, oh yeah, lest she forget . . . *he claimed he was from another time*! How much more bizarre did this adventure have to get?

"The fare is not to your liking, Lady Margaret?"

Startled, Maggie turned to Robert who was staring at her.

"Oh, it's . . . *it is* very good, thank you." She jabbed a vegetable with the two-tined fork and popped it into her mouth. "Delicious," she muttered between bites.

Robert nodded and leaned in too close for comfort. "One would have to maintain a healthy appetite to heed such rapturous form," he said with a low laugh.

Was that supposed to be a compliment? Hmm . . . that one could go either way.

He was staring intently at her mouth moving over the morsel. *Great*, Maggie sighed mentally. *This is the last thing I need now, some arrogant admirer who thinks I'm someone I'm not coming on to me.*

Suddenly, she felt his hand grip her thigh. She swallowed and clenched her utensil. Stabbing him right then was an option, but she figured the small fork wouldn't make much of a wound, and she had promised Countess Elthea she would exercise her womanly wiles for everyone else's sake. She was a woman of her word.

"The wine gives you more courage than courtesy . . ." she said quietly through her teeth, not believing the words tripped so easily from of her mouth, ". . . m'lord," she added coyly with a smile, while firmly removing his hand from her leg.

The silence after her words was deafening. At first, she was rather pleased she'd come back with such an appropriate response, but for a moment she was rethinking the possible repercussions of her comment and actions.

Wait a second, what did she care? This was all some foolish charade carried on by a bunch of frustrated actors . . . she was *asked* to play along.

He burst out laughing. "The lady is virtuous with wisdom and wit," he stated loudly, backing off and raising his cup of wine toward the crowded room.

She saw Countess Elthea glance over approvingly, as

though to say she was pleased that Maggie's performance was going so well.

"I am to be married in less than a fortnight, good
ladies and gentle men! Let us drink and dance in celebration of my coming union with the most beauteous
Lady Margaret," Robert announced boldly, turning toward Maggie with a great smile.

She nearly rolled her eyes. This whole scene was really getting on her nerves. Her mind was a jumble as it
raced with ideas on how to escape this insanity.

"Hoorah!" the room cheered, and drank in unison. It
was all she could do in the midst of this madness. She
forced a weak smile and quickly looked toward Nicholas, who hadn't yet raised his cup.

It was as if he'd mentally called out to her. With de-
liberation he clutched his cup, raised it toward only her,
and mouthed, "Remember . . ." his gaze intensifying as
he brought the cup to his lips and drank fully.

What did he mean by that? her mind questioned his
message. "Remember . . ." what?

The sound of Robert thumping his empty cup on the
large wooden table jolted Maggie to tear her eyes away
from Nicholas.

"I am most pleased," Robert nodded toward his cronies.

She stifled a groan.

"I know I'll remember to pity the real Lady Margaret
when she steps into this role," Maggie muttered under
her breath.

"Minstrels, strike up a merry tune! I wish to dance
with my betrothed!" Robert grandly gestured to the
quartet as he stood and held his hand out toward her.

Countess Elthea rose abruptly. "My lord, I fear my
dear cousin Margaret may still be too weak to engage
in such joyous activities this evening."

Maggie could tell Elthea was attempting to keep her

from any further intimate involvement with Robert, who was by now becoming publicly intoxicated. Plus, not knowing Elizabethan dances, Maggie was saved from that embarrassment.

"Quite right, my lady mother." Robert motioned toward a servant to refill his cup. "What would thou suggest, my betrothed?" he slurred toward Maggie.

Elthea quickly interjected, "By chance, has the Master Layton, my good friend and most excellent bard of prose and poetry, a recital to entertain us?" Countess Elthea inquired, looking at Nicholas with a sly smile.

Maggie hoped he would quickly agree.

Nicholas grinned boyishly and looked up from his finished meal. "Compliments are only lies in court clothes, m'lady," he answered, beaming toward Elthea as though they were sharing a private joke. Rising, he added, "But thy words sing like sweet poetry to my senses." He then bowed theatrically.

From the corner of her eye she saw Robert slide down and slump against the back of his enormous chair. Must be the wine . . . her mental speculation was drowned out as a ripple of amusement went over the room.

That would be the only reason Nick's overacting didn't seem to irritate her right now. In fact, she found herself smiling and internally giggled at the thought. It was almost endearing. And charming. Really. He was much too charming. She had the experience to know that artists were experts at using charm to their advantage. She'd fallen for it once before and thought it better not to finish the mental fantasy she was having when they first got to this insane asylum and she had him pinned against the wall, face-to-face, while her blood pumped wildly.

Yeah, must be the wine, she thought with resignation, as a servant replenished her cup.

Elthea waved for Nicholas to take the center of the

hall. "The right is yours, kind Nicholas," she said triumphantly, then looked toward Maggie.

She appreciated the opportunity to mouth "Thank you" to Elthea with a sigh of relief for the save.

As Nicholas limped slightly into the middle of the huge room, Maggie fidgeted to get comfortable in her chair. She was about to hear more of what this man who was attracting her attention was all about now. Elthea certainly thought highly of him, Maggie reminded herself, and she had begun to respect the woman's opinions.

"With thy permission, Lord Amesbury." Nick bowed in a deep sweep toward the head table.

"Recite what thou will, Layton," Robert dismissed with another gulp of wine.

Maggie sensed tension between the two men. She couldn't understand why this guy Robert was so obviously agitated by Nick's presence. It seemed to go beyond this realm of theatrics. Men. Things sure hadn't changed much in the last four hundred years.

"A poem of love," Nicholas began.

Chapter Ten

following his recital, the entire room was held in silence as Nicholas rose from his bow. With his back to the head table, he could see half the room of guests awaiting Lord Amesbury's response before initiating their own typically subservient gestures.

Maggie tore her gaze away from Nicholas to see Robert looking up from his whispered conversation with a man next to him as though he were surprised the recital was over.

"Well spoken, Layton." Robert clapped slowly. The room joined with hesitant applause.

Ashamed for those in the room, Maggie slowly rose and began clapping more loudly. To hell with all of them and their fears of Robert. Her heart reached out to Nick, to be treated so poorly by his host.

Nicholas leisurely turned around just as Maggie was blinking furiously to stop the tears.

"I humbly thank you, m'lord," he softly stated, not removing his eyes from her.

Taking her seat, Maggie inhaled and hoped no one could see the dampness in her eyes as she regained her composure. Oh, he was good. Very good. Now she was beginning to understand why Elthea regarded him so highly. What woman wouldn't? He was a man with a great depth of emotion. To whom were these incredible feelings directed? Was she assuming too much to believe it could have possibly been written for her? Such yearning. She knew she had felt a pull when he looked right at her while he recited, that same pull she had felt last night in her chamber. How terribly tragic that he could unfold his heart and bear it before all these people, but not to the one who had inspired such intense love. Or had he? And why did she want it to be her?

The sound of Robert's chair grating against the stone floor rammed through her dreamy preoccupation. He did not look pleased . . . especially with her.

"I pray thee all a good eve," he abruptly announced as he pushed away from the table and rose. "I convene with my associates for immediate council and bid thee lords and ladies continued celebration." He turned toward Maggie and offered a hand to take hers.

Maggie's eyes widened. *Oh geez, am I supposed to leave with this guy?* She began to worry as she apprehensively lifted her arm.

"Till the morrow, Lady Margaret." With disinterest he barely kissed her hand and turned away. Relieved, she watched as he crossed the hall directly toward Nick, who was still making his way back to his chair.

Most all of the people in the room bowed as Robert walked by and ignored them. She saw Nick's worried face glance up to hers as hushed words were exchanged between the two men. Nick quickly looked away and moved back to his seat.

"Child, you look as though you are absolutely spent."

She felt Countess Elthea's comforting hands on her shoulders.

Without looking up, Maggie sighed, and responded, "Yes, Elthea, I've had enough of this play for the night. Is this our cue to exit, stage left?"

Elthea grinned down at her. "Aye, dear Margaret. Your scene here is finished."

It really was seductive . . . all of it. The clothes. The manners. The people. The intrigue. The pampering. The woman who attended her was young and silent. She played the role of servant within this madness and, as she unlaced Maggie's gown, Maggie asked over her shoulder. "Have you ever heard of a telephone, a credit card? An airplane? A television?"

"M'lady?"

Maggie turned around and was confronted with a person whose confusion was obvious. "You really don't know what I'm talking about, do you?"

The woman bowed slightly, not making eye contact. "I beg yer pardon, m'lady," she answered in a shy, worried voice.

"Never mind." Maggie shook her head and turned back, allowing the woman to continue unlacing her. It was surreal. They all couldn't be actors who played their parts so well that even at dinner not one had made a mistake, or flubbed a line. If anyone had messed up their role, it was she.

She stepped out of the wide skirt and removed the heavy bodice before handing it to the woman. Taking a deep breath, she felt lighter without the weight of the gown and walked over to the bed. She sat on the edge of it and removed her shoes, shoes she reminded herself, that had been made in her time yet were reproductions that no one here seemed to think were out of place. How odd that she had been dressed in such a fashion so that outwardly she fit right in as being of noble birth. When she saw how tired the servingwoman was as she began to lay out the beautiful nightgown and robe, Maggie held her shoes in her hand and stood up.

"What is your name?" she asked with a smile.

The woman seemed startled and bowed, while low-ering her head. "Gwen, m'lady. I beg your forgiveness if I have offended thee."

Walking closer, Maggie realized that had she not been dressed in such a beautiful gown when she'd encoun-tered Nick, she might have found herself in a much more terrible situation. Much more . . . Compassion filled her heart, and she smiled. "Please rise, Gwen."

The woman slowly stood upright and raised her frightened gaze.

"You have been wonderful to me since I awakened this morning," Maggie stated, and took the sheer gown of white cotton from the woman's arms. "You've been working all day and now you're done. Go rest, Gwen. I can dress myself."

"But, m'lady . . ."

"Hush. This is an order," Maggie stated with another smile. "It's late. Go to sleep, or visit with your friends or make love to your husband. I am quite fine alone."

"M'lady, I . . . I . . ." the woman stammered in aston-ishment, while an embarrassed blush appeared on her cheeks. "I am not a married woman."

Maggie chuckled. "I don't know whether to extend my sympathies or congratulate you. Do whatever you wish, Gwen. And if anyone asks, you may tell them that Margaret of Norreys has given you permission this night to live your life however you choose."

"Oh, m'lady," Gwen gushed as a smile spread over her face. "Bless you. May God grant you a long and happy life. You are an angel."

Maggie laughed. "Hmm . . . I know a few who would disagree, Gwen." She waved her hand toward the door. "Now go, be happy."

Again, Gwen bowed. "Thank you, m'lady." And then hurried to the door.

Maggie's heart felt lighter, and she figured that as long as she had this power she might as well use it for good. She had dressed herself since she was a child and didn't need the constant attention. Plus, if she were honest with herself, she would admit that she was anxious to be alone. She wanted to replay the last part of the evening's events, especially when Nick recited that poem *Muted Heart*.

She would swear he'd been talking to her!

As she removed the remaining underclothes, Maggie dreamily played back in her mind the scene, the way her body had felt as Nick stared into her eyes and played his lute, speaking of a love that could never be acknowledged. His words tore into her soul. Picking up the delicate night shift, embroidered with pale yellow flowers around the neckline and ruffled cuffs, Maggie again wondered what it would be like to kiss Nicholas Layton.

She felt like a teenager, and mentally scolded herself as she placed the shift over her head and slipped into it. Here she was, a mature woman, dreaming about being kissed by a man who was totally wrong for her. Instead of such ridiculous mental wanderings she should be figuring out her escape tomorrow. Elthea had promised.

She had done her part by playing Lady Margaret tonight, she thought, smoothing down the nightgown over her stomach and hips. The sensuous feel of the material against her bare skin brought thoughts of Nicholas, and she groaned. She'd known if she stayed she would be drawn further into their drama, and now here she was . . . craving the touch of him, the feel of him, the scent of him, the sound of his voice. Her fingers actually ached to run through his silky hair. Grabbing up the robe Gwen had laid out for her, Maggie refused to allow her hormones to override her good sense. She didn't belong here. She didn't . . .

She fastened the closings around her and walked over

to the mirror. Elthea's robe was almost as elaborate as a gown, with intricate gold embroidery in a subtle tapestry of vines and leaves on a deep green background. If anything could be said for this time, it would have to be the elaborate clothes, she thought . . . wishing that Nick could see her in this costume.

She did it again! Why was it that everything she thought seemed to lead back to him?

She would leave tomorrow, she vowed, and that would be the end of it. Almost as a punishment for slipping, Maggie tore the pins from her hair and began pulling her fingers through it as it fell to her shoulders. She was going to find her aunt tomorrow and somehow put this all behind her. No more daydreams about Nicholas Layton and what he might or might not think about her. As she pulled an ivory comb through her hair, Maggie almost welcomed the pain of tangles, for it took her mind away from Nick and his muted heart.

What would his heart say, if it were not muted, she again wondered. As soon as she realized her thoughts, Maggie threw the comb onto the dressing table and began pacing.

She was *not* going to allow this to happen to her. Of what use would it be to explore this path when she was leaving and would never see Nick again? None. Absolutely none. Stopping in front of the fire, Maggie stared into the flames as the thought refused to be denied.

She would never see him again.

Was she prepared to walk away from this attraction without ever finding out if it was returned? And what good would that do, if she did? It would only make leaving that much more difficult.

A knock on the door stopped any further mental torture, and Maggie was grateful for the interruption. Elthea had promised to come to her chamber and continue their earlier discussion.

Maggie opened the door to admit Elthea and Evan, the steward of the house. He was carrying a tray with a decanter, goblets, and fruit. Elthea smiled at Maggie and instructed Evan to place the tray on the small table before the fire.

"Good eve, child," Elthea said, touching Maggie's arm. "I saw thy maid had been dismissed, and so I thought we might enjoy this last night together and I may fulfill my promise to answer all your queries." She turned to the servant, and her smile warmed. "Thank you, Evan. Please stand guard in the hallway. If you are asked, merely say that it is my order as I attend the Lady Margaret, who is quite exhausted from this night's activities."

"As you wish, m'lady." Evan bowed and left the room.

Maggie watched Elthea's gaze follow the man and she would swear she saw something akin to love in the woman's eyes. She then remembered Elthea's reaction to Nick's poem and wondered if the closeness she had observed between the lady of the manor and the steward might just be something more.

"He's a very nice man," Maggie remarked, as the door to her chamber closed. "And he seems devoted to you."

Elthea sighed as she lowered herself to a chair and began pouring what looked like alcohol into goblets. "Evan and I grew up together since childhood. His mother served mine, and he was trained to run this home by his father. Here, child. Aqua vitae, a strong spirit to help thee sleep." She handed a goblet to Maggie.

Maggie brought it to her lips and inhaled the potent scent. "What is it?"

Elthea chuckled. "Truly, you are not familiar with our time. This is a brandywine, and I have not put anything into it as I have promised, so you may sit with me and not fear, Maggie Whitaker, that I have broken my word.''

Sitting in the chair opposite Elthea, Maggie grinned. "You people sure do like to drink. I think everything I've tasted has something alcoholic in it, even the food.''

"It purifies the blood and circulates it throughout the body. If thou would care for something else, I shall send Evan to the buttery for a pear wine, or perhaps a—''

"No, no,'' Maggie interrupted. "I was just making a comment. Brandy is fine, and I suppose after the night you and I have just had, we can use it.''

"Thy performance was well-done, child.'' She hesitated a moment, then added with a twinkle in her eye, "I was most pleased.''

The two women looked at each other and burst into subdued laughter.

Holding her goblet up in a toast, Maggie said, "Here's to everyone being pleased tonight, *especially* your son.''

They toasted and each sipped the brandy.

"Geez, I don't mean to be rude, but he is . . . well, arrogant, Elthea.''

The woman nodded sadly. "I fear my son's arrogance may be his downfall, yet his ears are closed to my counsel now. I have accepted that I cannot alter his will, though I do watch carefully that I might smooth any ruffles he may leave in the fan of time.''

Maggie didn't know if it was the brandywine or the sudden heaviness that seemed to weigh her down, but she felt tired of trying to figure out if something were meant figuratively, as in the poetic way everyone seemed to word everything, or it was literal. "Ruffles in the fan of time? I don't understand.''

Elthea put her goblet onto the table and spread her hands out like a fan. "Everything is connected to everything else. It is an old concept that is seeing a rebirth now as more and more information comes to us and rings true within our hearts. The actions of my son will affect many people and their history, perhaps even the history of this country. Tonight, you dismissed your maid, Gwen, with instructions to do whatever she wished. Had Evan not questioned her idleness and brought the matter to me, she would have been punished and fined by Robert. Sadly, he would not care that her mother would then not receive her daughter's wages and Gwen's lame brother would be on the streets begging to put food on their table."

Maggie clutched her goblet. "Oh God, I didn't know! I'm sorry. It's just in my time I have always dressed myself and she seemed so tired . . ."

"All is well now, child. Rest easy. I realize you are not familiar with our ways."

Maggie issued a self-deprecatory chuckle. "I think that was obvious a few times tonight. I almost died when Robert wanted to dance."

"You do not dance, child, in your home? What a sorrow to have lost that form of entertainment. It is one of the few we women are permitted to enjoy."

"Oh, we dance," Maggie quickly answered. "Only you wouldn't recognize it as such. You would probably be scandalized. It's a much more . . . hmm, free form, I guess you could say. Actually, unless one is slow dancing with a partner, dancing is less intimate. You just stand there and do your thing and hope your partner can follow."

"Do your thing?"

Maggie giggled. "It's an expression, Elthea. It means be yourself, do whatever your soul dictates, even if it isn't accepted by society."

"Ahh . . ." Elthea sat back and stared into the flames that licked the charred wood. "I think I should like doing my thing in your time." She glanced at Maggie.

"Women, too, are allowed this freedom?"

"Oh yes. In fact, more women than men dance in my time. Most men are intimidated by public dancing."

"Truly?" Elthea looked astonished. "Tell me more, Maggie. Tell me that in your time, four hundred years into the future, sanity has returned. That the marriage has taken place."

"Marriage?" What was Elthea asking? "Whose marriage?"

The older woman looked disappointed. "If you are asking that question, it has not yet happened. Four hundred years, and they are still quarreling, instead of uniting."

Maggie sat back. "Okay, now I'm lost. Who are you talking about?"

Elthea seemed to draw her strength, after being disappointed. "It has been said that when the Queen of Heaven unites with the King, then peace shall reign. Right now they continue to quarrel like spurned lovers, plotting against each other in jealous rages, wanting the other to be powerless, to feel the pain of betrayal. It saddens my heart to know that four hundred years shall pass, and still they have not reconciled."

"Elthea, I don't know if it's the brandywine, but I can't figure out what you're saying. The King and Queen of Heaven? Like in mythology?" Maggie shook her head in confusion.

"Child, have thee not heard that we humans play out the dramas, the comedies, the tragedies of the goddess and god, the male and the female faces of the One? In four hundred years have thy people not yet discovered this?"

"I guess not." Maggie could only stare at the woman.

Elthea seemed more than upset as she continued. "First the goddess spurned the god, who wanted to dominate her, when she would only consent to equal reign.

He rose up against her in a jealous rage and wiped her name from the earth, demanding all worship only him. The goddess was wounded but tended by a few faithful servants who hid her for safety until such a time came when she realized that alone she was incomplete as, he, in his rage, was incomplete. To be one, they needed each other. It has been written that a time of reconciliation will come, when goddess and god forgive each other their childish foolishness and all the pain they have inflicted on the other is healed, making way for the heavenly wedding of equals in power, in wisdom, in love. Thus humanity is healed. Woman is given her rightful place. This time at the side of man, to rule over earth as equals and together, in peace, we see we never left the heavenly garden, for it is right here. A time of sanity.''

Maggie sat back and stared. What Elthea was describing, this marriage, for some reason reminded her of the pair skaters in the Olympics, that graceful movement of male and female when synchronicity happens. Could that be possible in real life? Is that what her aunt and Malcolm had together?

''Wow . . . That's quite a myth, Elthea. I wish I could say that has happened in my time. I think we might be approaching it though.'' She shook her head in bewilderment. ''I can't believe I'm talking to you as though you really do live in the distant past. If it makes you feel any better, I will say that women have made great strides in equality, but the struggle continues. In my opinion, some of us have taken on more than we can handle as we've demanded equality. We thought we would get the help from the men, but it hasn't always happened that way, and a lot of women are burned-out.''

''Women are still being burned?'' The horror in Elthea's eyes was painful to observe.

Maggie quickly put her mind at ease. ''Oh, no. Not like that. It's more of an emotional burning and exhaustion. Kind of like Gwen, who has no time for herself."

"All women are like this? We have become servants?"

"Not all." Then Maggie thought about it, about working an eight-hour job and coming home to make dinner and do laundry, and she didn't even have any children which would add several more hours to the working day. "But many are weary, Elthea. I think you are right when you say that women and men together need to heal their differences and respect each other as equals."

Geez . . . it was beginning to sound like a NOW meeting! Maybe liberation had its seeds sown thousands of years ago?

Wanting to change the subject, Maggie leaned forward and said, "You promised you would tell me who you really are. I don't think you are working so much for the Protestants, as for something else. Will you tell me?"

Elthea sighed and picked up her goblet. "Oh, child, thou asks much. I do not know as I am working for anyone in particular. I am what is called a humanist." Her voice lowered a few octaves. "I have replaced the belief in a separate heavenly god with godliness in the human. I believe that humans can, and sometimes do, reflect those qualities we have said are only to be found in deities. Compassion. Forgiveness. Wisdom. Power. Balance. Love."

She again sighed deeply with introspection. "That is why I ask of the marriage of the male and female. I had hoped in the future humans would have guessed that if god . . . goddess . . . All That Is wanted to hide somewhere, to be invisible, what better place than within each of us?"

Stunned, she thought about it and admitted Elthea was right. Who would think to look for God in themselves?

What was that song the kids were listening to? A young woman singing the question . . . *What if God were one of us? Just a slob like one of us, just a stranger on the bus trying to make his way home?*

Elthea sipped her ale and smiled with affection. "You, Maggie Whitaker, have balanced the male qualities of strength, courage, logic with the female qualities of intuition, compassion, love. Nicholas has balanced those qualities, as his poem this eve hast shown us. 'Tis only, I suggest, when one recognizes and appreciates the qualities of the 'other' and balances within, that one may seek the marriage of like souls. Thus, twins of one soul, balanced with the eternal flame of the true marriage, are united. 'Tis quite a union!"

Maggie couldn't answer. Her mind was reeling. Besides picturing Nick in her mind the entire time, she simply could not get past the notion that this woman thought and sounded just like her aunt Edithe. And to make the picture clearer, Evan was as devoted to Elthea as Malcolm had been to her aunt. The comparison between the women was incredible. Here she was, stranded in a place and maybe a different time, listening to a woman who held the same beliefs as her relative who lived four hundred years into the future!

"I have upset thee, and I ask thy forgiveness, Maggie. I do get impassioned when I have the opportunity to speak on these matters. It is not often I have someone who might understand my heart."

"Don't apologize, Elthea. It's a lot to take in, I admit, but it isn't as though I haven't heard it before. The language might be different, but the concept is the same. My aunt speaks on these same subjects."

Elthea seemed interested. "The one you are seeking to find?"

Maggie nodded. "Yes. She is a holistic healer, helping those with learning disabilities."

"This sounds most encouraging. A woman healer and teacher. And she practices openly?"

"Yes. That isn't to say she's given the respect of the medical community, but no one is protesting that she's a witch or anything. So there is progress, healing, taking place."

"Thou art a most intelligent woman, Maggie Whitaker. May I ask a delicate question?"

"Certainly." Maggie brought the goblet to her lips and drank deeply of the sweetened brandywine to fortify her for the question, whatever it was.

"Why are you not married?"

Sighing, Maggie placed the goblet on the table. "I was," she answered in a low voice. "I am divorced."

Elthea gasped. "Divorced?"

Maggie almost giggled at the woman's reaction. "It is very common in my time, Elthea. In fact, almost half the marriages end in divorce. Your Henry VIII started something there."

"Husbands putting aside wives is a nasty business, indeed. My heart reaches out to thee, child." Elthea leaned forward and touched Maggie's cheek in a tender caress. "You are a fine woman and deserve your equal."

"Oh, Elthea . . . thank you, but my divorce was equally sought. I mean, my husband filed the legal papers, but I wanted it as much as he did. He just did it, while I was still dragging my feet about the whole situation. It was for the best."

"Women divorce their husbands?"

"Oh yes. Quite often, as a matter of fact. I think that is part of the reason the divorce rate is so high. Women are no longer bound to stay in a marriage that is not nurturing."

Elthea sat up straighter. "The Church has allowed women to terminate their marriages?"

"Well, not the Roman Church, but just about all oth-

ers. I know for a fact that in the Protestant faith, it is
common. Women do have some options in my time,
Elthea . . . so you see, progress has been made. Just not
exactly peace yet.'' Maggie's smile was filled with tenderness for this woman who was really a revolutionary
in her time—an undercover agent for peace between
men and women. How extraordinary! And what better
place to plant her seeds than with the wealthy, who made
all the rules the rest of society must live by. Her respect
for Elthea grew. This was one difficult time to be an
intelligent woman and stay alive.

"Tomorrow I shall arrange for you to return to the
wood where Nicholas found you. My son will be distracted with his political aims. He and several of his
allies are up to some intrigue, I dare say, and have
planned another hunting party. The presence of Nicholas
Layton at Greville Manor has forced Robert to seek pri-
vacy for his schemes, and he uses the ruse of a hunting
party to plot his next move.''

Maggie lowered her voice. "Elthea, what caused the
bad blood between Robert and Nick? I could tell tonight
that Robert barely tolerates him.''

Elthea nodded. "Nicholas is here by my invitation,
and even Robert would not deny me this, for he knows
Nicholas's mother was dear to my heart.''

"And Robert is jealous of your affection for Nick?
That's why he dislikes him?''

"It goes much deeper than that, Maggie. It is political.
There are . . . certain facts that few know concerning our
queen. Nicholas's mentor is Francis Bacon, and Robert
sees Bacon as a threat to his schemes. Rightfully so.
Since Her Royal Majesty has no legal heirs, Robert's
plans are to put a Catholic back onto the throne. Nicholas is merely caught in the middle, by his association
with Sir Francis. It is far too complicated for me to relay
now, and not my place to divulge state secrets about Her

Royal Majesty. Some have lost their positions, their holdings, even their heads for speaking of it.''

''Well, I don't want to get anyone in trouble,'' Maggie said, and sat back with her fingers laced over her lap. ''I just want to get back to my home again.''

Elthea nodded. ''I understand. You are in the midst of an intrigue and not of your doing. A wedding to gain power and finances. Were it not that my cousin Margaret suffered a nervous collapse at her husband's death, I wouldn't have agreed to bring her to this home and to my son. These are not peaceful times, and I agree you should leave quickly.''

''Poor Margaret,'' Maggie murmured. ''I wouldn't want to be in her shoes.''

''You are in her shoes, child. Though tomorrow you may step back into your own, I shall watch over my cousin as though she were my daughter. Robert's demands shall not be great upon her person, once he gets the money and prestige at court. And then she will be allowed to grieve as her heart demands.''

''She is still grieving?'' Maggie's heart felt heavy for this woman she impersonated.

''When one finds the other half to one's soul, and then is separated, I do not know that one ever stops grieving until they are reunited. Margaret shared a great love.''

Elthea's words reminded Maggie of Nick's poem, and Elthea's explanation of divine marriage. ''You really believe in that, Elthea? Soul mates?''

''Certes!'' The older woman sat up straighter and smiled. ''We have just discussed my reasons, and though I have heard that Germans woo like lions, Italians like foxes, Spaniards like friars, and Frenchmen like stinging bees . . . I do not hold with such nonsense. I think we have many soul mates, those with whom we bond in a deep, harmonious way, yet I think there is only one twin to our soul. Many times we go through life and never find that person, but when we do . . . when that magic happens and cannot be denied, our search is over and together the two realize their life mission and complete it.''

Maggie's voice was a low whisper. ''Did you find it?''

Elthea lowered her gaze to her lap and studied her hands. ''I know of that which Nicholas spoke of tonight. His words struck a chord within my breast.''

''The love? Or, the silence of the heart?''

''Both,'' Elthea whispered. ''There are many shades of love, child, and I have known the joy and the sorrow that it can carve into one's soul.'' She seemed to shake off her thoughts and looked to her guest. ''And this is also known well to thee. I pray when you return to your own home you might also find the joy.''

Neither woman said anything as they both stared into the flames, allowing their thoughts to take them away.

Finally, Maggie said, ''I need a friend, Elthea. My heart is heavy with a decision I feel I must make.''

Elthea didn't turn to her, just smiled as she continued to study the fire. ''I have bared my soul to thee this eve, Maggie Whitaker, more so than I have allowed in many years. The honor would be mine to be considered thy friend.''

''Yes,'' Maggie whispered. ''I, too, feel that we are somehow connected. I know it's strange, considering that in your mind and maybe even in mine, we are separated by four hundred years, and yet I cannot deny what I feel.''

''I am grateful. Now, how may I help?''

''Well,'' Maggie began hesitantly, ''it is a delicate matter. One of the heart, I'm afraid.''

''Nicholas?''

Maggie looked sharply to the woman. ''How did you know?''

A soft chuckle escaped Elthea's lips. "Oh, child . . . I may be old, but my vision is still clear enough to see two people who are irresistibly drawn to each other. I am surprised Robert did not challenge Nicholas to a duel for the manner in which he presented his poetry this eve. I do believe my young friend thinks he has found his dream after all."

"Me?" Maggie felt a blush of embarrassment and at the same time experienced the racing of her blood, thrilled to know that she hadn't imagined it. Nick *was* attracted to her.

"And thy query?"

She took a deep breath, hoping to find the words to express how she felt. "I mean, I know it's crazy to even be thinking like this. I have half a dozen reason why such a thing is positively insane, yet there's something inside of me that refuses to deny it, and if I leave tomorrow I'll never know."

"You wish to remain?"

"Yes, no . . . I mean, yes, I have to get back to my time, but I don't want to spend the rest of my life wondering what would have happened if I'd had the courage to find out."

"What is it that you wish to discover?"

Maggie sighed. "If he's the one. The one I've been talking to since I was a child. Even late in my marriage I would lie in bed and look out to the stars and talk to him, whoever he was. I know it sounds nuts, but when my marriage started failing . . . and when I look back it began years before it actually ended . . . but when I knew something was wrong, something I couldn't fix, I would think about someone who really loved me, for me, not for the life I could provide. I *knew* he was out there, but I didn't know if I would ever meet him, or if I even should try. Then when my marriage ended, I was so overwhelmed I forgot about love. I even thought it was foolish to believe in it. And now . . . *this*!'' Even to her own ears, her voice sounded desperate.

Elthea's smile was warm and motherly. "Oh, child . . . does thou think one directs where they shall find love? 'Tis my belief that love is a power that cannot be dictated. You do not find it. It finds you. And now you are wondering whether love has found you, Maggie Whitaker?"

She didn't answer. She couldn't. It seemed so ridiculous.

"It would make your choice to leave much more difficult, I understand, but you must leave, child. We are expecting Lady Norreys's arrival within this week, and thus your presence cannot be here. I shall avert my son's attention until Lady Margaret presents herself, but have you given thought to where you shall go if your trip to the wood is a disappointment?"

"I have to find my way back, Elthea. I can't even consider any other plan."

"I think you should speak to Nicholas and follow thy heart. He could accompany you to London."

"London?" Maggie was shocked. "What is in London?" There was that phrase again. *Follow your heart.*

"Mayhap answers, Maggie." Elthea rose and sighed deeply. "You have much to contemplate this night. I have kept you from your rest, and I am weary from all this activity. We shall speak again in the morn."

Maggie stood up and instinctively hugged the older woman. "Thank you so much, Elthea. Truly, you are a friend. If I don't envy Margaret this marriage, I do think she is blessed to have you as a mother-in-law."

Elthea pulled back and there was a film of tears in her eyes. "Bless thee, child. You have given me hope that one day peace shall reign. Until then, I shall do what my heart directs. It is a strange journey we are on, is it not?"

Maggie felt all the emotion she had been holding creep closer to the surface, and she could only nod.

"Sleep well, my soul sister. Mayhap one day you and I shall be reunited."

Maggie couldn't speak as she watched one incredible woman open the door and leave her alone with her thoughts. There was one that was beginning to torment her.

What if she couldn't find her way back?

Chapter Eleven

the trees created a canopy of green overhead as she rode next to him. Maggie again thought she had entered a seductive fantasy. She glanced to her side to see him sitting tall, his chin up, his gaze panning around the dense forest. She was sure he was making a concerted effort to avert looking at her. Maybe he was on the alert for more marauding bandits. What was that expression again?

Oh yeah . . . villainous hedge-borne miscreants. The woods were full of them.

Deep down she really was glad he had agreed to accompany her back out here. The countess could have sent any one of her servants to help. Dear Elthea.

Her mind was filled with images as she held the reins in her hands and put more distance between herself and Greville Manor. It had been difficult to say good-bye to the woman, yet each knew it had to be done. Elthea had been so kind to her. She had given her a small bag of coins to help her on her journey, and Maggie didn't know how to refuse. Both of them had tears in their eyes, and Maggie knew no matter what happened to her now, she would never forget Countess Elthea, one of the wisest women she had ever encountered. How she would love Aunt Edithe to meet Elthea. The two of them would get along famously. They were so alike.

" 'Tis most curious to be on this road once more."

Maggie knew exactly what he meant and nodded. "Yes," she murmured, not trusting her voice to say more. The last time they had been here, it had been a much different situation. They had each thought the other mad. Soon, only one of them would be sure of their sanity. She *had* to find that maze, even the village, a highway, a modern home . . . anything!

A part of her was wondering if she would see Nick again, once she returned to her aunt's home. Would he drop his role-playing and seek her out? How she would love to show up at Greville Manor in Edithe's cherry red Jaguar. In spite of her mood, she chuckled as she imagined everyone's shock.

"Thou art recalling the fool, backward upon his steed?" he asked, then shook his head with honest laughter. "What a spectacle, no?"

Maggie grinned as she glanced at him. "I guess it was. I apologize for the way I acted that day. Nothing made sense to me." Geez, he looked so handsome, with that green cape flowing from his shoulders and his blond hair catching the dappled sunlight.

"And does it now?" he asked with a smile, as his horse neared hers and his leg lightly brushed against her skirt.

Maggie felt his brief touch and inhaled sharply at the sensations racing through her body. She had never felt this strong of an attraction in her life! How could she just walk away from him?

"Mistress . . . . ?"

His voice brought her out of the confusion. "Please, Nick. Call me Maggie," she answered, gripping the reins tighter. Everyone had been shocked when she'd insisted on straddling the horse, and now she wasn't so sure it was such a wise decision as the slow, undulating

movements of the horse beneath her created sensations
that only added to her torment.

"I was inquiring if things felt more in order . . . Maggie."

He added her name hesitantly, yet almost intimately,
and the sound of it seemed to inflame her already warm
blood. She shifted in the saddle.

Taking a deep breath, she said, "Actually, nothing
makes sense to me, Nicholas. I don't understand anything. Elthea and I spoke last night and . . . and I don't
know what to believe any longer."

"You are not alone in your confusion, m'lady," he
replied, and then added, "The spot where I happened
upon thee is not much farther. Soon, we may begin to
explore the wood for your labyrinth."

"I don't think you exactly *happened upon* me," she
said, wanting the record straight.

"You happened upon me?" he asked, grinning with
amusement.

She shook her head with a smile. "Okay . . . perhaps
we ran into each other." She looked out onto the path,
pausing to speculate. "But just think about the timing,
Nick. If it had been even an instant later you would've
ridden by and never fallen. You might not have seen me
at all . . . we would never have met."

Glancing at him, she added, "I've never thought so
much about the subject of time before in my life." In
truth, that was only one of her consuming thoughts.

"Aye, the theory of time and its relevance haunts us
all, Maggie." Now it was his turn to pause thoughtfully.
"A most excellent friend of mine avows that nothing is
accidental, that all is meant to unfold at exactly the right
time . . . even if the reasons behind it are unknown."

"Your friend sounds just like my aunt. She would say
just relax and enjoy the adventure." Maggie couldn't
wait to find her aunt and tell her about *this* adventure.

Without any safety, she was free-falling into a bewitching attraction to a totally unsuitable man.

"Thy relative is someone I would like to meet."

Maggie quickly turned to him. "Oh, she would love to meet you, too. I know she'd be as fascinated as . . . well, as anyone." She stared down at the path to help hide her near slip. "I mean, I don't think many people can say they've met a person who claims to be from the past. They're usually locked up for that sort of thing."

He chuckled. "And yet, Maggie Whitaker claims to be from the future . . ."

Okay, so he had a point. There are two sides to every story, she reminded herself.

"Countess Elthea seems to believe you . . . and she is a brilliant lady."

"Yes, she is." Maggie agreed.

"*But for the blessed unknown, I go in grace.* That expression always reminds me there are no detours on the road to grace, Maggie. There is purpose for and in everything, even if the explication is not readily at hand. Such a thought is inconceivable to thee?"

He lost her on that one.

She shook her head and sighed. "Time travel? I don't know . . . it's so far-fetched. Science fiction." They rode in silence for a few moments, each thinking over what the other had said, until Maggie blurted out, "But you know, I've heard that all time is concurrent. Probably in college. Einstein, or someone. It was many years ago, but I do now remember a demonstration of an old phonograph record, something about the grooves representing time lines and so time travel might be that somehow you jump a groove, or something."

When she turned, he was staring at her. "You must meet Bacon."

She laughed. "I'm sorry, I was rambling, but that memory just popped into my head."

"I was not able to comprehend many of thy words, yet I did hear something most interesting. You are educated? Where might this university be?"

"Yes, Nicholas Layton. You are speaking to a woman who attended the University of Pennsylvania and graduated from Wharton School of Business, though a lot of good that did me in the last year." She wasn't going to spoil the moment by thoughts of what awaited her in New Jersey. She had enough to do staying right here next to Nick and not blurting out what her body was screaming. Again, she shifted in the saddle and almost groaned as it only increased her desire to touch him. It was absurd to be feeling like a teenager again!

"You are from the New World?" He seemed shocked.

"The New World," she repeated and laughed. "It ain't so new any longer."

He glanced at her and seemed surprised by her answer. "There is much talk of the tribes of Indians. Have you any news of Simon Ferdinando?"

"Who?" Maggie couldn't believe where this conversation was going.

"A Portuguese navigator working for the English Crown. He is looking for treasure."

"Ah, no. Haven't heard of him."

"It is feared Indians have killed him. It must be a very wild, dangerous place."

She shrugged. "It is. Not because of the Indians."

He didn't say anything for a few moments. Clearing his throat, he said, "There is something I must ask thee, Maggie Whitaker."

Glancing at him, she grinned. "Yes?"

" 'Twas only last year Parliament passed an act allowing deportation of convicted criminals to the colonies. I should want thee to know, I do not hold with others' judgments."

She laughed. "I'm not a criminal." Unless not answering her phone or opening her mail was criminal.
"And what's with this New World? I'm an American."
A part of her was amazed that even now, he insisted that
he was living in 1598.

"Yes . . . that explains much. You are an adventurer,
to have crossed the ocean!"

Was there almost envy in his voice?

"This is where we turn," he said and pointed to the
right.

Maggie looked in the opposite direction. "Can we just
ride up this road a little? I swear that's where the parking
lot is."

"Parking lot?"

"A place to park cars, ah . . . vehicles of transportation."

He looked confused, yet shrugged. "I suppose a brief
detour would not impede our mission." He turned his
horse to the left, and Maggie followed.

She had never been a great horsewoman, yet was
grateful for the summer she'd spent at camp and had
learned to hold her own. Giving the horse the command
with her knees and the reins, she managed to stay upright as the gait increased. Nick kept up with her, allowing her the lead. She was anxious to turn the next bend
in the dirt road and see the parking lot.

She reined in the horse and stared at the thick forest
where a paved parking lot should have been. Her gaze
was riveted to the trunks of mature trees and the heavy
undergrowth. Where was it? She would have sworn this
was the road. Turning to Nick, she smiled sadly. "I'm
sorry. I was mistaken. It couldn't have been here."

He merely nodded as they turned the horses around
and headed back to the fork in the road. Maggie was
trying to concentrate on the horse, yet her mind was
turning all kinds of crazy thoughts around in her head.

How could she have been so sure? Parking lots don't just disappear. It had to be the wrong road. She refused to allow any other answer. Again, she urged her horse forward, past the fork in the road, down the narrow and rutted dirt path toward where she had entered this nightmare. The wind caressed her face, as though trying to soothe her chaotic mind. The sun shone on her with brief moments of dazzling light as she raced through a canopy of trees toward sanity. She *had* to find that maze. . . .

"Maggie!"

His arm reached over, and he grabbed her left hand. Startled, Maggie realized he was pulling back on her reins while slowing his own horse. She immediately felt embarrassed.

"We are here," Nick said, as both horses came to a trot.

"Already?" Maggie asked, and looked around to the woods.

He chuckled. "*All ready,* aye. The lady keeps her seat well upon a steed." He turned both horses and then removed his hand from hers. "In fact, we have passed the place when first we met, a goodly length back."

Slowly, they rode back several yards until Nick stopped and looked to the woods. "Here," he said, and pointed. "This is where thy pearls were discovered missing. That tree is familiar. Aye, I remember well . . .'Tis there," he hesitated slightly, "you disrobed, removing thy underblouse."

Touching the stiff, high collar under her chin, Maggie looked at the tree and remembered taking off the underblouse behind it. Yes, it did seem familiar. "Okay," she said, and began to dismount.

"Heed caution," Nick called out, and slipped from his horse to the ground.

Maggie saw him wince as his injured foot hit the dirt. "I can do it myself," she insisted, yet found that the voluminous skirt made dismounting a struggle.

Suddenly his hands were upon her waist, and she had no other recourse as he pulled her down but to hold on to his shoulders. Slowly, almost as if he couldn't bear to let her go, Nick allowed her to slide down the front of his body.

When her feet felt the ground, Maggie was sure the earth was made of quicksand as she seemed to sink beneath him in dizziness.

He held her tighter. "Are you *all right*?"

She forced herself to stand upright on her own. "It's just that . . . well, I haven't been riding in a long time," she muttered, and managed to take a step backward as his hands left her waist. It was the first time they had such intimate contact, and her entire body was reacting to him.

She took a deep steadying breath and walked away from him. The woods did look vaguely familiar and, if she was to find that maze, it was now time for her to say good-bye. She should just do it. Taking another deep breath, she stopped at the side of the road, turned to him, and said, "I want to thank you for bringing me back here, Nick. I don't know, saying good-bye seems—"

"Good-bye?" he interrupted, and came forward to tie the reins of both horses onto a tree branch. "Verily, I would not leave thee out here alone." His eyes seemed wide with disbelief. "Together, we shall search for thy maze . . . but should it exist not, have you a thought for such a contingency?"

She felt tortured, to leave him without ever finding out what was in his heart was slicing through her soul. "I can't think like that," she answered. "It *has* to be here. I must find my way back . . . to my life."

"And should that prove impossible this day, pray tell, what will Lady Margaret Whitaker do then?"

As he moved closer to her, Maggie took a step back,

her mind refusing to entertain such thoughts. "I have to try. Can't you understand I'm fighting for my sanity here? If I don't find it, that means you're right. Elthea's right. I'm lost in time and . . ." Her voice faltered. ". . . I just can't even think like that."

"I am with you, and together we shall discover the truth. You are alone no longer in this adventure, Maggie. I shall see thee to safety. Of this, I promise." He held out his hand. "Shall we . . . ?"

She had to bite the inside of her lip to stop the tears. Everything was running together, her fears and her attraction, and she wanted to just scream out her frustration. Didn't he understand she was struggling to find her sanity here? That if she entered those woods and there was no maze, she was insane? Had she somehow crossed over an invisible time line and entered another age? She was flying solo here. There was no one to tell her what was real, no one from her own time to help her understand what was happening. She was alone. Alone in a madness that was also the most incredible thing that had ever happened to her in her entire life! And now this man, this fascinating, talented, romantic, humorous, gorgeous man was staring at her, holding out his hand to her, offering her his help, his strength, his knowledge, his courage. Somehow she knew she'd be adding to that list of attributes if she stayed around him longer.

Was it any wonder her body seemed infused with an intense, gripping energy . . . a mixture of fear and anticipation? Courage. That was what she needed. Courage to continue this adventure. How does one get courage when there is no safety? She was on her own and had to trust herself now. No matter what happened once she entered the woods, she had to be prepared to accept it and deal with it. Even if it meant she was dead. For nothing while she was alive had ever compared to this adventure. Something had happened to her in that maze that rocked her world. Aunt Edithe and modern England didn't seem to exist. The answer was in those woods, and somehow she had to summon up the courage to find it.

She squared her shoulders and straightened her spine, feeling a calming energy balance out the fear enough for her to make a decision.

Slowly, as though knowing she was about to embark on what might prove to be *the* most important thing she'd ever done, Maggie put her fingers into his and tried to smile. "Thank you."

He held her hand tightly as he looked into her eyes. "Worry not, dear Maggie. No matter the outcome, I shall not abandon thee."

He led the way and she pulled her hand back to gather her skirt closer as they entered the woods. The underbrush was thick and several times as the velvet material caught a branch, she would have to stop and free it. Already she had lost many of the seed pearls in her travels and regretted the damage to the beautiful costume. Somehow, once she got back, she would make reparation, but right now it was all she could do not to tear at the skirt and hold it up over her thighs. She wanted to run, to end this madness, yet held back as Nick led her deeper into the woods. Something was wrong. They were walking too far.

"Nick . . ." She stopped and looked around her.

Turning, he asked expectantly, "Yes?"

"I ran from the maze and within seconds was on the road. It couldn't have been this far." Her gaze took in the surrounding forest and she felt the weight of dread come over her body. "This can't be the place."

"But I tell you, it is. Come, the forest thins, and I see a clearing ahead."

Hope surged then mixed with sadness that her adventure with Nick might just be over. This was it, then. Her heart began racing as she gathered even more of her skirt and hurried behind Nick as he held branches aside for her to pass.

Now he would see she hadn't been making it all up. Maybe he could come back with her and meet Aunt Edithe. Maybe it wouldn't be over. Maybe there would still be time to—

He stopped short and she almost walked into him. Stumbling forward, Maggie felt his hand on her arm to steady her. She looked up and stared at what was before her . . . a shaded clearing with rays of sunlight making an almost ethereal pattern through the canopy of deep green leaves. Wispy ferns dotted the carpet of tiny white flowers. It was almost magical to behold, yet there wasn't a maze in sight.

"This can't be it," Maggie stated in a strangled voice. "The maze must be farther down the road."

"I assure you, it is," Nick answered and looked around. "With great speed, you came running from this clearing, Maggie."

"No, there was a maze and I was lost and that little girl kept telling me to follow my heart and . . . and this can't be it!" She turned around in a full circle, staring at where there should have been a hedge maze. "We must have made a mistake. We need to find the faire. Where is the village?"

"The village Trowbridge? 'Tis a long ride from here, too far for thee to have walked. I vow there is no grand event taking place in that impoverished hamlet." He turned back to her, and spoke softly. "Maggie, how can it be even the possibility of unexplainable things, such as this phenomenon, is so impossible for you to believe?"

"You just don't understand, Nick. My life just couldn't have disappeared!"

"But thy life shines in front of me here, now Maggie,

in this moment. I cannot deny what mine eyes see. Thou art alive as my own flesh and heart . . .''

He stepped closer to her.

''Countess Elthea has also heard of such extraordinary events, yet neither she, nor I, can explain them. Nevertheless, I know of someone in London who could help you. Sir Francis Bacon. In a hard ride, we could be there before nightfall. Come, I promised Countess Elthea I would see you to safety and—''

''*I can't go to London!*''

Maggie walked farther into the clearing and found that her breath was coming in short gasps, as though she'd been running. Her heart was again racing and she thought she might just faint. ''This isn't happening. This isn't happening . . .'' she kept muttering, until she felt his hand on her upper arm.

Turning around, she gazed at him and could no longer contain her tears. ''I cannot accept this! I have to find my way back,'' she whispered in terror.

His finger barely touched her lips. ''Shh . . .''

''You don't understand,'' she whispered, staring into his eyes and feeling a peacefulness enter her body. ''I have to find my way . . .'' Her words trailed off as she watched him study her mouth.

''Perchance thou hast, sweet lady,'' he said in a low, soft voice, holding her now with both hands on her arms to steady her. He was staring into her eyes, beyond her eyes, and into her soul. ''It could be you have come back . . . returned, to remember this . . .'' He lowered his head to hers and captured her mouth in the softest, most gentle kiss Maggie could have ever imagined. Her body seemed to come alive, to feel more vital than she could ever remember. Suddenly, she felt herself waking up . . . for the first time in her life.

His hand came up and cupped the side of her face as his lips continued to softly explore hers, and Maggie thought she moaned in the most intense pleasure as he tenderly nibbled on her lips, demanding a response.

She gladly gave it.

She'd waited so long to feel this, to feel like this. It was as if her soul was soaring beyond her body, awakening to a long-remembered passion, yet one that she knew she had never experienced in her lifetime. Her head was spinning as she clutched the material at his chest and hung on, for he was taking her to an uncharted place in her heart, and she had no direction, only instinct.

His lips created an electricity that coursed through her as over and over and over again he kissed her as though starving for the taste of her. She felt his heart pounding against her breast and moaned as she flung back her head and gave in to what she had been craving since she'd met him. She wanted the taste of him imprinted on her mind, branding her skin and her lips so she would always remember this wonderment, this sensual intensity, this heaven on earth.

"Oh, Maggie," he murmured against her mouth. "I prayed once we kissed you would remember. Long I have waited for you to appear in this life." And he captured her mouth and took possession again. This time tenderness was replaced with passion, one kept long under control.

Maggie felt herself being taken to places she had only dreamed of as she ran her hands over his chest, feeling the beating of his heart against her palm, his wide shoulders, feeling the strength of his hardened muscles, his face, feeling the faint scratch of his beard under her fingertips. She felt everything she had ever wanted to feel with someone, as emotions long suppressed burst forth inside of her, taking her higher until she thought she was no longer touching ground. It was as if they were voracious for each other and when she pulled back and gasped for breath, the most amazing thing came forth from her lips.

"Where have you been all my life?"

His face was filled with passion as he stared at her mouth, her hair, her eyes. "Oh, my lady . . . I have been here . . . waiting only for thee."

Again, they came together, touching, inhaling, as their tongues darted, mated, and their bodies longed to follow suit. He pulled back and with one hand untied his cape and tossed it to the ground.

She didn't care if she was crazy, or if she had died and was in heaven. Every nerve ending in her body seemed to be screaming to go for the adventure. All her life she'd been the responsible one, the one who did whatever was right. Well, nothing in her entire life ever felt as *right* as this! To hell with whatever anyone else thought. . . .

This one's for me.

She needed no further urging to lower herself upon the cape. She sank down as he knelt before her and pulled her against him as they fell together. Feathering ferns bowed under their weight and when Maggie looked up to the tree limbs, the sunlight, the bed of soft green that surrounded her, she knew she had found paradise.

Her heart sang out with the joy of freedom.

Nick pulled back and leaned on one elbow while his fingers caressed her lips.

"Thou art the most enchanting creature I have ever known, Maggie Whitaker. Is it no wonder my heart was locked, when thou art the key."

"Oh, Nick . . ."

He leaned down and reclaimed her lips. Maggie wound her arms around his shoulders and pulled him closer. She wanted to prolong this moment of heaven. If she never experienced this bliss again, she wanted to capture the memory of it . . . for nothing in her life had prepared her for this intensity, this longing, this yearning to meld with another and lose herself in his arms.

When she opened her eyes, he was staring at her with such a serious expression that Maggie pushed on his shoulders to see him better. "What's wrong?"

"Wrong?" His smile melted her heart. "Everything is right finally." He brushed a stray lock of hair away from her forehead. "I shall protect thee, my love. As long as I live and breathe upon this earth, I vow nothing will ever harm thee. It matters not who you are or from where you came, whether in jewels or rags . . . whoever you are, Maggie Whitaker, I thank you for finding me and ending my anguish."

His eyes shined with emotion, and Maggie felt her own tears of joy resurfacing. She reached up and touched his cheek. "I thought we ran into each other," she whispered with a smile. "Thanks for running into me, Nicholas Layton, and changing my life." Her fingers traced a line down to his lips, as she added, "I wouldn't have missed this for anything."

It was in that moment, as their gaze connected with an electrifying jolt of recognition, of seeing beyond the eyes and into the soul, that Maggie *knew* Nicholas Layton.

She had loved him forever.

"Nicholas . . ." she breathed, seeing that his eyes were a mirror of such an eternal love. "Do you understand this?"

He slowly shook his head while smiling with tenderness and wonder. "I do not, yet it seems the most natural thing I have ever done, for being in thy presence I have finally come alive. Come with me now to London, my sweet Maggie. Let us leave this place and begin . . . this, our adventure, together."

The agreement was sealed with a kiss that took away Maggie's senses and left her breathless. His body covered hers and she groaned at the barrier of thick velvet material that separated them. When his hand cupped her breast, she arched against him and felt her body melt with an intense, primal longing. Maggie held on to him to anchor herself to the earth as they vowed in a language older than time to become one mind, one heart, one soul.

It was indescribable, miraculous and real. The future was staring right at her.

And it felt so familiar . . .

Chapter Twelve

It was ethereal. Brilliant lights danced on a thick sea of emerald green flowing above them. The cooling afternoon air lingered sensuously in the wooded shade. Their path was illuminated with myriad beacons cast down by the midmorning sun. Birds sang music her heart knew. Her instincts were alive with everything around her. It was magical. Maggie couldn't stop smiling as she rode next to Nick toward their future. She couldn't believe she was saying good-bye to everything in her past, to her aunt, her mother, her home . . . everything, and following her heart. It was crazy. It was wonderful. It was *real*.

It seemed the most intelligent thing she had ever done, nor could she deny how right it felt. She belonged with this man, in whatever time they found themselves, and she was determined to stay at his side.

His hand reached over and squeezed her arm. "You shall find London most interesting, and I am anxious for you to meet Francis Bacon. He will be overjoyed to make your acquaintance."

"Sir Francis Bacon?" Maggie vaguely remembered his name in history, but hadn't a clue why. Imagine, she would be meeting someone famous. If possible, her smile widened, with anticipation for this joint adventure.

No longer was she alone. She had found what Elthea talked about last night.

Her twin soul.

She only had to travel four hundred years to do it!

"I can't wait," she said honestly, as the horses trotted together almost in unison.

"My beloved," he said with a sexy twinkle in his eye, "neither can I."

She moaned and looked back to the road, again wishing that Nick hadn't stopped making love to her in their magic clearing. He had insisted that it was for her protection, and that they must travel quickly to reach London before nightfall. Nicholas Layton had become her knight in shining armor and Maggie felt protected, cherished, and loved. Yes, she could think the word . . . Love, no longer did it frighten her, for she was with a man unlike any she had ever known. It didn't matter if she had known him for three days or thirty years. He could be trusted with her heart, for they had somehow known each other for eternity.

Together they rode in a peaceful silence for what seemed like a half hour. It crossed her mind that soon they would reach the village and she wondered if they could stop, for her body was on fire and to just touch him and feel his arms around her would be enough . . . for now. A part of her was anxious about making love to Nick. He was younger than she and quite frankly, gorgeous. Immediately, she shook off the moment of insecurity. This man was like no other. What he saw in her went beyond the physical. It was as though they were connected . . . her mind froze on one word, the only fitting one. They were connected through the soul. She had to believe that. But didn't she luck out that her twin soul was everything she had dreamed and *way* more? Talk about the bennies.

Somehow, she had traveled back in time. No longer

could she deny it. Congratulating herself for having the courage to cross that line and go for the adventure, Maggie was totally unprepared for Nick's hand to come up and motion for them to stop. She was so lost in her daydream that she just now noticed the way his face was set with a mask of seriousness. She looked down the road and her breath caught in the back of her throat.

There were a group of riders ahead and one of them, the one in the lead, prancing upon a white horse, appeared to look a lot like Robert.

Maggie glanced back to Nick.

"Remain calm. I will speak with him."

"Nick, what about Elthea? I don't want anything to happen to her, or to you!" She forced her mind to function. "There's no need to confront him now. It won't serve anything. Just play along. We'll find another way."

He looked as though he were in mental anguish as he stared back at her. Maggie could hear the sound of the approaching horses and looked at him pleadingly. "Please, Nicholas. Let me deal with Robert. He still thinks I'm his betrothed. He won't harm me."

Nick looked to the men and then back to her. "This charade continues? I cannot bear thoughts of that man near you again."

"Now isn't the time," she warned. "I just found you, Nick Layton. I am not about to lose you over some grudge you two seem to have. Please . . . let me handle this with Robert. You play along. We will leave this place together. I promise."

She had no idea how she would accomplish it, but she vowed that she and Nick would do it. Maggie sat up straighter in the saddle, flung her hair back behind her shoulders, and waited for Robert and his men to ride up to them. If she ever wanted to be good at role-playing, the time was now. She was flying by the seat of her pants, yet she knew she'd do anything to save Nick.

"Good day to you, m'lord," she called out as the group neared. She could see now that Robert was holding a large hooded bird on his gloved forearm and a string of dead birds was attached to his saddle.

He led his friends, more a gang of unsavory thieves, up to them and stopped a few feet away. "M'lady," Robert acknowledged, and looked suspiciously at Nick and then back to her. "Where is thy escort? I was informed by my stable boy your destination this morn is the village Trowbridge of my bailiwick."

"Nicholas Layton agreed to accompany me. I am tired of wearing this dress," she said, feigning a pout, "and Countess Elthea spoke of a draper that might accommodate me sooner than your own could." Where did that come from? She remembered Elthea speaking about drapers and staplers. She figured she might cool it on the personal digs.

"And it was thy desire Layton sing a while en route? Most unusual, cousin." He looked to the lute, strung to Nick's saddle.

Maggie forced a laugh. "I asked Master Layton to show me the place where he found me, that I might search for my jewels. He was kind enough to act as my guide."

"And presently . . . you are traveling to my village?" Robert didn't seem to believe her.

"Yes, I . . . I was going to see if anyone there had information that might lead me to my things." There. That sounded semiplausible. The bird screeched, and Maggie jumped in fright.

Robert paid no heed to the sound. "Then it is fortunate indeed we have come upon thee, cousin. My entourage and I shall accompany thee and question the villagers. Here, Layton." Robert untied the dead birds and held them out. "Take these back to my manor and tell my mother I am attending my betrothed on the re- covery of her personal things.''

There was a strained moment of silence, and Maggie mentally pleaded with Nick to ignore the insult and just take the birds. No one moved as all waited.

Slowly, without any outward show of emotion, Nick urged his horse forward and accepted the birds from Robert. Maggie let out her breath. As Nick turned his horse around and stopped by her, she said in a voice to be overheard, ''Thank you for your kindness, Master Layton. I shall see you when we all dine on my be- trothed's bountiful game.''

''Thank you, m'lady.'' Only she could see the torment in his eyes as he nodded and rode off, holding the game out as though it were contaminated. Her heart ached to hold him in her arms and really thank him for not giving into his male instincts. The very last thing any of them needed right now was a fight. She would tell him that it took more strength to walk away than to stay and play in to Robert's schemes. He had wanted to humiliate Nick, and Maggie was going to make sure that Nick knew Robert hadn't succeeded.

''M'lady?''

Maggie smiled into the eyes of a man that she almost couldn't stand and positively couldn't trust. Gently, she urged her horse forward. She was immediately sur- rounded by Robert's men and refused to look at any of them. She kept her eyes on the rump of the horse in front of her as they proceeded down the road. She was on her own now and would have to use her wits to get back to Nicholas at the manor house. How could every- thing have changed so quickly? One moment they were racing toward their future and in the next they were parted. Now that she had accepted her time travel, she understood the gravity of her situation. Hers, and Nick's and Elthea's.

"M'lady rides like a man," Robert remarked, and stared at her bared ankles. " 'Tis not proper."

Maggie stiffened at the chastisement. " '*Tis* completely acceptable in my country," she lied. *Geez, I hope that doesn't come back to haunt Lady Norreys*, she mentally apologized. "How would you like to ride sidesaddle, m'lord? 'Tis most uncomfortable for any distance." She was getting the hang of this formal speech and prayed she would find all the right answers until she was reunited with Nick again.

He looked as though he were pondering her answer. Finally, he proclaimed in a voice to be overheard by his men, " 'Tis the latest fashion in France. Very well, I am most pleased."

Maggie was so relieved that she couldn't even smile. For once she was thrilled that Robert was pleased. Now, how to get back to Greville Manor and Nick? Somehow they would make their life together. Even though fates had conspired against her, she knew she and Nick were meant to be joined. Together they could face anything.

She had to believe that now.

They entered the nearly destitute village and Maggie felt like she was part of a band of outlaws as people scattered in all directions. Their faces were full of fear as the group on horses rode among them. She saw women dressed in thin dirty clothes with children huddling about their knees in rags. Men were hurrying to shops to get out of the way when one of Robert's men quickly slipped off his horse and grabbed a man by the arm only to throw him against a wooden wall.

It happened so quickly, Maggie could only stop her own horse and stare as Robert dismounted slowly, almost casually, and walked up to the terrified man.

"I should like to introduce my betrothed, the Lady Norreys of Rycote, soon to be known to all as, Lady Margaret of Amesbury, thy new dominion."

A few of the village men bowed.

"I value her greatly," he announced for all to hear. "And someone, or some parties, took it upon themselves to cause my lady much distress. I demand any man who knows of such mutinous deeds or can identify the perpetrators of these crimes to come forward."

No one moved.

"I will not ask again," he yelled, walking toward the man who was still being held against the wall. "You, man . . . What might thee know of this? Verily, there must be a peasant or two amongst you who has bargained for grain or other provisions with jewels, or clothing only a lady of nobility would wear?"

Not one mouth uttered a sound.

"N . . . no, m'lord," the captive man finally stammered. "I've not seen such a one."

Robert quickly put a dagger to the man's throat. "You had best not be deceiving—"

"Robert . . ." Maggie called out faintly, her own heart beating wildly within her breast. "Please, don't do this. You have no proof anyone from this village was involved."

Robert didn't move an inch, neither did anyone else.

"I . . . I feel faint," she called out, realizing it was the truth. "May we please return to the manor?" She couldn't believe what was happening, and it was all her fault!

Robert sheathed his dagger at his waist. He glanced over his shoulder to her once and then announced to the villagers, "Let all be well advised, I value what is mine. Should I apprehend whoever is involved, I swear they shall be dealt with in accordance with their heinous crimes. It would serve as an example to stretch some necks around here for such an affront upon a noble."

"Robert," she said in a faint voice. "Please, may we leave?"

He nodded to his man and the villager was released. Maggie watched as Robert mounted. His lead crony and right-hand man, simply known as Montague, addressed all.

"Let it be known Robert of Amesbury is not pleased."

He turned his horse and together they rode slowly out of the village. Maggie caught the gaze of a small girl, covered in tattered clothing, her face smudged with dirt and dark circles under her eyes. Something in Maggie cracked and split open at the sight of so much suffering. Impulsively, she untied the small drawstring pouch Elthea had given her and tossed it to the child. The sound of coins could be heard when it landed in the dirt.

"My gift to the village," Maggie said, and looked Robert right in the eye. "I do not want my first appearance to be remembered as fearful."

He didn't say anything, yet she could see he wasn't pleased, that she might have undermined his authority. Maggie didn't care. As soon as possible, she was leaving this place with Nick and getting as far away from the dangerous Lord Robert of Amesbury. She was in this adventure now, and planned to ride it all the way through.

She could do it, and she wasn't alone. She had found the other half of her soul. Together they would make magic happen and find some kind of future together. They had to, for now she believed they'd been brought together to complete something.

Maggie and the uninvited entourage were coming back along the path near the spot where she and Nick had shared their "reconnection moment." She almost groaned aloud with the ache in her breast for the memories that were still dancing through her whole body.

What was it Nick said back in the fern grove? We shall leave an impression on the universe, my beloved, and the stars will shout bravo . . . or something like that. Her heart knew it was something divine, even if she couldn't remember it verbatim.

Elthea had said when twin souls unite, it is to accomplish their life mission and nothing can stop them from it. She glanced to her side at the rigid form of the man. Not even Robert held that power.

No one spoke on the return trip, and Maggie was grateful for the silence. Somehow she had to come up with a new escape plan. Would Elthea go against her son even further? Would she help them? She had to believe they would find a way.

She remembered the last time she had come to Greville Manor, and Nick had said it was to be her new home. Now the thought filled her with dread. Soon the real Lady Margaret was going to show up, and now Maggie had gotten her into trouble.

Evan and two other servants ran out of the large home as the horses crossed the wooden bridge and Maggie could see Elthea standing in her rose garden. Robert's mother was clasping her hands together at her stomach, as though it might keep them from shaking.

She allowed Robert to help her dismount. He held her waist longer than necessary and Maggie managed a weak smile as she stepped back. "Thank you for coming to my aid today, m'lord."

"I suggest, Lady Margaret, in the future, should thou desire to travel beyond the gates of Greville, my men and I shall accompany thee."

She curtsied and lowered her eyes. "Yes, m'lord." She would say anything to pacify him now. "I find I am exceedingly tired from this adventure and ask that I may be excused to my chamber."

"It is well, Lady Margaret, for I have decided that on the morrow, we shall *discuss* the terms of our betrothal, so all matters may be consistent between us. Thy continental manners may seem charming to most, but take heed, I am a man who adheres to the old ways. Should thee ride, pray do so as befits a lady of standing from Amesbury.''

She was acutely aware of the men dismounting and staring at her. Last night they had toasted her arrival and today they witnessed her disgrace.

''Yes, m'lord,'' she stated meekly. Now was not the time to let pride override good judgment . . . and seeing Nick again was her immediate priority.

''Good day, Lady Margaret.'' He left her curtsying, never offering his hand to rise.

Elthea rushed forward as the horses were led away and wrapped her arm around Maggie's shoulders. ''Oh, child,'' she whispered, ''how I have worried since Nicholas returned.''

Her public humiliation over, Maggie rose and looked at the woman's expression of concern. ''Is Nick all right? Where is he?'' she asked, as they began walking back to the house.

''He rests in his chamber, yet I must say his dark mood could challenge Robert's. Come, we must retire and expedite our plans, for it would not do for you to be at Greville when the terms of the betrothal are discussed. I fear they would unmask you for certain, dear Maggie.''

''So do I,'' Maggie muttered, as they entered the home and quickly made their way to Elthea's chamber. They passed servants who seemed to know about Robert's black mood and averted their gazes. It appeared word of her humiliation had spread quickly. Elthea pushed the door open.

''In my chamber, you are safe . . . for the moment. Come in, dear Maggie. Rest. I know I must.''

Maggie fell into the nearest chair and stared at the

fresh logs in the fireplace. "I don't know how I just got through that," she sighed.

Elthea walked to a low chest where there was a tray set for drinks. " 'Tis a woman's innate balance, child. Thy wits were about thee . . . applaud thyself for that, as I applaud thee. Consequently, there are greater issues we must discuss." She set the tray down on the table in front of the cold fire.

"I have to see Nick," Maggie stated, and looked up to the older women. Poor Elthea seemed to have aged with worry.

"You cannot be seen with Nicholas again. His life already lies in danger for Robert's wrath. I know my son. Presently, he is verily displeased with thee, and should he come to know another meeting has taken place, his father's vengeful nature will surely possess him." The countess poured them each a cup of honey ale. "It is not my intention to cast judgment on him, but it is certain, Robert is plotting even as we speak. I've witnessed his retribution in the past." She took a great swallow from her cup. "We must, in some way, arrange for Nicholas to leave before the next dawn."

"He can't leave without me!" Maggie sat up straight and clutched Elthea's hand. "I just found him. I won't lose him now."

Elthea sat down in the chair next to Maggie. She looked weary, and closed her eyes, pausing a long moment. "And he feels likewise, Maggie." She sat up and looked knowingly at Maggie. "So, it has come to pass. The recognition and acknowledgment of each other. I was hoping this would happen far from this manor."

"It happened in the woods, when we tried to find the maze," Maggie said, releasing Elthea's hand and sitting back. "Everything suddenly made perfect sense. I traveled back in time for us to be together and I'm not going to settle for anything less. He is my twin soul, just as you described, Elthea. I know this.''

''I feared as much last night. 'Tis why I sent thee both away. It can no longer be hidden. Once discovered, the light of twin souls will not be extinguished. It burns hotter and brighter than any fire.'' The countess looked down to the hearth.

It sounded like good news. So why did she look so sad?

Elthea inhaled deeply. ''Robert fears his betrothed is unfaithful, and worse, in love with his enemy.'' She shook her head, as though weary of the drama. ''I will have to calm his fears, for in all good conscience, I cannot allow my cousin to enter into a marriage under these conditions. She has had her share of sorrow in her life and deserves this not.''

She was right. Ever since she arrived, Maggie knew every turn of event she had been a part of and every encounter she'd made, had changed the future. Not only hers, but changed for others . . . for although she and Nick had finally aligned with each other, the true Lady Margaret had an entirely new dynamic in her contract with Lord Amesbury. Maggie nodded. ''I'm afraid I may have made it even worse, and you should know this . . . when I was in the village and saw how poor those people were, I gave them the coins you gave me, Elthea. Robert was not pleased, and I'm so sorry . . . but I couldn't help it.''

Elthea smiled sadly. ''I might use that information to my advantage in convincing Robert of the Lady Margaret's pure heart.'' She turned and walked toward the door. ''So much discord . . . and I must conduct this drama to its end.'' She sighed. ''Remain here, child. I must see to my son.''

''What about Nick? I don't want him to worry about me.'' Maggie stood up.

"I sent Evan to inform him thou art safe, having returned." She lifted the door latch.

"Elthea . . . ?" Maggie pleaded. "Tell him thank you for riding back to Greville. I know what that cost him."

"Had he not done so, it just might have cost him his life," the woman said, nodding in agreement that it would have been certain. "Prithee, caution, Maggie. At once, for more than a happenstance is afoot."

The countess was nearly out the door, when Maggie heard a weary mother's voice, "Creating heaven on earth is no easy task! Makes one ponder why one agreed to this mission." The door latched behind her.

Maggie stared at the closed door for some time before sitting back down. She wished Elthea luck, then wrung her hands together in frustration. Nick was somewhere within reach and she had to remain alone and wait for Elthea's directives. And what did Elthea mean about creating heaven on earth? The fern grove in the woods. Wow. To live the rest of her life, feeling just as she did in those exquisite moments, would certainly be heaven on earth for her. Could that have been her mission? The reason she'd traveled back in time? Was she to meet Nick and discover that anywhere can be heaven if you're open to love? It was more than her mind could handle, and she mentally called out to Nick, to let him know that she was waiting.

She vowed, she would wait forever.

Hours seemed to have passed and still she received no word. Earlier, the servant, Gwen, was sent to Elthea's chamber to escort Maggie back to her room. She knew better than to ask the young girl anything about Nick. She couldn't endanger anyone else by the wrath of Robert. Not a word was spoken during her relocation.

Maggie sat on the sill of her window, which looked

over the beautiful rose garden. She was hoping she might see Nick or Elthea. Once, one of Robert's cronies, the one who had cornered the villager, was walking with another man and glanced up. She knew he had seen her and although Maggie pulled back, she still heard the men's laughter.

Some people just got off on being mean. It gave them the illusion of power, she thought sadly, and pitied Lady Margaret. Perhaps Her Ladyship would be able to handle it better, but Maggie also knew if she, herself, had to fake it much longer, she would probably be killed just for her big mouth. It felt as though she had exhausted every ounce of willpower to remain silent when she watched Robert push his weight around. She tried. She couldn't hold back the judgment anymore. He was an ass.

Elthea was right last night. The misuse of power was really historic. This was a time when control was omnipotent and anyone who threatened that was eliminated. Human rights were not even considered. These were rough times. Actually, she realized, not much had changed over the centuries. One still did what one had to do to survive. No wonder Elthea was a . . . what did she call it? A humanist? Was that Elthea's mission here, to hold the energy of balance, of sanity, for those who came in contact with her?

She was always led to believe the past was much simpler, but now Maggie realized no age is uncomplicated in its time. Nick and Elthea were navigating through a sea of souls lost in their own fears.

Yeah, lost in fear. She'd been there, and recognizing it put her on the other side of that concept . . . clearly. Damn. It really takes a lot of courage to walk this journey of life. She could credit herself for being a lot stronger than she had thought before.

Have faith the bridge is there, Maggie . . . and cour-

age to walk across it. Nick's voice from the morning in the grove echoed in her head. She had crossed the chasm.

When she had faced her biggest fear, just trusted the way was there and took those first steps, she crossed that bridge with ease and discovered the strength in herself. Now she had to continue to trust that the way would be shown, as long as she remained calm, watched, and listened for signposts along the way. Nick was skilled at making her see things much more clearly. The man did have a way with words. And his English delivery didn't bother her anymore. In fact, she now thought it made him even more romantic.

She stood and stretched as she watched the picturesque setting sun in a sky that could only be painted by angels. Streams of white, that appeared dryly brushed over shades of purple and light tones of blue were all illuminated in iridescent orange and pink. As the room darkened, Maggie walked to the edge of her bed. The myriad thoughts shooting through her brain made her feel like her mind was about to overload. What she would give for an aspirin, yet she was thankful for the sunset portrait.

She considered lying down. Getting lost in thoughts of Nick was a lot more appealing than a headache. Once she was reunited with him, she would share all these new insights spinning in her head. A big part of her felt like when she was little . . . the electricity of being alive was running through her again now. It was a refreshing energy. She smiled. Nick would understand that.

Within moments a knock sounded on her door and Maggie jumped in reaction. Elthea said to be prepared for anything, she thought as she raced across the room. Pulling the heavy door, she saw Evan holding a tray of food. Disappointment descended upon her, as she forced a small smile and opened the door completely.

"Your supper, m'lady. The countess requested it be delivered to thy chamber."

"Thank you," she said, as the man entered and placed the food on the small table in front of the darkened fireplace.

He dutifully stooped to light the fresh logs. Maggie watched in silence, wondering if she dared ask the man a question. Finally, when tiny flames were licking the wood, she cleared her voice and found her courage.

"Has Countess Elthea given you any instructions for me?"

"Aye, m'lady," he softly answered as he rose and turned toward her.

It was the first time she had ever really looked closely at him. He was tall and thin, with wisps of gray hair around a benevolent face. Maggie thought he must have been very handsome when he was young. His devotion to his work and Elthea was something she had to admire. This was a man with dignity, and he had her respect.

A soft knock was sounded and Evan moved quickly to open the door. Two women entered, carrying a narrow copper tub. Maggie turned to inquire aloud, but saw Evan was busy instructing the troth be set near the growing fire.

Maggie stepped away from the group and motioned for Evan to follow. At the window, she whispered, "What did she say . . . ? Anything about Nicholas?"

The elderly man lit a thick candle on the table beside her bed and replied in a low voice, "Aye, Lady Elthea has composed the agenda for Master Nicholas. It is not for me to say, m'lady . . . perchance, his arrangements shall include a discreet rendezvous, anon."

"Not later. Please, can't you take me to him now?" Maggie pleaded, then lowered her voice when she saw the maids returning with steaming, heavy buckets. "Evan, I must see him before he leaves."

"Would that I could, m'lady, yet I am duty-bound. The countess has bid me specifically . . . I am to serve thee supper, and these good ladies"—he gestured toward the women who were coming back in carrying steaming heavy buckets—"will attend thy bath. I may impart no more to thee at this time." His mannerisms spoke louder than his words as he clasped his hands behind his back. This man wasn't going to be deterred from his loyalty.

The moments away from Nick suddenly felt eternal.

Frustrated, she walked back to the table. Sitting down, she began voraciously nibbling at the fruit and coarse bread. She wasn't going to touch the game bird, for her own convictions. It had to be one Robert killed.

Evan came forward and poured her ale, and Maggie gratefully accepted the goblet. With her mouth full she could barely swallow the ale to wash it all down. Her anxiousness to see Nick was obvious as Evan tried to hide the hint of his knowing smile.

Gasping for breath when she had finally gulped, Maggie managed to ask, "Thank you. Wow. That was great. I'm so full," she winked, patting her stomach.

The man stood stoically.

Maggie glanced toward the women, and whispered to Evan, "Can you at least tell me if everything is all right? Please, Evan . . . can't you tell me anything?"

He replenished her goblet. As he lowered himself closer to her he whispered, "At present, Master Nicholas rests, although his impatience to be reunited with thee is commensurate, m'lady." He turned to see the maids leaving for more hot water. "I am to escort thee to his chamber when Lady Elthea instructs the hour."

He must have sensed her anguish and taken pity on her.

Maggie sighed with gratitude. "Thank you, Evan. I needed to hear that."

Okay . . . she could relax with that hope. Realizing she

had no option but to wait, she tore off another chunk of bread. She ate in silence as Evan stood nearby, watching the tub being filled. Studying the flames before her, Maggie found she was becoming drowsy. Must have been the relief and the fact that she was starving. She also realized, this might be the last chance she had to sit a while . . . quietly.

The adventure she had accepted with every essence of her being, would continue.

And how like Elthea to think of everything, even in the midst of chaos. She was one cool cookie. Grace under pressure was the way to describe her.

Finally, Evan cleared his throat, and said formally, "I shall leave m'lady to her ablutions." The tub was full, and the ladies stood waiting.

Maggie looked up as Evan reached into a small pocket in his vest and brought out a piece of paper. Handing it to her as he bowed, he whispered, "Pray, keep the fire going when thou art finished reading."

Taking the folded parchment, Maggie nodded. She was to read it and then throw it into the fire. "Thank you, Evan . . . for everything."

He smiled kindly at her, then left the room.

Maggie turned to the fire's light and slowly opened the paper. The handwriting was in decorous script and she guessed it was written with a quill pen. It was not hastily scribed.

My Beloved Angel, Verily, and with no uncertainty, I feel thou art quite with me, in heart and spirit, We are One— Proof of this will be presented to thee on this very eve. Our benefactor has been most generous in providing aid to our sacred cause—The journey of our eternal love shall be the adventure we write together. I rest your loving Nicholas

Greville at Amesbury
this 23rd March 1598

The cryptic message was definitely clear to her. First of all, he was okay . . . he hoped she got this letter . . . Elthea had a great plan . . . not to worry . . . for she would be with him . . . once and forever . . . Her Nicholas.

She read it again, memorizing each word, then with reluctance turned to the fire to destroy it as Evan advised. Wait. It was the first *tangible* memento of his love and devotion to her. And it was written on her birthday! How could she burn something so precious? It was the gift tag on the greatest present she ever got in life. Her twin soul.

She had to save it in a box for posterity. That's it! If she ever got back to the future, and she would only go if he was by her side, she would have it to verify everything that had happened to her. She bent down to her left shoe and slipped it off. She lifted the sole lining and carefully tucked it underneath.

Proof. Time travel was real.

"M'lady?" The interruption startled Maggie. "Thy bath awaits." The woman smiled imploringly.

Sighing, Maggie removed her other shoe, and with the pair safe in one hand, she began untying the back of her gown with the other. The older woman hurried to help her. Maggie didn't protest. She was too tired to make any more points. All she could do now was go along with the story and be ready for anything. When she felt the fabric loosen from its laces, she exhaled and walked to the tub.

"Thank you, m'lady," she said to her kindly assistant.

A hot bath was not a bad idea, considering all she'd been through today. Talk about your life-altering days. She almost groaned out loud when her mind flashed back to riding through the woods with Nick. She spied a stool that had been placed near the foot of the bath.

She put her shoes on the small wooden seat and began removing the heavy velvet outer gown. The fabric dropped slowly to the floor and sent shivers up her arms and neck when she felt the caress against her skin. The woods . . . the fern grove. She drew in a breath between her teeth. And there was still later tonight.

The woman assisted Maggie to pin her hair up and helped remove her underclothes. It amazed her that she felt only marginally self-conscious about being nude in front of this kind stranger. She'd discovered a new freedom today. Those old fears seemed of little importance to her now . . . she was learning life and love were so much more than physical.

It was like playing the childhood game of connecting the dots. She couldn't predict how any of it was going to turn out, or what picture was going to be presented. From here on, it was dot to dot . . . and waiting, being aware to see her next move. Patience had never been a strong point for her, yet now she was forced to practice it.

The tub itself was hot because of the metal, and when Maggie leaned her back against it, the heat entered her pores, and she deeply exhaled with a sigh of pleasure. Steam rose, creating tendrils of hair to curl as she sat very still and looked into the fire. From the corner of her eye, she saw the women bend down and pick up her gown and shoes.

"By thy leave, m'la—"

"No . . ." Maggie sat up quickly. "Where are you taking my things?"

"To be cleaned and aired, m'lady, as is procedure every eve." She turned and started for the door. "Fret not, thy fineries shall be returned 'fore mornin', good as—"

"Wait!" She was nearly standing in the tub. "You can't take them. I . . . I may need them when I've finished my bath . . . and I might go for a walk later. Thanks for the offer, but really, it's fine.'' She reached out insistently to the woman for the gown and shoes.

The woman approached her hesitantly. "As ye wish, m'lady.''

Maggie smiled at the lady, while returning the shoes and gown to the stool and slipped back into the soothing water, "Thank you, dear lady. You've been very kind.'' And she closed her eyes.

"God reward thee, m'lady.''

She heard the latch click and allowed the tears she'd been holding back to finally come. Oh, she had been rewarded already . . . she had never in her life expected to find such happiness. Her heart was bursting with joy.

Truthfully, since her own marriage was such a miserable failure, she thought a love like she shared with Nick was just a myth. But she had seen it with her aunt and Malcolm and so she knew it was real. She vowed to do whatever it took to protect such a love, even if it meant taking a bath when all she wanted was to run down the hall to Nick's room and throw herself into his arms.

She picked up a small cloth and soaked it in the hot water. On a narrow ledge were tiny glass vials and she chose one. Sniffing the stopper, she recognized lavender and poured a small amount into the water. When she was reunited again with Nick, at least she would smell nice even if she was in the same dress. Laying her head back against the tub, Maggie relaxed into the dream.

'' . . . is it you? . . . is it you? . . . is it you?'' She woke with a jolt.

She had no idea how much time had elapsed as she reached for the thick cloth to dry off. She glanced around the empty room. Whose voice spoke? Maggie stood to pat herself down. It was the dream . . . the very same dream she had had on the plane before she arrived in England. Then the thought slammed into her. Aunt Edithe. How she must be worrying.

Maggie stepped out of the tub and finished drying herself off. It wasn't like she'd been purposely avoiding the memories. She was just slowly beginning to accept the fact she might not be able to get back to her life.

All the people she knew and loved. All those that loved her, too. She had to keep believing there was purpose in everything. Even the unknown. Just as Nick had said.

Somehow Aunt Edithe knew that, too.

Maggie replayed in her head the afternoon in that clearing. It had been magical and soon they would be joined, traveling to London and visiting Nick's friend, Sir Francis Bacon. What would it be like to meet someone who was written about in history books? She tried to remember what she had read, but it was useless. Whatever Sir Francis Bacon had done to deserve being remembered by those who followed him was lost to her. She would question Nick about it. He had so much to teach her about this time, and she had so much to tell him about hers. Maybe Elthea was right. Together they might accomplish something. Their lifelong magical adventure was about to begin.

The door opened just as Maggie dropped the towel. She expected the maids, but the figure she saw caused chills to run down her spine, despite the heat of her bath. Immediately, she grabbed her undergown and held it over her breasts.

"Get out," she commanded in a strong voice.

Chapter Thirteen

*R*obert walked farther into the room and closed the door behind him.

From somewhere in her frenzied mind she heard Elthea's words . . .

Be prepared for anything.

Surely no one expected this!

"What do you want?" she demanded, as he silently walked to the side of the bed and sat down.

Damn. No way. Not this. She didn't care if he *was* lord of the manor!

"I demand that you leave," Maggie stated in a voice that she prayed would not reveal her terror. The man was far too silent to suit her. And he looked drunk.

"Thou art a picture of feminine beauty, dear cousin," he whispered. "Your appearance pleases me even if your demeanor does not." He invitingly patted the fur cover on the edge of the large bed.

"You had better leave before I scream," she threatened, realizing she was butt naked, save for the damp undergarment clutched to her chest, and helpless to do much of anything more.

"As ye wish, m'lady. Scream. There is no one in Greville manor who would disobey me and incur my displeasure . . . including my dear lady mother."

Maggie took several deep breaths to calm her frantic mind. "What do you want then?"

He smiled wickedly and paused. "I wish to discuss our betrothal, cousin."

"You said it would be tomorrow. This is not the time or place for such a discussion. Now, *I* am not pleased, Robert."

His attention was drawn by her last statement. "Thou art my betrothed, and as such, thy pleasure is of utmost importance to me, Margaret. Nevertheless, I am Lord and Dominion, therefore, all-important."

She almost laughed with nervousness. Dot to dot, but she never would have figured this picture forming! "That makes you feel so much better, doesn't it? That everyone should run around trying to please you? Who are you, Robert . . . really, to act so spoiled? Because of your birth? Perhaps I've learned that if one is so blessed as to be born with privileges, then one might devote his or her life to service of those not so blessed."

"Thy speech is rightly brave for a woman, yet I care not of thy opinions or what manner of acceptable customs have been acquired in your travels. When you are my loyal wife, you shall act in accordance to the proprieties befitting a noble husband." He leaned back on the huge headboard and folded his hands behind his neck. "Forthwith, as my betrothed, I forbid thee to consort with that recreant, Master Nicholas Layton. . . . He will ne'er be seen, ever again."

His pompousness made her want to vomit. She would not respond to his insult of Nick. That would be just what Robert was looking for to provide him with ammunition to use against them. She had to remain calm. The best way to play chess was to relax and allow your mind to function.

Taking a deep steadying breath, Maggie closed her eyes briefly and said, "You are wearying me, m'lord. I shall not discuss the betrothal while I am at my bath. I ask you to leave.''

He quickly sat up. "And I ask thee to answer my query . . . Why is thy speech so foreign? Why have your manners lapsed, as to laugh at me in public? The price of indiscretions can be very dear to thy life, and thy purse, cousin." His face looked mottled with anger.

Maggie knew whatever she answered would affect Lady Norreys's life. Suddenly, she came up with a plan. She hoped she wasn't creating a monster.

"Would you mind if I dressed?" She figured it was a beginning.

"The maids are not present to assist thee, and I am quite pleased with my view . . . But change if you must." He continued to stare directly at her.

Okay, it's a standoff, she thought, and lowered herself to the small stool, draping the undergown over as much of herself as she could. "I'm thirsty. Hand me my ale, and then you and I shall come to an agreement." She hoped he would take the bait.

He seemed suspicious for a few moments, then walked to the table. Maggie squirmed to avoid his stare as he refilled the goblet and handed it to her. She accepted it and sipped, praying what she had planned would work.

"Thy agreement, Lady Norreys?" He poured himself a cup.

She nodded and looked him in the eye. "Let us drop the formal language and just speak truth. Let's be honest, you and I. You need my money, and I . . ." Maggie had no idea what Lady Margaret's reasons were for entering into this marriage. "I need to be with my family now. I have traveled and am truly weary of the world. Too many tyrants, like you, Robert," she said with a forced smile. "Should I marry you, I will promise to behave according to your wishes . . . in public. I shall be a credit to your name. However, in private, you must earn my respect, and barging into my bath is not the way to achieve that.''

''And that is all?'' Robert asked, sitting back and taking a deep gulp.

This time Maggie did laugh, despite the pounding of her heart. ''Hardly, for you will have access to my money, after all. I shall want a precise accounting of your intentions and investments with my holdings, and it must be reported to me directly.''

''That is outrageous!'' he jumped up from his seat. ''I am lord of this manor and as such—''

She held up her goblet as she interrupted. ''*As such* you will have ample funds, but you will not squander my fortune, Robert. In my . . . my travels I have had an extensive training in finances and you will not be pulling the wool over my eyes. Come, all I ask for saving you and your home is the peace I now seek and that you earn my respect before again viewing my person in such an intimate manner. This shall be a partnership, Robert, or none at all.''

Wow, she was impressed with herself for coming up with that one.

''The betrothal contract has been signed and none of this was stated prior,'' his voice was agitated. ''You cannot—''

''I can do whatever I please,'' she again interrupted. ''I am not married to you yet. I do so want this to be a peaceful marriage. All I am asking is that you—''

Before Maggie could finish her thought, the door was flung open and Elthea came into the room. Evan stood behind her and averted his eyes.

''Have thy senses been lost?'' she demanded of her son. ''You have ingested more than a sufficiency of the drink, Robert, and it has dulled your senses! Bear witness to your own deplorable behavior, Robert, as has the steward of this house.''

"My witness and good servant, Evan, do you think me drunk?''

Evan looked up from the floor. "I have no eyes nor ears this evening, m'lord.''

"Remove yourself at once, sir!'' Elthea sounded disgusted with her son. "Must I remind you, this marriage contract may be breached by your actions?''

"As ye will, my lady mother,'' Robert said with a sarcastic tone, as he began to sway.

"My son, thy character is most fulsome—''

Robert interrupted. "Continue thy fanciful orchestrations for the forthcoming event, my lady mother . . . an agreement has been struck between Lady Margaret Norreys of Rycote and Lord Robert of Amesbury.''

Elthea looked furious. "Depart this chamber at once, I say.'' She pointed to the door. "Forget not our cousin is highly favored by the Queen. Breath of this scandal would be cause for forfeiture of more than thy marriage, Lord Robert of Amesbury.''

From the look on his face, Maggie knew Ethea's dig pried hard into Robert's side.

Elthea glanced around to everyone present. "Nothing of this shameless calamity shall be spoken henceforth,'' she instructed.

Maggie breathed easier, yet kept her gaze on Robert as he made to leave on unsteady feet. Thank goodness Elthea had arrived when she did!

Robert passed his mother without answering. He seemed to stagger, as though fighting to maintain his balance. Once at the doorway, he turned back, and said, "My sincerest apologies, Lady Margaret, for disrupting thy ablutions.'' He bowed clumsily and stumbled out.

"Evan, prithee, see that my lord son gets to his chamber in good speed.''

"As ye wish, m'lady." Evan hurried to Robert's side and supported him as he closed the door behind them.

Finally, the two women were alone, and Elthea turned to Maggie. "What transpired here? When Evan informed me Lord Robert was in your chamber I nearly lost my senses. I came as quickly as my feet would carry me."

"Here." Maggie held out her goblet. "Drink something to calm your nerves."

Elthea, wearing her own dressing gown with her graying hair braided down her back, accepted the goblet and sank into a chair before the fire, saying nothing.

Still squatting on the stool, Maggie pulled the linen gown over her head. She was grateful that Elthea kept her gaze on the fire, as she rose and straightened down the fabric. "I'm sorry I've been so much trouble; none of this would have happened—"

Elthea interrupted. "Maggie," her voice nearly trembled as she spoke, "the course has been set."

"But listen, Elthea, I need to tell you something important. I . . ." Maggie stammered, "I told Robert tonight that his wife would behave and not embarrass him, but I also said that in return he would have to account for any money he spends and he would respect his wife and never force himself upon her." She drew in a deep breath. "I figured it was the least I could do for Lady Margaret, since I've messed up so much already."

In spite of the situation, Elthea chuckled. "Somehow, I shall explain this comedy of errors to my cousin. It appears the advantage will be hers, and she may likely wish to thank you for it. In truth, I was concerned that in her grief she would not protect herself. The agreement may have been made vicariously, but it is struck," she finished with a wink.

"For her sake, and yours, Elthea . . . I certainly hope so." Maggie smiled. "And I wish the woman good luck with Robert. Your son can be a *fulsome character*, at times, can't he?''

''My son is my blood, but he is first my lord. For a mother, that is the way of precedence, yet, this is my worry. There are greater worries ahead for thee, Maggie.'' Elthea sipped the ale and continued. ''The plans have been made. It is certain the Lady Norreys shall arrive soon, and I fear the comedy of two ladies betrothed to Robert would not be taken in much humor.''

''Hey, there's only one lady getting stuck with him . . .'' Maggie stopped as she realized the possible insult in her words. ''What I mean is, Lady Norreys can have him, I'm already spoken for.'' Maggie grinned as she warmed her backside to the fire.

'' 'Tis done. On the morrow, Nicholas shall escort thee to London, dear Maggie.''

''Why can't we just leave right now? Robert's drunk. He won't know a thing.''

Elthea stood up. ''Robert has seen to it that Montague is on garrison duty this eve.'' She walked toward the window, and continued, ''It would be impossible to ready the horses until he takes rest at morning's light. 'Tis then Evan may ready the horses, and Nicholas shall escort thee far from Greville Manor.''

Maggie followed her to the window. ''And Robert will be nursing a hangover while all this is going on?''

Elthea chuckled. ''If you imply he shall be taken ill by the drink, it is not likely. Robert never deviates from his itinerary. He would sooner die than be known for slovenliness. 'Twould be as unseasonable as snow in summer for him to do so. My son has good qualities in him, Maggie, though I regret his actions toward you have not revealed them.'' She turned her gaze from the moonlit garden and smiled apologetically at Maggie.

Suddenly, Maggie felt great sympathy for Elthea. The woman was a mother, and although Maggie had no children of her own, she knew that a mother's love was eternal, regardless of the child's deeds.

"I know you love him," Maggie reassured.

"I do, very much." Elthea turned back to the window. "And I shall do whatever I must to protect him. It pains me deeply that should include deception, but it is for his benefit, and thus, the good name of Amesbury."

Maggie consoled Elthea, rubbing her arm tenderly.

"As for our itinerary tomorrow, child," she continued, taking a deep steadying breath, "Nicholas shall have thee nearing London before nightfall. When Robert discovers thy absence, too much time will have passed to form a reconnaissance. London will offer many places for you both to safely disappear within the city."

"Then I guess we won't be coming back here again," Maggie said as she felt a lump coming to her throat.

Elthea turned to her and nodded. "Aye, it appears your time with us is finished, dear Margaret Whitaker. I think not, after this night, that I shall ever see you again in this lifetime. When next we meet, may we both remember we have fulfilled our purpose together in this time here."

Maggie could see tears beginning to well up in Elthea's eyes.

"I think I'm going to miss you most," Maggie managed to say through the tightness building up in her throat. She suddenly felt like Dorothy in the *Wizard Of Oz* when she said good-bye to the Scarecrow.

"And I, thee, child." Elthea maintained her composure. "Come, Maggie," she insisted, quickly changing the subject. "Rest thyself from worry now." She gently led Maggie to the bed.

"But I'm not really tired right now." Maggie tried to dissuade the woman.

" 'Tis best to rest while you can, child. Much strength

is required for the adventure that lies ahead . . . and forget not, there are no detours on the path to grace, Maggie. Rest and repast is necessary for the balancing of our human selves.''

Maggie watched as the woman turned down the fur cover and continued, ''One should always derive pleasure and comfort from these essentials, for they provide balance to thy spiritual self.'' She turned toward Maggie, patting the straw-filled mattress in invitation. ''Life offers many luxuries, save that of passions, child,'' she said with a wink. ''I assure thee, indulgence of rest now shall assist you in fortifying not only your courage, but your spirit on its ultimate journey home.''

Maggie giggled with a blush as she crawled into bed. ''Okay, I think I get it, Elthea.''

Elthea smiled, pulling the heavy fur blanket around Maggie. ''Aye, child. I know my words have struck chords in your mind and heart. I can only hope they resonate long and true.'' She smiled. ''The maids will arrive anon to retrieve the tub. Then in a small while, Evan shall come to escort thee to your beloved's chamber.'' She lit the candle as she spoke. ''For tonight, Margaret Whitaker, you are born again. I celebrate this day of your birth, for my life is much richer now, having had you in it.''

''Oh, thank you for remembering, Elthea,'' Maggie whispered while fighting back tears.

''This night is thine, my present to you, that you may truly be born once again spiritually and reunited with thy twin. Cherish it, dear one, for after this I know not what your future may bring.''

''It is one of the greatest gifts I have ever received, Elthea. Thank you for being instrumental in all of it.'' Maggie sat up and quickly hugged the woman.

''Aye, and the gift is mine for receiving so gracefully, child. Now rest.'' Elthea began tucking Maggie in once more. She was forty years old yet felt much younger.

"Oh, and please tell Lady Norreys I'm sorry, okay, Elthea? Tell her any problems I've caused were unintentional, and I truly wish her a long and happy marriage." Maggie shook her head. "She'll understand, won't she?"

"Who knows that answer, child? I have not seen my cousin in many years. I know not what her travels have taught her about life. Perhaps, she will."

Maggie looked up at the countess and smiled sadly. "I can never thank you enough, Elthea, for everything you've done. Please know you have a place within my heart forever. Bless your soul, for it is wise and compassionate. You really are helping to create Heaven on earth. I'm just sorry I've been so much trouble—"

"Hush now, Maggie. I call thee child as an endearment, not that I might be elevated, for is it not true we are all students and teachers to each other?" Elthea smiled and, bending down, placed a sweet kiss upon Maggie's cheek. "Until I bid thee farewell, rest easy."

She walked away from the bed and opened the door. The maids were waiting to enter. Elthea directed them to make haste and turned once more to Maggie. "I shall miss thee most as well, dear child." Elthea smiled lovingly and closed the door.

Maggie was again alone, wondering what her future might bring. It didn't matter as long as she was with Nick.

Somehow, some way, they were going to face it together.

Chapter Fourteen

"Come, m'lady . . . the time has arrived."

Maggie quickly picked up her gown, her underclothes, her shoes and hose, and followed Evan from her chamber. She looked back over her shoulder and tried to memorize everything. The time she had spent in this house had changed the way she viewed life.

"Hurry, m' lady," Evan urged, holding his candle higher.

Maggie didn't need further coaxing. Her future waited for her down the hall. She followed Evan into the darkened hallway. Deep shadows were cast along the stone walls as they hurried, and Maggie felt a shudder of fear. She still didn't trust Robert. Even his own mother worried that he would demand retribution from Nick. Such silliness, Maggie thought, the way these men prized their reputations. In this time, one would even kill for it. Once they left this place, she and Nick would be fine. She had to believe that, but right now she couldn't wait until Greville Manor was just a memory.

Evan lightly knocked on a door, then stepped aside, and Maggie's heart pounded in expectation.

The old door creaked open slowly and when Nick saw Maggie, he flung it wide to clasp her in his arms. She felt his body against hers and his heart beating against her breast as he pulled her farther into the room.

"Thank you, Evan," Maggie murmured with a blush as she turned back to the servant.

The man smiled slightly and nodded before closing the door. Nick took the clothes from her arms and set them on a chair. Again he pulled her into his arms and whispered against her hair, "Verily, I have worried for thy safety. I promised to protect you, then I was forced to desert you to my enemy."

His eyes looked tortured, and Maggie brought her finger to his lips. "Hush, my love, it was a very courageous thing you did today. We would not have this moment right now had you resisted Robert." She kissed his lips and smiled. "A small price to pay for this, isn't it?"

Nick grinned, and Maggie saw the worry and anger leave his expression. "I would bear anything to hold thee, to love thee again . . ." And his mouth captured hers in a breathtaking kiss.

Maggie felt her senses reel with passion and, as her knees actually buckled beneath her, Nick reached down and did something no other had. He picked her up, as if she weighed nothing, and carried her to the bed. His chamber was dark, save for one candle on a table and the light from the fireplace. In the low amber glow, Maggie looked into Nick's eyes and knew she was home, that place of belonging she had been struggling to find all her life.

"Nick . . ." She breathed his name when he laid her down and bent over her. Brushing a lock of blond hair away from his eyes, Maggie whispered, "Make love to me . . . please? I don't know about the future, but I do know that right here is where I belong. With you, wherever you are."

"Oh, my lovely lady," he said, bending down and kissing the tip of her nose. "Verily, I have wanted to worship thy body from the moment I met thee. I grant thy wish with gladness . . . t'would be a pleasure of discovery and recollection, for my mind tells me that we have loved many times, in many lives, and our reunion was destined."

"I don't understand it, but I feel I have known you forever," she whispered.

He stripped the ruffled shirt from his body and Maggie gasped as he looked at her with an expression that she had known forever. It was love. *Love.* And it was a love that she recognized. She didn't need to understand it, yet she couldn't deny that in his eyes she saw a passion they had shared before.

She held out her hand and welcomed him back into her heart, her mind, her body.

He came to rest with his knee between her thighs on the bed and untied her robe. Seeing the thin gown beneath, Nick sharply inhaled as his fingers traced a line to her breasts. "You are so beautiful," he breathed.

Maggie smiled and raised her fingers through the air. "I'm sprinkling faerie dust in front of your eyes," she whispered. "I hope you always see me like this."

He captured her hand and kissed her palm. "My eyes need no magic to behold the woman I have waited for my entire life. Thou shalt be always beautiful in my eyes, my sweet, sweet lady."

She pulled him down to her and kissed him with all the love she contained. He answered her love with his own and added passion to bring her higher. Gasping when they parted, Maggie pushed herself into a sitting position and began to pull the robe from her arms. "I don't care anymore . . . I have to feel you against me." It was a bold and honest statement. She had waited long enough for this moment.

Nick laughed. "As ye wish, my lady," he complied and began to unlace his tightly fitted breeches.

Within moments they were together, skin against skin,

under a fur cover, shivering in each other's arms with cold and anticipation.

"Ahh . . ." Maggie couldn't contain the moan of pleasure as she was pulled against the hot length of him. Immediately, she wound her arms around him and caressed his back, using her hands to memorize each muscle. She raised her chin and looked into his eyes.

"I love you," she whispered. "I don't understand it, but I know it's true. You and I have been like this before. I know you, Nicholas Layton . . . as I have never known another. You truly are the other half of my soul."

His eyes closed briefly, as though taking in her words. "I am so honored," he answered, lightly caressing her back, her hip, her thigh with such tenderness that the small of her back arched in response . . . "Honored, thou has recognized me, accept me, and allow me to share my love. I would die for thee, Maggie Whitaker. I cherish you that much."

She shook her head. "I don't want you to die for me, Nick. I want you to make love to me. I've waited a lifetime for you."

Words were no longer needed as hands became instruments of discovery and mouths tasted skin aflame with desire. They stared into each other's eyes, watching the changes upon each other's faces as new discoveries were made. It was as if he knew exactly how to touch her, what would excite her and build her passion, and Maggie thrilled to see that instinctively her hands, her body, would do the same for him. This was the rediscovery of each other.

When Nick slid on top of her, Maggie closed her eyes and held him closely, never wanting to let go. His hot breath was in her ear, whispering her name over and over as she arched her back and invited him into her. "Not just yet," he gasped. "Patience, my beloved, I must adore every bit of you."

She moaned as he slid down her body, capturing first one breast and then finally, mercifully, paying homage to both. She clutched his shoulders and wound her fingers through his silky hair as she ground her head into the pillow. Her hands dropped, clutching the fur blanket to anchor her, while charges of exquisite pleasure raced through her body, inflaming her already hot blood. His lips traced an intricate line down her belly, around her navel, and Maggie was shocked to discover the intensity of her reaction. No longer did her mind torture her with insecurities. She belonged to him and surrendered to an ageless, timeless passion.

He worshiped her completely, bringing her to the very edge of rapture, only to stop and slide up her body. She felt tears run down her cheeks and clasped him tightly against her, as if just the pressure of his body might ease this exquisite pain in hers. Her legs entwined with his as he breathed deeply into her mouth, ''Now we shall be one. One mind. One heart. One body. One soul . . . Come dance amid the stars with me, my precious . . . for surely that is where this love began.''

Her legs encircled him in a sensuous movement and he entered her gently, slowly, almost reverently, allowing her time, as his eyes spoke to her with such love that again, Maggie arched her back and this time he entered her fully as together, as one, they were joined completely and eternally. She was inflamed, hungering for something that was just out of reach, and her movements matched his as he took her higher and higher into uncharted territory, beyond the candlelit chamber . . . beyond bodies where lovers of old meet and dance amid starlight. And all the while, he stared into her eyes, watching her, speaking to her, guiding her, promising to love her not just now . . . but forever.

Their movements quickened as the pace of the ancient dance increased. He was leading her now, and she surrendered everything, save the exquisite pulsing sensation that seemed to build in intensity with each thrust of passion.

"Please," she cried out, wanting to end the magnificent torture.

"As ye wish, m'lady," he whispered in a low rumble of passion, and brought her back to the edge and then, suddenly, together, they broke free of all earthly bounds and soared beyond themselves, holding on tightly as wave after wave of pleasure crashed over them.

Maggie felt herself shattering, coming apart into thousands upon thousands of fragments of such intense pleasure that she cried out his name in awe.

"*Nick . . .*"

He quickly followed, holding her so close that when his body arched, Maggie melded into him, grabbing her shattered fragments and merging with his.

It was a wondrous and extraordinary reunion of souls.

They held each other thus, prolonging the moment of passion as aftershocks rippled through them. Finally, as they gazed into each other's eyes with awe, he collapsed onto her breast, and Maggie lightly brushed his hair back from his damp brow.

"Thank you, my love," she breathed, slowly coming back to the room and reality. Never had she even imagined that such a fusion of souls was possible.

He was shaking his head slowly as he raised it to gaze at her once more. "Thou art everything to me now. I pledge to thee my life and my love. Thank you, thank you, thank you . . . I am truly alive!" He kissed her lips with tenderness. "This is an ancient love, Maggie. I feel it deep inside . . . can ye feel it as well?"

"Yes." The admission was easy for her. She knew him as she had known no other.

"We have loved this way before, my angel."

"Yes."

"And we shall love again. I ask thee, Maggie Whitaker . . . Do you accept me as thy one true love throughout all eternity?" The intensity in his eyes was riveting. "No matter what may come to pass, wherever our souls may travel, we shall find each other again and again and remember each other, support and love each other from this moment hence."

"No one will ever love me like you do, Nick . . . I know that." She stared back, opening her soul to him. She wanted him to see the truth of her words. "I accept you as my mate, my twin soul, my true love, and I will never want another. This I promise. I will always know you. You're a part of me now."

"I believe we were and always shall be a part of each other, Maggie. Equally, it has been our eternal quest . . . to find each other again in this lifetime. To bring a face, a voice, a touch to that lonely part of us." He smiled. "And thou art *so* beautiful, my love. I am truly blessed."

She giggled. "Hmm, and if my looks didn't please you, would you still love me?"

He moved slightly and rested his cheek against his raised fist. His grin increased as he used his other hand to caress her face, "I would know thee anywhere and though I am blessed that you are beautiful, I would love thee even if you were not. This love, sweet lady, goes beyond the physical union. This is of the spirit. Whatever we are made of, you and I, 'tis the same."

Maggie remembered her aunt saying almost the same thing to Malcolm. She reached up and brought Nick's face down to hers. Kissing him thoroughly, Maggie sighed with contentment. "I am very pleased," she announced and laughed along with him.

"Prithee do not remind me, my lady, of that scoundrel Amesbury," he growled through his low chuckle.

Maggie pulled out from beneath him and curled into

his body. She ran her hand over his back, the slope of his bottom, and asked, "What is it between you and Robert? Why such antagonism?"

"And how am I to remain in such serious mind when thy touch is once more inflaming me?"

She laughed and kissed his shoulder. "Just tell me."

He rolled over and slid back against the velvet pillows. Pulling her to his chest, he held her in his arms and kissed the top of her head. " 'Tis a political game Robert and I play."

She curled her leg over his legs and wound her arm over his waist as her head lay on his chest. The strong beat of his heart matched her own and she sighed with a deep fulfillment. "Politics . . . I've already heard so much from Elthea. She says we will leave by daybreak and then you must promise me to put whatever it is with Robert behind you. I do not intend to lose any more time with you, and he would make our lives miserable. Promise me?"

He didn't say anything, and Maggie raised her head to see him. He looked serious.

"Allow me to quench my thirst before answering thy query?"

"Of course," Maggie said, and moved away. She almost groaned when he left the bed and she lost his sensuous warmth. Of course, she was rewarded with the delicious sight of him walking naked across the room. His incredible form was bathed in the golden glow from the firelight as he bent over to stoke the embers.

He returned with a filled goblet and Maggie wanted to pinch herself to make sure she wasn't dreaming up this fantastic man. He was hers . . . for eternity!

Nick offered her the goblet and Maggie sipped the bitter ale. Handing it back, she straightened out the pillows and waited for him to join her. He slipped under the fur cover next to her and leaned back.

"There is a story that needs to be told. I may open my heart to thee, my beloved, and know it shall pass no further, for this is the stuff one can lose one's head over. Allow me to begin without interruptions, for it is tangled and weaves its way in many directions."

"All right," Maggie whispered, and leaned her head on his shoulder as she hugged his waist. "I can't promise not to interrupt, but you may tell me anything, and I will keep your trust, Nicholas."

He stroked her hair tenderly. "Of that I am sure, precious one, but it is for thine own safety that I warn." He took a deep breath and began.

"This involves many and begins with the story of young lovers, much like ourselves. I know not what may already be known to thee." He sipped the ale. "The tale of fact and woe begins with our queen, when she was but a princess, committed to the Tower under suspicion of treason, for it was alleged she plotted to secure the throne to the Protestant Succession. At the same time, already in the Tower, was Robert Dudley, later known as the Earl of Leicester, who had attempted to aid his father, the Duke of Northumberland, in declaring Lady Jane Gray as Queen of England. He was sentenced to death, yet it was not carried out and thus he met the young Elizabeth in the Tower and they fell in love. It has been said that Elizabeth and Dudley were secretly married for the first time there. A year later, Queen Mary died, and Elizabeth ascended the throne. She was twenty and five with an empty treasury and a nation divided by religion. One of her first acts was to appoint her secret spouse Master of the Horse, an honorable and valuable post which conveniently gave him lodging at court and personal attendance on the Queen."

"So they were able to be together?" Maggie asked, attempting to keep all the names straight in her head.

"Much to the displeasure of the court. She became

so unduly affectionate with Dudley, it was not long before rumors began stating the Queen was with child.'' He paused. ''There have been several people who have been sent to prison for saying this, so by making thee privy to such knowledge, my love, endangers thee further.''

''Who am I going to tell?'' She almost laughed.

''Merely possessing this knowledge, even if kept to oneself, is enough to endanger you if we are together.'' He held her tighter.

''We're in this together, Nick. You should be able to share everything with me, as I will with you. Okay, so tell me more,'' she asked, kissing his chest. ''Before I become distracted.''

He stroked her hair and she listened to his voice reverberate against her ear. ''It is said that there is an official record stating that our Queen Elizabeth was again secretly married in the house of Lord Pembroke before a number of witnesses. The rumors began to fly from Spain to Rome and back again. All of this is to say that many, including Robert of Amesbury, our reluctant host this night, know that in 1571 a statute was passed by Parliament at the behest of the Queen which makes it a penal offense to speak of any successor to the crown, save her *natural issue*, for she had rejected the term legal heirs.''

Maggie raised her head. ''Did she have a child, or not? And who's the father?''

''She did. A son was born at York Place, a royal Tudor, and given to Sir Nicholas Bacon and his wife to raise as their own. Francis does bare an uncanny resemblance to the Earl of Leicester.''

''Francis Bacon?'' Maggie was struggling to understand this complicated tale.

Nicholas nodded. ''I came to this knowledge when my childhood friend, Anthony Bacon, stepbrother to

Francis, spoke of Her Royal Majesty visiting Francis many times, and taking Francis under her wing, sending him to Cambridge for education and to Italy and France for further education. It is only in the last few years that I have formed a close alliance with Francis and have heard his story and of what he learned in his world travels. He was promised legitimacy by his rightful mother for many years, yet has been made to keep silent that he is the Prince of Wales and heir to the throne.

"When his adopted father died, he was left nothing, although Anthony was well endowed. Perhaps, Sir Nicholas Bacon was giving a mute indication that Francis's expectation lay elsewhere. His mother, our Queen, has treated him poorly . . . first dangling the treat before his eyes and then withdrawing it as she played her lengthy and delicate political game with all of Europe."

"Francis Bacon is the heir to the throne? Does Robert know this?" She sat up straighter and pulled the fur blanket around her breasts.

"There are two heirs. Bacon and the Earl of Essex, another issue from Her Royal Majesty's body. Many know of it, and Robert would like nothing better than to see Bacon in the Tower and a Catholic back upon the throne when Elizabeth dies. Already Essex is gaining disfavor with the Queen, for both mother and son are prideful and hot-tempered. Francis, as the older son, would be the rightful heir."

"Why does Robert hate you?" she asked.

"He knows of my close association with Sir Francis and that I am part of a . . . a group of individuals that encourages the departure of Rome's influence in this country."

"What does this . . . group do?"

"We are a clandestine society, dedicated to the elevation of man's mind and thus his station in life. We encourage the seeking of knowledge, the practice of wisdom, and the freedom of the soul. We follow the tenets of the Rosicrosse, a secret literary society based on a very old mystery school. Sir Francis has been vocal in his opposition to control by Rome and also is averse to all corruptions, advocating free parliaments. He says laws were made to guard the rights of the common, not to feed lawyers, and should therefore be comprehensible to all.''

Maggie watched him sip more ale. She smiled. ''It sounds like Francis would make a good king. I guess I understand why Robert is so opposed to you and him, especially if the good of the common people is important to you. Robert has no time for anyone common.''

''Robert of Amesbury has no time for anyone who would not further his own cause. Already he has begun to sway the Queen against Bacon again. Francis was denied access to court, his allowance from the Queen cut, and for years, he survived financially by selling his works of recreation. He has a fine mind and a rare gift for comedy and tragedy.''

''He's a writer?''

''I may reveal to you that he is, indeed, a writer of plays and great philosophical works, though Her Royal Majesty has made him swear never to write or speak or print secrets under his own name. And he has kept his promise. It was Lady Bacon, Anthony's mother, who unwittingly provided the means.''

''I don't understand. Francis is a writer who swore never to write?''

Nick laughed. ''It is an intricate web, I agree, but allow me to unweave it for thee. Francis's works of recreation *were* beginning to be performed. Lady Bacon, Francis's adoptive mother was horrified that her son, Anthony, and her adopted son, Francis, were involved in such mummeries and demanded that they cease. Francis then knew he needed a *mask* to continue writing his dramatic performances. He had been trained by masters in the art of cleverly concealing truth, the greatest teacher being his own mother, and so he devised a brilliant plan to publish his thoughts while concealing his identity. His muse is Pallas Athena, a Greek goddess representing the intellectual aspects of challenge. She carries a spear and is helmeted. Pallas means 'to shake' and William is from the German meaning 'helmet of' . . . his mask is perfect. He writes from the helmet of the spear shaker, and uses codes and ciphers, tenets of the Rosicrosse, to identify his true authorship.''

Maggie held her breath for a moment. ''Wait a minute. You are saying *O Romeo, Romeo! wherefore art thou Romeo* was written by Francis?''

''Yes. A talented man he is as either the Prince of Wales, denied legitimacy by his own mother, or a lawyer championing the common, or a writer of works where he delves into the minds and machinations of nobility.''

Maggie's mind was spinning and she sat up straighter. ''Wait . . . wait . . .'' She held her hand up to interrupt him. ''Shakespeare wrote *Romeo and Juliet.*''

''Yes. Shakespeare is Bacon's name for the stage. A fine name for a playwright.''

''*William Shakespeare*, from Stratford-upon-Avon wrote it,'' Maggie insisted.

Nick startled her by throwing back his head and laughing. *Laughing.*

She could only stare at him as he collected himself and continued. ''Oh, sweet one, if you are speaking about a certain actor, William Shakspur of Stratford, I think the man would know more about an odd yard land, buying up farms, than the machinations of the nobility. He is barely educated and not such a finished actor, either, if truth be told.'' He looked at her strangely. ''How would you know of this man?''

Maggie didn't know how else to answer him. "Nicholas, this actor, is given the credit for all of Shakespeare's or Sir Francis Bacon's work. It is history. We're taught—"

"Then you have been taught incorrectly," he interrupted in a serious voice. "Francis Bacon is the author of *Romeo and Juliet, Henry the VI, Taming of the Shrew, A Midsummer Night's Dream, Love's Labour's Lost . . .* why . . ." he almost stammered in his frustration, ". . . the play even impressed Lord Campbell by the author's accurate knowledge of the law! Shakspur might have saved himself being returned as defaulter in subsidy tax in St. Helen's, if he were the true author and knew anything at all about the process of law!"

"Calm down, Nick," Maggie interrupted. "I'm as frustrated as you are. I've been taught one thing, the whole world has been taught one thing, and now you're telling me the greatest writer in the world is a *hoax*?!"

Nicholas stared at her with the strangest expression, as though putting together something in his mind. His voice, when he spoke, was a mere whisper of shock. "Pray that I have misunderstood thee. Four hundred years into the future, it is not yet discovered that Sir Francis Bacon is the true author of the works? This cannot be so!"

"But it is," Maggie answered. "Everyone, everywhere, for hundreds of years, has believed that William Shakespeare, a sometimes actor and brilliant playwright, is the author of *Hamlet, Romeo and Juliet, Macbeth . . .* and I don't know how many others. I don't really know that much about Shakespeare, so I can't tell you a lot about him, but I've never heard of Sir Francis Bacon being the author. I don't even know why I remember Bacon's name at all . . . but I do. I just don't remember why."

"Bacon has left his authorship," Nick stated. "From

the very beginning, he has been using ciphers and codes, in the word *honorificabilitudinitatibus*—''

Maggie laughed, as the language rolled off his artistically trained tongue. "What in the world is that?" She wouldn't even attempt to repeat it.

'' 'Tis a game, the making of long words . . . it means honorable and was being used at court at the time Bacon wrote *Love's Labour's*. He used the original Latin ablative plural when he had Costard, the clown say to the servant Moth, 'I marvel thy master hath not eaten thee for a word, for thou art not so long by the head as honorificabilitudinitatibus'.''

He paused while she giggled again. '' 'Tis a code, Maggie . . . for the rearranged letters form the Latin sentence, 'These plays, born of F. Bacon, are preserved for the world.' ''

She stopped giggling and stared at him.

"Francis Bacon is not given credit for the plays, Nick. I don't even know if anyone has discovered this.''

'' *'Tis an ill discover who thinks there is no land when he can see nothing but sea.'* ''

She shook her head. "I am sorry, Nick, but I can only tell you my truth. And that is Francis Bacon is not known in history as the author of the works . . . it's Shakespeare.''

He suddenly grabbed her shoulders. "That is why you have come back . . . to tell Bacon . . . he must be more obvious, or declare himself author now to stop this madness. A sorry lot like Shakspur is renowned throughout time as the author of *Henry VI*. It should not be so!''

Maggie could only blink in disbelief! She was supposed to tell the person, the brilliant mind of Sir Francis Bacon, illegitimate son of the Virgin Queen, that he must declare himself author of *Hamlet*, *Macbeth*, and every other work bearing the name William Shakespeare!

She leaned back, shaking her head, and muttering, "I don't think so." Reaching for the shared goblet, she sipped the ale.

Nick became very still. "You think not . . . ?"

"Look, Nicholas Layton, I came back in time for *you*. That much I have fully accepted. I'm not into changing history or any other heroic insanity, okay?" Handing the goblet to him, she sat back and folded her arms over her breasts. "You'd better understand that right up front on this adventure."

Nick stared out to the darkened room. They each had a few moments to integrate the extraordinary events that had just taken place. They had made the most exquisite love and joined in mind, body, and soul. Neither could deny it. They had each acknowledged the other as the one they wanted to spend eternity with, over and over to meet and join and love unconditionally. It was not their first mental duel, nor would it obviously be their last. Each respected the other and yet held their own beliefs, and the air was almost tangible with the strain of emotions between them.

Finally, Nicholas said, "I have no wish to place you in danger, my sweet one. I have vowed I would die for you and, willingly, I would. You must believe my word, and yet I must also follow mine own heart in this matter. This is a mission one of us must accomplish. We came together for it! Can you not see this? Did not Countess Elthea say that twin souls reunite to fulfill their mission?"

"My mission is love," Maggie stated, as tears came into her eyes. She sounded exactly like her aunt Edithe. She had said love was her agenda.

"As is mine, my beloved," he whispered, turning to her and gathering her into his arms. He gently stroked her hair and kissed the top of her head. "Can you not see we were traveling to Francis in London this morning before we were stopped by Robert? We already knew where we should go, we merely didn't know the entire reason why until now. Do you not speak of adventure? *'He is an ill discover who thinks there is no land when he can see nothing but sea.'* It takes courage, my love, to have an adventure, to believe the land is out there beyond the sea of fear. And now, on your adventure, you have your own devoted knight who would die for you. Would you ask for more confirmation that you are well suited to the mission?''

He was starting to make sense, or at least stir up something inside of her that said she *was* experiencing one hell of an adventure, something she had never in her life imagined. What could it hurt to tell Bacon her story, and while doing it relate that William Shakespeare happened to be known as the most respected writer in history?

She took a deep breath as she continued to hold him. ''All right. I'll do it, but I'm not getting more involved in all this political madness. And I don't want you caught up in it, either. You must promise me that.''

She felt him nodding above her.

''I promise I shall not become involved with political madness.''

''Ever.''

He chuckled. ''Ever. I am but a poor minstrel, after all . . .''

His words trailed off, and Maggie felt his muscles stiffen. ''What's wrong?'' she asked, and lifted her head to see him.

Nick appeared startled. ''How shall I provide a life befitting such a glorious adventurer?'' He looked into her eyes. ''What have I asked of thee, Maggie Whitaker? I am not a man of wealth.''

She giggled and slapped his chest playfully. ''Oh, stop it! If it makes you feel any better, I'm not of wealth either. I was waiting for an eviction notice on my home any day before I left! Now don't be ridiculous . . . we shall live, Nicholas Layton, for as long as it lasts . . . happily ever after.''

His words, when they came, seemed filled with awe. "Such a woman of courage thou art. Like no other I have ever known. Happily ever after is how most tales end. Life does not always comply, my love, as we both have known.''

"Well ours begins there, mister,'' she announced. "For once in my life I'm going to go for it with everything I've got.''

Maggie felt such love that she couldn't contain her smile. "This isn't courage, my love . . . this is a knowing I can't deny. Besides, it's my birthday today, and that's my wish. Happily ever after.''

"Happy birthday, my love. When we get to London tomorrow, I shall buy thee a fine gift.'' He gathered her completely into his arms, muttering into her neck, "Come back with me, my beloved . . . let us again free ourselves of these earthly bounds and soar into the heavens.'' Picking up the candle, he whispered, "Make thy wish proper.''

She closed her eyes and, for a moment, wished with everything in her heart that she and Nick spend eternity together. Opening her lids, she smiled like a kid at the best birthday party of her life. "It's done.''

"Blow the candle, love . . . send thy wish out there.''

She did, and the room was cast into the soft, warm glow from the fireplace.

He pulled her back into his arms and whispered into her ear. "I have a gift for thee . . . one of love, my precious one.''

She melted.

Chapter Fifteen

She was given Elthea's long brown hooded cloak to obscure her face, and Maggie felt like a journeyer into the unknown as she hurried after Evan, down the stairs and out of the manor house. Her new life awaited her, and she was filled with hope. Nick followed closely behind and they found around the side of the house Countess Elthea, dressed in a similar hooded cloak and holding two horses by the reins.

"Praise be you are safe!" she whispered, handing the reins to Evan and walking up to Maggie and Nick. She reached into her pocket and withdrew something white. Opening her hand, Elthea held out to Nick a pearl necklace that gleamed in the fading moonlight. "Your dear mother gave these to me many years ago. I believe it is time I returned them to her son, for I think you shall have need of them."

Nick accepted the necklace and then hugged Elthea. "I thank thee, m'lady, for the many kindnesses thou hast shown me throughout the years."

Elthea pulled back and placed her hand upon Nick's cheek. "Be safe, dear Nicholas. Protect this guest of the future."

He nodded. "With my life, dear lady. She is most safe with me." And turning, he smiled with love as he held out the necklace to Maggie. "Gather your pearls, my lady . . ."

"Nick . . . ?" Maggie stared at the necklace, stunned to see that save for a different clasp, they appeared to be the same as the ones she had lost. The same size pearls and the same length strand. It couldn't be . . . ! She didn't move as Nick gently pushed her hood back and placed them over her head. They fell to her breast, and Maggie clutched them. "I don't know what to say . . ."

"Thank the gentleman for his gift," Elthea said, and pulled the hood back up to cover Maggie's face.

She looked to Nick and smiled with more emotion than she knew she should acknowledge at the moment. Tears threatened, and her throat closed. "Thank you," she whispered. "I shall treasure them always."

"I promised you would have your jewels again." His smile was filled with emotion.

How she loved him. She would never forget those words. *Gather your pearls, my lady.* She had so many memories. Stuffing the pearls down the front of her gown, she swore this time she wouldn't lose them!

"Now bid me farewell, child. For I do not think we shall again meet."

Maggie looked at Elthea and couldn't stop the tears. "I don't know how to say good-bye to you," she mumbled. "We tried once, and it didn't work."

Elthea smiled and gathered her into her arms. "Oh, child . . . I do not think we shall meet again in *this* lifetime, but I know we shall again be together. We are soul mates, you and I, and we shall play this game again, perhaps with much different roles. If we are fortunate we shall again remember and again do whatever is necessary to follow our hearts. You are deep within mine, child. Take that knowledge with thee now."

Maggie held the woman tighter, and in a flash she

wondered if Elthea was her aunt Edithe in the present time. Days ago she would have thought it crazy even to contemplate such a notion, but now she knew there were things going on that she couldn't possibly understand. Now, anything was possible!

"I love you, Elthea," she whispered against the woman's hood. "Thank you for being my friend when I needed one so badly."

Elthea pulled back and looked Maggie straight in the eye. "*Namaste*, Maggie Whitaker."

"I don't understand . . ."

"It is a word that has come from the East and it means *I recognize and honor the spark of divinity within thee.*"

Maggie wasn't sure she completely comprehended the meaning, but found herself whispering, "*Namaste*, Countess Elthea." And she bowed deeply with recognition of a friend, a friend of her soul.

"Now, hurry," Elthea urged, and motioned for Evan to bring forth Maggie's horse. "Do not use the main roads, Nicholas. The house remains quiet, yet I think prudence is required still."

"Aye." Nick mounted his horse as Evan assisted Maggie.

This time no one argued with her about riding like a man. The horse snorted loudly, and Maggie's heart stopped with fear for an instant.

"*Go!*" Elthea urged in a forceful whisper. "I bid thee travel in love's protection."

Together Maggie and Nick left Greville Manor again, this time knowing neither would ever return. They traveled slowly until they were across the wooden bridge, and then she followed Nick's lead as he took her into a field of damp clover toward the forest. She was in it now . . . the adventure . . . and could only surrender to a force that seemed to be directing them both. Whatever this force, love even, she was now helpless to stop it.

She had to believe there was land beyond the sea . . . She also had to give the man credit, whoever he was. Francis Bacon knew about faith!

Maggie held her seat as the sun rose in the east and the humidity started to make her sweat. She pushed back the hood and allowed the wind to cool her as she continued to follow the man of her dreams through the forest. Neither of them spoke, and Maggie had time to replay the incredible night in her head. Still, she could not believe that she was on her way to meet the greatest writer the world had ever known. Everything Nick said made sense. They had spoken of it at great length during the night as they waited for the call to leave. William Shakspur of Stratford couldn't have written about nobility, the law, philosophy. The man hardly had an education and had never left England. Nick said that Shakspur could barely write his own name and never claimed to have written any plays. He wasn't even a good actor and was more involved in trying to keep himself out of debtors' prison than in writing about *Two Gentlemen from Verona*, *The Merchant of Venice* or *Taming of the Shrew*. Now that she had heard Nick's story about Francis Bacon and his lineage, it seemed more than probable that the man would easily be able to write about kings and queens and all the manipulation of the nobility.

It made her wonder what else she had been taught that was false? What other things had she taken as truth, written in history, and just accepted? Like time travel . . . Well, she was an authority on it now and no matter what anyone said to her, she couldn't deny what had happened. She was living four hundred years into the past and more in love than she thought possible with the most wonderful man in any age.

Elthea had said that history is written by the victors. She didn't want to tell Nick that she never heard of a

King Francis of England, so Bacon never was acknowledged by his mother or ascended the throne. Someone else had won that fight and written the history.

They had been traveling for some time when they rode up a small hill and, as they crested the top, Maggie pulled on the reins and called out to Nick. He stopped and rode back to her.

"What is it, my love? Soon, we shall rest."

She continued to stare at the large circle of stones in the distance. "It's Stonehenge," she whispered in awe. "Can we stop there?"

Nick looked down the hill and nodded. " 'Twould be a good place to rest."

Excited to finally have the opportunity to see Stonehenge, Maggie kicked her horse into action and yet slowed down as she approached the huge neolithic structure. She was filled with awe as she continued to stare at it. It was far larger than she had imagined, and it seemed to have more erect stones. *Pictures can't do it justice*, she thought, as she stopped and just took in the energy of the place.

Nick dismounted and came to her assistance. When her feet touched the ground, she had to hold on to his arm for a moment as she regained her footing.

"My beloved, thou art weary from lack of sleep," he said with tenderness as he pulled her closer.

She rested her head upon his chest and sighed. "Oh, Nick, I wouldn't give up one moment of last night for sleep." She raised her head and smiled into his eyes. "Would you?"

He looked deeply at her and grinned. "Not a moment, dear lady." He kissed her forehead, and added, "Now, come . . . Countess Elthea was most gracious and has provided us with nourishment. Let us sit upon these ancient stones and replenish our bodies, for we have a long ride ahead of us."

Maggie nodded and moved back to follow him to his horse. She watched as he removed a sack and untied a leather skin. He held out his hand and she placed hers inside his as together they walked toward the giant circle.

"Oh, Nick . . . how I have wanted to see this place. It's famous in my time. People come from all over the word to see it."

"Truly?" he asked, as he stopped at a huge overturned block of stone and placed the sack and skin upon it. "Thy table, m'lady . . ."

Maggie removed the cloak and grinned. "I cannot believe I'm about to have lunch *on* Stonehenge," she said, and sat down. Running her hand over the gray stone, she murmured with awe, "I wonder who built this."

"There are many theories here in Salisbury. The most common is the Ancient Ones. Druids," Nick answered, unwrapping a thick round pastry and handing it to her. "Some say it was built before the Celts ever arrived on Briton, and the Druids used it as their temple. 'Tis a mystery."

Maggie bit into the pastry and found that it contained meat. Hungry, she continued to look around the structure while wondering how whoever built it got the giant stones from a quarry and all the way to this plain. It really was a mystery.

Nick unplugged the leather skin and handed it to her. She had to be careful as she brought it to her lips and squeezed. Warm honey wine filled her mouth, quenching her thirst. Handing it back, she asked, "Exactly who are the Druids? I know I've heard the term, but the best I can remember is that they're like wizards or witches, or something."

Nick chuckled. "Four hundred years have passed, and that label persists? It isn't too hopeful if any group of people we don't understand, or who believe differently than we do, are still labeled witches."

"I'm sorry." She meant it sincerely. "I guess you're right. That thinking does still exist. So what did they do here?"

"I'm not an authority," he said, and drank the wine. Licking his lips, he smiled. "The Druids were an earth-based religion, honoring the sun and the moon. Eclipses would be observed. It is said that here is where the solstices and equinoxes were celebrated, along with Beltane, Lughnasadh, and Samhain, the Celtic New Year. Have you heard of them?"

Chewing, Maggie shook her head.

"Most have been assimilated into the Christian religion now and bear other names."

"Wait," she mumbled and held up her hand until she swallowed. "You're saying that . . . well, like Christmas is actually a pagan holiday?"

He laughed. "I'm saying that most of Europe celebrated these pagan holidays that are marked by astronomical events, when the sun enters a certain sign . . . for example Yule is the day when the sun enters Capricorn. 'Tis the winter solstice. The minor pagan holidays came after the Roman occupation of northern Europe and the British Isles. When the Catholic Church became the official church of the Roman Empire, the people were literally forced to submit to Christianity, or perish. Many people refused to succumb and held off with incredible force and it was not until the church modified its own holidays to fall on the pagan ones that the people submitted. Thus, the European pagans were converted when they could celebrate such holy days as Yule as the birth of Christ."

Maggie was trying to understand. "What is Yule then?"

Nick was munching on his meat pie and smiling.

When he swallowed he said, "You have an inquiring mind, Maggie Whitaker. Francis will be most pleased to meet you."

She grinned. "I guess I'll be most pleased to meet him. It still blows my mind to think that I'm going to be talking to the greatest writer in history and that—"

"Blows thy mind?" he interrupted. "I do not comprehend these words."

Maggie laughed and playfully poked his arm with her elbow. "It means that I will be astonished, amazed, astounded . . . it will, quite frankly, blow my mind to meet the author of the Shakespeare works."

"Ahh," Nick answered with a laugh. "Well, Francis is better informed about these mysteries. Yule was the original celebration of the return of the sun, or rebirth of the God and it was only when Christians took that opportunity to use the birth of the *Son*, Jesus the Christ, to convert the so-called heathen Europeans who still practiced pagan beliefs that they were successful. Most ancient texts agree that Jesus was born in the spring, yet the church adopted the pagan holy days in order to convert. The true meaning of Yule, existing thousands of years before Christianity, is the celebration of the return of light."

"More history written by the victors," Maggie muttered. "Geez, what else have I been taught and accepted as truth that just isn't so?" She bit into her pie with near anger.

"Be at ease, Maggie," Nick said, observing her mood. "The truth has a way of surviving. Even in the darkest period of history, such as the Inquisition, there are always those who secretly hold the light of truth and pass it on. It is but thy impatience that makes you angry."

"I'm angry because I'm coming to realize that what I have been taught isn't so."

"It was thy choice, was it not, to accept those teachings?"

She thought about that. "Well, I guess you could say it was, but I didn't even realize there *was* another explanation. I just accepted . . ."

"Do not berate thyself, dear lady," he said, while smiling into her eyes. "I, too, was raised with those beliefs, and to challenge the Church was heresy and a crime punishable by death. It takes courage to look beyond the obvious, and to refuse to give away your power to another's version of history without investigation. That is why Francis shall be pleased by thy queries. You are not fearful of using your mind to think and question. That is a sign of the seeker of truth."

"Truth . . ." Maggie murmured, looking at the tall columns with huge stones on top. "Who would believe I have time traveled, and yet it is my truth."

"I have heard such things as possible," Nick said, and handed her the wine. "The Celts had a strong belief in the spirit world and were said to have spoken of an in-between time, a non time or place where this world and the other worlds were the closest, and ancestors and the physical world could travel easily to each plane. Francis knows of these things and will better answer thy inquiries." He looked around the circle, and whispered, "He is a master of the mysteries."

She merely nodded, and they continued to eat in silence, each caught up in the majestic stones that surrounded them. There was a mystical quality to the place, as though not just the stones but the very ground itself held something undefinable by man, something that no one could attach a label to. It went beyond explanations. It was just *there*, to be felt and held in awe. And Maggie thought it was holy, if for no other reason than that.

When Maggie finished eating, she stood up and wiped her hands on the cloth that had held her meat pie. "I'm going to explore," she proclaimed. "This is a once-in-a-lifetime opportunity, and I'm not going to miss it."

Nick grinned up to her. "My beautiful adventurer . . ." He pulled her closer and held the backs of her thighs through the heavy velvet skirt. "How have I been so blessed that you should wander into my life and create such magic in my heart and mind?"

She grinned down to him. "Hmm . . . just in your mind and heart?" she teased as his hands started caressing. "The way I remember last night, my love, the physical became more than magical." Stroking back his silky blond hair, she whispered, "I will never, ever forget it."

"We shall make more memories," he promised, obviously pleased by her words. "We have forever."

She bent down and kissed him, tasting the wine upon his lips. When she raised her head and looked into his eyes, she again felt him go within her and connect to her soul. "Forever," she committed in a serious voice.

He held her gaze for a few precious moments, and then patted the backs of her legs. "Now, go . . . explore, for I do not know if we shall return to this place again."

Smiling, Maggie caressed his face once and walked away. She sighed with a deep contentment, knowing she had been blessed. No matter what anyone else thought, she knew that what was happening to her was extraordinary. Somehow, from a very ordinary life, she had been given this opportunity to find the most awesome, magnificent love.

This was the stuff of legends, what poets would write about, she thought as her palm brushed across the surface of a huge gray stone. She wasn't anyone extraordinary. She wasn't wise or very knowledgeable in the unexplainable. She wasn't even religious, so piety was out the door, too. There wasn't one single reason why this exquisite gift had been presented to her.

It had just happened, and she accepted it into her heart without question now.

As her hand continued to touch the stone, Maggie was filled with gratitude. How she had fought this adventure, even thinking she was crazy, but now she knew without a shadow of a doubt that Nicholas Layton was the other half of her soul, that she had traveled back four hundred years to find him and know that kind of love was real.

A smile came to her face as she walked farther amid the stones. She sure had been bitter when she arrived here. Even her aunt Edithe sensed it and had tried to make her see that the only safety *is* in love. Nothing else was lasting. The love she had shared once with her ex-husband was real, though it was nothing like this. *The love lasts*, she thought with conviction, knowing that her memories of her ex would no longer be tainted ones. Thank Heavens she *was not* married now! In her mind she pictured her first husband and actually smiled. Once they had shared something real and memorable, and she found that, if possible, her heart was lighter as forgiveness entered and transmuted the bitterness into a mere memory. She felt free, more free than she could remember being since she was young and believed the world was a wondrous place.

"Thou art so beautiful in this moment," Nick whispered.

She heard his voice coming from her right and turned to see him on the other side of the stone, peeking at her. Grinning, she began to raise her hand, as though to sprinkle faerie dust again to keep him thinking that, when he quickly reached out to capture her wrist.

Pulling her to him, he met her, and continued, "You fail to recognize your own beauty, m'lady." He enclosed her in his arms and leaned back against the tall stone. Sighing deeply, he looked out to the surrounding plain, and said, "Some may say that is a virtue, to be so humble. I think humility is seeing the truth and not denying it, with the gracious ability to thank the observer. Perhaps that is what I might teach you . . . not to give your power away so easily.''

"You may teach me anything,'' she answered, hugging him tightly and kissing his chest as she snuggled into him. ''I trust you with every cell of my body.''

"Cell?''

She listened to the way his voice resounded within his chest and smiled. ''It's a term used in . . . in my time. It's what our bodies are composed of, tiny cells you cannot see without great magnification. The blood, the bones, the muscles . . . are just cells arranged in organs and . . . bones and everything, I guess. But beyond that our bodies are magnificent machines that science is finding out is mostly space and in that space is atomic energy . . . light. And in those cells of light, I feel I can trust you, Nicholas Layton.''

He didn't say anything, and she raised her head. He seemed lost in thought, and she didn't disturb him. Finally he said, ''You blow my mind, Maggie Whitaker.''

Laughing, she hugged him again, and answered, ''Touché!''

He grinned as they mentally connected and within moments their expressions became serious. Maggie read the passion in his eyes as she lifted her chin and offered her lips to him. He gladly accepted the invitation and lowered his head.

''Forever,'' he breathed into her mouth before capturing it in an intense kiss. He pulled her even closer and wound his fingers into her hair.

Maggie felt herself surrendering again to a force much stronger than her, one that was leading her in this adventure. The muscles in her body relaxed with the capitulation, and she clung to Nick's body as the kiss deepened and she melted into him.

"Ah, Maggie, my precious one . . ." He kissed her cheeks, her eyes, her nose, and grazed over her lips. "If I be dreaming such a woman, do not ever let me wake. Come, there is something I want you to see."

He took her hand and led her back to their neolithic table. "Sit, love," he directed, then walked to his horse. He pulled something from his saddle and came back to her. Opening it up, he flipped a few pages and then handed it to her.

She saw it was a leather-bound journal of some sort. Looking up, she said, "You sure you want me to read this?"

He nodded. And waited . . .

Maggie looked down at the script and within moments found her eyes filling with tears.

Journal Entry
15 May 1598

Long have my inner notes been lulled to whisper . . . until now, as I have been aroused by the reverberation that you, my ancient love, are approaching.

I have always loved you, I love you still, I always will.

And I know you are more than a dream, for I remember your tones, even in my waking, and your exquisite vibrations fill the very corners of my being.

We have orchestrated this, our music, for a thousand years or more. Our harmonizing chords striking deep within this One Soul shall serenade all things into infinity—a heavenly resonation—leaving such an impression upon the universe that the stars call out a billion ovations.

Listen now, My Beloved, our symphony seduces and implores, we return to us.

We are One Mind, One Heart, One Soul.

I reach to embrace you gently, but the sun's rise chases another dark velvet thief who has stolen my sleep, our song, and you from me, as I am left in these, my long waking hours, with only haunting echos of our refrain.

Yet I know I will find you, and our music will rise again, through eternity . . .

Once and Forever.

Speechless, she looked up to him, and he smiled as he slowly sat back on his heels before her.

"Thank you for waiting, my love. Together we shall serenade our love into eternity."

Maggie stared at his face, his full lips that just spoke those words, his high cheekbones, his perfectly aristocratic nose, his deep soulful eyes, and felt honored, privileged, to experience the moment, for it was one that was sacred. She had never felt such union with another human being. "Thank you, Nicholas," she whispered, and wiped away a tear that was running down her cheek. "Those are the most beautiful words I have ever read."

"It was written for you, Maggie, though I knew not who you were then."

She couldn't help it. The tears increased and flowed without stopping.

"Now that is not the response I was anticipating," Nick stated as he rose and sat next to her. Gathering her into his arms, he kissed the top of her head. "Hush now, my love . . . 'Twas only meant to show you my conviction that you are my beloved."

Maggie nodded and wiped at her face. "I know," she murmured. "It's just that no one has ever honored me like that. These . . . these are tears of joy."

"Ahh . . ." He stroked her hair. "Then we shall allow them, but only briefly, for I wish you to tell me of your time, of these new thoughts, like body cells being of light. What else does the future hold? With all the room to roam, how could I not dream a greater future, such as you have described?"

Sniffling, she raised her head and smiled. "Oh, Nick, you should just see it. I drive a car, a machine that has the horsepower of a hundred horses, then there's television, and—"

"It cannot be so!" he interrupted. "A hundred horses? No one can ride a hundred horses."

Wiping her face, she laughed. "Well, I can! It's the power of the horses, Nick, not the actual horses. Don't ask me to explain how it works, but it does. It was called a horseless carriage when first invented. Think of it that way. I control a horseless carriage that, to you, would seem faster than anything you have ever seen or imagined. In fact," she said, sitting up and pushing her hair back off her face, "we have sent men to the moon."

He merely blinked at her in disbelief.

She giggled. "It's true. At least I saw it on television, but I really believe that men have walked on the moon and safely returned to earth."

Nick looked to the sky. "I don't understand how such a thing could be possible. How did they get there? Like you, traveling in light?"

"No, by machine. They flew an aircraft." She lifted her arms to make wings. "It's how I got to England. I flew in an airplane across the Atlantic. It took seven hours."

"Surely you cannot be correct. You traveled across the Atlantic Ocean in less time than it shall take us to get to London now."

Nodding, she smiled. "I'm telling you the truth, Nick. I would never lie to you."

"But . . ."

She patted his hand. "I know. Time. It's only a present illusion. I'm sure in 2050, someone will hear about it taking seven hours to cross the Atlantic and laugh at such slow travel. Everything is speeding up, Nick. At least that's the way it felt to me when I was living four hundred years from now. There was so much . . . to take in, to understand, to accomplish in what was feeling like a short time. We call that stress." She again giggled. "I had to travel four hundred years back in time to learn to slow down, to smell the roses." She stopped laughing and looked deeply into his eyes. "And when I did, I discovered *love*!"

It hit her like a thunderbolt from the sky.

What a great reason to drop out of the rat race!

She had been miserable trying to keep it all going . . . the house, the job, the marriage. She had driven herself almost crazy attempting to be Superwoman, and she couldn't do it alone. The only way it could have ever worked was if she was with an equal partner, someone who shared her dreams and balanced out the load. But she had thought she needed the smart town house, the clothes carrying a prestigious label, the cars, TVs, VCRs, the designer furniture, the pedigreed dog, the prestigious job, the money to buy it all! She wanted *the good life*.

Didn't everyone? Wasn't that what life was about? Struggling against time to make it all happen? Damn, talk about stress! Time, a merchant's invention, had been killing her!

"What is it, love? What startles thee so?"

She shook her head. "Nothing. I mean, I just didn't see how foolish I had been, buying into someone else's story again. Giving away my power. I guess I had to be startled, shocked into seeing what I was doing, and that's part of the reason I'm back here. Not just to find you, Nick, but also to stop worrying and fighting time and just surrender to it and allow it to bring me the good life." Touching his cheek, she smiled. "For there is no life better for me than right here with you, right now. It doesn't matter what tomorrow brings, where I am, or how I live. No possession, no job, nothing is more important than what I am feeling with you now."

He cupped her face between his hands and returned her smile with one of deep affection and love. "The universe is a wondrous place to have an adventure, is it not, Maggie Whitaker?"

"*Who are you*, Nicholas Layton?" she breathed in awe, not knowing if it was the energy of the stones or her own mind, expanding into something she wasn't sure was possible. "This is magic."

"This is life," Nicholas answered with an even deeper grin. "This is a return to the garden, where everything seems like a miracle. Have thee not heard magic is natural in Heaven?"

"I'm in Heaven?" Even though he was smiling, Maggie was shocked by his words. "Have I died?" It was a possibility she hadn't wanted to consider, one that terrified her.

He laughed, throwing his head back, and Maggie relaxed again.

"Ahh, my precious time traveler!" he said between remaining chuckles as he looked into her eyes. "Did you not hear me? I said this is *life!* This is the way life is supposed to be . . . joyous. Francis has been saying much the same to me for years, and it was not until I found thee that I began to understand that precious truth. What an angel you are!"

"Angel?" Now Maggie's voice was filled with disbelief.

"Angels are messengers. I think we both have assisted each other with some remarkable messages since we have met."

"We have, haven't we?" She pondered it for a few moments. "Who would have thought? I'm in love with an angel."

"As am I, my beloved. You expected wings?"

They both laughed until Maggie tapped his chest.

"Elthea's an angel, and Evan and my aunt Edithe and Malcolm and . . . and—"

"And everyone who has ever given us a message that we are more than what we've been told," he finished her sentence. "Anyone who assisted us in remembering our angelic nature. How else would we know we could have Heaven on earth? Remember, we each were taught a different belief."

What a miracle Aunt Edithe's letter had been. That remarkable angel had saved her life. So she had to travel into the past to discover she needed to heal the present, just to stay alive? All she needed was a little faith and courage to live the adventure?

She burst into laughter.

And *laughter* . . . oh yes! All she had needed was faith there was land beyond the sea, courage to keep going forward and laugh at her fears. Aunt Edithe had been right. Everything is evolving at exactly the right time.

She was with the love of her life, having a private lunch at Stonehenge, waking up from a nightmare of stress and learning to trust herself now. Not a bad gig!

She burst into chuckles, and said, "Give me a piece of paper."

Nick had been watching her, seeing the many different expressions cross her face, and his heart expanded with love. He would know her in any time, any place, as his beloved. He felt blessed that she was so lovely, intelligent, courageous with the most capacity for love that he had ever imagined. He wished in his heart that he had the means to treat her as a queen, as was her right. This was a woman of incredible faith in love and deserved the best life could offer. An angel who had come back into his life to remind him that joy was also his birthright.

He reached for his journal. Withdrawing a blank page, he handed it to her. "Shall I get the quill?"

She shook her head and smiled as she held the paper in her hand. "I don't need this written, you already know it."

He watched as she placed the paper on her lap and, using her finger, pretended to be writing. . . .

"I love you now," she whispered as her nail traced the letters. "I love you forever."

He smiled, seeing her pleasure and she began folding the paper. "Infinity," he whispered.

"Now, watch," she said, as she continued to fold the paper into more angles.

"What are you making?" he asked, fighting the desire to pull her back into his arms. He had never wanted to touch a woman more, to feel the texture of her skin, the scent of her hair, the warmth of her body. But it was more, he knew . . . It was the connection they had made beyond the physical senses. It was the reconnection with eternal love.

"You'll see," she stated, and giggled as she concentrated on her folds.

When she finished, Nick saw that she was holding something that looked like a bird, something with wings. "What is it?"

She turned to look at him and his heart expanded with awe. What he saw reflected back to him took his breath.

"It's an airplane," she said, looking very pleased with herself. "A paper airplane."

"An air plane?" he asked, confused, yet chuckling at her excitement.

"Yes, this is just a model, a poor model, of the one I flew in for seven hours to reach England. Now, watch this." She tugged on his sleeve and spoke to his heart.

"We are bound together now . . ." And she pulled back her arm and flung the paper model out into the air.

He watched in fascination, as she whispered, "And wherever we land."

He sat in awe as the wind caught the paper and took it higher, only to dip and glide above the tall grass. It was magnificent! "How is that done?"

"I didn't really do it, Nick," she said, giggling at his pleasure and hugging his arm between her breasts. "The material was already here. I just applied a bit of ingenuity and energy to it to allow it to soar. That's us," she proclaimed with a nod. "Out there . . . soaring."

"We've just landed," he said with jolt of disappointment as he watched the model crash into the earth.

"Well that does happen, love." Maggie put her head on his shoulder.

He felt something stab his chest, as though when he saw the paper crash it had stabbed him in the heart. It was foolish, he reminded himself, lowering his head and inhaling the scent of the wondrous woman who clung to him. He was experiencing Heaven on earth right then and refused to allow an invasion of worry.

"Thou art the most remarkable human being I have ever met," he said with sincerity.

She chuckled. "I'm not remarkable, Nick. Far from it. I can't explain why that paper plane flew. I don't have the technical knowledge about thrust and Newtonian physics. I just know it does. Your friend Francis would probably be able to figure it out. Now, there's a remarkable person."

"Thou art remarkable to me, Maggie Whitaker," he said, studying her lips. "And I love thee with my life. I shall honor thee always, in everything I do." He didn't know if she truly understood the depth of his love. "One day I shall write a sonnet about it," he whispered.

"You already have," she said in a low voice. "I just read it."

"It is understood? We are one."

"Yes, Nicholas Layton. I don't need a wedding or some official to pronounce it legal in the eyes of God.

I have never felt more in the eyes of God than in this moment, and I vow to be your beloved forever. I want no other mate.''

He felt his eyes filling with emotion and tried to swallow it down. "I am filled with gratitude, and I, too, vow to want no other. I have always loved thee, I love thee still, I always will, my precious one.''

"Then let's spit on it,'' she said, holding out her hand and grinning.

He laughed at her antics. She wanted a ritual after all. "Spit on it?''

"Yes. You know, to seal the deal.'' Her almost childish delight was precious.

Nodding, Nick held out his palm and barely spit.

Maggie followed suit.

"Wherever, however, forever,'' she whispered with all seriousness.

How he adored her. "Wherever, however, forever,'' he repeated, and shook her hand.

They grinned at each other and then sealed their deal, and their fates.

"You may think of me as your husband, madam. And as soon as we get to London, I shall place a ring upon your finger so all others may know.''

She pumped his hand again. "Deal. You may think of me as your wife, sir. And if you lend me some money until I figure out how to earn some of my own, I shall buy you an identical gold band so all these unmarried ladies don't swoon over you and make plans to marry you.''

He threw back his head and laughed. How precious she was! Picking up the piece of cloth that had wrapped their repast, he chuckled, and said, "Here, give me your hand,'' and wiped hers with it. "My angel has a spark of jealousy, hmm?''

She took the cloth and wiped her other hand with it,

then playfully threw the cloth to his chest. "Do not even attempt to tell me you were not aware that Lady Marjorie was all but throwing herself into your lap at that betrothal dinner!"

"I had eyes for none but thee, wife." He laughed as he wiped his own hands.

"Hmm . . ." Maggie said, and looked at him slyly. "Well, I can't blame her for trying, but it would be very nice to have a ring on your finger that stated you are committed."

"Anyone who sees me knows, Maggie. Even Robert was most suspicious. I cannot hide this love, nor will I ever try." It was the truth. He no more knew how to conceal what he was feeling than to fly in one of her airplanes.

"Let me retrieve your model. I want you to show me how it's done," he said, standing.

She stood with him and wrapped her arms around his shoulders. "Okay, you can play for a few minutes. You go get the plane, and I'll clean up our mess here." She kissed his chin. "Don't want to piss off the Druids, ya know?"

He joined her laughter. "This has been the most delightful interlude, my love. I shall treasure the memory. But thou art correct; we have stayed here longer than I thought we would."

She placed both hands to his face, each palm resting upon one of his cheeks. "Thank you, thank you, thank you, Nicholas Layton. It has been a magical time. I feel . . . healed somehow."

Her eyes seemed to pull him inside of her, illuminating her soul, and he was stunned by the brilliance of what he saw. It was the future! He could see himself, staring into her frightened eyes, and he was so shocked he immediately blinked to stop it. "Thou art my trea-

sure," he whispered, smiling. "I'll get thy creation and
we shall fly it for Francis."

"Or, you can stay right here. I can make another,"
she stated, smiling at him with a very challenging smile.

"Are you flirting with me, my luscious, unpredictable
wife?" he asked in a voice that could not hide his pleasure. He pulled her closer and her breasts crushed
against him.

Her beautiful eyes widened, and her brows arched in
feigned innocence. "Why, my lord Nicholas," she cried
with a coy smile and pushed away from him, only to
surprise him by bowing before him and adding, "If I
have startled you, I beg your forgiveness. I am but a
mere woman who is learning *precedence, preferment,
and attainder.* I can only—"

"You shall pay for this, Maggie Whitaker," he interrupted with a laugh, immediately reminded of the night
in her chamber when they had not just clashed wills but
began to recognize each other.

"Is my back erect?" she muttered without looking
up.

Laughing, he said, "Oh, rise."

"I'm practicing. Gotta get used to the customs of this
place if I'm gonna fit in."

He held out his hand and waited for her to look up.
Moments passed, and when she finally raised her head
and looked at him, Nick found his breath caught in the
back of his throat. She looked so *happy*!

"I love you," he whispered, as she placed her hand
in his.

"That's why I'm thanking you. You're some angel,
Nickie." She must have seen how startled he was, for
she quickly added, "Now go play with the airplane for
a few moments. We have a future to ride into . . . places
to see, angels to meet, history to write . . . whatever. I'm
ready."

"Aye, m'lady time traveler." With a kiss on her adorable nose, he left her and headed for the model lying in the tall grass. As his boots crushed the thin stems, he smiled to himself and thought how Francis was going to fall in love with his wife. What a fortunate man he was to have fallen for the woman who had shown him that once his eyes were opened, angels really did exist and they appeared in their own form, which is the human form. He looked forward to speaking with Francis on this weighty philosophical subject. He had so much to look forward to now . . . life with his beloved.

As he bent down to pick up the paper model, he resolved also to focus more on his writing. He knew through Francis that theatrical performances were profitable. He was learning his craft from a master and now he had the inspiration, his own muse. How much more fortunate can a writer be, to be married to his muse? He had only to live with the woman to receive inspiring information. He heard Francis's voice in his head, reminding him over and over . . . *A message is accepted more readily in entertainments than anywhere else. We communicate with words. Use the words and the truth will be recognized.*

Holding the airplane in his hands, he thought . . . *I shall write our story of angels. Some will hear my message, and I shall provide for my lady with every—*

His thoughts immediately ceased as he felt an imperceptible rumbling beneath his feet. Looking up to the crest of the hill, he saw three riders, and immediately his heart began racing.

"Maggie!" He shouted her name and watched as she dropped his journal back onto the stone where they had been sitting. Running back, he yelled, "Get to the horses!"

She seemed stunned and didn't move as she stared at him with frightened eyes.

"Mount up," he yelled, yet she was still staring at him with horror upon her face.

Her hands reached out to him, grasping, as though he were fading before her eyes!

"Nick! Hurry!" she yelled, looking terrified.

His heart clenched in fear.

Chapter Sixteen

Elthea sat at her writing table, checking over her list of chores for the coming festivities. "Give this to Will, Gwen, and then make certain Lady Margaret's chamber is aired."

The woman accepted the paper and curtsied. "Yes, m'lady."

Elthea heard the knock on her door and absently said to Gwen, "Please admit whoever that is and then inform Will of my desires for the betrothal feast."

Gwen turned and quickly went to answer the knock. Elthea tried to center her thoughts on the feast and not grant allowance to the persistent shadow of gloom that was broiling in her belly. Worry most certainly never alleviated a concern, and yet she could not deny what she felt.

"M'lady?"

She turned from her writing table and saw Evan standing before her. Immediately, her heart lightened with his presence . . . then she saw his expression. "What troubles thee, Evan?"

Her dear childhood friend and confidante seemed most distressed.

"The courier thou hast sent to find Lady Margaret has returned. Thy cousin is en route and will be arriving within hours."

"Thank heavens Maggie and Nicholas have left for London," Elthea announced, and then her instincts kicked back in and demanded her attention. "There is more? Something is troubling thee."

Evan seemed reluctant to speak.

"Tell me."

"The courier saw three of Lord Amesbury's men traveling toward London at great speed. One was Montague."

Elthea immediately rose and clutched her stomach as fear raced through her body. Montague was Robert's henchman, a soul without principles who felt no remorse at killing another, especially if ordered by his lord, her son . . . Robert.

"If there is more information, I need to know everything."

"Only that I questioned the boys in the stables and they reported that Montague and the others were heavily armed. I fear this is not mere chance. Grave circumstances may lie ahead, m'lady."

Elthea came forward and grabbed Evan's arm. "What has my son done?" she asked, as she pictured Maggie and Nick, unarmed, alone against such a force of violence.

Evan gently placed his hand upon Elthea's and held it tenderly. "M'lady . . . I will support thee in whatever you desire."

Elthea smiled briefly and nodded, then turned and began pacing her room. "I must confront Robert and see if I can untangle his machinations, whatever they may be. I cannot allow those innocents to come into harm's way." She stopped pacing and faced the steward, who was far more than a household servant to her. "That is it. I shall confront my son. I see no other option until I find out the facts."

Evan nodded. "I implore thee to exert caution,

m'lady. Thy son . . ." His words trailed off.

"Aye . . . he is my son, and I am well aware of his distorted perception of truth. I shall be cautious, dearest friend." Elthea hurried to the door and flung it open.

She raced through the large house, passing servants without acknowledgment, until she came upon Robert's inner chamber and house of office. She tried not to imagine any impending disaster, not to give it power, yet her heart was racing, and her belly was twisted in knots of fear. She didn't even knock.

He was sitting in a chair before the large arched window, his legs crossed and resting upon the stone sill. Holding a goblet in his hand, he stared through the glass as though lost in his thoughts.

"You disappoint me, Mother. It took you longer than I thought to discover I, too, have 'eyes' in *my* home."

"What have you done, Robert?" Her mind seemed like a swirling pool, and one thought seemed to emerge.

"*Gwen!*" she blurted out with the sudden knowledge. The young woman had been playing both sides of the fence.

He didn't answer, nor did he move a muscle.

Standing behind him, she repeated, "What have you done?"

"The golden angel creates miracles, no?" he asked. "From the right person, ten shillings can buy anything, even devotion."

In her mind's eye, she could see him smiling. "You are master of that, my son," she answered with sadness. "Upon what mission have you sent Montague?"

Robert sipped his wine and slowly said, "Why, to retrieve my honor, my lady mother. I sacrificed the pleasure of watching it extracted from Layton's body, for this very meeting with thee . . . *Mother.*"

She felt a stab of fear in her back, as though someone had taken a knife and thrust it into her spine. Attempting to stay calm, Elthea called upon every force of light in the universe to come to her aid. Lives rested upon the outcome of this encounter. "You have sent your henchman, Montague, on a mission of death?"

He spun around so quickly Elthea was startled, yet held her composure as she faced her son. Her heart tightened with a mixture of fear and sadness as she awaited his reply.

"Why do you fight me so?" he demanded, his face distorted with anger. "I shall never see the world through your eyes. Mine are opened to what must be accomplished in order that our ways be restored. My mother deceives me and aids others in *my home* to disrespect me. Am I to allow my betrothed to shame me before my house and to run away with a spineless troubadour who is also my political enemy?"

"Have you ordered Montague to kill Nicholas Layton?" she demanded, no longer afraid. She stepped closer to her son, and said as calmly as possible, "Have you shamed *my* home with such a blatant act of desperation?"

They stared into each other's eyes, and Elthea felt the force of Robert's challenge. Perhaps such a meeting was destined, as mother and son faced somber matters.

"I am the Lord of Amesbury. This is my home, and you have disgraced it by abetting mine enemies."

"Robert, Nicholas is not your enemy for this woman's affections. Love cannot be dictated," she said, trying to break beyond his wall of anger.

"Love!" Robert scoffed and shook his head as he turned back to the window. "Do not deceive yourself now, Mother, by entertaining thoughts I might have loved the woman. She was but gold and silver to me, a means to victory. Love is a myth. Women refuse to see it as such." He paused for a moment. "Did you, Countess Elthea, love my father?"

"Yes, Robert, I did," she whispered. "Though the love I shared with your father was not the love shared by Nicholas and this woman, I did. Love is real, my son, and in the name of love I ask again, have you sent Montague on a mission of death?"

"Surely you do not think I would answer that query and indict myself? My honor shall be renewed and one more political spider . . . spinning its own web shall be swept away. That is all you need know."

Elthea felt the wounding of his words. "You have taken much upon your shoulders, my son," she said with deep sadness. "This action shall ever alter you, and you shall surely see it revisited, for that is the way of the world. I pity thee."

He turned from the peaceful view. "Pity me? Pity thyself, dear mother, for I am considering a nunnery for thee!"

She inhaled with shock and recovered blessedly quickly. "This is my home, Robert of Amesbury, son of my womb, who would not be breathing God's good air had I not given thee life. Beware your words, for they shall resound throughout the universe and already you have a large debt to pay in the balance. Your church in Rome with its nunneries is not welcomed in this land, nor in my heart. 'Tis a delicate game you play, my son, aligning with the darkness when it is so desperate to keep its power that murder is condoned." She paused. "Never forget, your own end may be in its future, for there is no leash on this mad dog now."

"You speak in riddles, trying to disguise your deceit. You work against me, in my home, in my political ambitions, in my duty to my God . . . who has been cast down by heretics intent on destroying his one true church!"

"Robert," she pleaded, wishing with all her heart he would hear her. "You are fighting a natural law from which you have no defense. Time. Change. The forward-thrusting movement of all things. Do you actually think there is one true church? One chosen people? Is it not the same arrogance, cloaked in a different robe? Are not wars fought with those issues held on banners? And all with such . . . such a desperation to be proved correct? To believe *they* are the only beloved of God and no other? Do you worship such a jealous God of war?" She paused for only a moment to catch her breath. "Is that why you have ordered someone's murder?"

"Thou art a woman," he almost growled. "You know not of such things which grip a man's heart. I am living in a country where a *virgin* whore sits upon the throne, whose father committed murder time over to achieve his end by divorcing himself and his people from my God. I will see another ruling this country, one who will listen to reason. And not one of her bastards!"

"Reason? Do not speak to me of it, nor that I am but a woman," she said in a controlled voice. "Heavens above I have my wits about me or I wouldn't possess my sanity, surrounded by men who are blind. It is no wonder Elizabeth remains unbound by a man. His terrified mind alone would drive one to proclaim herself again virgin! You, Robert of Amesbury," she said, pointing her finger, "are living in an illusion that you can turn back time for it is where you feel safe . . . in the past. Time is always moving, like wind across a pond creating ripples. The Roman Church will never regain its dark hold in this country. Minds, thoughts, have expanded, like a bladder of wine . . . once expanded it can never shrink back in size. I pray that the day will come when all are free to choose to worship the One by following their own heart."

"Thou *art* a witch," he pronounced with a snarl. "I have overlooked your rhetoric in the past, but now you have declared thyself. Beware, mother. For I—"

She held up her hand and interrupted, "I have no need to know what you might do to me. You cannot make my mind a prisoner. I thank the heavens the Inquisition is over in this country and a renaissance of thought is emerging. And that is your fear, my son. Thoughts are not being controlled any longer by Rome. Queries are being made. Answers sought. Freedom should not bring you such terror."

Robert slammed his fist against the stone wall. "I will not speak on this any longer." He turned toward her quickly changing his tone. "Know that should we receive any . . . news of an unfortunate nature, I fully expect you to do what is in the best interest of your lawful, *rightful* heir."

"What is this you speak of now?" Elthea demanded. "Already you have taken ownership of my home. What else do you expect? My jewels, my garments? Take it all, Robert. I care not any longer." She was fighting tears, her throat burned, and she had to remind herself such emotion would not serve now.

His laugh wounded deeper than she thought possible. "Keep thy possessions. I am speaking of our dear cousin and her . . . her value. As her closest relatives, we would inherit."

"Are you mad? You are speaking of killing Lady Margaret!" A wave of dizziness washed over her, and she held on to a nearby table to regain her balance.

"I am only saying should the opportunity arise, that our dear cousin's estate is passed on to us, I shall expect—"

"Your greedy expectations affirm thy madness," she interrupted. "You are absolutely unaware . . . you have not a clue, have you?" She paused, shaking her head in disbelief. "The woman with Nicholas Layton is not my cousin. The true Lady Norreys of Rycote arrives this day, with a full entourage."

"Now thou art speaking madness," Robert stated. "She left this very morn with Layton on horseback. Montague reported it, along with others. I will not—"

"You *will* listen," she again arrested his words. "The woman with Nicholas is not my cousin Margaret. Granted, I too believed for a short while Lady Margaret met some grave misfortune and arrived under dire conditions. Yet, the woman did not proclaim herself to be my cousin. She bore a remarkable resemblance, enough that I thought her delirious and sedated her to rest. Before she awakened, and I could question her, you had returned from a hunting party, boasting to all your betrothed had arrived and it was to save you, my son, the debacle of feasting a stranger as your future wife, that I implored the woman to play your betrothed for one night."

Robert ran his hand through his hair. His eyes were wide with bewilderment. "What are you implying? This woman in our house was an impostor?"

"Aye, Robert. 'Twas a deceit necessitated by your own selfish ambition. Your betrothed is very much alive and beloved by Her Royal Majesty, Elizabeth. Should Margaret decide to proceed with the marriage, know that I shall watch over my cousin and her *value* with my life."

"Do not blame the miscarriage of your own deception entirely on me, Mother," Robert interjected. "Evidently, you are as much to blame for the events which are taking place . . . even as we speak. Such treachery is punishable by—"

"How far does this God of war you worship demand that you go . . . far enough to condone murdering the woman who gave you life? Ask thyself which master you serve, my son."

Her last words hung in the room, like stale air, as they continued to stare at each other.

"You will not kill me, Robert," she finally whispered. "Already your crimes are too many to hide. I would suggest, my son, you call back your men posthaste before you see yourself in the Tower, or worse, without your own head."

Robert said nothing for a prolonged few minutes. Finally, he sank back into his chair and, looking out the window, muttered, "It is too late. Montague left shortly after them. What has been put in motion cannot be altered."

The silence in the room was charged with meaning.

"Then God help them," Elthea said with great shock and sorrow as she forced herself to walk toward the door. "And God help thee, Robert, for thou shall most certainly reap the harvest of what thou hast sown this day."

"There is a greater cause," Robert stated in a sullen voice.

Elthea turned back to look at him. "Yes, there is," she said quietly. "There is no greater cause than the light of truth. I pray, my son, one day you find it."

It took every shred of strength to keep walking, and Elthea focused her attention on each breath, each step, as she made her way through her home. Home . . . suddenly the stone halls were no longer welcoming. They had taken on the deep shadows of her son and she wanted to order water-bowled candles lit in every chamber, every hall, every stairwell and fling open the windows to allow air, light, earth, water for cleansing. Somehow, her heart was telling her it was not her place any longer to keep the energy of this home. Robert had placed his mark this day upon it with his dark deeds. No quantity of candles could burn away his actions.

"M'lady, Will requests thy presence." Gwen curtsied quickly before Elthea.

Stopping, she looked at the young woman, wondering

if she should dismiss the servant who had betrayed her and aided her son in an unforgivable crime. Elthea's mind filled with the image of Gwen's mother in the village and her lame brother. Suddenly the fatigue deepened, and she nodded before saying, "I shall see him later."

She walked past the woman. It was Gwen's choice to ally with darkness, and she was too weary to confront this issue at the moment. She must get to her chamber as quickly as possible and collect her senses. As though her wishes were now to be tested, several others stopped her on her path, seeking attention. Each one she postponed, determined to reach her destination. When her hand raised the latch on her chamber door, Elthea almost cried out with thankfulness.

Opening the door, she stood for a moment staring at the large room where she had lived for most of her life. She saw her mother's furniture, the tapestry on the wall her grandmother had created . . . all the memories . . . of birth, love, work, learning, contemplation. What once held such memories now felt foreign. Suddenly, she saw she had been in a nunnery, one of her own choosing.

"M'lady . . . ?"

Startled, Elthea spun around to see Evan, holding a tray. She moved aside and allowed him entrance before closing the door. Neither said a word as the steward placed the tray on the writing table and Elthea sat in a chair by the window. Looking out to the countryside, she sighed deeply, wanting to abort the flow of tears that demanded release. Helpless to suppress them, she allowed the cleansing as her thoughts took her to two journeyers of life who were fulfilling their purpose. She could not understand what purpose such an injustice would serve, yet she knew that in the grand tapestry of life it was an integral thread. Her heart went out to Mag-

gie and Nicholas, thrusting her strongest wish that somehow their love survive this madness.

She sensed Evan at her side, and whispered, "Montague is on a mission of death."

She heard his intake of breath and reached out her
hand. He clasped it between his, and when she turned
to look up at him sorrow was reflected in his eyes.

"I grieve with thee, my friend," he said in a voice
filling with emotion.

"Oh, Evan . . . whatever shall I do? I cannot stop this
madness of Robert's. Two innocents . . ." Tears rolled
down her cheeks, and Elthea pulled a silk scarf from the
table to wipe them away.

Without word, Evan came closer and wrapped his
arms around her shoulders and head, pulling her into his
body and allowing her to weep. She clung to him, sobbing for the loss, for the senselessness of it all and the
pain it would cause. She had participated in a great story
of love, of twin flames uniting. And she had also participated in the deception. If she had only gone to Robert, sent word while he was on his hunting trip that
something was amiss with her cousin . . . anything to
have prevented *this*! She pushed away from Evan.

"Oh, what good does this?" she asked, though not
expecting a reply. Wiping her face, she shook her head.
"Weeping shall not be of assistance."

"Grieving can be of assistance. It's all in the balance
of things," Evan said kindly, pouring her a goblet of
wine.

She accepted the silver goblet with the Amesbury coat
of arms engraved upon it. Staring at it, she said, "I shall
grieve at a later time when it has all played out. Now I
must gather my wits to be of assistance to those whose
lives are endangered."

"What can you do?" Evan asked, sitting on a stool
beside her.

Sighing, Elthea laid her head against his shoulder, and said, "I can only send my prayers that their love survives this challenge."

Above her, she heard him say with regret, "I should have seen that Master Layton had protection, a sword at the very least!"

She shook her head. "We can both blame ourselves, and that won't serve the moment." Handing him the goblet, she said, "Drink."

He pulled back. "M'lady!"

"Oh, Evan . . . do not look so affronted." Wiping at her nose, she added, "We have shared baths as babes and tutors as children. We swam in the River Avon together and hunted imaginary dragons in the woods. Not to mention that thou hast been my confidant, my mentor in many ways, my lover for more years than I care to remember at the moment." She pushed the goblet toward him. "Surely, drinking from my cup will not shock thee now."

He smiled tenderly into her eyes. "As you wish, m'love," he answered, taking the goblet into his hands. "Though I do wish you to recall that neither you nor I chose our stations in this life. And it wasn't until you were a widow that I permitted my love to show. I honored thy marriage."

She nodded. "Drink. We both need to be fortified for the thoughts that are swirling through my mind."

Evan drank deeply and held the goblet in his hands. "What are thy thoughts, Elthea?"

"This is going to sound mad to you," she began as she looked back out the window. "Though since we are operating in a house of madness now, 'tis no surprise such a notion comes to my mind."

"Elthea . . . ?"

She heard the plea in his voice to just state it, and so she did, allowing it out there and giving it more power.

"I wish to leave Greville Manor. 'Tis my home no longer."

"Where shall you go? How shall you live?" Evan sounded concerned but not incredulous.

"How long before my cousin arrives?"

"At least two hours more of traveling."

She looked at him and knew that her eyes were wide with the magnitude of what she was considering. "I shall leave here posthaste and meet Lady Margaret in transit. I am my cousin's only family, or she would not have agreed to marry my son. I cannot allow her to make that decision without full disclosure of this situation. Should she decide to abort the betrothal, I shall ask to be her companion. I can no longer live in this house."

Once she had said it aloud, she heard the truth in her words. This was not her home.

"Think of it, Evan," she continued. "We shall be wanderers. Explorers . . ." She stopped. "Unless you wish not to accompany me. Thou art the steward of this house."

He reached out and cupped her chin. "Dear lady, I was but a child when I knew my true purpose was steward of thy heart. Have we not agreed long ago that wherever you go, I shall follow?"

In spite of her tears, she smiled into his eyes. "Thank you for your trust. Perhaps it is time for us to leave everything behind and have our own adventure."

"Thou shalt leave everything?" the steward in Evan needed to know.

"Oh, no . . . not everything. I shall not come to my cousin in need. We shall gather my jewels and a few sentimental belongings. The rest Robert is welcome to, for I shall only take one carriage when I leave." Elthea reached out and clutched Evan's hand.

"Do not allow anyone to assist us. No one is to be trusted. Gwen has betrayed us, and I no longer wish to rely on others. When I have gathered my things here, and the carriage is waiting, then I shall call the servants to carry everything down. I am determined to leave without another scene with my son.''

She sniffled and again wiped her nose with the tip of her scarf. ''We have said all that needs to be spoken aloud. I shall write him of my plans and leave it here.''

Elthea rose, feeling drained . . . very old and weary. She knew she couldn't allow this fatigue any more power over her now. She had to summon her strength, she thought, as Evan rose with her.

''I shall do as ye wish.''

''Then it is done,'' Elthea said, looking around her chamber and feeling the memories wash over her. ''We shall leave as quickly as possible and join my cousin.'' Once that decision was made, she felt a measure of relief . . . but only briefly as her thoughts returned to the two souls most in need of strength.

She looked out the window and covered her eyes as the tears returned.

''Elthea . . .'' he whispered as he came behind her and held her in his arms. '' 'Tis a decision of great import. To leave thy family home and—''

She shook her head. ''I am thinking of Maggie and Nicholas, and my heart is breaking at this injustice my son has set into motion. If I could but fly like one of Robert's falcons, I would warn them, but I am too dense for flight and thus only my prayers may reach them now.''

She stared into the sky, beyond the clouds to the space beyond, and sent out her intent. ''Robert is my son and my blood runs in his veins as surely as his father's. I have loved him since I carried him in my womb, but I swear, Evan, by all that I hold true, one day the scales will be balanced. I shall make restitution and do everything in my power to see the love of these twin flames is never extinguished.''

She clutched his hand at her shoulder. ''Of this, I vow!''

Evan blew his breath out in a long sigh as he realized the intent of her words. ''And I shall assist thee, my lady, my love . . . in any time to balance those scales. As I have always done.''

She leaned back against his chest and knew she had written it in the universe.

So mote it be.

Chapter Seventeen

"I... I thought you were disappearing! Everything seemed to be breaking up again into light!" she cried, clutching his hands as he shoved the airplane into them.

"Maggie, we must hurry. Get on your horse!" he commanded, pulling her toward the animals. "We are alone no longer." He looked to the riders and knew he didn't have the time to explain.

"Who are they?" She immediately went into action, and he watched her stuff the airplane down the front of her bodice as she hurried to the horses.

"They could be anyone, though my guess is Robert of Amesbury is not pleased."

"Oh, shit . . ." she muttered in fright, as he assisted her in mounting. "Honey, I'm so sorry for getting you into this."

"Nonsense. We are in this together," he muttered, mounting his horse. "Now ride!"

They raced across the tall grass, away from the huge stones, away from the magic they had found there. He saw she was having trouble keeping up with him, and he slowed the horse to stay at her side, yet saw that the riders were gaining. His heart contracted with fear when he recognized one. Montague.

No longer could he think with fear. Now was the time for clear actions. "Keep riding, Maggie! It's Montague," he yelled to her. "There's the road. Follow it. Don't stop until you reach the village of Aideine!"

She nodded, urging her horse into a deeper gallop. He knew she was frightened of Montague, yet he also knew she would do whatever it took to outrun them. He saw she was focused and, for her, nothing would detract from their escaping.

Nick dropped back and allowed her to ride ahead, while slowly bringing his horse to a stop. With one last loving look to his beloved, he turned the horse and faced the approaching riders.

Think clearly, his mind commanded. He had been trained by the best tutors in fencing and logic. Suddenly a plan came into his head, and he whispered to Goliath, "If ever I needed you, my friend, it is now."

Nick lifted his foot from the stirrup, as though to dismount. Gripping the saddle gullet firmly, he swung his right leg over the animal's back and, locking his knee into the cantle, he gave a quick and silent command to lunge forward. The faithful steed bolted.

Balancing himself upright, supporting himself in just the left stirrup, he charged the first of Amesbury's henchmen yards away. He allowed his body to move in heaving rhythm to the gallop, while leaning over his saddle and grabbing the leather fender to the right stirrup.

Pulling it up, he was sure the forged steel at the end would be weight enough.

With steady aim, he swung hard.

The blow of the makeshift mace whacked the man's forehead and sent him crashing to the ground. Nick jumped from his horse to the side of the unconscious man. Seizing his advantage, he picked up the man's sword and turned to the other. In the distance he heard the third rider hurry after Maggie. Hopefully, he had bought her enough time to reach the road.

He stood ready, challenging his opponent to single combat.

Montague dismounted in assured movement. He slapped the flank of his horse to move out of the way. Slowly, Amesbury's man withdrew his heavy sword and walked with confidence toward Nick.

No words were spoken, nor needed, as the two men filled the air with the clashing of wills and the clanging of metal.

Nick knew he was in a fight for his life and Maggie's.

Maggie was riding furiously toward the road. Sure Nick was right behind her, she dared not look back. Just get to the road. Follow it to the village. That was all she knew as she raced away from Robert's men. Montague! Never in her life had she been so terrified by human beings and the horror they could create. She reached the road and slowed to make the turn when a hand reached over and grabbed her reins.

Her mind refused to accept what her eyes were revealing. It was not Nick, but a huge man who looked at her with evil in his eyes. He slowed both horses and turned them around. "Please," she begged, gasping for breath. "Just . . . just let me go back to Nick."

The man didn't answer her and the blood raced wildly with fear through her veins. Her heart was pounding from the exertion as she looked back to find Nick. Farther off in the field, she could see he was engaged in a sword fight.

It was her fault. She had delayed them at Stonehenge. She couldn't ride well enough to keep up with him, slowing them down. "Oh, Nick . . ." she whimpered, fighting tears. "What have I done to us?"

Determined to help the man she loved, she fought for

possession of her reins. She would *not* abandon Nick now. Not ever!

The man slapped her so hard on her face that her knees instinctively jerked and her nervous horse bolted into a run. Stunned, she grabbed the saddle for balance as the man was jerked off his horse and, still holding her reins, was dragged beside her.

She kicked at the struggling man and immediately felt the weight leave as the reins were freed from the burden. Scrambling to grab them again, Maggie cried out in fear as she raced back toward Nick.

She saw Nick retreating, backing up to a tree and then with the grace of a ballet dancer, intricately avoid a thrust. In spite of her terror, she had to admire his skill, yet something in her was pleading as she galloped to the fighting men.

Her mind was screaming *be careful, my love*, yet her voice was mute with dread.

Speeding past a man, his face covered in blood, Maggie noticed he struggled to his feet. She gasped when she saw from the corner of her eye that the man had pulled a dagger from his waist and was running toward Nick's back.

"Nooooo!" . . . she screamed and pulled hard on the reins, so hard she almost fell.

Nick spun around at the sound of her voice and, seeing the assassin, ran him through with his sword. Maggie was so stunned, having never seen death before, she could only stare in horror as the man fell to the ground. Montague ran over and grabbed her horse's halter.

"What say thee now, Layton? The decision is yours," Montague breathed out, while holding his sword up to Maggie's chest.

She stared at the man, at Nick . . . and then saw the one who had caught her speeding back on his horse. They were outnumbered with weapons and as the second man slowed to dismount, she watched as Nick's shoulders slumped.

Dropping his sword to the ground, he said, "It is over."

She knew he was doing this for her, and her heart constricted with pain. But they were alive, and that's all that mattered. Somehow they would go back and talk to Robert and—

All thoughts ceased as she watched the man who had hit her exchange places with Montague, who was now walking back to Nick.

"Not quite over, Layton," the man sneered as he kicked the sword Nick had been using out of the way. "Lord Robert of Amesbury and all those who support his cause have a final message for you . . ."

Maggie looked at Nick. Across the space she saw a puzzled expression on his face, moments before Montague lunged forward and drove his sword right through the center of him. There was a mixture of horror and disbelief on his face, and Maggie was sure that time stood still as her mind refused to accept what she had just seen. . . .

His gaze never left hers as his knees buckled with the withdrawal of the sword. He fell hard to the ground, swaying on his knees, holding his chest as blood seeped through his fingers.

Maggie leaped from her horse and ran to him. She didn't care if they killed her. She had to get to him! Running, she stared into his eyes and saw something she refused to accept. As though his weight now was too much to wait for her, he fell forward into the tall summer grass. She whimpered in denial as she dropped to her knees and gently turned him over.

This nightmare cannot be real! It just can't . . .

"Nick!"

He opened his eyes and looked up to her. Even though

he was still alive, her entire world was stopped by what she saw in his gaze.

"Sweet Maggie . . ." he gasped, as she cradled his shoulders and head in her arms. "Please accept my apology, I'm so . . . sorry . . . the ethereal calls."

She watched his lids slowly close as he dryly swallowed down his pain.

"Nick . . . !" She shook his shoulders to stop him from going. "Nick, no . . . no, no . . . stay here," she encouraged through her tears. She looked to the man holding her horse and screamed, "Get some help! He needs help!"

Montague came forward and took her arm, dragging her away.

"Leave him . . . he is well killed."

She stared at the man and broke free of his grasp. "He dropped his weapon! We surrendered . . ." she whispered, cradling her beloved again in her arms. Clinging to him, she urged, "Nick . . . you promised. Come on. Stay with me. Don't go . . ."

He gasped and opened his eyes.

Gazing down into his beautiful, incredible blue eyes she could barely hear his whisper. *"Remember me . . . my love."*

"Nick! *No*! You can't die . . . you're my twin soul. I just found you," she pleaded through her sobs.

Nothing existed for her in the moment, but the love she saw reflected back to her . . . It was a timeless instant of recognition beyond the physical, as though they had always been a part of each other and always would. She broke free of it and refused to accept what was happening.

"Nick! *You promised!*" she screamed in desperation. "We spit on it! You and me, husband and wife . . . we have plans, our adventure! You can't go now!"

Her brain fought off the inevitable as she gasped, the

sobs cutting so deep within her soul that she too felt mortally wounded. A feeling of impending doom seemed to wrap itself around her and strangle her.

"Remember me . . . remember . . . re . . . member . . ."

Rocking him slowly, she watched the light slowly fade from his eyes. She felt his warm body go limp as his breath was expelled with his last word. How was it possible to know such fulfillment of love and hope only a short time ago and in an instant of cruelty, feel such indescribable loss? She continued to rock him as the memories of joy seemed to disappear and she was engulfed in agony. She felt saturated in grief, as she watched the light of life extinguished from the windows to his soul.

He was gone.

And she was alone.

Slowly, reverently, she laid his precious head back in the tall summer grass and rose to her feet. Her body was shaking, and she stumbled away, putting distance between herself and the horror . . . *horror* she had witnessed. Tears were streaming uncontrollably down her face and blocking her vision. She clutched at her skirt, making fists of material. Her mouth opened, and the depth of her anguish seemed to come from the very pits of hell as a wail of heartache and pain echoed out into the air and reverberated into the universe.

"*Noooooooooooo . . .*"

The sound of movement brought her back to the present, and she spun around to see a carriage and many horses traveling on the road. Instinct took over and she started waving her arms and screaming, "Stop! Help me! *Help!*"

Her legs started moving, faster and faster, all the while she was waving her arms. She heard the sound of Montague and his man cursing and mounting their horses, yet she kept running and yelling and pleading in her mind for the carriage to stop. She stumbled, slipping on the high grass, and felt her shoe leave her foot, yet she crawled upright and grabbed her skirt to continue. Nothing could stop her now. Her entire being was fused with one emotion.

Justice.

She saw the entourage slow down and three riders coming quickly across the field. Within moments they were upon her.

"They killed my husband!" she screamed, pointing at the retreating murderers.

The formally dressed men looked at her strangely, as though confused by something, and then immediately set off after Montague. Dazed, Maggie stumbled closer to a tree and sank against the trunk, sobbing, not caring any longer whether she lived or died.

Nick . . .

She couldn't get out of her mind the look in his eyes . . . the regret, the love, the acceptance . . . the void. Maggie knew if she allowed her mind to replay what she had just experienced, there would be no sanity left. Her precious husband . . . lying in the grass . . . dead . . . gone . . . He wasn't there. She was all alone.

She heard the snorting of horses and dragged her head up to focus upon the road. Just as she did, someone pulled back a ruby-velvet curtain on the window of the ornately decorated carriage.

Face-to-face, their eyes met in disbelief.

A woman with a sad expression stared at her as Maggie stared back in stupefaction. Her mind tried to wrap around what her eyes were revealing . . . a woman, older than she, yet looking so much like her that she couldn't breathe, or think, or see anything else.

Suddenly, as though she knew she was dying, Maggie watched as her vision began to fill with shadows, first around the edges then narrowing into a tunnel that closed everything out but the woman's face. Lady Margaret's face. Her face. It was all disintegrating, this time into darkness . . . and without Nick, she just surrendered her broken heart and her broken mind. It was the end, and she wanted to join him . . . wherever he was.

Chapter Eighteen

for a time nothing existed for her save warm, peaceful, beautiful darkness.

There was no sensation of wanting anything. There was no sensation at all, except of peace, of a weightless floating, though slowly, as though knowing she was now something, Maggie began to observe flashes of light forming in her mind. She didn't really want to focus on them, for she was content to just drift in a warm swirling sea of black-purple . . . nothing. The bursts began to alter into shapes, glimpses, designs of deep rose and dark blue light, catching her attention, calling her away from the peaceful warmth of nothingness. . . .

Annoyance was her first reaction but was quickly replaced by curiosity. Her mind seemed to be awakening more and more, and she focused her attention on the myriad colors and lines and then suddenly, from out of nowhere, a picture flashed for only a brief instant, shocking her farther away from the warm darkness.

Eyes. A man. A profile.

It took great effort, and she wanted to return to the peaceful darkness, yet again the pictures flashed before her, this time more quickly. A red dress with pearls. The smile on an older woman's face. A fur cover on a high bed. Intricate tapestries hanging on stone walls. Crying before a fireplace. She wanted to stop the confusion, yet sensed she was helpless as the images seemed to increase. A hand holding a two-tined long fork. A blanket of green wispy ferns, dotted with tiny white flowers. Pieces of a puzzle raced before her and demanded attention.

She had no sensation of breathing, not even the need, yet there was a desire now to connect the pieces.

Quickly they came, each one pulling her further toward something larger, an expansion. Walking in a maze. A black horse pawing the air in terror. A woman dressed in a long blue gown sitting at a banquet table. A naked man, smiling, and offering her a goblet of wine . . .

There. The man. Something about the man called out to her, yet before she could place him, more pictures assaulted her, flashes of movement showing riders on horses, swinging swords, and faces of horror. Hers. And his . . . the man, the one who held her so tenderly and made love to her with such passion that Maggie knew she had to save him, to do something to stop the images from continuing for she knew now she didn't want to see how it turned out. It wasn't a dream at all. She had been there, holding his head in her arms and . . . he . . .

She refused to think of it as sensations invaded and bombarded her. Pain. Grief. Anger. Fear. She couldn't get back to peaceful darkness now. She was lost in the illusion as a great weight descended upon her, crushing her, demanding that she breathe, and Maggie felt her chest heaving as she gulped in huge amounts of air.

"Nick!"

She didn't know if she said the name, or only thought it, but she knew now how the pieces fit together in the puzzle, and she didn't want to see it played out. Then other scenarios formed . . . being held in a warm, loving embrace, lying against a hard chest, hearing a heart beat and knowing that she was totally loved. Her fingers ever so slightly caressing a firm thigh and *feeling* a connection that reminded her of home, of belonging.

She breathed in the memory of pleasure and joy, and it was then that she knew him.

She called forth his face, wanting to see his blue eyes reflect back to her the love that was within her and, immediately, she felt her heart expand with exquisite intimacy that led her to experience a rapture of memories, all of it now filling her with such bliss that she didn't mind any longer leaving the darkness.

She allowed her mind to enter into moments of tenderness, communication, certainty, wonder, awe . . . and she began to hear something . . . music in the distance.

"You who are on the road must have a code that you can live by."

Again, she felt tiny flickers of annoyance, as though the noise was trying to pull her away from her joy. She wouldn't give it her attention, she resolved, focusing more intently upon moments of love. The more she tried to bring forth those images, the more difficult it seemed as the lyrics became momentarily clear.

"Teach your children well . . . "

The sound of the music grew along with something else that sounded like screams of approval, and Maggie tried to shut it out, to stop it, though she was losing control.

Like snippets of movies, the images flashed against the screen of her closed lids, each one jolting her with confusion. Malcolm, looking at himself in a mirror. Robert's hand on her thigh. Aunt Edithe hugging her when she'd cried. The little girl in the maze extending a rose. Racing through the forest. Robert standing in the doorway as she bathed. Nick throwing his cape onto the ferns. Evan holding the reins of a horse. Elthea holding out a pearl necklace.

From somewhere beyond herself, she experienced her

hand reaching up to her chest and finding the small pearls beneath her clothing. She had them!

Aunt Edithe's pearls.

Elthea's pearls.

Hers . . . Nick gave them to her . . . Nick . . . *Nick!*

She clutched the pearls and lost herself in his memory, drifting with the distant music as it ended and muffled appreciation followed. . . . Then it happened. A sudden jolt of separation.

The music rose in volume, increasing her fear of what she knew was coming. No longer could she suppress the memory of it. He was dead. She had seen it, the duel, the thrust of a sword into his chest, words, the dying vow to remember, the way the light left his eyes, and then she was alone.

"Wonders what's goin' on . . . down under?" Lyrics seemed to break through the crescendo of anguish and noise.

A great surge of turmoil rose up in her belly, demanding release, traveling up her chest into her throat and burning with such intense grief that she opened her mouth and screamed to let it out! A wail of sorrow filled her ears and she shot upright, staring wide-eyed into the gray darkness as her cry was absorbed into a calliope of sound.

"If I'd ever been here before, I would probably know just what to do, don't you . . . ?"

Stunned at the refrain, Maggie tried to make sense out of the madness surrounding her. As her ears continued to receive an assaulting barrage of chords, lyrics seemed to mix with a roar of screams. Her eyes adjusted to the new darkness, and she distinguished the shape of framing, pipes and beams of gray against the blackness. Her hands were on the earth, and she felt grass against her palms as she tried to push herself up, to stand and leave this place of utter confusion.

She felt her clothing. Velvet. She was still wearing the gown, she thought, using every ounce of willpower to push down panic and rise. Her head hit something before she could stand upright, and she fell back down to her knees. Swallowing a frightened sob, she lifted her hand to her head and then stretched it farther. Again, she slowly rose, gathering her skirts and attempting to stand. Moments before she could, she felt something hard above her vibrating with the intensity of noise.

" *We have all been here before* . . .

We have all been here before . . . "

Nothing made sense and, as she crouched, fighting the paralysis of panic, Maggie started pounding on the low ceiling. "Let me out! Help!" she screamed, hearing her voice get lost in the excruciating level of sound above her. Over and over she pounded, demanding release, then pleading and finally begging. Her fists felt raw and her voice hoarse as she sank back to her knees and collapsed against a box.

She couldn't think, not now, not yet . . . she had to block out the noise and pull herself together. Gasping for breath, she felt her throat begin to close with emotion as each intake of air was a struggle.

It was just like in the maze.

Everything started to close in on her, the hard framing, the strange boxes, the noise, the darkness, and she felt that same panic of claustrophobia return with a vengeance. It was as if she were buried alive!

"*We have all been here before* . . . "

Again she heard the refrain coming from above and something in the back of her brain was desperately trying to identify it. As the music ended and screams began, Maggie felt suspended in fear.

She sensed in every cell that she was losing control. Something inside of her snapped, and she began crawling, stumbling when her knees caught up in the long

skirt. Help. She needed help. Nick . . . Aunt Edithe . . .
God . . . Anyone. Banging headfirst into another beam,
she barely felt the pain as she clawed at the grass to
regain her balance.

The deafening music resumed, and Maggie again felt
the fear gain power. She couldn't breathe . . . *breathe*!
Basic human instinct, survival, jolted in her. She started
kicking and screaming at anything in her path, barely
aware that she had lost a shoe as pain mixed with terror.
It was then she saw a small light, a crack of white amid
the black, and she moved on her hands and knees toward
it, all the while gasping for breath, for life . . .

"We are stardust. We are golden . . .

And-we've-got-to-get-ourselves back to the gar-
den . . ."

She distinctly heard those lyrics as the crack widened
to a wedge of light streaming from the most chaotic
place she had ever seen, where machinery, bizarre-
shaped boxes and cables were strewn in wild confusion.
As the music died out amid the growing crescendo of
screams, she thought she saw shadows blocking the
light.

People!

"Help me," she whispered, slumping against the side
of another hard beam, exhausted. Her heart was slam-
ming into her ribs, resounding in her fingertips and ears
as she watched the light shift around the boxes until it
shone on her.

Relief swept through her, though she was blinded and
covered her eyes. "Thank you," she kept whispering
amid sobs of gratefulness. "Thank you, thank you." She
heard them coming toward her, and the light flicked back
and forth with their movements.

She wasn't going to die.

The knowledge lessened the tightness in her chest,

and she was able to take a deeper breath, though her lungs still felt like they were collapsing.

The screams were receding, and the music had stopped as two crouched figures, one after the other, made their way closer.

"Damn, 'ow do these birds get in 'ere?"

The angry words were muttered in a very English-accented voice.

Modern English.

Maggie kept breathing, swallowing air, as her brain tried to make sense of it while watching the men close the distance between herself and them.

"Let's get a move on with ya. Ya won't be hidin' under this stage anymore and . . . ah, Jeysus . . . I'm ruinin' me good shirt under here." The second man had a distinct Irish lilt in his voice, and she winced when she heard his yelled exasperation.

"Shaddap, Seamus . . . who gives a damn about your shirt when we've got us a stage crasher? Come along, I don't fancy breakin' my back down here either."

Maggie couldn't concentrate as the one with the Irish accent shouted.

"Come along, ya say? And how much faster am I to be when me back is folded in two, like a flippin' leprechaun, I ask ya? Sweet mother of God in Heaven, when ya said we was to be backstage security, I was thinkin' minglin' with the bands, not fetchin' crazed women from under the bloody stage!" He cursed, not quite under his breath. "And me, missin' seeing the goddess herself, Joni Mitchell, singin' the song she wrote, one of the bloody hymns of this spectacle!"

The light shone on her face again, and Maggie held up her hands to shelter her eyes. "Thank you for finding me," she said with as much volume as she could muster.

Two men sat back on their heels before her. From the illumination of the flashlight, she was able to see that both the tall, thin one and the shorter, stockier one were angry.

"How'd you get under here?" the short muscular one demanded, breathing heavily.

"I . . . I don't know," she mumbled, shocked to be speaking with them. "Where am I?"

"Ah, Jeysus . . ." the tall one muttered as the music began again. "We're right under one of the left speakers. Let's get her outta here."

The strong, shorter man grabbed her arm and pulled her forward. Stooped over, she held on to his hand as she clutched the material of her skirt and stumbled after him. The tall Irishman led the way, shining the flashlight before them.

Several times she was so disoriented by the deafening music above her and the cables on the ground that she tripped, and by the time they reached the low doorway, both of them were nearly pulling her through it into the light and dropping her.

Her ears and eyes closed in reaction to the barrage of sound and light, and she rolled over onto the ground, her hands on either side of her face, gulping in fresh air.

"Well, will ya look at what we've caught, Raul . . . some woman in a costume taking an asthma attack or somethin'! What'll we do with 'er?"

She wanted to tell them she didn't have asthma, yet the one who spoke was checking out his shirt and looking none too pleased. She sensed people rushing about, and the shorter one again grabbed her under her arm and forced her to stand.

"Who are you and how did you get under the stage?"

Dazed, she stared into his angry face while feeling the fear return. "I . . . I'm Maggie Whitaker," she answered, gulping in air. *Where was here?* "I don't know how I got here."

"A Yank!" the Irish one almost spat. "Dressed like

the Queen herself, she is! Though a bit tattered, I'd say.''
In the light she saw that he was older, in his forties.

"Shaddap, Seamus!" the one called Raul ordered, as
he continued to stare at Maggie, as though trying to figure her out. "Pick up our headsets from the ground, ya
bloody fool, and we'll take her to the Security Office."

"Ya can't do that," Seamus yelled to be heard over
the music. "Ya have to take her to that holdin' area they
told us about. Backstage it was!"

Gripping her arm tightly, Raul glanced to his companion. "You're only saying that because you want to
be there yourself. I didn't hear—"

"Oh yeah," Seamus interrupted, putting on his headset and adjusting it over his mouth. "It was in that
bloody long orientation class yesterday. Ya told me to
remember anything you didn't get, cause you dozed off
on account of you and Sheila stayin' up half the night
shaggin' and—"

"All right!" Raul interjected, while trying to maintain
control. He also looked highly annoyed at the whole
situation. "Where is it?"

Maggie watched as Seamus seemed startled for a moment, and then pointed to a white tent where crowds of
people were milling about. Her gaze took in men wearing jeans and T-shirts and women with short skirts, long
skirts, heels, and platform shoes. Even though she was
forty feet away, there was no mistaking it now. This was
not the Renaissance.

"Where?" Raul yelled in exasperation.

Oh, black night, silhouette me in the sky . . .

She shut out their bantering and concentrated on the
song. She *had* heard this music before . . . When she was
fighting claustrophobia, the music had been Crosby,
Stills, Nash and Young. Her brain now labeled it. This
was . . . her frazzled mind tried to make the connection.

"Come along then," Raul stated in a gruff voice, nodding toward the crowd. "You had better find that holding station, Seamus, for if you're leading me into trouble again, I'll be wiping that smacked-ass grin off your face before this night is out."

Seamus's voice sounded almost childish with glee. "Oh, you'll be thankin' me, Raul, before this night is over. Just you watch. I told ya some kinda magic is in the air tonight, didn't I? Here we are, in this most ancient of all places, and this is it, I tell ya. Why, we have us a . . . a prisoner, a gate and *stage crasher* no less! We got this important job to secure the very rights of these fine people deliverin' their message under the stars. Why . . . why we'll be heroes, Raul. Just you watch!"

"Bloody hell!" Raul cursed. "I'm in a freakin' three-ring circus whenever I work with you, Seamus Farley!"

Maggie stared at them. It was like watching a Cheech and Chong movie.

Take me high, high . . . higher than I've ever been . . .

Seamus led the way, and she held up the hem of her gown while brushing back her hair and wiping her face. She walked with them toward the tent and as people passed them and stared at her with curiosity, she would have sworn she was at a rock concert! It couldn't be! What about Nick? Elthea? *Four hundred years ago?* Her life was there with her beloved, her twin flame, her—

She passed a large poster, hanging off the side of a yellow-plastic fence. A white bird of peace was flying over a picture of—

All thoughts ceased as she read the large print.

Stonehenge: Rock Reunion 2000

It couldn't be! From some place in the back of her mind, Maggie remembered Malcolm talking about it . . . Malcolm . . . She stumbled, and the guard held her up as she clutched her chest and gasped. *She was back!*

Her lips again started trembling, and she felt as though she were walking on the edge of a razor. On one side was Nick and everything she had experienced. On the other was . . . this. People screaming, music blaring, no job, no love, no Nick!

It had happened! She had been there!

Hadn't she . . . ?

Chapter Nineteen

She tried to keep herself together as they entered the crowd. Dazed, Maggie felt the tears returning, the pounding of her heart, the deep sorrow that descended over her body like a heavy blanket. The shock of grief made her start shaking again as she walked with only one shoe toward the crowd. She barely noticed the people staring at her, some slack-jawed, some chuckling in amusement as they passed.

"Where is it?" the man holding her yelled to his coworker.

Seamus appeared to be looking around in awe. Maggie followed his gaze and saw Sting and a young girl with long wild hair shaking hands.

"Seamus!"

The tall man jumped at the yell along with Maggie. She watched as the Irishman came closer, and shouted, "Ya see that? Sting and Alanis Morissette!" He punched Raul's arm with relish and grinned like a leprechaun. "I told ya this night was magic!"

Maggie watched as Raul looked at the singers and nodded. Suddenly, he seemed to pull himself back to his job. "Yeah, so what? Where's this holding area?"

Maggie couldn't believe any of this was happening!

Seamus again appeared startled and looked back to the crowd. "It's over there," he shouted and pointed.

"On the other side of the buffet tent. Come along, I'll lead."

"Use your headset to call and confirm it."

The taller man looked down to the other, and replied, "Where's yours?"

"Ya didn't pick it up?" Raul let go of her arm and checked his chest, his neck, his head. "Damn! I must have lost it under the stage."

Seamus shook his head sadly, "Ah, too bad. And here they said we could keep them." He adjusted the mike by his lips, as though getting ready to speak into it.

Raul glared at her, assigning the blame for losing his bonus headset. "Damn the bad luck!"

Maggie was so startled by the entire scene that she was unable to respond while Seamus tapped at the battery pack attached to his belt while shouting, "Code 110 . . . code 110." He then removed it and began slapping the small black box. "It ain't workin', Raul. Static. Maybe we're too close to the big microphones."

Raul dropped his shoulders in frustration. "Gimme that thing!"

Seamus pulled the headset and battery pack off and surrendered it. Raul was trying to make it work, and Maggie lost interest in their situation as she noticed a tall handsome man walking toward her. The closer he came the more familiar he looked, and she searched her brain to connect a name with the face. He looked at her and the two arguing security guards and smiled. Gazing right into her eyes, he nodded in acknowledgment as he passed.

She was stunned.

"Jackson Browne," she said to the man's back as the name came into her head.

Seamus spun around. "Ah, Jeysus! I missed Jackson Browne?" Looking highly disappointed, he slapped at Raul's arm. "Go back and get yers under the stage."

The shorter man scowled. "Let's just hand her over to security and be done with it."

Seamus's jaw dropped. "And have some bloke who's only work this night has been having to watch over the likes of Jewel and the Indigo Girls take all the credit for this? I think not. Get your headset or just follow me."

Raul seemed indecisive. Looking around, he bit his bottom lip, then threw the headset back at Seamus's chest. The Irishman easily captured it in one hand and shrugged his shoulders.

"If this is another of your live-in-the-moment, freaky schemes, I'll not be havin' it, Seamus."

"Your choice, Raul. Go get your headset and then reap the reward." The man hesitated and looked at the piece of technology. "I can get this fixed. Reap your reward, or you can hand it all over to another and let them have this moment. Myself, I'll be stayin' here, thank you, and walkin' through these fine folk to the holding area." Seamus stuck out his thin chest.

"Look, I need to sit down," Maggie said to break the tension, yet it was also the truth. Her legs were giving out on her, and her head was pounding with pain, sorrow, and confusion. "I'm going to be sick," she added to the standoff of choices, pushing her hair back off her damp face. The tears were too close to the surface again, and she swallowed hard to stop them. Somehow, she had to hold it together.

"Fine," Raul decided, pushing Maggie toward Seamus. "You take her to that chair, right there . . ." Raul pointed to a corridor beyond the tent that seemed to lead to the other side of the stage. "Take her there and wait for me. Have her sit down and don't leave her side for a second."

Seamus grinned and did an impromptu salute. "Aye, sir."

"This is serious business, you daft bloke! Just do it,

all right?'' Raul looked like he, too, just might be ill.

Seamus became very serious as he grabbed Maggie under the arm and said in a loud, official voice, ''This way, Yank . . . This ain't no picnic you've wandered into, I'll tell ya. You'll have to answer for yer actions, ya know.''

He pulled her away, and they began walking toward the crowd. She wasn't sure if she wasn't dreaming. How could any of this be real?

How could any of what she'd experienced four hundred years ago *not* be real?

''Hey, look!'' Seamus called out next to her in an excited voice. ''Bono from U2 is over there talking to Stephen Stills and George Harrison. And there's Seal comin' to join 'em.'' Awe was in his voice when he added, ''Did ya ever think you'd see that in person? That you'd be witness to the greatest reunion since Woodstock or the Isle of Man?''

''I have to be dreaming,'' she muttered, identifying members of groups from the last forty years. She watched in disbelief as Bob Dylan, Tracey Chapman, Joan Osborne, Graham Nash, Art Garfunkel mingled around her. Some even smiled or chuckled at her costume.

She felt suspended in time.

''Yeah,'' Seamus breathed deeply. ''If you're dreamin', lady, then so are over half a million other dreamers havin' the same dream. And about four billion over the planet on the telly. This is one fantastic dream we're sharin', huh?''

Maggie couldn't answer as she continued to stare.

''Come along,'' Seamus said, nudging her with pressure on her arm. ''I don't want Raul to get back and bust a bloody vessel when he sees we ain't where he told us.''

She allowed him to lead her and she saw performers

that she recognized, but couldn't name. Younger ones from MTV and VH1. Seamus stopped, and Maggie leaned into his side briefly to regain her balance.

"There she is . . ." he said with awe again in his voice. "What I wouldn't give to meet her."

Maggie saw him looking at the back of a blond-haired woman.

"Joni Mitchell." He said the name with great respect.

Maggie found herself saying, "Go meet her."

He turned to look at her. "You think?"

"You may never have another chance." Thoughts of Nick passed through her mind, and she immediately stopped them. She could not think about him now. She had to find a place where she could stop to figure everything out, and it wasn't here. Her throat closed with emotion and she added, "Don't ever put off following your heart." She knew the truth of those words now.

He took a deep breath. "So you think I should just do it, huh?"

Mentally, physically, emotionally exhausted, Maggie nodded.

Seamus looked around to make sure Raul wasn't anywhere in sight, before saying, "The woman has the voice of an angel, and wrote some of the best stuff to come out of the sixties and seventies. I was in the States then."

Again, she merely nodded.

He pulled a screw from his pocket and held out his palm for her to see. "You and me, we're both alike in some ways, don't ya see? The headset wasn't broken at all. I only took this job to get back here for this," and he nodded to the crowd. "Course, for some of us, our choice of attire leaves a wee bit of room for ponderin', don't ya think?" He looked pointedly at her gown and grinned.

She had no words and tried to smile back. It took too much effort.

"Okay, here's the deal . . . ya got yerself in this mess, and I can't change what ya put into motion, but I can trust ya to just pretend you never seen me show you that battery screw and to just go along with whatever happens. Ya really don't have much choice here, darlin', but I figure anybody that goes to the outrageous extremes you did deserves some credit somewhere."

Pulling what strength she could, Maggie said, "Seamus, if you let me in sit in the chair Raul pointed out, I promise I won't move until you come back. I've got nowhere to go. I just need to sit down before I faint. Being under that stage almost killed me."

Seamus looked sympathetic, and asked, "How *did* you get under there?"

"If I told you, you wouldn't believe me."

The man shrugged. "Fair enough, and I don't want to waste any more time before Raul gets back. Come along then. I'm a man about to take yer advice and follow me heart. I trust ya, Maggie Whitaker. There's somethin' about ya."

She smiled weakly into the merry Irish eyes. "Thanks, Seamus. I won't betray your trust." Hell, she hoped the authorities could help her. Somehow, she needed to find Aunt Edithe in all these people. Over half a million people! It would be like looking for the proverbial needle in the haystack.

"Then let's do it," Seamus announced and much more gently led her past people tasting hors d'oeuvres and drinking bottled water and juices. Some were smoking and others were chewing gum. Many were waving large paper fans to keep cool in the close area, yet everyone seemed happy. Faces were beaming, and the mood was one of celebration.

They left the crowded tent area, moving slowly since

Maggie found walking with only one shoe difficult. She almost tripped again over all the cables closer to this side of the stage. Finding the folding chair against a canvas wall, Seamus stopped and Maggie collapsed into it.

He gave her a moment and then said, "You'll be all right?"

She nodded. "Yes. I have to rest. Go follow your heart, Seamus."

"I trust you," he said, looking deeply into her eyes. "You won't let down this silly fool? Just a shake of her hand or a smile from her lips is all I ask."

"I won't let you down. Go meet your goddess." It felt so wonderful to be sitting and breathing without difficulty that she didn't know when she'd be able to move. He could come back hours from now and still find her here. If he would just go, so she could calm down!

His smile was wide. "Be back in a jiff."

He turned and was gone for no more than thirty seconds before he came back. Holding out a container of bottled water, he said, "Ya looked like you can use it."

Maggie found her eyes filling with tears of gratitude. "You're an angel. Thank you."

He winked at her. "Ah yup, that would be me, all right. Tell it to Raul."

He disappeared back into the mingling crowd.

Her hands were still shaking as she struggled to open the bottle. Finally, she broke the seal and unscrewed the top. Using both hands, she raised the bottle to her lips and drank deeply. It tasted heavenly. Water . . . It was then that she realized in all the time she had spent in the past she'd only once been offered water. *Don't think about it. . . .*

Pulling the bottle away, she held it in her hands as she sat back and without warning those images began to race through her mind again. Nick. Elthea. All of them

. . . how could it all have happened? How could she have left Nick in 1598, dead on a field, and wind up in the present . . . at a rock concert? Her mind couldn't handle the paradox, and she knew she couldn't think about any of it right now or she would run into the night screaming.

She looked down to her feet and saw her big toe was bleeding. Her shoe. She'd lost her shoe. Her left shoe . . . Nick's note! The one she had saved. Gone. She had nothing, nothing to prove it had all happened!

Something *had* happened to her. She believed it. She knew it.

Malcolm had talked about this concert. She remembered that. Looking to her right, she saw another poster on a tall canvas wall opposite where she was sitting. She concentrated and read the dates.

She had been missing for days in this time. Surely, they were looking for her. What would she say when asked? Who would believe her? She had to find her aunt! With thoughts of Aunt Edithe, Maggie reached up and pulled the pearls out from her dress. When she did, something crackled, and she reached inside her bodice to remove the crumpled parchment airplane model!

It was *real*!

Emotion filled up inside of her. Love, tenderness, devotion . . . She couldn't relive it now. She had to distract herself until she was alone, for once she began grieving, she didn't know when it would ever end.

Avoiding the memories and what she knew was going to be painful, she looked back to the poster and held the precious paper airplane close to her heart. She read on, seeing the long list of performers . . . hearing the music of a familiar song playing on a stage behind those canvas walls . . . Reading, listening, her mind took her back to a nostalgic time when she was full of hope, young, believing that the world could be something better.

"We shall all meet and love again."
Her vision seemed to scan down the list.

U2, Seal, Pearl Jam, America, Collective Soul, Dan
Fogelberg, Indigo Girls, Simon and Garfunkel, Aiden
Harley, Rolling Stones, Jewel, The Eagles, Goo Goo
Dolls, Fleetwood Mac, Melissa Etheridge, John Fogerty,
and Creedence Clearwater Revival, Hootie & the Blow-
fish and it even announced Jethro Tull was coming out
of retirement. The list went on and on. She leaned closer
and squinted her eyes to read the smaller print. . . .

*Featuring Steve Miller's Fly Like An Eagle anthem of
Stonehenge: 2000*

Maggie continued to read names that were blowing
her mind even farther out there. It was incredible how
many people were involved. Stunned, Maggie continued
to read the poster announcing its message was one that
continues through time.

The strength of the human spirit.

It was too much, after listening to Elthea for days.
What was happening? She goes back in time and hears
the same message from Elthea and returns to find there
are millions upon millions of people who are not only
hearing it, but celebrating it!

She was very still for a moment, as a thought raced
within her.

What did Elthea say she was waiting for? A marriage
of something. She couldn't remember, but she wished
with all her heart that Elthea could see this, be a part of
this reunion. Still, she felt like she was truly losing her
mind as thoughts flashed one after the other, refusing to
be denied. . . .

How could she have not known about this? It was
happening all around her, and she had been blinded by
. . . by worry, shame, and bitterness. And she had felt
alone.

These people were celebrating! It couldn't be that

these millions of people were living such great lives that they never had a problem. The time she had left had not been utopia by any means. They just knew there was another way . . . what she had traveled four hundred years into the past to find out!

Follow your heart.

Aunt Edithe had first shown her it was possible. She was here, somewhere in this crowd, and Maggie's heart lifted a tiny bit. She could breathe deeper now. She would find her aunt and then—

"I did it!" Seamus almost popped in front of her eyes, blocking out the poster. He looked like a tall, skinny elf, grinning from ear to ear. She would focus her attention on him, she decided, until the authorities claimed her. If she tried to figure anymore of this out right now, she might just have a nervous breakdown!

"Joni Mitchell shook my hand!"

Maggie concentrated on him and making her lips move. "What did you say to her?"

He leaned back and bent slightly so she would hear him better. "I thanked her for sharing her remarkable gift with the rest of this mixed-up world we find ourselves in."

His words seemed to break through the pain around her heart, and she smiled more genuinely. "What a beautiful thing to say to her," she murmured. "She must have been moved."

Seamus started laughing. "I don't know if she was moved, but that's when she up and shook me hand. Imagine, Joni Mitchell shook me hand and said thank you to *me*." Shaking his head, he added, "I could die a happy man. Surely, if Heaven were a moment, this would be it."

Stunned, Maggie stared into his eyes. Nick had said those exact words to her!

It was as though the pain made another assault on her

as memories came flooding back, squeezing at her heart
and demanding recognition. She couldn't. Not now.
Forcing herself to unscrew the bottle, she brought it to
her lips again and gulped. When she finished drinking,
she pulled some inner reserve of strength and looked
back to the man at her side.

Inhaling, she blurted on the exhale, "So what's this
concert all about, Seamus? You might as well fill me in
while we wait for Raul." There. Let the man ramble and
divert her. She would do whatever it took right now,
anything to avoid memories that would only torture her.

"Well," he answered, pulling himself up to his normal height, "I don't know that I'm the one who could
speak for this thing. I just knew as soon as I heard about
it, I wanted to be a part of it somehow." He looked to
his right with a slight laugh. "Raul must still be sear-
chin' for his headset."

"Why?"

He looked back at her. "Why what?"

"Why did you want to be a part of it?" In that moment, Seamus was the most important person in the
place. She had to keep him talking, for if left alone with
her own thoughts, she would lose it for sure.

"Hey, your toe's bleedin'."

She pulled the long skirt over her feet. "Forget it.
Tell me why you wanted to be a part of all this." She
wiped her face with her hands and pushed her hair behind her shoulders as she waited with great concentration for his answer. *Talk to me*, she mentally pleaded,
anything . . . tell me anything so I don't have to think!

" 'Cause it's like the greatest event that's happened
in my life. Bigger even than men on the moon. That was
technical, but this"—he looked around him and then
touched his chest—"this is about in here. Stuff you
knew when you were young and then forgot when the

going got tough and ya didn't believe in yerself any longer and so ya bought somebody else's story. Ya know?''

She nodded. How well she knew. "So it's a reunion with the music?''

"Where ya been, Maggie Whitaker? You obviously went through an awful lot of trouble to get to this place. Why would ya be here if you didn't know?''

"Know what?'' she insisted, not daring to answer his question.

"What this is all about. It's been advertised everywhere and is on the telly all over the planet right now. It's about a reunion of the music but more. It's for those who used to hear the message and the kids who hear it now. Ya know . . . reuniting the baby boomers with their kids. I mean, heck . . . look around ya. They're wearing our clothes and even platform shoes. Their music may not be Earth, Wind and Fire, or Joni Mitchell, but the message is the same. Maybe we actually have something to teach each other, ya think?''

He laughed, as though at the notion that it could be anything else. "Parents maybe remember what they already knew and some of us forgot, and the kids find out their parents had the same hopes, the same dreams . . . fer a better future.''

She stared at him.

"Ya know, the human spirit?'' He was looking at her as though she had forgotten something important and then chuckled.

"Right . . .'' she mumbled, and remembered hearing something about it, but she'd been too wrapped up in her miserable life to pay attention. She had been killing herself with worry over a job, a failed marriage, and a stack of bills.

"It's our only hope now, in my humble opinion.

We've tried everything else, besides what's right inside of each of us," he said in a serious voice while moving back against the canvas wall as the corridor began to fill with people. He leaned down and finished his thought. "Maybe together, two generations united, can make this here new millennium a better beginning to a brighter future. This is about peace, Maggie. Ya never know until ya try."

She noticed that the heavier Irish lilt left his voice while he was speaking. It was now more . . . well, intelligent. Instinct told her Seamus knew how to lay it on thick when the mood suited him.

"Watch your dress there, Lady Maggie," he called out to her as men in uniforms began to race about.

"What did you call me?" she demanded, pulling her soiled gown to the side while people with towels and bottles of water ran to stand down the corridor by the stairs to the stage.

" 'Twas only a joke, cause of the way you're dressed. I gotta say, you do stand out." His smile was innocent.

She had no more time to think about his answer as she sat in amazement, surrounded by the chaos of technical staff running about and yelling at people and into more two-way radios to "get ready to move the set, clear stage three, cue the lights, the band, and go, go *go*! We're almost ready here."

Maggie couldn't make any sense out of it. When the music on the main stage she had been pulled out from under reached an earsplitting, body-pounding crescendo, she heard masses of people applauding, screaming, and whistling in such unison that she was riveted by the sheer power of it. The sound seemed to mesh into a dull hum that began to fade as she closed her eyes and drew inside herself, the only place where she could find protection from the unexplainable chain of events.

She opened her eyes and saw that the back stage was

now almost lined with a different set of security guards as a group of musicians started exiting the stage and hustling through the corridor.

"Hey, man, incredible set!"

"They loved you! Great set!"

The accolades were being yelled by people slapping the backs of the musicians dripping by her. She couldn't help but gaze at the long-haired, sweating, heavy-breathing, vein-pumped, muscular bodies and towel-wrapped necks of the band players passing her. A handsome drummer, with sticks in hand, grinned at her as he walked through the crowd. Another man, tall and lanky, passed with an elaborately painted electrical guitar in hand and winked at her.

Seamus was cheering loudly, having a terrific time, high-fiving everyone who would slap his hand.

At least the band players didn't seem to mind she was there. She didn't even know who this band was, but so far they didn't seem to think she was some crazed fan who had crashed the backstage area, was being detained by security, awaiting concert police and dressed in a filthy Renaissance costume.

But then again . . . maybe she really was nuts after all.

Aiden Harley stood on the stage, looking out to a sea of people, knowing he was experiencing a peak moment in his incredible life. This concert had been his focus for the last four years and to have caught up with the future he had envisioned so often was blowing his mind! He continued waving and, when he felt the burning at his eyes, he knew it wasn't from the sweat pouring down his face. He'd better do something fast or he'd be crying in front of four and a half billion people across the planet.

"Thank you!" he shouted hoarsely over and over as

the applause and yells and whistles continued. People were throwing flowers, and he walked a few feet, picked up several, and threw them back out with thanks. They still accepted him, graying hair and all.

He saved a single pink rose with a white ribbon. Waving it, as the sound grew in approval, Aiden just took it all in. All of it. . . .

Within moments, his whole life ran before him as he time traveled into the past with emotion . . .

After spending a childhood in the grasp of a misdiagnosed illness, he'd played the guitar for company and peace. It was all that time alone going inward, instead of playing outside with other children, that enabled him to think beyond the box and question life. Then he really found his place in front of a piano. Never could he have imagined that playing with others would lead to a record deal, success, fame. He was just a kid. All he was doing was living his life and singing about what mattered to him. In the late sixties he sang about peace. In the seventies he expressed his disillusionment. The eighties taught him about balance and the nineties about focusing beyond himself. All he was doing was singing.

He was just one voice in the crowd, but somehow he was heard . . . and he never took that for granted. Semiretired, he'd thrown most of his attention toward pulling off a reunion of baby boomers with their best creations, their kids. There was something for everyone, friends, lovers, family to remember. What better time to make a pitch for peace than at the birth of the new millennium? And the response all over the globe exceeded their expectations.

Waving good-bye to the crowd, he walked backward to the exit, wanting to acknowledge the energy he was receiving. Yeah, it was an incredible life, and to be a part of this was simply overwhelming. Whoever was writing this in the universe had perfect timing, for the crowd estimates were bigger than Woodstock. Something *big* was happening, and it was like a wave reaching its peak potential before crashing with power. People had had enough craziness and were remembering.

Aiden swore that if he died right then, his life would have been complete, and, throwing a kiss, he left the stage. Energy like he had never felt was racing and buzzing through him. He barely sensed the floor beneath him. Every muscle, every organ, his entire being seemed like it was operating in perfect symmetry. He heard the wild enthusiasm continue to vibrate as he neared the stairs. Somehow these people had opened up and let him inside. They had for over thirty years. No matter how much he explored, no matter the adventure, nothing could have prepared him for this one. Again, he realized what a great gig his life had been.

"Man . . . what a set! You never sounded better!"

His road manager threw him a towel, and Aiden wrapped it around his neck while wiping his face and running it over his hair. The sweat really started pumping now that he had stopped singing and someone handed him a bottle of water. Stopping briefly, he drank deeply and looked for his band. He wanted to thank each one of them for pulling out all the stops and jammin' like they were twenty years old again.

When, suddenly, it was as though his entire focus was drawn to a frightened woman dressed in the most outrageous costume, a security guard standing next to her. Walking down the steps to the ground he thought if she wanted to crash and get attention, she certainly picked a surefire way.

"Great set, Aiden. Let's get together and talk. It's about time for a new CD, isn't it?"

He shook hands with Mike Anderson, vice president of one the biggest labels around and one of the major sponsors of the reunion.

"Sure, Mike," he answered, while being slapped on the back by strangers who also were trying to talk to him.

All the while, he kept looking for the woman. He could only catch glimpses of a tattered-looking ruby dress. The crowd parted for a few moments, and his gaze was drawn to her eyes, the most beautiful eyes he had ever seen. Her face was flushed and dirty, but it was those eyes . . .

They looked . . . hauntingly familiar.

He watched as she seemed to realize he was staring at her.

Something happened, so eerie that despite the sweat, he felt the hair rise on his body as her eyes got wide with astonishment. As though in slow motion, as if time had slowed down, he saw her gasp and clutch the pearl necklace at her breast. He could actually feel her bewilderment as the pearls scattered down to her lap, rolled over the soiled velvet gown, and hit the ground.

She tore her gaze away from his while reaching down to the trampled grass at her feet, and time seemed to return to normal. The security guard next to her bent down to help as the intriguingly lovely woman scrambled around picking up her pearls. Suddenly, people started to crowd around him again and he held his hand up to keep them back.

"Wait a minute. Hold on," he called, walking toward her.

When he was a few feet away, she stopped and looked up at him. Her expression tore at his heart, her tears at something deeper. She wasn't young, yet to him she was so vulnerable and yet achingly familiar that he bent down. Grabbing a fistful of pearls, he extended his hand.

Slowly, as though unsure, she extended her hand and, as he emptied his into it, he found the words, "Gather your pearls, m'lady," coming out of his mouth.

They stared at each other in stupefaction.

Why ever would he use that language, he wondered, kind of embarrassed since this was so public. Two more security men pushed their way through the small circle of people surrounding them, and he noticed the tall one who was with her held them back, motioning to wait.

Aiden looked back at her and it hit like a bolt of lightning, shaking him to his very core. In an instant he knew her, just as he saw the recognition burst into her eyes and once the connection was made it all fell into place. He felt the longing, the yearning, the loss and painful separation, the promise to remember. It was as though his heart burst open with an ancient knowing . . . indescribable, demanding his attention. Confusion gave way to trust, faith, certainty. He knew that his life may have been incredible, but one thing had always been missing. Even though he'd had great loves, he hadn't found *her* . . . the mirror to his soul.

His mate throughout eternity.

At the same moment, as his own eyes filled with emotion, they spoke for the first time on this part of the adventure, saying the same words, asking the same question. . . .

"*Is it you?*"

He held out the rose.

Somewhere, in all the surrounding chaos, Aiden Harley swore he heard an impish, childish giggle.

Epilogue

She had never been so happy. It was finally her turn, and she didn't take it for granted. Grateful for every miracle in her life, she realized she had never felt more whole, complete . . . peaceful.

Holding that last thought, of peace, she finally surrendered to the sweetness of the dark and allowed herself to drift into sleep. She wasn't aware of anything for some time and then suddenly she was walking, through a mist, hand in hand with the little girl from the faire. It seemed natural, serene, and she enjoyed the sensation as the dream grew in clarity. They were walking toward a room, lit in the most beautiful soft white gold. The little girl was laughing, delighted with herself and the direction they were heading. Maggie went along willingly, since the child really was irresistible, and she sensed those in the room were happy she was coming. She felt welcomed.

She halted when she realized there was no room, just pockets of people . . . laughing, communicating with great intensity of pleasure, though no one was actually speaking or opening their mouths. Its was as though everyone could hear everyone else's thoughts. It was surreal and, like most dreams, anything was possible . . . Besides, it *felt* so good she wanted to proceed.

Focusing more attention, she was stunned to make out

Aunt Edithe in a group with Lord Robert, congratulating him on his excellent performance. And there was Malcolm, patting the back of the man who killed Nicholas. Montague! Elthea was beaming at Maggie's ex-husband! There was her mother laughing and shaking her head and holding on to Gwen's arm. Her favorite teacher from third grade was talking to the doctor who stitched up her arm when she was twelve. There was Evan, grinning with pleasure at Seamus. So many . . .

The place was packed!

Confused, Maggie felt her attention drawn to a solitary figure, a man dressed in a Renaissance costume. He looked familiar, yet she couldn't place him. Suddenly, the name came, as though he allowed it in her mind.

Sir Francis Bacon.

The greatest writer in history nodded to her in recognition, as though she had earned the right to discover him in the party of her life, and all its players. She was showered with recognition as the author of her own adventure and Maggie knew she was dreaming, yet no dream had ever been this clear, this incredible. Nor had one ever felt this good! As she looked once more around her, she saw in an instant how everyone, and everything that took place in her life had served her in some way, even those things that were painful. Filled with instantaneous understanding, she knew she could never really put it into words. It was just a flash of seeing how all the puzzle pieces of her life fit together and made sense.

Feeling a tug, Maggie looked down to the beaming face of the adorable child who was still at her side. The rosebud wreath encircled ringlets of shining blond curls. She smiled into the little girl's eyes and suddenly heard her excited thought. . . .

I'm going to be born soon. This is my party, too!

Maggie felt joy for the child and finally learned her name. Carolyn. There was another mystery solved. She was about to ask the child why she had helped her in the maze when, suddenly, from behind her she felt fear creeping up and tapping her on the shoulder.

Where were Nick and Aiden?

Any sense of this being a dream vanished.

She had seen *Titanic*! Holy shit, was she *dead*?

This was *not* fair . . . if she was the author of her life, this would make such a lousy ending! She wanted to protest, but saw all the characters who played roles in her life fading. Fear increased, and there was a moment of terrifying darkness where she didn't know what was real. Gasping, she bolted upright in bed and clutched the sheet to her chest while desperately trying to find sanity again.

It was then she felt his gentle touch on the middle of her back.

"Shh, it's okay. The nightmare returned?" he asked in a sleepy voice and slowly sat up next to her. Continuing to stroke her back in soothing circles, he added, "It's been a long time since you had it."

She looked at him in the moonlight and her thundering heart began to slow down. "It wasn't the nightmare. I haven't had it in . . . in over a year. This was . . . it was different, Aiden."

He pulled her into his arms and slowly lay back down, taking her with him. "Tell me about it, love."

Curling into his arms, she wrapped hers around his waist and wound her leg through his, pulling his thigh closer to her for grounding. "It started out so great. The little girl from the maze was holding my hand and she led me into this . . . gathering of people." She sighed, trying to remember and to tell it before she lost it, like so many of her dreams.

He continued to stroke her in silence, running his hands down her bare arm ever so slightly, soothing and supporting her.

She snuggled into his chest. "Everyone was there. Aunt Edithe and Malcolm. Elthea and Evan. My mother and my ex were laughing together. Sheesh, that was weird."

She felt him chuckle as she went on . . . "And so was Robert and that assassin, along with Joe, my old boss. Even Seamus. So many I can't remember them all now."

"Seamus, huh?" Aiden asked, and Maggie could imagine his grin. Seamus now worked for Aiden.

She continued to explain it as best she could remember, especially the part about Sir Francis Bacon, not wanting to leave out important details for she felt it was an extraordinary dream. Aiden stopped her when she said she could see how it all had served her.

"And what did you learn?" he asked softly, brushing the hair back from her face.

She thought for a moment. "That I can't so easily judge anything anymore. Some of the hurtful ones were there to challenge me, I guess. Maybe to show me not to give away my power so damn easily."

"Was that what frightened you?"

"Ohhhh," she murmured and then chuckled. "Wait till you hear this. It suddenly dawned on me that you aren't there. And neither is . . . well, Nick, and I got so scared. I thought I had died and it was like the movie *Titanic*, or something. Remember that scene at the end where everyone is applauding her and—"

His laughter interrupted her, and she couldn't help smiling. It was pretty ridiculous.

"Oh, Maggie . . . the way your mind sometimes works," he breathed in appreciation and kissed the top of her head. "I'm sorry you had such a fear."

She nodded, seeing the dream now in a new light. It was when she had questioned the dream that her fear had ended it, and it had been a great one! Too bad.

Again she gave her power away to it. "Damn."

"What?"

"I did it again," she muttered. "Gave away my power."

He squeezed her. "We all do it, Maggie. We all have our buttons. Right now, yours is death."

"I don't want to talk about it. I was so happy when I fell asleep." She kissed his chest and ran her hand down his thigh, feeling his energy and making her skin tingle with pleasure.

"Are you attempting to change the subject, or just shut me up?" he asked with amusement in his voice.

She raised her head and looked at his handsome face in the moonlight. "Ya think I can?"

He laughed. "You can, m'lady, anytime you want. I think I've made that clear in the last year. All I have to do is touch you, and I want you."

She sighed with pleasure. "Me, too," she murmured, laying her head back down on his chest and stroking him.

"All I was saying, Maggie, is that you have this . . . this trauma about death since Nick."

She groaned. "You're going to do this, aren't you?"

"What better time, my love, to rid yourself of this fear? You, of all people, know death is not an ending, an annihilation. I am living proof of it." He chuckled. "Now there's a paradox you can chew on for months."

She sighed. "Falling asleep in one world and waking up in another? Let me tell you, it's disorienting."

"Until you learn the balance. When I was a child, Maggie, I was so sick sometimes I thought I was dying. Funny how even that served me, getting me in touch with my inner self years earlier than I would have had I been healthy. And once . . ." His words trailed off. "I think I've told you about this."

She nodded. "You felt at one with everything."

"It was . . . there are no words to describe it. The closest is joy. It isn't an ending. It's another beginning. There is nothing to fear, my incredible time traveler."

"I don't fear it," she whispered. "Well, not the experience so much as leaving you. Life. It's just starting to be everything I always desired. And way more. Talk about the bennies of this union. I just don't want it to end."

He hugged her tighter. "Why ever would it end now? You are finally living your life *on purpose.* Now is the time to live fully and do whatever you came this time around the wheel to accomplish. And it shall never end with you and I, Maggie. You know that. We have said it over and over, in lifetime after lifetime, and we're saying it again right now."

Tilting her chin up, he looked down at her and smiled with love. "As I remember more and more of my connection to Nick and life with you in the Renaissance, I know that no matter what happens in the future, or the past, we are irretrievably connected by a twin flame, bound to create our own light and leave our impression upon the universe."

"Into eternity," she breathed, touching his face with tenderness. "Adventure after adventure. Time after time. We'll always find each other."

"Aye, m'lady," he whispered back, turning his face to kiss her fingertips.

She smiled with such love that all thoughts of death, of fear, vanished as she reaffirmed that no matter what happens, the love never dies. It continues. He was right. He was proof.

"Hey," she asked, "wanna make an impression upon the universe?"

Laughing, he pulled her up on top of him and her hair made a tent around their faces as she eased in between his legs. "I can't think of a better way in this moment to affirm life than by making love to you.''

"Oh goody," she remarked, leaning down and kissing him soundly.

He quickly held her head when she pulled back. Staring into her eyes, he said, "I want to worship every inch of you tonight."

Again, she groaned as delicious sensations raced through her body. Smiling seductively, she whispered, "And you think I'm going to make this difficult for you?"

He laughed. "I'm serious."

"I know you are. That's why I groaned. I have received your worship, my love . . . and it's anticipation I'm feeling right now."

"To put it in the words of one of the most intelligent women I have ever encountered . . . oh, goody."

It was her turn to laugh. She pulled back a little bit and tried to see his eyes more clearly. "Do you really think I'm one of the most intelligent women you have ever encount—"

He gently tackled her and turned her onto her back. "Oh, hush. I shall stroke your ego, m'lady, if that is your wish," he said with a laugh, while he traded positions and wound up between her legs, using his forearms to support himself as he looked down to her. "You *are* brilliant when you let go of your fears. Can you leave your insecurities this night? Your questions and deep excavations into your mind? Don't think."

"Don't think?" she asked in surprise.

"That's right, don't think. I want you *to feel*, to follow your instincts."

As soon as she heard the words, her body reacted. Making love with Aiden Harley was like nothing she had ever experienced. He took her places in her mind and body that she didn't even know existed. Now he was saying to turn off her mind.

"How?" she asked, knowing her trust in him was complete. That was one thing she knew without a doubt. With twin flames there isn't even a discussion of trust.

Their gaze connected in *that* way. She knew she could never really explain it . . . the closest was the intimate, eternal spark of their flames uniting. In Aiden's eyes was Nick staring back at her with such love that it left her in awe.

"Hi . . ." he breathed with the most tender smile, as the timeless recognition was made.

Her breath caught in her throat as she smiled back with wonder. "Hi . . ."

"Allow me to worship you . . . you, that infinite spark of you that is eternally connected to all that ever was or is. Your emotional body is vibrating with unresolved emotions from your past. Thinking isn't helping. See if feeling does."

She would have laughed except her body was sending some pretty strong feelings to go along with the suggestion and shut up, even mentally. "Oh, you're good, Aiden Harley. No wonder all those women buy your CDs and write you those letters and—"

"Hush, Maggie," he said, right before his mouth captured hers and she couldn't remember what she was even thinking.

His kiss deepened, demanding her response.

Surrender was sweet.

When he lifted his head, she was gasping with her reaction. He rolled to his side and leaned up on his elbow, resting his head on his hand. Tenderly, he began using the tips of his fingers to caress her lips, her cheeks, her eyes, her hairline . . . down to her chin. He had done this many times in foreplay, yet this time there was something more in his touch. His energy was stronger.

"You don't have to do anything," he repeated in a

whisper. "Just feel. I'll take care of your emotional body."

She knew he had studied with Buddhist monks, with native Indian shamans and a mahatma from India, but this . . . this was incredible. He was barely touching her, sometimes only the tiny hairs on her skin, and yet she was saturated with an energy of love that was stunning.

"Wow . . ."

"Shh . . ."

Closing her eyes, she allowed him to continue without interruption as Aiden seemed to soothe everywhere he touched. The lyrics of the Marvin Gaye song, "Sexual Healing," raced through her mind, and then she reminded herself that she wasn't supposed to be thinking.

Right . . . feeling.

No words could ever describe what she was feeling. There weren't any. Not in any language. The closest was bliss. She settled on that word and let it drift from her mind as all her attention seemed to be on her skin and right above it, in the fraction of space between the surface and his hand. That was where she was being drawn as wave after wave of pleasure spread through her body, blocking all thought.

There was nothing but the experience of him . . . and of her.

He slowly made his way down her body, not missing an inch of her. There was something reverent in his magical hands. Her shoulders, her breasts, her arms, hands, seemed to vibrate with his ministrations, and she moaned as she felt herself weightless again, this time wide-awake yet floating beyond herself.

His touch was filled with such love and respect as he paid homage to her belly, and she experienced the purity of it center between her hips. When her thigh felt his hand, it twitched in instinctive response. He paid slow careful attention to her knees, her calves, her ankles her feet . . . everywhere. As he traveled up her inner thigh, she couldn't stand anymore and grabbed his hand, pulling him up to her.

"My physical body is telling my emotional body that enough is enough, Aiden Harley." Her gasp of pleasure was genuine.

His smile was tender. "As you wish, m'lady."

Kissing her nose, he then gently pushed her back down to the pillows.

It was a sensuous dance of legs and arms, the electricity of skin against skin, the thrilling impression of intimate contact. It was old. Ancient. Primal. Life-affirming, and Maggie felt him merge into her, become one, and they both moaned at the exquisite homecoming. Together they danced in perfect unity, graceful and passionate to sustain the union. Each wanted to prolong the present and played with the illusion of time, continuously drawing it out until it lost definition and, suddenly, they went beyond the beautiful white room on the California coast. They were out in the universe, making their glorious, unique impression.

It was a timeless fusion, a marriage of male and female, light and dark, right and left, all opposites harmoniously blended until there was only love left to dance amid the stars.

Life, with all its innocence and passion, was honestly, profoundly affirmed.

Holding each other through the aftershocks, they slowly returned, and Maggie opened her eyes to moonlight and Aiden smiling at her with such love she felt tears burning for release.

"How I love you, Aiden Harley," she murmured, touching his lips, his square jaw, and the tiny cleft in his chin.

He kissed her fingers, and whispered, "And I adore you, Maggie Harley. You are the most incredible human being I have ever known, or ever will . . . and we belong together. Thank you, thank you, thank you for waiting for me. You *are* my beloved.''

Closing his eyes, he inhaled deeply, and breathed, ''Sweetness of my days, goddess of my nights, angel of my mornings . . .''

Lying on her side facing him, she buried her head under his chin and allowed the tears to come. He remained calm, stroking her hair, her shoulder, as though sweeping away the charge of intense energy. Moment by moment, she felt lighter as she cried for the pain and sorrow, everything she had put herself through in order to reach this oasis in paradise. It had been quite an adventure to get home, to where she had always belonged.

How could she now be afraid of death? If her life ended tomorrow, she wouldn't regret one single bit of it. This was just one chapter in an endless book. Yet she knew her fear had kept her away from really living while she was here, in this moment, and it was for that she cried, releasing the gripping hold terror had on her. Someday she would be tired and fall asleep again. Then she would dream the next chapter and, when she felt herself being awakened, she would remember the characters, the motivation. She might not remember the whole plot, but that was the adventure . . . to re-member, to put it all back together, to have the courage to live with purpose and recognize faith as the invisible bridge . . . to know without doubt there is land, paradise, beyond a sea of life's confusion.

Who ever said you had to die to live in paradise?

Her tears instantly stopped when that thought entered her mind with such clarity that Maggie lifted her head and stared at Aiden. Sniffling, she used the side of her hand to swipe at her nose, and said in an awe-filled voice, ''I'm not afraid anymore.''

He smiled with love, and whispered. ''Oh, goody.''

Bringing her closer, he hugged her so tightly she had to hold her breath. "Let's really *live* now!"

"Yeah," she agreed with a long exhale.

He pulled back, and said with a boyish grin, "After all this impression upon the universe, I'm hungry. How about you?"

Giggling, she sniffled and nodded. "What about ice cream?"

"Yeah," he said, sitting up and getting excited. "Ice cream and . . . pickles?"

She laughed and skooched back against the pillows, collapsing in giggles. "Gimme a break, Aiden. I'm not that bad . . . yet. Plenty of people eat peanut butter–and-marshmallow sandwiches, and I would say a very small percentage are pregnant. My cravings are more . . . more primal," she said, and grinned at him with a seductively arched eyebrow.

In the moonlight, his handsome face lit with playfulness. "I have read that women in their second trimester are highly sexual creatures."

"Oh!" She sat up and pushed at his chest. "I'll get the ice cream! Really," she muttered, dropping her leg over the side of the bed. Reaching for her robe, she added, "I was speaking about something more substantial, like chicken salad or something."

"And touchy," he said with a laugh. "Chicken salad on ice cream? Hold the chicken on mine. Hey, I was teasing you, Maggie. I'll get your ice cream and chicken salad."

Standing and tying the silk belt around her expanding waist, she stopped the tinge of weird energy. This balancing of hormones was something!

"I'm sorry, hon," she said, and walked around the bed to his side. Bending down, she kissed the top of his head, while he kissed their child growing within her. "I know you were teasing."

He looked up and grinned. "I'll get your munchies. It was my idea."

She tousled his dark hair, and then gently stroked his graying temples. "I'm up and I need to use the bathroom *again*. Besides, you were up late writing the album liner notes. You rest, my healing husband. Your impression upon the universe tonight was powerful and deep."

"You sure?" he asked in a tired voice that said he would gladly go if she wanted.

"I'm sure. Now what do you want with your ice cream? I think we have some leftover broccoli from dinner," she offered teasingly.

He patted the back of her thighs. "Off with you, woman. Raid the fridge and create a midsummer night's repast, then. We have a lot to celebrate."

She chuckled. "We do, don't we?"

As she left, she asked, "What do you think of the name Carolyn?"

He didn't say anything and she looked back to watch him reach over and turn on the nightstand lamp. "Hold on. Let me look it up."

She mentally shook her head as she saw him pick up the book of names that he kept with him all the time now. This naming of a new soul was of utmost importance to him.

"Carolyn . . . Carolyn . . ." He ran the name over his tongue while flipping through pages. "Here it is. In Latin, the name means strong; womanly. The Old French say Carolyn is a song of joy."

He looked up from the book, and his gorgeous blue eyes widened. "I like it."

She laughed. "Me too."

"Where did it come from? You just thought of it?"

"I'll tell you when I get back," she threw over her shoulder as she walked out of the room. "I have a more pressing need."

She headed straight for the bathroom. This pregnancy stuff was an adjustment. At forty-one years old, though, she wasn't complaining. She was thrilled.

Feeling like a woman well loved, Maggie strolled through the rambling single-story Mission-style home. What a sanctuary Aiden had built overlooking the Pacific Ocean. He had given her full rein to redecorate and add her own imprint, yet she had been so impressed with his taste that very few changes had been made. It was comfortable, beautiful, and welcoming.

She walked through his office to turn off the light at his drafting table. He sometimes left it on, in case he awaked with inspiration. Well, she had some inspiration for him. He thought she wasn't going to return with pickles and broccoli, huh? Chuckling, she was about to push the base button and cast the room into darkness, when her gaze caught the words written on a piece of scratch paper . . . He was already starting a new song.

> Trying to hear my own song
> I searched my life for you
> Sweetness of my days
> Goddess of my nights
> Angel of my mornings
> Now and forever more . . .

She had never told Aiden that Nick had said those words to her. Sweetness of my days, goddess of my nights, angel of my mornings . . . When he had spoken them tonight, it was then she couldn't hold back the tears and had finally broken down to release her fear of death. He was writing this one for her, and her heart expanded with awe.

She turned off the lamp and stared out the huge picture window at the ocean. It was as though she had left the light and instantly entered the world of darkness, of the moon casting shadows and stars bursting through the soothing shades of black. She finally could appreciate the beauty of the opposite. The light of the sun creating shadows as it bathed the earth with warmth, and the shadows of the night as the cool light of the moon coaxed them out.

Elthea must love this marriage of opposites.

She thought of the wise woman with a surge of gratitude welling up inside of her for those who came before her and held the light until she, herself, could see. The real illusion was that this moment wasn't *The Garden*.

We never left. We've just been, well . . . shitting in paradise.

She burst out laughing and hugged her gently rounded belly. "Welcome, Carolyn . . ." She chuckled. "This is one heck of a ride, but leave your seat belt unbuckled. You don't really need it." Not bad advice, coming from someone who had followed her heart and found an ancient happiness.

Her joy was such that when the tears again entered her eyes, she allowed them without judgment. With a sacred love, her hands began caressing her belly as Aiden had done earlier. The connection was made with her child, and she knew she would be talking to her every chance she got. She wanted to tell her everything she knew. What worked and what was a challenge. She wanted Carolyn to hear soothing music to coax her into life. Her eyes would serve as a mirror to entice her daughter into the sense of beauty. Her hands and nose would reveal the sensuousness of the earth. And her tongue would delight with taste and textures and—

Suddenly, she felt a faint flutter in her belly like butterfly wings and jumped. She also really wanted the ice cream now.

Aiden had said don't think. *Feel.* Geez, he was some angel in disguise. If someone had told her her own story, she would have said it was a fairy tale. That it couldn't be true. But it was . . . she was living it with a man who was creative and handsome, tough enough to have finished all the carpentry work in the house himself and so talented he played five instruments with passion. He was romantic, bitingly funny, handsomely *older* than she by eight years, and so full of respect for her he had made her a partner in his company. And he had more integrity than anyone else she had ever met.

Nick certainly wrote himself a great gig this time around.

Aiden was her friend, her lover, her partner. Her twin flame. His light and warmth supported her own flame, and somehow she did the same for him. Now, inside her body, another being was creating itself. If there was one thing she had learned it was not to wait to say anything that was deep within her heart, but to follow it always. Always to live her truth.

It was her first clear communication with her child, and she felt the importance of the moment. Filled with the awe of life, Maggie smiled tenderly and whispered what was in her heart.

"*Namaste*, sweetie . . ."

is it
THE END
?

Afterword

Where I am gone, be not afraid . . .
It is a place that Life is made.
In a New Beginning, not an end . . .
We all will know and Love again.

—CRISTOPHER CORNELL STERLING

Author's Note

Before I acknowledge others who have inspired or assisted me in writing this story, I would like to thank you, the reader. I figure this is the best opportunity I have to communicate directly to you, so I'm taking it. *Carpe diem*, and all that. To those who have bought my books, shared them with others, written me such beautiful, articulate letters that I have been rewarded beyond anything public . . . to all of you, thank you from my heart.

The only time I call myself a writer is when I'm filling out a legal form. I think of myself as a storyteller, a communicator, and I wish to express to you my personal acknowledgment for allowing me into your head and assisting me to do something I love. Create. I am honored you have consented for a short while to drop your disbelief and have allowed me to take you on an adventure of the mind and heart. Together, we've ventured into a few mysterious and sometimes misunderstood subjects. I'm learning all the time just how much there is to learn. I guess that's why when you read my perception in a novel I am honored that somehow I can communicate with you. So many have written and said they feel like they know me through my work. It's a friendship that has lasted thirteen years and, again, I am honored.

I started writing for myself when I was a reader, just like you. My novels were part of my budget. I learned so much in those imaginary worlds, about history, re lationships, balance, and love. I considered myself a fairly intelligent woman and when I sat down to write that book I wanted to read, but couldn't find . . . I thought of you, and wondered if you'd like it, too. It was just a story, not literary fiction, but then I always knew I was a storyteller. Since childhood I would read to anyone who would listen, for I couldn't think of a better way to be entertained and to learn. Originally that's why I liked history, and it wasn't until I started to question the story that I learned there just might be another perception, another view. Once in a while, following the paper trail really can lead to some surprising clues. That happened in this book and my imagination took off, yet that is merely my perception and this is, after all, fiction. You, the reader, will assess for yourself how it feels.

Personally, I think every single person who has ever entered into this adventure of life is writing a best-seller just by showing up. Often, it takes courage to keep writing our stories. Again, my perception, and yet that could change at any moment since change is sure. We all seem to agree on one thing though. Free will. The ability to make choices. Thank you for making this one, and holding my hand as together we dreamed a slightly different dream. I'm already excited and thinking about the next one. See you there.

Namaste
Constance O'Day
New Jersey, January 1999

All the world's a stage,
And all the men and women
merely players.

SIR FRANCIS BACON (1561–1626)
AKA WILLIAM SHAKESPEARE

Acknowledgments

Gary L. Wade—for providing me with information on healing herbs.

Tara A. McGovern—for technical support and the laughter shared.

Maggie Pierce Secara—for her invaluable research on the Renaissance, available at renaissance.dm.net.

Lyssa Keusch—my editor, for her insights, expertise and her support of this book . . . and all the staff of Avon Books who have contributed to this publication.

Patricia Trowbridge—the inspiration for Edithe and Elthea. I cherish our friendship and am so glad we reconnected. What a hoot to come full circle and realize we know nothing.

Francis Carr, and all those who contributed to the bountiful research available on the Internet concerning the Baconian Evidence for Shakespeare Authorship.

Cristopher Cornell Sterling—for his patience and encouraging me to venture into the Renaissance when I was intimidated by the time period. So glad I listened to his wisdom.

Finally, to all those, too numerous to mention, who have held the light throughout time and questioned the answers . . . I acknowledge your courage.

Have you ever wondered why opposites attract?

Why is it so easy to fall in love when your friends, your family ... even your own good sense tells you to run the other way? Perhaps it's because a long, slow kiss from a sensuous rake is much more irresistible than a chaste embrace from a gentleman with a steady income. After all, falling in love means taking a risk ... and isn't it oh, so much more enjoyable to take a risk on someone just a little dangerous?

Christina Dodd, Cathy Maxwell, Samantha James, Christina Skye, Constance O'Day-Flannery and Judith Ivory ... these are the authors of the Avon Romance Superleaders, and each has created a man and a woman who seemed completely unsuitable in all ways but one ... the love they discover in the other.

Christina Dodd certainly knows how to cause a scandal—in her books, that is! Her dashing heroes, like the one in her latest Superleader, SOMEDAY MY PRINCE, simply can't resist putting her heroines in compromising positions of all sorts . . .

Beautiful Princess Laurentia has promised to fulfill her royal duty and marry, but as she looks over her stuttering, swaggering, timid sea of potential suitors she thinks to herself that she's never seen such an unsuitable group in her life. Then she's swept off her feet by a handsome prince of dubious reputation. Laurentia had always dreamed her prince would come, but never one quite like this . . .

SOMEDAY MY PRINCE
by Christina Dodd

Astonished, indignant and in pain, the princess stammered, "Who . . . what . . . how dare you?"

"Was he a suitor scorned?"

"I never saw him before!"

"Then next time a stranger grabs you and slams you over his shoulder, you squeal like a stuck pig."

Clutching her elbow, she staggered to her feet. "I yelled!"

"I barely heard you." He stood directly in front of her, taller than he had at first appeared, beetle-browed, his eyes dark hollows, his face marked with a deep-shadowed scar that ran from chin to temple. Yet despite all that, he was handsome. Stunningly so. "And I was just behind those pots."

Tall and luxuriant, the potted plants clustered against the wall, and she looked at them, then looked back at him. He spoke with an accent. He walked with a limp. He was a stranger. Suspicion stirred in her. "What were you doing there?"

"Smoking."

She smelled it on him, that faint scent of tobacco so like that which clung to her father. Although she knew it foolish, the odor lessened her misgivings. "I'll call the guard and send them after that scoundrel."

"Scoundrel." The stranger laughed softly. "You *are* a lady. But don't bother sending anyone after him. He's long gone."

She knew it was true. The scoundrel—and what was wrong with that word, anyway?—had leaped into the wildest part of the garden, just where the cultured plants gave way to natural scrub. The guard would do her no good.

So rather than doing what she knew very well she should, she let the stranger place his hand on the small of her back and turn her toward the light.

He clasped her wrist and slowly stretched out her injured arm. "It's not broken."

"I don't suppose so."

He grinned, a slash of white teeth against a half-glimpsed face. "You'd recognize if it was. A broken elbow lets you know it's there." Efficiently, he unfastened the buttons on her elbow-length glove and stripped it away, then ran his bare fingers firmly over the bones in her lower arm, then lightly over the pit of her elbow.

Goosebumps rose on her skin at the touch. He didn't wear gloves, she noted absently. His naked skin touched hers. "What kind of injury are you looking for?"

"Not an injury. I just thought I would enjoy caressing that silk-soft skin."

She jerked her wrist away.

*What could be more exciting than making your debut...
wearing a gorgeous gown, sparkling jewels, and enticing all
the ton's most eligible bachelors?*

*In Cathy Maxwell's MARRIED IN HASTE, Tess
Hamlin is used to having the handsomest of London's eligible men vie for her attention. But Tess is in no hurry to
make her choice—until she meets the virile war hero Brenn
Owen, the new Earl of Merton. But Tess must marry a
man of wealth, and although the earl has a title and land,
he's in need of funds. But she can't resist this compelling
nobleman...*

MARRIED IN HASTE
by Cathy Maxwell

"*I envy you. I will never be free. Someday I will have a
husband and my freedom will be curtailed even more,*"
Tess said.

"I had the impression that you set the rules."

Tess shot him a sharp glance. "No, I play the game
well, but—" She broke off, then admitted, "But it's not
really me."

"What is you?"

A wary look came into her eyes. "You don't really
want to know."

"Yes, I do." Brenn leaned forward. "After all, moments ago you were begging me to make a declaration."

"I never beg!" she declared with mock seriousness and they both laughed. Then she said, "Sometimes I wonder if there isn't something more to life. Or why am I here."

The statement caught his attention. There wasn't one man who had ever faced battle without asking that question.

"I want to feel a sense of purpose," she continued, "of being, here deep inside. Instead I feel . . ." She shrugged, her voice trailing off.

"As if you are only going through the motions?" he suggested quietly.

The light came on in her vivid eyes. "Yes! That's it." She dropped her arms to her side. "Do you feel that way too?"

"At one time I have. Especially after a battle when men were dying all around me and yet I had escaped harm. I wanted to have a reason. To know why."

She came closer to him until they stood practically toe to toe. "And have you found out?"

"I think so," he replied honestly. "It has to do with having a sense of purpose, of peace. I believe I have found that purpose at Erwynn Keep. It's the first place I've been where I feel I really belong."

"Yes," she agreed in understanding. "Feeling like you belong. That's what I sense is missing even when I'm surrounded by people who do nothing more than toady up to me and hang on my every word." She smiled. "But you haven't done that. You wouldn't, would you? Even if I asked you to."

"Toadying has never been my strong suit . . . although I would do many things for a beautiful woman." He touched her then, drawing a line down the velvet curve of her cheek.

Miss Hamlin caught his hand before it could stray further, her gaze holding his. "Most men don't go beyond the shell of the woman . . . or look past the fortune. Are you a fortune hunter, Lord Merton?''

Her direct question almost bowled him off over the stone rail. He recovered quickly. ''If I was, would I admit it?''

''No.''

''Then you shall have to form your own opinion.''

Her lips curved into a smile. She did not move away.

''I think I'm going to kiss you.''

She blushed, the sudden high color charming.

''Don't tell me,'' he said. ''Gentlemen rarely ask before they kiss.''

''Oh, they always ask, but I've never let them.''

''Then I won't ask.'' He lowered his lips to hers. Her eyelashes swept down as she closed her eyes. She was so beautiful in the moonlight. So innocently beautiful.

Across the Scottish Highlands strides Cameron MacKay. Cameron is a man of honor, a man who would do anything to protect his clan...and he wouldn't hesitate to seek revenge against those who have wronged him.

Meredith is one of the clan Monroe, sworn enemies of Cameron and his men. So Cameron takes this woman as his wife, never dreaming that what began as an act of vengeance becomes instead a quest for love in Samantha James's *HIS WICKED WAYS*.

HIS WICKED WAYS
by Samantha James

Cameron faced her, his head propped on an elbow. His smile was gone, his expression unreadable. He stared at her as if he would pluck her very thoughts from her mind.

"It occurs to me that you have been sheltered," he said slowly, "that mayhap you know naught of men . . . and life." He seemed to hesitate. "What happens between a man and a woman is not something to be feared, Meredith. It's where children come from—"

"I know how children are made!" Meredith's face burned with shame.

"Then why are you so afraid?" he asked quietly.

It was in her mind to pretend she misunderstood—but it would have been a lie. Clutching the sheet to her chin, she gave a tiny shake of her head. "Please," she said, her voice very low. "I cannot tell you."

Reaching out, he picked up a strand of hair that lay on her breast. Meredith froze. Her heart surely stopped in that instant. Now it comes, she thought despairingly. He claimed he would give her time to accept him, to accept what would happen, but it was naught but a lie! Her heart twisted. Ah, but she should have known!

"Your hair is beautiful—like living flame."

His murmur washed over her, soft as finely spun silk. She searched his features, stunned when she detected no hint of either mockery or derision.

She stared at the wispy strands that lay across his palm, the way he tested the texture between thumb and forefinger, the way he wound the lock of hair around and around his hand.

Meredith froze. But he stopped before the pressure tugged hurtfully on her scalp . . . and trespassed no further. Instead he turned his back.

His eyes closed.

They touched nowhere. Indeed, the width of two hands separated them; those silken red strands were the only link between them. Meredith dared not move. She listened and waited, her heart pounding in her breast . . .

. . . Slumber overtook him. He slept, her lock of hair still clutched tight in his fist.

Only then did she move. Her hand lifted. She touched her lips, there at the very spot he'd possessed so thoroughly. Her pulse quickened as the memory of his kiss flamed all through her . . . She'd thought it was disdain. Distaste.

But she was wrong. In the depths of her being, Meredith was well aware it was something far different.

Her breath came fast, then slow. Something was happening. Something far beyond her experience . . .

What could be more beautiful than a holiday trip to the English countryside? Snow falling on the gentle hills and thatched roofs ... villagers singing carols, then dropping by the pub for hot cider with rum.

In Christina Skye's THE PERFECT GIFT, Maggie Kincaid earns a chance to exhibit her beautiful jewelry designs at sumptuous Draycott Abbey, where she dreams of peacefully spending Christmas. But when she arrives, she learns she is in danger and discovers that her every step will be followed by disturbingly sensuous Jared MacInness. He will protect her from those who would harm her, but who'll protect Maggie from Jared?

THE PERFECT GIFT
by Christina Skye

Jared had worked his way over the ridge and down through the trees when he found Maggie Kincaid sitting on the edge of the stone bridge.

Just sitting, her legs dangling as she traced invisible patterns over the old stone.

Jared stared in amazement. She looked for all the world like a child waiting for a long lost friend to appear.

Jared shook off his sense of strangeness and plunged

down the hillside, cursing her for the ache in his ribs and the exhaustion eating at his muscles.

He scowled as he drew close enough to see her face. Young. Excited. Not beautiful in the classic sense. Her mouth was too wide and her nose too thin. But the eyes lit up her whole face and made a man want to know all her secrets.

Her mouth swept into a quick smile as he approached. Her head tilted as laughter rippled like morning sunlight.

The sound chilled him. It was too quick, too innocent. She ought to be frightened. Defensive. Running.

He stared, feeling the ground turn to foam beneath him.

Moonlight touched the long sleeves of her simple white dress with silver as she rose to her feet.

He spoke first, compelled to break the spell of her presence, furious that she should touch him so. "You know I could have you arrested for this." His jaw clenched.

Her head cocked. Poised at the top of the bridge, she was a study in innocent concentration.

"Don't even bother to think about running. I want to know who you are and why in hell you're here."

A frown marred the pale beauty of her face. She might have been a child—except that the full curves of her body spoke a richly developed maturity at complete odds with her voice and manner.

"Answer me. You're on private property and in ten seconds I'm going to call the police." Exhaustion made his voice harsh. "Don't try it," Jared hissed, realizing she meant to fall and let him catch her. But it was too late. She stepped off the stone bridge, her body angling down toward him.

He caught her with an oath and a jolt of pain, and then they toppled as one onto the damp earth beyond the moat. Cursing, Jared rolled sideways and pinned her beneath him.

It was no child's face that stared up at him and no child's body that cushioned him. She was strong for a woman, her muscles trim but defined. The softness at hip and breast tightened his throat and left his body all too aware of their intimate contact. He did not move, fighting an urge to open his hands and measure her softness.

What was wrong with him?

Imagine for a moment that you're a modern woman; one minute, you're living a fast-paced, hectic lifestyle ... the next minute, you've somehow been transported to another time and you're living a life of a very different sort.

No one does time-travel like Constance O'Day-Flannery. In ONCE AND FOREVER Maggie enters a maze while at an Elizabethan fair, and when she comes out she magically finds she's truly in Elizabethan times! And to make matters more confusing, the sweep-her-off-her-feet hero she's been searching for all her life turns out to be the handsomest man in 1600's England!

ONCE AND FOREVER
by Constance O'Day-Flannery

Maggie looked up to the sky and wished a breeze would find its way into the thick hedges; she couldn't believe she was in this maze, sweating her life away in a gorgeous costume and starving. Thinking of all the calories she was burning she wondered, who needs a gym work out? Maggie stopped to listen for anyone, but only an eerie silence hovered.

Suddenly, she felt terribly alone.

Spinning around, she vainly searched for anyone, but saw and heard nothing. "Hello? Hello?" Her calls went unanswered. She stopped abruptly in the path. She felt weak. Her heart was pounding and her head felt light. Grabbing at the starched collar, she released the top few buttons and gasped in confusion. Okay, maybe she could use that shining knight right about now. She didn't care how or where he appeared, as long as he led her out, for the air was heavy and still, and Maggie found it hard to breathe.

"Help me . . . please."

Silence.

Her heart pounded harder, her stomach clenched in fear, her breath shortened, her limbs trembled and the weight of the costume felt like it was pulling her down to the ground.

Spinning around and around, Maggie experienced a sudden lightness, as if she no longer had to struggle against gravity and push herself away from the earth. Whatever was happening was controlling her, and she was so weary of struggling . . . flashes of her ex-husband and the alimony, her failed job interviews, the bills, the aloneness swirled together. It was bigger, more powerful than she, and she felt herself weakening, surrendering to it. The hedges appeared to fade away and Maggie instinctively knew she had to get out. Gathering her last essence of strength, she started running.

Miraculously, she was out. She was gasping for breath, inhaling the dust and dirt from under her mouth when she heard the angry yell that reverberated through the ground and rattled her already scrambled brain.

She dare not move, not even breathe. If this were a nightmare, and surely it couldn't be anything else, she wasn't about to add to the terror. She would wake up any moment, her mind screamed. She *had to!*

Drawing upon more courage than she thought she had left, Maggie slowly lifted her head. She was staring into the big brown eyes of a horse.

A horse!

She heard moans and looked beyond the animal to see a body. A man, rolled on the side of a dirt path, was clutching his knee as colorful curses flowed back to her.

"Spleeny, lousey-cockered jolt head! Aww . . . heavens above deliver me from this vile, impertinent, ill-natured lout!"

Pushing herself to her feet, Maggie brushed dirt, twigs and leaves from her hands and backside, then made her way to the man. "How badly are you hurt?" she called out over her shoulder.

The man didn't answer and she glanced in his direction. He was still staring at her, as though he'd lost his senses.

Shoulder-length streaked blond hair framed a finely chiseled face. Eyes, large and of the lightest blue Maggie had ever seen stared back at her, as though the man had seen a ghost. He was definitely an attractive, more than average, handsome man . . . okay, he was downright gorgeous and she'd have to be dead not to acknowledge it.

Wow . . . that was her first thought.

Everyone knows that ladies of quality can only marry gentlemen, and that suitable gentlemen are born—not made. Because being a gentleman has nothing to do with money, and everything to do with upbringing.

But in Judith Ivory's THE PROPOSITION *Edwina vows that she can turn anyone into a gentleman . . . even the infuriating Mr. Mick Tremore. Not only that, she'd be able to pass him off as the heir to a dukedom, and no one in society would be any wiser. And since Edwina is every inch a lady, there isn't a chance that she'd find the exasperating Mick Tremore irresistible. Is there?*

THE PROPOSITION
by Judith Ivory

"Speak for yourself," she said. *"I couldn't do anything"*—she paused, then used his word for it—''unpredictable.''

''Yes, you could.''

''Well, I could, but I won't.''

He laughed. ''Well, you might surprise yourself one day.''

His sureness of himself irked her. Like the mustache that he twitched slightly. He knew she didn't like it; he used it to tease her.

Fine. What a pointless conversation. She picked up

her pen, going back to the task of writing out his progress for the morning. Out of the corner of her eye, though, she could see him.

He'd leaned back on the rear legs of his chair, lifting the front ones off the floor. He rocked there beside her as he bent his head sideways, tilting it, looking under the table. He'd been doing this all week, making her nervous with it. As if there were a mouse—or worse— something under there that she should be aware of.

"What *are* you doing?"

Illogically, he came back with, "I bet you have the longest, prettiest legs."

"*Limbs*," she corrected. "A gentleman refers to that part of a lady as her limbs, her lower limbs, though it is rather poor form to speak of them at all. You shouldn't."

He laughed. "Limbs? Like a bloody tree?" His pencil continued to tap lightly, an annoying tattoo of ticks. "No, you got legs under there. Long ones. And I'd give just about anything to see 'em."

Goodness. He knew that was impertinent. He was tormenting her. He liked to torture her for amusement.

Then she caught the word: *anything?*

To see her legs? Her legs were nothing. Two sticks that bent so she could walk on them. He wanted to see these?

For anything?

She wouldn't let him see them, of course. But she wasn't past provoking him in return. "Well, there is a solution here then, Mr. Tremore. You can see my legs, when you shave your mustache."

She meant it as a kind of joke. A taunt to get back at him.

Joke or not, though, his pencil not only stopped, it dropped. There was a tiny clatter on the floor, a faint sound of rolling, then silence—as, along with the pencil, Mr. Tremore's entire body came to a motionless standstill.

"Pardon?" he said finally. He spoke it perfectly, exactly as she'd asked him to. Only now it unsettled her.

"You heard me," she said. A little thrill shot through her as she pushed her way into the dare that—fascinatingly, genuinely—rattled him.

She spoke now in earnest what seemed suddenly a wonderful exchange: "If you shave off your mustache, I'll hike my skirt and you can watch—how far? To my knees?" The hair on the back of her neck stood up.

"Above your knees," he said immediately. His amazed face scowled in a way that said they weren't even talking unless they got well past her knees in the debate.

"How far?"

"All the way up."